# BLUES UNDER THE
# GREY SWEDISH SKYLINE

# Blues under the Grey Swedish Skyline

A novel

by

**RAGHE DULANE**

Adelaide Books
New York / Lisbon
2021

BLUES UNDER THE GREY SWEDISH SKYLINE
A novel
By Raghe Dulane

Published by Adelaide Books, New York / Lisbon
adelaidebooks.org
Editor-in-Chief
Stevan V. Nikolic

For any information, please address Adelaide Books
at info@adelaidebooks.org
or write to:
Adelaide Books
244 Fifth Ave. Suite D27
New York, NY, 10001

ISBN: 978-1-952570-17-9

*This is for Galib, my son, with love and affection. It is also to Loving memory of my grandmother, Aulo Gutale, and Fadumo Yere, my sister.*

# Contents

BOOK ONE

# Chapter One

# *1982*

As he sat on a rickety bed, inside a little room he had been sharing with a tenant, Kore gave thought to his position in life and was overwhelmed with a feeling of misery. The stone house he lived in, its plaster peeling off walls, had a corrugated iron roof. The house had a courtyard surrounded by rooms, set apart by cardboard sheets so thin that in a clear silence of the night, one could hear neighbours expressing their sorrows in tears, their joy in laughter and their happiness in songs. Families cooked meals in the courtyard, where children ran around and played with each other. As one looks at the courtyard one gets a feeling that it is a cross between a refugee camp and a place hit by a natural disaster.

Kore had been a refugee in Nairobi, Kenya, for several months now. The United Nations High Commission for Refugees (UNHCR) had offered him a status of political refugee, and had forwarded his case to the Swedish Embassy to be considered for a resettlement there.

What Kore had no way of knowing was that, far off in Sweden, inside a brightly chandelier-lit room, at a headquarters of the Swedish Immigration Department, a group of politicians and bureaucrats have been in a meeting to discuss the fate of refugees that had sought political asylum in Sweden.

Just as a slightly-built middle aged blond woman, chairing the meeting, sitting at the head of the long conference table, dressed in a straight-skirt, a blouse and a jacket, was getting ready to address the meeting, a younger-looking man, in a maroon-coloured jacket, said to a man sitting on his right, "Watch out; here comes panic incarnate."

The lady's major duty, as head of the Immigration Department, was to devise and implement policies on immigration. She gave her colleagues a sweeping glance; as she did so, she let her grey-looking eyes move with ominous overtone, from side to side. "Ladies and Gentlemen," she said, "the subject for today is refugees. She took a short breath. When she resumed her speech, a moment later, she looked quite upset.

"Needles to mention to you," she said, "is the fact that this country is going through a period of great economic hardships. Therefore, here is my question to you. How far can we afford to accommodate people, in the name of promoting diversity, or saving humanity from suffering, without putting both the economy and social cohesion of this country in great jeopardy? Enough is enough."

"Your point is well taken," said a man who had a thick drooping moustache that looked like a handlebar. He paused briefly to have a look at his colleagues; meanwhile, his colleagues stared at him, to see if he had something more to say.

"Let us not forget that both Vietnamese and Poles are victims of communist persecution," he said in a hurry. "I am sure," he added, "if we grant asylum to these poor people, our American friends will be pleased with us. However, when it comes to economic refugees – I am having in mind people coming from Africa and the Middle East - I would like to advice caution"

"Oh," a woman with thin sandy-blond hair exclaimed. Unable to keep excitement, she said, "Have you said, 'Our American friends?' Let us not forget that this is a neutral country. In our eagerness to please the Americans, I fear we may fall foul of our Russian neighbours. Since we can't afford to do this, therefore, let asylum seekers try their chance elsewhere, I say."

An elderly-looking man, conveying impression of a highly learned man, in a baggy grey-sweater, a round wire glasses and a goatee that had turned grey, was getting ready to address the meeting. As he did so, he neither displayed in his speech a sign of banter nor mock.

"The previous speakers have spoken well," he said wisely. "However," he added, "I beg to differ with both. Whether these people are running away from communism it is beside the point. To me, it is important that we offer them asylum on a humanitarian ground."

The elderly-speaker picked up a glass of water; he was intending to have a sip when someone requested him to speak about the state of Africa's political conditions. He put down the glass on the table and sighed; he knew he had been asked to tread on a slippery ground. All eyes were focused on him; it was quiet in the room.

"Almost all African countries are in a state of great turmoil," he said; he posed briefly to have a sweeping look at his colleagues. When he resumed his speech, seconds later, he painted a morbid picture of the African continent.

"People in Africa are going through a great deal of hardships," he said. "Those hardships," he added, "are caused by an incompetent and corrupt group of leaders, thanks to a support they draw mainly from the West."

There was a murmur of discontent in the room.

At a far-end corner of the conference table, filled with a burning anger, was a man who shouted, "Ought we to give a blanket approval to applications we receive so as to ingratiate ourselves with those accusing us of a political felony we have not committed?"

The elderly speaker took the challenge headlong.

"The answer to your question," he said firmly, "is both yes and no."

This time he managed to take a sip of water before responding. "I am not for free immigration," he said. "However," he added, "I am totally opposed to a kind of attitude encouraging policies denying genuine refugee chances for resettlement here."

He took a pause; later, directing his gaze at the woman chairing the meeting, he said, "It seems to me, at the behest of the UNHCR, our country has been regularly offering political asylum to a group of a highly educated people, only to have this one important quality in them not given its due attention here. Ladies and Gentlemen, this is wrong; morally wrong, to say the least."

This final statement had not gone unchallenged. Facing the chairperson, across from the table, was a middle-aged man; he was short and dressed in a dark-blue suit. As the elderly-looking man in a baggy grey sweater gave the speech, the man had made facial gestures to indicate that he begged to differ with the speaker.

Finally, when the time came for him to speak, he used a lucid language to express his point. "The security that we offer to refugees, more than anything else," he said, "is what makes our action morally correct; all other factors are beside the point. Individual refugees who are lucky enough to have landed here on our shores," he added, "could attest to this fact. I hope, in future, we shall continue to provide the security they need, to enable them to lead a fulfilling life in this country.

What is more, extending asylum to refugees for reasons of promoting human rights is a good thing; however, let us be careful not to allow this to open the refugee floodgates to our country. We must act with caution, and so let moderation be a major guiding principle of our refugee policies."

As he went on with the speech, the chairperson looked at the short man with a rapt attention. From the way the chairperson looked at him, it was quite clear that she held him in high esteem. Oftentimes, she agreed with his views, just as she was bound to do so now. More discussions followed before the Chairperson finally closed the meeting.

# Chapter Two

# *Nairobi*

As he sat in his room reading a book by a shaft of sunlight, getting through a crack, in a ramshackle wooden window, Kore heard a knocking at his door.

"The door is open. Come in please," Kore said.

A young boy who was eleven years old entered the room; the boy ran errand for tenants in an exchange for food.

"Good morning," he said politely. "There is a call for you at the manager's room," he added.

"Thank you," Kore said.

At the manager's single sleeping room, which also served as an office, there was a telephone that the manager had constantly kept under a lock and key, its use being available to tenants only when receiving calls, for which they were made to pay. The manager, who also owned the building, had no patience with tenants that did not pay their rents on time.

One time, when a family had failed to promptly pay their room-rent on time, she threw them out in the rain.

"I scrubbed floors, washed dishes, and had worked in chicken farms in USA to get where I am. Go scrubbed floors,' she had told people who implored her to have mercy for the troubled family.

Tall and heavily built, the manager was in her mid-fifties; she sat on a chair, her thick legs sprawled out; she made a point of listening to telephone conversations made in the room; the word privacy never existed in her world; for this, Kore hated and despised her.

At the manager's office, Kore picked up the telephone and said, "This is Kore. Good morning."

"Hello Kore. This is Wijewardena. How are you?" Wijewardena said.

"I am fine; thank you," Kore replied in a most cheerful manner.

"I am calling to let you know that my office has received a word from the Swedish Embassy. They wish to see you. Go now; hurry up and good luck," said Bob Wijewardena, who was from Sri Lanka, and had been working as a Legal Officer at Nairobi's UNHCR office.

Kore wanted to take shower before going out. For quite some time, water inside the bathroom had not been running smoothly. Outside the bathroom, he waited impatiently to have the bucket now in use. Once he got it, he went to the communal water supply station, several meters away from where he lived; while there, he had to stand in a queue in order to secure a fair share of the water. The whole process of taking shower had become somewhat a tedious, cumbersome and frustrating ritual that took the thrill out of what should have otherwise been a joyous occasion.

After he showered, he put on a pair of jeans, a jumper, a jacket, a pair of tennis shoes and then left his dwellings in a great hurry. He had every reason to believe that today was the day. The UNHCR don't let people visit any embassy unless there is a valid reason for doing so.

He had never been asked to visit the Swedish Embassy before. When he got off the bus, fifteen minutes later, he continued to his destination. The Swedish Embassy was situated at the heart of the city of Nairobi, inside one of those most imposing multi-story buildings.

It had rained late at night; the sky was overcast, and the day was getting colder by the hour. After all, it is not uncommon for the city of Nairobi, as well as areas surrounding it, to experience cold weather. The name Nairobi, named after a river the Masai called Engare Nairobi (a river of cold water) has been derived from the Masai language, meaning a place of cold water.

Before the advent of 20th Century, the Masai had grazed their cattle where now the city of Nairobi stands until their ability to do so has been rendered ineffectual by a city that slowly but surely was growing into becoming a metropolis that it has turned out to be today.

At Nairobi city centre there were frantic efforts made, to give its buildings a new facelift; however, since some roads were still full of potholes, Kore had to take cautious steps, as he navigated his way through numerous pools of rain water.

To get inside the embassy, one was required by security personnel to go through a light searching security measures that Kore went through quite successfully; later, he was directed to the Swedish Embassy, which had its offices on one of the top most floors of the building. He took a lift. Seconds later, he was talking to a girl receptionist with a pleasant smile that he assumed was Kenyan.

"What can I do for you"?

"I need to talk to someone."

"Do you have someone in mind?"

"No."

"What is your mission?"

"I am a refugee."

"What is your name, please?"

"Kore is my name."

She looked Kore in the eyes as she spoke over intercom, using a lower tone. Later, she offered Kore a smile and said, "If you care to go to the sitting room and wait, someone will see you."

Thank you," he said.

There was a waiting room, a few steps from the reception-desk, where thin but elegant brown set of chairs were made available for the visitors to use; in the middle of the room, there was a long wooden table, on top of which were brochures of all sizes and colours. Framed beautiful pictures of Swedish lakes, green meadows, children at play-parks, as well as outstandingly beautiful Stockholm's waterways, adorned the walls of this brightly-lit waiting room. Kore had set up his mind to go through some of the brochures when he caught sight of someone approaching.

"Mr, Kore?" The man said.

"Yes," Kore said, and stood from the chair.

"You must be Kore. You look just the same as in your photos. My name is Erik; Erik Nilsson. I am the First Secretary here," he said as he shook hands with Kore.

Erik was tall and lean. He had a crew cut on a long narrow head. He was not elaborately dressed. His simple mode of dressing, Kore thought, could be a sign that he was a man of modest character. He had put on a white short sleeved shirt, a tie, a beige coloured pair of trousers and a pair of black leather shoes.

"Come with me, Mr. Kore," Erik said cheerfully as he led Kore deeper into recesses of the building.

Seconds later, they entered an office room that Kore guessed to be a place of the interview. One of the room's notable features was a large glass-window. From that window, one could catch a mind-boggling view of Nairobi.

"Mr Kore, what would you like to have; tea or coffee?" Erik said the moment they got inside the office.

"Tea, please," said Kore politely.

Erik went out and returned with the drinks in a wooden tray; he offered Kore the tea and kept the coffee. Erik sat in a chair, his back against the window. Kore sat facing Erik across the table. Erik took out a file from a drawer of his desk. "This file, 'he said, pointing to it, "contain an important information concerning the interview that the office of UNHCR has had with you. This information helps us to assess your situation correctly, while your case is getting considered for resettlement in Sweden."

He took a short pose afterwards. "Even though we collaborate closely with UNHCR," he said further, "and rely on their judgements on all cases they forward to us for consideration, we feel it is important that we do our interviews to supplement what we receive from UNHCR."

Before proceeding on with the interview, Erik wanted Kore to give him brief information about himself.

Kore gave his name, and then went on to explain the meaning of the word Kore. He said, in his native language, the word Kore comes from the verb Kor. When applied to a male child, he told Erik, Kore means one who must find a way to climb up in the ladder of life. As he was born not in a hospital, where births and deaths records are kept, hence the exact date of his birth day is unknown to him, he told Erik. But the name Kore also belonged to his grandfather after whom he had been named, he said.

For convenient sake, he went on, believing that he was born between 1950 and 1955, his parents had chosen 1952 to be the actual date of his birth. His parents, he told Erik, had attached a great significance to the date, because it reminded them of the time that Coca Cola got introduced to their town.

He wanted to say more, but Erik told him the information he gave was enough. Addressing Kore further, Erik said, "I am interested in the account of your life-situation that has landed you here in Nairobi, which has made you to also seek political asylum at the UNHCR office.

Be concise; but try, if you can, not to omit any point that would likely help to bolster your case." After a brief silence, he added, "Do you mind if I have your statements recorded?"

"I don't have any objection," Kore said; whereupon, after turning the tape on, Erik told Kore to go ahead and talk.

Below is the statement given by Kore, in his own words, and recorded by Erik Nelson of the Embassy of Sweden, in Nairobi.

"My life undoing," he began nervously, "had started on the day when I and Bobe Haigan became friends."

"Who is he," Nelson inquired.

As he went on talking, he lost nervousness, and even enjoyed giving the account of his life to someone eager to know the ups and downs of his life.

"Bobe Haigan," he said "is an old friend of mine. Today, in the country that he rules, in association with his cousin president, friends and cronies, he is everything. He holds so many ministerial portfolios that sometimes he forgets what they are.

He is a man of peculiar character. He has a high opinion of himself. To people he considers below him, he has no any regard for them, whatsoever. As for those people he considers to be above him, he has a special hatred for them.

Haigan acquired an American education. After returning from his studies in America, he was lucky to find that his cousin, who was in the army, had become a president, following a coup he had engineered along with other army men.

In my case, when I got back home from studies in India, I secured a job in the ministry of foreign affairs.

Haigan and I once again met and picked up our friendship from where we left. I discovered, to my dismay, how changed Haigan had become. Nowhere was this change more evident than in the way he dealt with people. At restaurants, he was impatient with waiters; he shouted at them for no apparent reason; the waiters accepted the humiliation with a spirit of meek resignation,

Once, while sitting in a restaurant, having a conversation with him, I told him that I had a nostalgic feeling for the past. He chuckled; he told me to forget the past, and reminded me to think of the present, instead. He told me that the country was on a right path.

I begged to differ with him; I mentioned several government policies to him that I disagreed with. If Haigan had got annoyed with me for being so forthright in my views, he said nothing.

After dinner, promising to meet each other, more often, we parted. I continued to work for the ministry, and had kept a sporadic contact with Haigan.

Several months later, Haigan visited me in my office. This had never happened before, because Haigan had often relied on phone calls to arrange meetings with me.

Haigan asked me to take a ride in a car with him. He told me he had a surprise for me. We took a stroll to a parking lot, where Haigan had kept his car. The car was the latest kind of Mercedes Benz, furnished with all kinds of luxury gadgets. We got inside the car and drove away, in silence.

Suddenly, from out of the blue, Haigan broke the silence by telling me that he knew exactly how I was feeling about the car. He said I was wrong to assume that he had no right to own such a luxurious car, being a citizen of a poor country. The car, he said, was a reward he deserved to have for the kind of job he was doing for the nation.

I stayed quiet, because I wasn't willing to engage in an argument with someone whose mind is up. I listened to him, instead. A half an hour later, the car pulled into a front-yard of a large white-washed bungalow, situated in one of the most exclusive posh areas of the city, facing the ocean.

We could feel the ocean breeze on our faces. Far off on the horizon, fishermen canoes were visible in large numbers. We got off the car, and together we approached the building. At the main gate to the building, Haigan offered me the keys to the house. I was surprised, but remained quiet. Haigan told me to go ahead and open the door.

Though the house looked empty of furniture, nevertheless, it was exceptionally clean. A single refrigerator stood at the far-end corner of what appeared to be a dining room. Haigan approached the fridge to retrieve two bottles of soft drinks. He handed me one and kept the other one.

Since everything took place quickly, I had many thoughts crossing my mind. One thing that had never occurred to me, however, was that the country's president would give the house to me as a present.

Haigan told me the president was greatly fascinated with my work; therefore, he had made up his mind to offer this house to me, as a token of appreciation for my contribution to the development of this nation.

It occurred to me then that getting a free house was not something which happens every day to a person; but when such a thing happens, there must be a reason for it. I have always believed that no one gets anything for free, in this world.

Nevertheless, to show my appreciation for the gesture made by the president to me, I told Haigan that I wished to thank the president for his generosity, and hope I will be worth the trust that he had bestowed on me.

Haigan smiled lightly and told me that I have a splendid sense of perception. He further told me that I couldn't have been more accurate. Trust and loyalty were all that the president wanted from us, Haigan told me. The president, he said, did not put pressure on us more than we can bear.

Although, at the time, I was unable to understand the motive for the presidential largesse, yet I was filled with a sense of apprehension. Very soon, I would come to know the reason.

One day, a special arrangement was made to have all my household goods transported to a new house - courtesy of Haigan.

I lived my life comfortably in the house given to me by the president; it was in the same house that I wedded Hadio surrounded by Haigan as my best man. The marriage had attracted the elite of the society, who came in large droves to the wedding ceremony. Even the president had found time to grace the occasion with his presence, as the guest of honour.

The marriage had been a culmination of a courtship period that had lasted for quite a long period of time. It had been postponed several times to allow Hadio to complete her nursing education. Haigan had been a regular visitor to my home, and had even eaten his meals there, quite occasionally.

Life went on without any sort of interruption until, one day, a year later, when I found a letter on my office desk, bearing presidential seal. I opened the letter in a hurry to see what was in it. From my previous position of a legal adviser in the ministry of foreign affairs I learnt that I got transferred to a High Court, where I was expected to act as a judge. The letter bore the signature of the president himself. I became somewhat surprised; I didn't know what to think

There was no doubt, as a trained lawyer, I could do the job to the best of my ability. But I felt I would have done a much better job had not the country's legal system been already perverted. As it was the case now, the country lacked a well-established body of law, all of it having been scrapped away in favour of presidential decrees. Thus, I felt lost about how I could arrive at a correct verdict, on cases presented to the court for adjudication.

It took quite some time before I met with the first challenge of my career.

A group of small farmers, related to each other, had been evicted from their lands. Subsequently, they forwarded their case to the court for redressing. In due course of time, I would come to know that the people who had deprived the farmers the right of ownership to their lands were either related to members of the ruling class, or they were acting on their behalf.

Unfortunately, neither of the contending parties had been able to furnish the court with a proof of a legal ownership of the land in dispute. But unlike the accused, the plaintiffs had been able to base their claims on a long-term period of occupation of the land in dispute. This fact had been confirmed by witnesses.

To me, as a judge, that alone had the effect of validating the claims made by the plaintiffs.

I believed then that the success made by the plaintiffs in the court of law would have the effect of discouraging future attempts that could be made by well-connected group of individuals wishing to rob the farmers of their land. I had hoped that this would be the case, after I declared the verdict in favour of the plaintiffs.

In my decision to award the farmers the right of ownership to the disputed lands, in the absence of a proper set of laws, I had made use of both tact and logic. The decision would annoy many people.

Talking to each other, after dinner, in one of the beach-side restaurants, Haigan expressed his feelings concerning land issues to me.

He told me in a voice that was laden with angry emotion that land is of paramount importance to the development of a nation. Whether he was angry with me or the farmers I couldn't tell, at that point in time. If left exclusively in the hands of small farmers, he went on, the land becomes useless. The small farmers, by nature, are a conservative lot; they abhor change. If they can grow food, enough to last them a season, they become more than happy, he concluded.

In reply, I told him that I understood his point well, but that I doubted whether his views that were more political than legal in nature could in any way nullify the peasants' right to own those lands that belong to them.

Since the nation was determined to move forward, he told me, no one should be allowed to hold it to ransom, on a spurious claim of maintaining legal niceties

That evening, we parted amidst a state of gloom. On my way home I realised the reason for which the government had bestowed so many favours on me, including the house, the loans, the job, the farm etc. For each of the favours that I had received, I was now expected to repay them in kind.

Was I willing to play the role? I asked myself. If could bring myself to do it, I would get along well with my life. But if not, the future would be too ghastly to contemplate.

I didn't want to put the life of my wife and two children to jeopardy. I could never see myself as someone willing to sacrifice the life of my family for a principle. I could never rise to the occasion, like other people who had sacrificed everything for a principle. History is replete with such figures. Buddha is one such a person; he left his family to seek enlightenment. Mandela was another one; he spent years in jail in the hope that his country will be free.

What does it require for someone to give up his family? I asked myself. Is it courage or conviction? To this question, I had no answer. Yet I had known all along that something must soon give.

It had all started with Haigan cutting off all communications between us. I was convinced, sooner or later, a gesture much greater and worse in magnitude than the mere cutting off of the links was going to happen.

One day a group of seven men, in tattered clothes and haggard looks, were arraigned before the court. They had been accused of treason. However, for want of clear evidence against them I sent them back to their cells, pending further investigation.

Later in the evening Haigan paid me a visit in my houses. I had just come home from work, and was looking forward to have a rest. He was accompanied by state security personnel. These were young men in platform shoes; they had a habit of wearing dark glasses, even in the darkest of nights, and had preferred wearing bright colourful shirts and trousers so wide at the bottom that they looked comical in them. Their loyalty was to no one, but Haigan.

Haigan gave brief favourable comments about how beautiful everything looked in the house. He never sat down. Like a cat playing with a rat, I realised those words were a preliminary stage of an act that was bound to turn nasty, at any time. A moment later, Haigan changed the subject; He was straightforward in his speech by making his intention clear.

As he spoke to me, Haigan paced the ground. Haigan approached me eventually, and stood so close to me that I caught on his face the scent of the after lotion.

Directing his gaze at me, he appealed to my sense of understanding; he told me not to play a hero. I have a splendid future, why waste it, he told me.

Finally, using an intimidating tone, he wanted to know whether I was going to find the accused guilty of the crime for which they had been arraigned before the court.

This time, I was beside myself with anger. I looked Haigan straight in the face and told him categorically that the defendants are innocent until proven guilty. I presume myself a judge, I told him, not a murderer of people.

If he was so eager to have the men dead, why put them through the charade of court procedures? I asked him. I told him that he has the means at his disposal to do whatever he may wish to do with the prisoners without involving me. I was not going to smear my hands with the blood of innocent people, I reminded him.

As ruthless as he seemed to be, Haigan was not that reckless or silly enough to make him commit a broad-day act of political blunder for the all the world to see. He wanted someone to give his foul action a legal credibility; it was obvious he had chosen me for the job.

In response to my principled stand, Haigan called the security personnel and ordered them to take me away. He would not allow me to have a word with my wife or my children who, lurking behind the walls, heard everything said between us.

It was obvious to me that I sacrificed my life, as well as my family's life, for the sake of principle. I wondered what that had made me into. Did it make me into hero or a fool? I asked myself.

I was sent to a special prison designed to deal with people that had been accused of high treason. In a newspaper where my photograph was printed, I was declared a traitor. I had been conniving, the paper wrote further, with the defendants to overthrow the ruling regime, through a support that I was getting from a neighbouring nation.

To support the allegations that had been made against me, my photograph was printed in the country's major newspaper, showing me as I shook hands with the ambassador of the said neighbouring nation. The caption above the picture had read,

"The Face of a Traitor can't hide." Immediately below the picture was the following statement: "In this picture, Kore is seen passing over some sensitive information to Mr. Andergatchew Meshesha, the bona fide ambassador of the nation hostile to this country."

In fact, there was no any truth whatsoever at the allegation made against me. Instead, Mr. Meshesha had been extending a personal invitation for me to take part in a celebration, commemorating the defeat of the Italian Army by Abbyssinians in 1896, at the Battle of Adwa.

In prison, in a crowd of approximately twenty people crammed inside a small cell, of four by three meters, with high ceiling, and a single window placed high up on one side of the wall, I met all kinds of people, including, businessmen, students, and religious leaders. In this place, prisoners were almost starved to death.

The sense of humiliation we had been made to undergo had made our suffering hard to bear. Any of us could be hauled to a torture chamber, situated at the middle of the building, to enable the screaming victims of torture to be heard by other prisoners.

To the prisoners, life meant either undergoing a continuous moment of torture, or hearing the horrible screams of the torture victims. Naturally, in such a place sleep never come easily; this, of course, was intended to be the case. Occasionally, Haigan himself had tortured the inmates. Although he didn't have a direct hand in torturing me, yet on more than one occasions Haigan had been there watching as I got tortured.

One time, I was hurt so badly that my kidneys were affected. This had required sending me to a hospital for treatment. While in the hospital, a group opposed to the regime smuggled me out of the country, and took me to Kenya for further treatment. In Nairobi, I applied for a refugee status.

At this point, he reached the end of the story of his life.

Erik gave him what had amounted to sad look; he turned the tape off, and got up from the chair.

"You have had more than your share of troubles in life," Erik told Kore.

"The Embassy," he told him, "would get in touch once a word about the fate of your application is received from Sweden."

They shook hands. Kore thanked Erik and left the Embassy.

On his way back to his little room, Kore thought about Erik whom he found to be quite thorough, as a person. One thing that Kore noticed about the man was that he was the embodiment of the fine qualities that are associated with people of his country.

After the interview, each time he contacted UNHCR to inquire about the fate of his application for asylum, Kore received a favourable review of his case, something which often gave him a dose of hope, allowing him to have fortitude to live his life, to continue to dream about a change that would come, one day.

The life of a refugee is a mixed bag of hope and despair. The refugee is hopeful that life will get better, one day, yet, not knowing when that long-awaited change would come, the refugee is a desperate person. Several months had gone by and still there was no word from the Swedish Embassy; then suddenly it happened. One day, he got a call from Wijewardena of UNHCR, requesting him to visit the Swedish Embassy. At the Embassy, once again, he met with Erik Nilsson.

"Congratulations. I am happy to let you know your application for a resettlement to Sweden has been |accepted. I have it all here," he waived the piece of paper at Kore.

The news was so overwhelming that all Kore could manage to do in response was to give Erik an ecstatic smile. For a moment, it was quiet inside the room. Kore never knew what to say; he felt words were not enough to express his feelings of joy. He knew what the word resettlement means, but he wanted to hear from Erik himself what that word means, as if he needed to reassure himself the word is what it says it is.

"What does resettlement mean?" He asked.

"It means you will have a permanent right to live and work in Sweden. Furthermore, your family members, including your wife and two children, will have the right to join you there. After couple of years, if your record allows it, you would be entitled to a Swedish citizenship." Erik said easily.

"I am happy to have the opportunity to work and live in Sweden," Kore said sincerely.

"Mr. Kore, when do you wish to leave?" Erik said quite abruptly, ignoring Kore's remarks.

"Anytime soon," said Kore.

"I understand that you don't have a passport. The Red Cross office will provide you with one. As soon as you get it, come and see us so that we could set to motion the process of getting you to travel to Sweden. Do you have something you wish to say, Mr Kore?" He asked.

"No." Kore said.

"Well then, it has been nice meeting you, Mr, Kore," he said. He stood up and offered to shake hands with Kore.

As Kore was about to leave, Erik drew his attention.

Kore turned around to face Erik.

"May I ask you a question, Mr Kore?" Erik said in a hesitant tone.

"Feel free, please," said Kore eagerly.

"What picture of Sweden do you have in your mind?" He asked.

"Many blond blue-eyed people, believing in liberal ideals, living in an exceedingly cold place," Kore said readily.

Erik appeared to be a little surprised; he adjusted the knot on his tie, pursed his lips, gave Kore a subtle smile and said, "Your knowledge of Sweden is great, Mr Kore."

"Thank you, Mr Nilsson," Kore offered in response.

"Good luck," Erik genially said.

"Thanks a lot," Kore offered sincerely.

Kore left the embassy premises, looking happy. He was happy that his ordeal seemed to have at last come to an end. But he knew well his current state of happiness was merely a temporary thing. He had a feeling of a person, who finds nothing about him has changed, even after realising his goal of getting on top of a highest mountain. In his case, even the pain in the stomach, which he had forgotten about in the moment of joy, now it was back in full force.

A week before his departure, Kore's friends held a farewell party for him. Later, the Red Cross issued him with a travelling document, while the Swedish Embassy gave him a Lufthansa plane ticket bound for Stockholm, via Frankfurt.

# Chapter Three

# *Flight LG600*

It was little past 10 p.m., on a chilly August night, at Nairobi's busy Jomo Kenyatta International Airport, when Kore took Lufthansa Flight No LG 600 that would take him half-way across the world to a place he had never dreamt about. Inside the plane, having gone through all the airport formalities, Kore searched for his seat and found it. He was happily surprised to discover that he had a first-class seat reserved for him. Yet given circumstances that made him to be one of the passengers on flight LG 600, he doubted if the seat was indeed his. He beckoned at a flight attendant to see what she would say.

A tall blond German air-hostess whose smile could not hide the state of a physical tiredness approached him carefully. She kindly requested to see his ticket, inquired his name, nodded her head in the direction of the seat, and then said, "Mr Kore, seat No. 10C is yours. Please take your seat and enjoy your flight." Soon the departure of flight LG 600 was announced, and the passengers prepared themselves for a long flight, with a stop-over of several hours at the Frankfurt Airport.

Sitting next to him was a short and frail looking man that Kore assumed to be in his late thirties; the man introduced himself to Kore as Johan Bjorkman, and further said that he was from Sweden. Pointing to a woman sitting beside him, he told Kore, "Meet my wife, Susan."

Susan gave Kore a light smile that he reciprocated with a smile of his own. Later, Kore graciously introduced himself to the couple. In contrast to her husband, Susan was quite big.

As soon as the introduction was over, the couple resumed their conversation, punctuated with ripples of laughter. Occasionally, quite discreetly, they kissed each other. However, in-between conversation with his wife, to while away the time, Bjorkman would choose to engage Kore in a light conversation.

Addressing Kore in a cautious manner, Bjorkman said, "By the way, I live and work in Nairobi for United Nations Educational, Scientific and Cultural Organisation." (UNESCO) He posed briefly to see if Kore would say something. Kore remained quiet.

After a moment of hesitation, he said, "Education holds a key to the development of Africa. It has served other continents well. It could well do the same for Africa."

He met Kore's eyes with dogged stares. His baritone voice belied his slight physical feature. His receding hair was the colour of sand, and his bulbous nose gave him a funny look.

Kore remained quiet.

As the man continued engaging Kore in conversation, a stewardess approached to offer them a light dinner. The man from Sweden resumed his conversation with his spouse and ate his dinner, and Kore dug into his food with relish.

Making efforts not to allow chain of thoughts that he feared to evoke memories of a torture he had undergone in his country to take control of his mind, Kore became quite glad when Bjorkman drew his attention, moments later.

"What is your destination?" He asked in an affable manner.

Kore adjusted the pair of glasses to sit well on the bridge of his nose, lowered his voice, looked at his sides, as if to discourage eavesdropping, and then said,

"Sweden is my destination; there I have been offered political asylum."

"Why does it have to be Sweden, of all places?" Bjorkman said.

"What is wrong with Sweden? Kore asked. "Don't you know," he added, "Sweden's good name has always been preceded by its reputation abroad?"

"Are you happy?" he cautiously asked.

"What," Kore asked.

"Sorry." Bjorkman said hurriedly, and further said, "Are you happy that you have gained political asylum in Sweden?"

As the conversation between the two men was taking place, Bjorkman's wife remained silent. Occasionally, however, if something of interest in the discussion caught her attention, she nodded to indicate her involvement.

"I am happy, of course. I have every reason to be happy," Kore spoke with an accustomed playfulness.

Taking a sip from a drink he had just ordered, Bjorkman nodded his head. He put down the glass on a small makeshift table, and then said, "What more do you know about Sweden?"

Kore took a long look at Bjorkman, turned to look across the window to catch a glimpse of the night. Slowly, and quite thoughtfully, he rubbed his chin and then said, "It is not so much what I know about Sweden, but what I don't know which is important to me."

This conversation was followed with a long silence. A moment later, Kore sat upright in his chair, took a critical look at his fellow passenger, and said, "Do please tell me something about your country; anything will do."

As a proposition, the statement might have taken Bjorkman by surprise, since he could never have imagined he would be expected to give a reply to such a question, without having to add his own value judgements on his observation.

"What should I do to impart a piece of information about my country to someone who, sooner or later, would be confronted by a reality to which he alone would best know how to deal with it?" he seemed to think.

Giving Kore a determined look, Bjorkman said, "Sweden has many forms of reality and mine is only one among many others. Let us assume that I tell you that there is no country better than Sweden? Would you have believed me? I doubt it very much"

Kore saw logic in Bjorkman's statement and subsequently kept quiet. Except for a dim-light shining above, it was totally dark inside the rest of the cabin. By now all passengers were fast asleep, and so they too went to sleep.

In the afternoon of the following day, the plane landed Arlanda Airport, after a stopover at Frankfurt for a change of plane.

Kore was relieved to find someone at the airport waiting to receive him, and thereafter convey him to a refugee camp, at Flen. Acting as a holding ground, the camp was a place refugees were required to learn Swedish language, as well as acquire other few rudimentary knowledge of the Swedish culture. His escort turned out to be an elderly Swedish man with lively happy dispositions.

On the way to the refugee camp, situated scores of kilometres away from Arlanda Airport, Kore realised how the world he had left behind differed from the present one. Throughout their journey, not once have they come across a pedestrian, either crossing the road or walking alongside the road.

It was one car after another to which Kore's sight was treated; some came from behind in full speed, while others came from the opposite direction, all of them looking brand-new, leaving no plume of smoke behind.

This stood in great contrast to where he came from, where vehicles are made to stop, after every while, in order to let people and the cattle they tend to cross the road, at their own convenience.

However, given differences pertaining to levels of material development, climatic conditions, as well as racial types, between the two continents of Europe and Africa, some of the differences one could see in trees, buildings, people and farmlands, had made sense to Kore. What his mind was unable to fathom, however, was a pervasive extent of silence present both in social and physical spheres.

After long tedious hours of driving, finally the driver arrived at a small town, where he carefully drove through its narrow and twisted lanes. In the end, they stopped at a parking lot, in front of a huge single-story building, painted in a broken-white colour, surrounded with large trees.

From the colour of the leaves that had turned golden brown, green and red, it was quite easy for him to determine the season of the year as autumn. He thought his new home had pleasant surroundings. Not far from the building, there was a lake; he promised to develop his swimming skills there.

Kore and his escort got off the car and together they entered the building; everything regarding this building was exceptionally large in size, including the walls, the rooms and the corridors in it, Kore had noticed.

From the look of the building, kept a long distant away from the surrounding buildings, he assumed it must have once been a place for taking care of people with some sort of health problems – be it physical or mental. Inside, it held units of social amenities, including a dispensary, class rooms, an administration unit and a nursery school.

It was dinner time; the dining hall was full of people that he believed were refugees, majority of who were from the Far East. Later, he would come to learn that they were the so-called "Boat People," whose fate he had followed closely in newspapers.

In the dining hall, to his surprise, he discovered that the oppressive state of silence he had experienced earlier, on his way to the refugee camp, had suddenly dissipated against the background sound of laughter and children's cries.

Apart from "Boat People," there was a group of Europeans also in the dining hall. It turned out, later in the evening, during a conversation he had had with some of them, in English, they were from Poland.

As he entered the dinning-hall, escorted by his host, who would join him for dinner, all eyes were directed at him, for a moment. The amount of food, in the dining-hall, had staggered his imagination.

There were all sorts of food for the refugees to have. Available also, there were loads of butter and varieties of cheeses on the tables, covered with oil clothes.

Baskets of sweet smelling freshly baked-breads were placed at the most convenient points, across the dining hall, for the diners to take with them, on their way out, if they wished. Meat, chicken, fish and pork dishes were also available to choose from.

Korea had never been to a place where such a large amount of food had been displayed in a single place. Of course, in his community, there were occasions when large amounts of foods had been made available to people. But then, such occasions had often been far and wide in between.

In the dining hall, he gave thought to a paradoxical view about the nature of food consumption and was amazed at what he found out. He believed one is likely to have greatest desire for food when it is least available. Yet that desire is bound to disappear when faced with a mountain of food. This should have explained to him the reason for so much food going into the wastebasket, as the refugees streamed out from the dining hall.

From the dining hall, he was directed to an office where he met an elderly woman of grace. She welcomed him in perfect English, and then inquired briefly about his trip. He studied the office as he talked to the lady.

The office had a few set of furniture, which gave the place its spacious look. The windows, whose green curtains had been drawn apart to reveal a picturesque landscape outside, were large and clean, albeit, like the building itself, they were old fashioned. There displayed on top of the table was a framed photograph of her family members. There was something about the office which gave impression of its occupant as someone who was quite meticulous, as that sense was also evident in the way that she dressed.

Facing Kore across from a table, and over a cup of black coffee, she formally introduced herself as Annika, and said she was the camp's Assistant Director. Afterwards, she asked Kore questions to see if they matched the record that she had of him in the office.

Satisfied with the information, she took pain to accompany him to a nearby building, across the road, from where she identified a room for him that she said would be his. Before she left, she told him that someone would come to fetch him, early in the morning.

Although the room that had been reserved for him had a simple look, yet it had everything necessary for adequate living. The bed was covered with a white sheet; on top of it was placed a red blanket made of wool. Somehow the way the bed had been made, and the blanket that covered more than half the bed-space, had reminded him of his home, where he had once been hospitalised, following a fractured leg.

His room was in a middle of a three-storey building, overlooking a main road. He could see from the window of his room, in the playing-ground, filled with zeal and zest, how the children were enjoying themselves. It was hard for him to believe that these same children, along with their parents, not a long time ago, had been sailing on rickety boats, searching for a country that could offer them asylum.

He was glad to see the children amusing themselves with games that children like so much to play.

His first night in Sweden had proved to be like any other night; night-time it is a time when worrisome thoughts come jostling for attention in the minds of most people. He tried to free himself from those ominous thoughts that came knocking as he searched for sleep.

On this night, he had many worries crowding his mind for attention; he thought mostly about his family which he left behind in Africa; he thought of the future, and had many other worrisome thoughts to deal with besides. After a long tossing and turning he fell asleep.

# Chapter Four

# *Peter Sellers*

Just as promised by Annika, a woman came to fetch him early on the morning of the following day. She was tall; she seemed to be in her early thirties; her long thin blond hair sat in total disarray on her long narrow head. She had put on a pair of blue jeans and a wind-breaker that had matched the blue colour of the jeans.

Even though beauty is culturally determined, and it was clear to Kore that one should not use the standard beauty measurement of one culture to determine beauty in another culture, Kore considered the woman beautiful, by any standard of judgement.

To him, however, she seemed to be in a constant state of someone in a hurry. She walked so fast that he was forced to trot behind to catch up with her.

In due course, he would discover this to be a trait common to people living in Sweden. He thought it might have something to do with extreme low temperatures outside, which makes people want to run away from.

It was autumn now, and the temperatures at 5 degrees centigrade outside could generally still be considered as warm, by Swedish standard. He shivered with cold.

If someone had told him that in future he would be able to put up with minus 18-degree temperatures, he would have laughed at the suggestion.

"You must come with me; I am taking you out for shopping," she told Kore in a cheerful tone. "My name is Anna," she added in the same spirit.

"Thank you," He said.

"Don't thank me," she said smiling.

"Why not," He asked.

"I am simply doing my job; however, I understand your desire to be grateful," she said.

"In this case, why don't you accept my expression of gratitude to you," He said, showing signs of frustration.

"To begin with, I am not the right entity for you to direct your gratitude. But if the state is what you have in mind, I am sure you must have already given your thanks where they are due. You can't go offering gratitude to someone throughout all your life" she said with less effort.

"I don't know about that," He said.

"You have duties and rights here in this country," she said.

Now they were approaching the building with the dining hall inside.

"One of your major duties is to be a law-abiding citizen of this country; in return the state must protect and promote those rights that are yours," she said.

They had just entered the dining hall; since his mind was on breakfast, he kept quiet.

"What sort of a person is Anna, who wouldn't accept expression of gratitude easily?" He asked himself.

Different people act differently whenever they will meet someone new, he realised. Some may want to assert their mark; some will compromise, while others will remain indifferent. To him, Anna belonged to the first of the three categories of people. He wasn't sure he would like to meet her often.

Anna accompanied him to the dining hall where he took his breakfast of bread with cheese, omelette and tea. She took black coffee and smoked. From the dining hall they took a short walk to a parking lot, where the two got inside a car that Anna drove.

A few blocks down the road Anna stopped the car, and then parked the car in front of a building that would hardly impress someone who was a casual observer of things, since nearly all buildings in this small-town lack some of those most imposing qualities often associated with buildings of other similar towns in the developed world; nevertheless, there was something that had betokened a sense of grace and age about them that are rare elsewhere, Kore assumed.

The two entered a shop, where a well-dressed young-looking woman took time to welcome them in. After an exchange of warm regards, the two women went on talking to each other. Kore, meanwhile, attended to a business that had brought him there. There was so much to choose in the shop that he never knew where to begin. Finally, he saw a pair of trousers and a shirt that he liked. He picked them up, intending to show them to Anna, when he caught sight of Anna approaching.

"Ah," she said pointing at the clothes in his arms "is that all you have managed to choose?"

He remained silent; he felt embarrassed. Anna took him by the hand, and led him into a section where there were largely clothes meant for gents.

"Here you will find clothes for this season as well as the coming season," she said.

After that, she provided him with a list of each item. The list was so long it could fill in a page or two of an exercise book. Anna made sure that she stood by, in case he needed any assistance.

He made his choice well. Incidentally, among the clothing items he was expected to own, there were two dressing gowns and two pairs of pyjamas, as well as two pairs of slippers. The thought of wearing such apparel made him laugh.

Anna noticed the smile and looked inquiringly at him. He told her the clothes reminded him of Peter Sellers.

"What about him?" She asked.

He wanted to tell the reason but had remained quiet, instead. In fact, the reason that had caused him to laugh was that he knew Peter Sellers as an outstanding actor of comedies; one of his memorable acting scenes that had remained etched into his mind is in one of those hilarious PINK PANTHER film series, in which Peter Sellers is getting ready to engage his Chinese-looking valet in a mock fight.

In that scene, Peter Sellers had a dressing gown, worn over a pyjama-suit, and had sandals on his feet.

"Oh, nothing of importance," he said in response to her question.

"Suite yourself," she said.

After she finished paying for the items, Anna helped Kore to place the clothes in the van; from there, they drove back to the camp. At the camp, she helped him to unload the items. Later he took the clothes and carefully placed them inside a wardrobe.

The rhythm of everyday life in the camp had a precision of the proverbial Swiss-clock. The camp came to life early in the morning, every day. Breakfast was served between eight and nine, followed with language classes that ended at half past eleven. Lunch was served immediately thereafter; at one in the afternoon, all classes were resumed. Four o'clock was the end of a normal working day, every day. Afterwards, the refugees were free to spend their time any way they liked.

Kore would always keep fond memories of his Swedish language teacher; in her mid-fifties, she favoured plain gowns, boots and sweaters as her favourite mode of dressing; she had buck teeth, had low cropped-hair and had an unassuming character.

But hold on there; don't be cheated by her simple manners. As a language teacher, she had no parallel. Every word, every sentence that she taught her students, she gave a life to it, drawn either from her country's historical legacy or the cultural practices of its people.

She made the language speak to her students. Once, for example, when she explained the meaning of the word migration, she reminded the class how Swedes left for America, trying to escape from the 19th Century abject poverty of the Swedish rural life.

Her venturing into different fields of knowledge was a way of bringing to life the language she was teaching, thus enhancing in her students a desire to even learn more.

One time she talked to her class about meatballs. To prove to the class that it was a type of food dearly loved by Swedish people, she recounted how Ingmar Johansson's mother had welcomed her son, fresh from boxing victory over Floyd Patterson in New York, by having meatballs for dinner.

In her class room, one was instantaneously transported to a time when one was a young child, and learning was a process of rebirth into a new world, full of fascination. She had a reassuring way of dealing with people. She had a knack for making people feel comfortable.

Whenever she helped a person with something, she would never make that person feel she had an upper hand. For example, she would avoid saying to a person she was helping words such as, "Oh, poor you," (Stackers du)

In future, Korea would come to remember his teacher as one of the most lovable persons in the world.

The camp had no organised activities to keep its inhabitants engaged as a group. Hence, there was little interaction outside the context of ethnic associations. The Poles, like the Vietnamese and the Chinese, had each kept to themselves, and so did Kore, who never associated himself with any group.

Irrespective of one's ethnic background, however, everyone had made serious endeavours to visit room number eleven, which was Maria's abode. Maria was a young Polish woman. She told the future to whoever wished to know something about it. Although she never requested to have money for the services that she offered, yet she never rejected a contribution of money given to her. Fortune telling was only a hobby to her. Maria was concerned more with political future of her country.

The Chinese and the Vietnamese fought each other over the first right of access to Maria's room. The Poles, who made claims of close affinity to the priestess of fortune telling, contested the claims of both Vietnamese and Chinese.

One day, a Vietnamese old man, who had a long thin beard that touched his breast, came up with a clever proposal. He proposed, for each nationality, a day should be reserved for them to pay Maria a visit.

Incidentally, Kore was not in a procession of people paying Maria a visit. It was not because he was less gullible that had made him to not visit Maria; rather, the reason was that he had had an experience with a palm reader that had opened his eyes.

When he was young, he had a crush on a girl in his class. A well-known palm-reader had promised that he would win the love of the girl. When that didn't happen, he lost confidence with all fortune tellers.

Once when Maria met him in the dining hall, she told him, "Are you not curious about your future?"

"Are you?" He replied with a question of his own.

She blushed and looked down. "Would you mind coming over to my place this evening? I have something important I wish to talk to you about," she told him.

Saturday, being a day of rest, he decided to pay her a visit. Maria lived not far from where he lived. She lived in a single room, in a two-storey building. On his way there, less than a hundred meters away, he walked under the canopy of maple trees; meanwhile, he tried never to speculate about how the evening would turn out. Naturally, he was not interested in what she would have to say about his future; after all, he never believed her prediction to be necessarily an accurate reflection of future events.

As he followed his thoughts, he found himself at a doorstep to the now famous room, number eleven. He hesitated, straightened his pullover, which was one among many other clothing items that he had recently acquired. He wished he had a full dressing mirror in his room, to enable him to see how he looked.

Kore looked younger than what his thirty years of age would suggest. He was six foot tall. He had a jet-black complexion; he had kept an afro hair style, and had a beard that covered only his chin. He had put on a pair of glasses that easily rested on the bridge of his nose. His thin waist gave his shoulders a much broader dimension. In connection to his general appearance, a few women he had met in his lifetime had considered him a good-looking man.

This evening, however, he was extra conscious of himself. He swallowed; he was about to give a knock when the door was opened; he was caught in a frozen posture of someone about to give a knock on the door. Maria opening the door could not help smiling.

"I was beginning to suspect that you were not going to come," she said.

She was in a jubilant mood. "Come in," she said in perfect English, as she held the door wide open for him to get in. Once he got inside the room, she locked the door. She sighed and went to sit on the bed, facing Kore.

Maria had put on a black-satin evening dress that added shade to what otherwise was a milky white colour of her skin. The long-heeled shoes had accentuated her height of five feet ten inches to make her appear almost at par in height with Kore. She had done her hair in a ponytail style, which had the effect of displaying well her gypsy cheekbones - a gift she had acquired from her gypsy mother - adding a shade of brilliance to her beautiful face.

Maria's dream of future success was reflected in the way she had her single room decorated. The floor had a carpet from Samarqand. Hanging on the walls were paintings, some of which were imitations of the works of great European masters of past centuries.

A wooden bookshelf was attached to one side of the wall; it seemed, from the list of the books in it, not only was Maria an avid reader of books, but she was someone who made a good choice of all the books that she read.

Next to one of the bookshelves was a small table; mounted on top of the table was a small fridge that held an assortment of drinks in it, including bottles of priceless brand of whisky and wines.

Maria owned a music system that had an elaborate mechanism installed in it, to produce a wonderful sound. After a brief surveying of her records, Kore found that she also had a sophisticated taste in music; she enjoyed listening to jazz, after all; how much more sophisticated could one be.

All the other items, except for the drinks, Maria had bought them in Stockholm, from dealers of used items!

"What would you like to drink?" She asked Kore.

He requested for a glass of red wine.

She took out a bottle of wine from the fridge, opened it up, and then poured the drinks into the tumblers; she carried the tumblers and gave one to Kore, sitting on a leather chair; she sat on the bed.

"What do we toast to?" Maria inquired impatiently.

He gave her a bright look and then said, "Let us say," He hesitated, leading Maria to look at him with anxious eyes.

He said finally, "Let us drink to happiness?"

Maria smiled and said, "To happiness."

She approached the music system, picked one of the jazz albums by Charlie "Bird" Parker, and let it to play in a low volume.

"I like to listen to Parker, because the fury in his music touches my body and soul in a way that is comparable to only when someone is making love to me," she said merrily.

"What about Henry Miller? He said.

"What about him? She asked.

"Well, I see you have the copies of his books," said Kore.

"Why do you ask?" Maria said, giving him a lavish smile. "I am afraid, you have a dirty mind. Do you have a dirty mind, Kore?" She said in a playful manner.

"No, I am simply curious," he replied.

"Well, in this case, if you must know, I think Miller was in a class of his own," she said. She took a sip from her drink, put down the glass on a coffee table and then further said, "I read Miller, because I admire him for his courage in making the story of sex and sex-making into a literature form with both quality and taste."

A few moments later, she said, "Have I answered your question adequately enough to satisfy your curiosity?"

"Yes," he replied almost obediently, and further said, "I must agree with you that for someone to have to consider his work in the same light as the cheap pornographic literature, while forgetting other aspects of his writings, dealing with Parisian working class, was a foolish thing to do."

"Splendid. You have an acute sense of perception," she said with a feeling of elation.

He smiled lightly, took a keen look at her, but remained quiet.

"What? Say something," said Maria.

"Why do you hate communism in Poland? For no reason, Kore felt a strong inner compulsion to ask the question.

Maria posed to look at him, and with a touch of irony said, "You ask strange questions. Perhaps you enjoy challenging people, or are you not?"

Kore gave a hilarious laughter. "Not at all, I don't mean to bother you with questions you may not want to answer. I am sorry," He said.

"You don't have to be sorry. Your last question is a typical question which many people want an answer given to. That answer, unfortunately, is not what they hope for," she said, as she gave Kore a warm smile.

"What is your answer?" He asked in a challenging tone.

"In Poland, most of us do not hate communism as an ideology. We hate the Soviet Union," she said in a firm tone.

"To me they are one and the same." he said.

"Wrong," she said. She smiled lightly and added, "Communism belongs to a corpus of knowledge offered as a critique of the capitalistic system of economy, while the Soviet Union is a totalitarian state driven by a desire to extend her hegemony over Poland."

They stayed quiet, for a short moment, each sipping their drinks and looking as if they were lost in their own thoughts.

"Why are you not consulting me about your future?" Finally, Maria said. From the way she put up the question, Kore felt that she was eager to know, like everyone else, why he hasn't shown any kind of interest in her work.

Kore let his eyes rest on Maria, but chose to stay quiet, which made Maria to give him an anxious look.

"With all due respect for you,' he said abruptly, to the happy surprise of Maria, 'I don't need to know anything concerning the future, and what it may hold in store for me; what is to be will be, after all. Besides, I am not as desperate as anyone else. People come to see you so that, in promising wealth, health, fame and love, you are saying that life is worth living; you promise the four-major pillar-dreams of life - so to speak. To me, that is a form of therapy that I can do without."

For the first time, Maria removed her hands that had been resting on her chin and then laughed loudly.

"I am going to have some more drinks," she said. "Would you like to have some?" She added.

He nodded his head. She refilled both their tumblers, offered Kore his drink, and then resumed her position on the bed.

"You seem to have quite original ideas. However, sometimes, I am inclined to believe you are quite obstinate, or are you not?" She ejaculated.

"You are not charitable in your tributes," he ventured to say. They both laughed hilariously.

By now the music had long stopped playing, and so Maria went and played some soft romantic music. Afterwards, she approached Kore; her arms outstretched in his direction, she asked him for a dance. Kore never considered himself to be a good dancer; he accepted the request, nevertheless. Soon the two were shuffling to the beat of the music, silently obeying the sound of their heavy-breath, promising to reach a rhythmic crescendo, at any moment now.

At this point, looking at Maria giving him a seductive look, as she danced with him, it occurred to him that the path he was taking would lead him to a place he may not want to be. He ought to put this thing to an end before it gets too far. He stopped dancing. The sign of uneasy feeling in him might have shown in his face, which had led Maria to inquire about how he was feeling. He mumbled something, subsequently; something about not feeling well before leaving the room in a great haste.

On his way to his room, he looked at the path he had taken and how that path had crossed Maria's path. Would their path ever meet again in the same way; where would that lead them to? Maria was single; she had no commitment to anything, save her politics. In his case, he had a wife and two children. Maria could afford to be infatuated with him, and if it went a step further she could even fall in love with him, too.

But what would that mean to him? Can he fall in love with her and yet pretend everything was fine? What chances are there he might fall in love with her? No one has an answer to such a question; certainly not him, who is married to his wife, currently in Africa, waiting to reunite with him.

And yet he couldn't pretend that his short encounter with Maria had left no marked imprint in his mind. Not only has he found Maria to be beautiful but she was nice to talk to; those are the same qualities that had attracted him to Hadio, his wife.

He had reached his home by now; minutes before he opened the door, he heard a sound of footsteps behind him; he turned around only to catch sight of Maria, two steps away from him, heading in his direction. Her arms outstretched, she fell into his arms, and the two kissed. Kore opened the door, meanwhile, and the two entered the room, kissing feverishly as they edged towards the bed.

They were now openly panting in a manner of people who had just finished running a long-distance race. Hence, the crush into the bed that had followed came as relief to both, since it stopped them from attempting an impossible task of trying to maintain a balance, where maintaining the balance was increasingly becoming an exercise in futility, with each passing moment.

They lay on the bed, facing each other, while their hands explored each other's supple bodies.

That night, Maria spent the rest of the night in Kore's room.

From that day on, every Saturday night was to become specially a night Kore visited Maria, in her room. In due course, besides becoming lovers, the two had also become good friends.

Kore had left the threshold behind; from now on, he entrusted the feelings he had been having for Maria on fate; what did he hope to achieve from fate? To this question he had no answer; he must wait and see; he had become a slave to fate.

After he came to know Maria well, he discovered that her family's history was quite a fascinating one. Maria was a product of a union of two very unusual people. Her father had been one of Polish Marxists intellectuals who had left Poland for the Soviet Union, in the twenties, to show solidarity with the Bolsheviks, but later became disappointed with the totalitarian form of the Soviet rule.

Her mother was a Gypsy from Moldavia. As a young girl, Maria's mother had taught herself how to read and write against the wishes of her parents and society in general. Through her readings, she became acquainted with claims made by the Bolsheviks about giving recognitions to nationalities in their aspirations; all of which had favoured her dream of one day becoming an actress.

She left her home, one day, and never returned to see her family again. She left for Moscow; there a communist youth organisation, after noticing her talents, had nurtured it accordingly. Subsequently, at the age of twenty-three, she became the best theatre artist in the whole country.

It was during this period in her life that she met a man who would become her husband, and later Maria's father, who had been a professor of philosophy at Moscow State University. In 1947 the family returned to Poland where Maria was born in 1949.

In Poland, Maria had been an editorial-board member of an underground press, critical of the Polish Communist-run Government. Being a professor of English literature, she also helped recruit students to swell the ranks of people who identified with the aims of the Solidarity Movement that would become instrumental in helping to bring the communists rulers of Poland down to their knees.

One day, a government-mole revealed her identity to the communist authorities.

A move to arrest her had been under way when a counter mole, serving in the higher echelons of the communist party, informed her organisation of the plan to have her arrested.

It was then that her organisation was forced to smuggle her out of the country, using a Norwegian cargo-ship that had docked at Gdansk sea-port. Once in Sweden, she was given a political refugee status.

# Chapter Five

# *Uppsala.*

At Flen refugee camp, life was not expected to last forever. By now Kore had spent nearly five months there, and had a month more left to stay in Flen. Maria had already left the camp, a month earlier; now she was living in Stockholm. On more than one occasion she had invited Kore to visit her there. Kore was pleased with architectural designs of the buildings, as well as the many waterways crisscrossing the city's beautiful landscape.

Although he found the city of Stockholm to have a beauty almost of a bewitching quality, Kore settled elsewhere, instead.

His new home – Uppsala - is an hour drive to Stockholm. Uppsala, in its own way, is a beautiful city.

Located at the city centre are three structures, placed in a triangular set up, symbolising power, both temporal and spiritual. These are the following: Scandinavia's tallest cathedral (DOMKYRKAN). Kept in its vaults are the remains of Gustav Vasa, the once charismatic King of Sweden, who had made Sweden a unified kingdom, from out of many smaller principalities

A short distance from the church is a big library with treasures of manuscripts and books - ancient and modern - unmatched elsewhere, in terms of their uniqueness.

Close to the library is the castle. A massacre of a group of aristocrats that once had taken place there, several centuries ago, is recounted with such unparalleled vividness that one could visualise it.

Uppsala is famous throughout the world as a home of learning. Although not half the size of Stockholm, Uppsala is just as cosmopolitan as the city of Stockholm is.

In Uppsala, one is likely to come across individuals from such remote places as the Kalahari Desert or the Amazon Forest, doing shopping in a business concern that belongs to either a Turk or an Armenian.

In the university, it is not unusual to have a class in which close to half of its student population have come from outside Sweden. Hence, because of many different nationalities found in Uppsala, it is not wrong perhaps to assume that the world has come to Uppsala.

Apart from foreign students on exchange programme, Uppsala also is a host to multitudes of other groups of people that were refugees once, or contracted industrial workers. Forever a student of man, nature and history, Kore had found the city of Uppsala, more than any other one, to have a special appeal for him.

This was a reason that had made him to disagree with Maria, who wanted him to move to Stockholm for them to live together. It was a big mistake he made; the decision will coast him much.

One fine Saturday morning, as he was getting ready to have breakfast in his two room apartment, at Sernandes väg student quarters, sitting on a chair by the window, his telephone rang; He picked up the phone and said, "Hello."

There was a moment of silence, and then a voice that belonged to Maria said, "Hello."

There was a gloom in Maria's voice that he couldn't fail to detect.

"I am happy you called. I have been thinking about you just moments before you called; talk of telekinetic."

He tried to sound happy, to hide the feeling of a foreboding nature that was beginning to take control of his mind. To his surprise, Maria didn't bother to comment further on what he had just said to her.

"I will be frank with you," she said, instead. "I don't want you to anymore come and see me in Stockholm," she added.

This last sentence threw his mental constitution off balance; he couldn't think clearly; he stayed quiet for lack of something to say. His silence wouldn't take him off the hook; if this is what he expected would be the case.

A moment later, he heard Maria say, "I don't wish to see you again."

Maria's voice sounded as if it reached him from inside a hole. To him it sounded muffled.

"What do you mean?" He said. "I am coming to see you," he added in a haste.

"There is no use coming over. I am finished with you," she said in a resolute manner.

"Finish with me, you said," he repeated her statement. For the first time, he became irritated with Maria.

"I am not a piece of bone that you throw away after scrapping the meat off of it. I am coming to see you," he insisted.

Maria hung up on him, leaving him lost on what to think.

Immediately after this conversation, however, he made up his mind to travel to Stockholm, to try to convince Maria to change her mind. She was angry with him; he was sure about it;

but it wasn't about something that can't be discussed between them.

He was so eager to get to see Maria that he felt the train to Stockholm was not moving fast enough. On the way there, he stopped at a small shop, inside Stockholm's train station to buy Maria a present of a chocolate box; he did this every time he paid Maria a visit.

Maria had been allocated a two-room apartment in a second floor of a building, situated in a block immediately behind Rinkeby square. Rinkeby suburb of Stockholm had over a period of time increasingly become home to successive waves of immigrants.

The first wave of immigrants who came from Greece, the Balkans and Turkey, took place in the fifties and the sixties of the 20th Century; these were industrial workers; the Chileans found their way there early seventies, as a result of a coup that overthrew Salvador Allende from power.

In the eighties political refugees from various African countries as well as Iran and Iraq arrived.

By early seventies, the Swedish original inhabitants had already moved out, leaving the area to the new comers.

When he got at Maria's apartment, to his surprise, he found the keys to the apartment not fitting the lock. Maria had given him the reserve key to the room for him to use.

He had to double check carefully the number on the door to make sure that the apartment was Maria's; the number on the top right-hand corner of the door clearly read 113.

There should be quite a valid reason for Maria wanting to change the lock, he thought. But just as he was about to give a knock, he thought he heard what sounded like voices coming from inside the apartment, which Kore assumed must belong to her friends.

He retrieved the box of chocolate from the plastic bag, held it in his left hand, and then gave a knock.

"Who is it?" Maria asked.

"It is me, Kore," he said.

Suddenly, the door opened, but kept half-ajar. Behind the door stood Maria, dressed in a large fitting male shirt; she was bare-foot. She held the door with one hand, and had the other hand resting on her hip. Kore was not surprised at her action. He moved forward, attempting to embrace her. She took a step back, and gave him a disgusting look.

The door became fully opened, meanwhile, revealing the sight of a white man, the lower half of his body covered in a bed sheet, bare-chested, reposing in a bed, laughing at him.

"Who is that man in your bed, Maria? He asked in a trembling voice.

His voice sounded different; it lacked its usual timber.

"Oh; I almost forgot. A formal introduction is what is called for here," said Maria, who sounded like a bureaucrat introducing a new colleague to a meeting.

Looking at the man in the bed with adoring eyes, she said, "Nestor, meet Kore." She kept quiet about Kore.

She took a hasty look at Kore and said, "Kore, this is my new friend, Nestor."

"But darling…" he said.

"Don't you ever call me darling again," she said loudly; she didn't give him time to finish what he wished to say.

She went to sit on the bed, next to her new boyfriend, Nestor, leaving Kore to stand in the middle of the room, clutching at his chocolate box.

Kore never wished to believe his eyes. Was he dreaming? He assumed that whatever was taking place there had to be the phantom of his imagination. How could Maria become suddenly quite so insensitive and so cruel to him?

"What have I done to warrant such a change of heart in her?" He asked himself.

For quite a long time he stood in the middle of the room, not saying anything; in the end he pleaded with Maria to change her mind.

"Please," he said."

At this point, he became so much agitated that it mattered little to him someone was there in the room watching him, as he asked for love from a woman who had mysteriously lost all feelings of love that she had been having for him.

He belittled himself once again by saying, "Please."

"It is over", she said quite vehemently; she added, "I am not anymore in love with you."

He would in future come to know how that statement has often been used by lovers to bring many loving relationships to a tragic end. Many such relationships had seemed initially to be quite unassailable as well as impregnable.

While still standing in the middle of the room, clutching at the chocolate box, he asked Maria to change her mind about him. If understanding is what he expected to get from Maria, she gave him none of that; instead, she told him "Stop it. Your theatrics do not impress me. Leave, or else I will call the police."

At the word police, he gave Maria a last dismal look. To avoid looking at him, Maria turned her face. She wouldn't accept the chocolate box he had brought for her to keep, as a present.

"Take away your chocolate; I don't need them," she told him.

On the way out, he threw the chocolate box in a waste basket, kept beside the door. He left the room quietly; he had a dazed look, such as the one you see on the face of a zombie. He took a train to Uppsala. It was an afternoon of a day in winter; the city was full of people making their shopping, in preparation for Christmas.

He wandered through the streets in the grip of a festive mood. Everything that once had seemed of interest to him now ceased to evoke the same feeling in him; instead, they irritated him.

The figure of Father Christmas, with its white flowing beard, dressed in red, found in every shopping centre, had stopped having for him the same fascination that it once had. Christmas Carols lost their charm, and people in the streets appeared to him as if they were operating in a world which had lost its force of gravity.

He found walking on snow, in an almost empty stomach, had become a difficult task to perform. His legs would not carry him any further. Not to bump into the floating figures of humanity that he had been imagining in his mind, he searched for a convenient place to sit and rest.

From Svertsbackgatan, he crossed St Olofsgatan, and was on Svartsbacksgatan once again, heading towards those modest-looking cafes standing in a row, opposite Uppsala's famous botanical garden, named after its founder, Carl Von Linne. He got inside of one of those cafes and served himself a cup of tea and pastries that he paid for in the counter. Next to his table, a young couple sat holding hands, talking in whisper, looking at each other, and then kissed occasionally; he envied them.

As he sat there alone, sipping mint-tea, savouring the sweat taste of pastries, his eyes fell on a roof-top of a building, demarcated by a wooden wall, its large iron-gate facing Svartsbeckgatan. Resting on top of the gate is an iron frame bearing a Swedish court of arms, symbolised by three crowns, which means the property inside is a government property.

Here in this compound, centuries ago, Carl Von Linne did his scientific work. Kore tried to imagine, with loving eyes and tender care, how Carl Von Linne would hold plants in his hands scrutinising each for the quality that makes it unique - a feat that had enabled him today to become one of the greatest scientific minds of all centuries and felt awe-inspired.

In spite of the gift of mind, could it have ever occurred to Carl Von Linne, Kore imagined, one day, centuries later, an African, whose race he didn't think highly of, would sit not far from his place of work to brood over the loss of a love he had had once for a European woman? The thought caused him to laugh for its irony, attracting the attention of the people in the cafe.

In his relationship with Maria, he never thought that one day he and Maria would go their separate ways; to him, after all, separation had meant something that could happen to other people, not to him.

Now as he sat there in the restaurant, feeling sad but also anxious and angry, quite at the same time, he acknowledged to himself that life with Maria had not been without its ups and downs.

There were occasions, he recollected, tears in her eyes, Maria had requested him to move in with her in Stockholm and take up a job. Every time she took up the issue, to distract her attention from the subject, he covered her face with kisses, and the matter was forgotten, until the subject resurfaced, once again.

"How could I not have foreseen it coming? How could I have not read the writings on the wall?" He asked himself.

Maria had presented him with many chances meant for him to change his mind; however, time and again, he had disappointed her. When she literally threw him out of her apartment, an hour ago, he had hated her for it.

Now, while enjoying the cosy-atmosphere of the cafe, sipping mint-tea, enjoying the taste of the pastries in his mouth, he could afford to be generous in his attitude toward Maria.

One thing he could never understand though was the reason that had made her not wishing to have anything to do with him, even as he broke down in front of her new lover, begging for her love.

"Did I not in the past forgive her when she had caused me to feel hurt?"He reasoned.

He recollected a time when she kissed his toes, licked his ears, and if he had shown any sign of anger she would sit under his feet, crying, asking him to forgive her. Of course, whenever she acted in such a slavish and demeaning manner, he would somehow become ashamed of himself. Subsequently, he would choose to forgive her.

"Why then would she not forgive and forget my sins, since now the tables have been turned on me?" He asked himself.

In relation to the spirit of forgiving and forgetting, which he thought was lacking in Maria, he recollected a conversation he had had once with a friend that had a misfortune of losing love; this friend had warned him against incurring the wrath of women. About women, his friend had told him, "When a woman loves, she loves with all her heart. However, once she turns her back on you, no amount of cajoling, backbiting, begging, blackmailing or beating would force her to change her mind."

He should have taken his lessons well, but he had been foolish enough to assume that whatever his friend was telling him, it has no bearing on his life experience. The only relevance his friend's speech had had on him, it occurred to him now, was of such a nature as when you are told of a car accident that you assume could not happen to you, but to someone else.

He sat in the café long enough for him to regain strength of body. Suddenly, he remembered the priest scholar from Africa that he knew. He decided to pay him a visit, after he phoned him, thinking of the solace he would achieve from meeting with him.

# Chapter Six

# *Augustine Mulembe*

The priest, Augustine-Mulembe Mohamed, was born in the highlands of a central southern African nation to a father who had converted to Christianity from Islam. His father had worked as a gardener for a Swedish family of missionaries. Mulembe, Augustine's father, slowly but surely, worked his way up to become a head cook in the same Swedish household.

Augustine was a third child in a family of six children. From a very tender age of seven, the young boy was able to impress his father's employers with his diligent mind. He could read the Bible, and remembered important passages from the Holy Book with such ease that everybody thought the child had a special gift that needed nurturing.

Hence, following a recommendation made by head of his local church, he was sent to study theology at a special seminary, away from his home. While there, he excelled in the study of philosophy; among the many luminaries he had come across in his studies he had a great admiration for Martin Luther, not only because he was a man of erudition, but also for the courage and conviction that led him to follow his intellect to its logical conclusion. He considered Martin Luther an example to emulate.

On graduating from the seminary, he never looked back. He was appointed to act as an assistant professor, at a local university, to teach history of the world religions. He acted also as a priest for his church. His summons aired in the country only radio station, on every Sunday, was admired widely in the country.

Amidst a busy schedule, meanwhile, Augustine had found time to fall in love with a lady diplomat from Sweden, acting as a First Secretary in the Swedish Embassy. Augustine had been a frequent visitor to the embassy, which also had a special relationship with the local Church of Sweden. Very soon, the two became known to each other well enough for them to formalise their relationship, through a wedding held at Saint Mathew Church.

In one of the most impressive hotels in the city, known as Metro Pole Hotel, a lavish party was held, inside a brightly lit hall with beautiful chandeliers. Malin's parents flew in from their home for the occasion, and were seated there quietly with the rest of the other guests, and in keeping with the etiquette smiled and clapped their hands whenever the audience did so. Malin's parents undertook the journey after a bitter discussion, with Malin's father put off by the idea of his daughter's betrothal to a neger. (Neger is a Swedish version of the word nigger in English)

On Malimbe's side, on the other hand, it was his grandmother who wouldn't have him marry any woman outside his home village; a white woman was the last woman she imagined her grandson would want to get married to. To stop him from doing such a thing, she had threatened to take off her clothes, so she could stay nude in front of him, which, according to the tradition of her people, is an expression of one of the most virulent and feared forms of curse a mother or grandmother can caste on a progeny.

When she insisted on having her way, however, the village elders forced her to give her blessings, which she did begrudgingly. Now, inside the hotel lounge, she was seated not far from Malin's parents, whom she met earlier.

Marcel Motoko, the country's President, graced the occasion and delivered a brief speech. "This marriage," he said, "between these two young dynamic people is a marital bond that is appreciated by everyone in this country including Ambassador Marcus and other staff members of the Swedish Embassy, who are here to celebrate this occasion with everyone else." He posed briefly and waved at Ambassador Marcus, who in return offered a smile and also waved at President Motoko. "The bond," he said further, "should be a symbol of friendship between our two respective nations."

When he stopped in order to take a short breath, the guest, seating in a group of five, at their rounded shaped tables, bedecked with white tablecloth, gave President Motoko their anxious look. He coughed slightly, took a snow-white handkerchief out from the pocket of his dark blue jacket and wiped his mouth. He gave a short cough and then requested Augustine, sitting next to Malin, surrounded by friends and relatives, to get to the podium from where he was delivering the speech.

The moment Augustine in a white suit and a red carnation on the lapel of his jacket stood before him, President Motoko got hold of his hand, pulled him towards himself, gave him a bear hug, after which in a playful manner he wagered a finger at Augustine, and said, "Let us talk of dowry between us. I know your woman did not ask for it, because it is not in her culture to ask for dowry."

Following that statement, the guests stopped talking; they directed their attention at President Motoko; standing in the podium, he looked big. Marcel Motoko was a giant of a man. He was found of making jokes, and so now the guests must have been wondering, what next.

Some of the people who didn't take liking to him chose to see him as a buffoon. "To cut the story short," he said suddenly, "Ladies and Gentlemen, if you may allow me, my government wishes to make this marriage adhere to certain cultural practices of our people." He sighed, gave the audience a contented look and then chuckled. "No, no; it is not what you think. No cows for Malin." He said.

He was at the point of saying something more when his speech was drawn in large applauds that lasted for some time. When it was quiet again, a moment later, he directed his chief of protocol to come forward, and show to the audience a gift he wished Malin to have.

Harris Pembe did as ordered. At the podium, he dipped his right hand into the pocket of his jacket, and fished out a little brown coloured box.

"Open it up and give it to me," the President ordered. At once Pembe complied.

Once the prize was in his hand, President Motoko raised the item high above his head, and, addressing the audience with a great measure of enthusiasm, said, "Ladies and Gentlemen, my government wishes to give this gift of diamond ring to the bride; it is a dowry this nation wants Malin to get. In this way, Malin will have two rings in her delicate finger; one of which she has received from her loving husband, and another from this great Republic of Panopia."

There was applause from the audience that lasted long. When it was again quiet, he handed the ring to Augustine, standing at the podium, and ordered him to go and put it in Malin's finger that he did, to the jubilation of the audience.

The band, in a standby, chipped in by playing a splendid sounding tune to the accompaniment of the ritual. When all was over and done, the President and his entourage left as the band continued to entertain the guests, who dined and wined until late hours in the night. Malin and Augustine had departed much earlier, dizzy with happiness.

Each day that went by thereafter, Augustine grew in stature in the eyes of Malin, his newly found love. Malin liked to listen to his sermons on the radio; much inspiring, especially, was his courage to speak his outrage against a government known for violating the rights of its citizens.

As if the act of marriage had further emboldened his resolve to speak against his government, Augustine took every opportunity to criticise it. He never spared the government even in the lectures he had been giving to his students.

The foreign embassy personnel much impressed with his declared political stand, on issues affecting his nation, showered him with much praise. Meanwhile, the government of President Motoko had been tolerating his radio programmes to prove to its critics that it was open to all kinds of criticism. What it could not tolerate, however, was the decision that Augustine had taken to lecture students on the need to stand up and fight the government; it was to become the last straw that broke the camel's back.

The government, one day, reached a decision to get him arrested. In the subsequent months that he was held in detention, without trial, Augustine could not envisage that Amnesty International would turn his case into some sort of cause celebre; he became a prisoner of conscience.

Most vociferous in its criticism of his government's actions was the Swedish Government. Having found itself beleaguered, his home government finally relented to a request made by the Swedish Government to have Augustine released under its charge. Augustine was sent to Sweden; there, his wife and daughter followed him.

Given his life-long connection to the Church of Sweden, Augustine assumed that in Sweden he would be the official guest of the church – a dream that never became true, to his disappointment. After a short stint in the refugee camp trying to learn the language, as well as other aspects of the Swedish culture, he finally left the camp to settle down in Uppsala.

He was met with morbid amusement when he sought a teaching job at Uppsala University. Nevertheless, in cooperation with the Church, the Labour Office got him a job that required him to work as a gardener in a church yard, at a small parish with a population of less than hundred people, most of who were well past their retiring age.

Augustine had used all his spare time to write articles on religious affairs, and had them published in prestigious peer research journals. However, lack of proper employment to fit his qualifications had made him to suffer from periodic bouts of depression. Whenever, he complained to his wife about the state of his waning fortune, he thought she seemed less concerned about his fate.

# Chapter Seven

# B.B. King

Kore found the main gate to the cottage where the priest lived with his family standing wide open. The house was in the outskirts of Uppsala, on the edge of a small forest. The red-coloured wooden cottage, common in these farming areas of Sweden, Malin had inherited it from her father, together with the farm that lay idle, ever since the day her father and mother went to live in a nursing home.

It had been snowing all throughout the week; the snow that had fallen during the previous night had almost blocked the narrow-path, leading to the front-porch of the house. Nobody, it seemed, had cared to remove the snow, severely blocking the narrow path. Kore negotiated his way carefully.

Now, standing at the front-porch of the house, he heard a faint music sound, coming from inside the house. Later, he was surprised to discover the music was not from any of the classic sounds the priest had enjoyed listening to. A few steps before reaching the door, leading to the front door of the building, he heard the loud, lamenting sweat-sounding voice of B.B. King, in the 1969 version of the famous blues song, "The Thrill is Gone."

He stopped to listen carefully to B.B. King passionately saying in that sharp but deep and sweet-sounding voice of his,

"The thrill is gone away…"

"I am free, free from your spell…."

"You have done me wrong baby and you going to be sorry someday…"

"Although I still live on, but so lonely I will be…"

"And now that it is all over, all I can do is wishing you well…"

As he listened to the words of the song, it occurred to him that those words belonged to a man, like him, hurting from a feeling of lost love. If he were to express his sorrows, those were the exact words he would have used. At that moment he liked and respected B.B. King more than ever before.

Meanwhile, through a window partially covered in snowflakes, the priest was able to observe Kore.

"I don't believe. Is it you, Kore?" He shouted from his position inside the house. "Come in you rascal? When have we met last?" He added joyfully.

Apart from the sound of music, Kore felt the empty silence inside the house was confounding in its magnitude. The silence stood in great contrast to a time when he visited the house, once before. The house had seemed to be full of life then, and no one had lightened the house with her smile more than a little girl who had opened the door for him.

This was Malaika. At eleven years of age, Malaika was quite tall for her age; she had brown thick bushy hair, soft skin with brown freckles, and a small nose on an oval-shaped face. Like all children of a mixed marriage, between black and white couples, Malaika was exceedingly beautiful looking little girl.

Malin, her mother, had been an excellent host; she had engaged Kore in all kinds of discussion. Kore had felt relaxed in a company of this family, which to him had seemed to embody happiness. Appearances, he would come to know, are not what they are.

Once he got inside the house, it was not hard for him to realise the priest was tipsy. Although it was getting late in the afternoon, the priest was still in his pyjamas; his large but ordinary looking face, covered in a day's beard, gave him a dishevelled look. He looked small; the last time that Kore saw him, Augustine had a robust look; he was large and full of confidence. The living room was unkempt and looked dirty; half empty glasses of drinks were scattered on the table covered in dust.

"Have some drink, Kore, will you?" Augustine, swaying to the tail-end of the song, shouted on top of his voice.

Kore hesitated briefly, but soon threw care to the wind by having a drink, just to calm down his nerves.

Presently, Augustine took a seat in a couch next to Kore; he picked up his glass of wine and drank the rest of the contents, at one go.

"Good God, how happy I am to have you with me here!" he said in an anxious tone, and added, "It seems as if God has answered my prayers. How much I wished God would send someone for me to talk to."

Kore never knew what to make of this confession. He had come to the priest to seek solace, and now it looked like the roles were about to be reversed.

There was no doubt in his mind that something was bothering Augustine. But whatever that may be, it could not have the seriousness of a lost love; after all, the priest's marriage, he assumed, had been firmly built on a firm foundation of a loving relationship. But the priest was also an excellent scholar. It could be perhaps that one of his articles had not received the raving reviews to which he had been accustomed.

As he was following his thoughts in his mind, the priest put his face close to Kore's face and said, "My wife has left me." He added, "She took my child away from me."

Since he has had had several glasses of beer by now, Kore had been slow in reacting to the news. However, when the truth finally dawned on him, he laughed until tears came freely flowing down his face.

"What is funny?" The priest asked.

"Oh, nothing," said Kore, feeling ashamed;

"I am afraid I couldn't bring myself to imagine, as the man of cloth, you could have a problem similar to mine - a common man," he added.

"The priest is a human being; he is also a common man, like anyone else," he put stress on the phrase "common man."

He remained quiet for a short while before saying, "I may be a priest, but I am not an angle. I am a social being, on whom the pressures and misfortunes of life could well take their hold on, just as much as they might do to you."

They took their supper, drank and talked to each other throughout the night, each consoling the other.

A month later, the priest, who despised life, committed suicide.

On the day when he was getting buried, Kore was at Domkyrkan to pay his last respects. Later, the priest was buried at Uppsala's main graveyard, in a section reserved for Ekdahl's family members, to which Malin belonged; it was an honourable send-off for someone disgusted with life that he chose to end it.

Kore's presence in the church presented him with an opportunity to meet friends he had not seen for quite some time. Joseph Mukongo was one of the friends that he met there. The two exchanged greetings and stayed quiet throughout the time it took to finish the rituals of getting the body ready for burial

People who were there to bury the priest came from all kinds of background, and belonged to different racial groups. Someone from the Church of Sweden, to which the dead priest belonged, was also present there. He delivered a brilliant eulogy, from the pulpit, couched in luminous words, all of which were made in praise of the accomplishments made by the priest, in his life time.

He spoke particularly of his intellectual prowess, the love he had had for his family, and his opposition to a despotic regime that he had once fought against, in his home country. He ended his brief eulogy by saying, "We shall miss him," to which point everybody was bound to agree with, even if in a subjective manner.

In a pew, in front of him, Kore saw Malin accompanied by Malika, her daughter; both were in black mourning dress. Outside the church, later, he offered his condolences to mother and her daughter, both overwhelmed with a feeling of grief, after losing a man in their life, who they must be missing, Kore assumed.

From the graveyard, Kore and Mukongo left together in the direction of the city centre. It was 12 noon. The two agreed to have something to eat somewhere. They ended up having launch at Gallienne, in a building, at a junction where St Johannesgatan meets Syslomansgatan. It was a restaurant favoured by students; the price was right and the food made up of famous Swedish dishes was excellent.

"You look tired," Kore said.

Mukongo shifted from his chair and shrugged his shoulders. He let his large protruding clear eyes rest on Kore and told him "You look tired yourself." After a short silence, he added, "Yes I am tired; the death of the priest has taken its toll on me,"

"I was overwhelmed with a feeling of shock on hearing the news; I didn't get a good night's sleep after that," Kore said.

For a brief moment it was quiet as they sampled the food they had just ordered.

"I had met the priest a month before he committed suicide," Kore said; as soon as he uttered the words, he realised the word suicide has left a bad taste in his mouth. "I wish he didn't do it, notwithstanding the fact that things hadn't been going on well for him," he added.

"So, you know the whole story," Mukongo said.

"We discussed our woes to each other," Kore said, wishing they were not going to discuss the death of the priest any further. "He said his wife and daughter had left him, but didn't tell me the reason," he added after a brief silence

"We all have our woes, but the priest went a step further by killing himself; he shouldn't have done it," Mukongo said, looking frustrated.

"Well, he did it; no one can do anything about it now," Kore said.

"I guess you are right, but I wonder if committing suicide has done the priest any good, the priest himself, above of all," Mukongo said.

"Some people might see courage in the action taken by the priest," Kore said.

"Courage or not, I don't know what it is," Mukongo said. He kept on the plate the knife he used to cut a piece of meat; he gave Kore's eyes a deeper look and said, "I miss him; the priest and I are from the same village; he was like a brother to me."

"Yes, he will be missed," Kore agreed.

"However," Mukongo said, "it is his mother, whom he had gone at great length in supporting her financially, against the wish of his wife, causing a friction to rise between them, that will miss him most. Malin said he didn't love her enough and that he loved his mother more."

"When I met him, a month had already passed from the day his wife left him. He had by then already seen the futility of running after what he had called a lost love," Kore said.

"He did," Mukongo said, his voice sounding in Kore's ears as if it belonged to someone expressing doubt and not affirming a point.

"He compared the love he lost to a shimmer of mirage," Kore said. "'The priest said both are elusive," he added.

"The priest, given to statements of hyperbolic dimension," Mukongo said, "was quiet right, I dare say."

"That statement had left a marked impression in my mind. I had been pursuing a love of my own that I had lost. Since I lacked the will which had made the priest to choose death over life, I gave up pursuing the love that I had lost, which to use the priest's statement, like a shimmer of mirage, had kept receding further and further away from me, the more effort I had made to get closer to it," Kore said.

"The priest in my eyes is no lesser of a person for doing what he did," Mukongo said.

"The priest asserted his freedom to choose; he chose death, for whatever reason." Kore said.

"No one can tell the exact reason that had made the priest to commit suicide. No doubt he suffered from a broken heart and felt that he had prematurely become redundant after he failed to work in a job as a priest and a scholar," Mukongo said.

"He is dead; the reason hardly matters now," Kore said.

"Of course it matters to me. What happened to the priest can happen to anyone of us," Mukongo said.

Kore had once trusted Maria with his love, and called it fate; he had asked himself what did he hope to achieve from fate? He didn't have an answer to that question but had preferred to wait and see to which end fate would take him; in a sense, he had become a slave to fate.

Now, however, he knew the path to which fate had led him; it led him to a dead end. If fate is what took him into the arms of Maria, the same fate took him away from her arms. He felt he had no alternative but to accept the path which fate had chosen for him.

Getting jilted by Maria left a big hole in his heart; however, in retrospect, Kore felt that what Maria did to him had become a blessing in disguise. After all, the separation had afforded him the opportunity to give serious thoughts about his family's affairs, and how to get them to join him in Sweden.

Even though Kore was a married man, he had a love feeling for Maria; he believed he had betrayed his wife, but tried to convince himself that whatever he did, it was done not intentionally. He was sure his wife wouldn't forgive him in case he chose to sincerely mention his escapade to her.

Is it right to ethically hold someone responsible for falling in love, considering that falling in love requires no prior planning, like going out to do shopping for the items one had planned for? Falling in love is not something one plans about; no one knows how to fall in love, or stop from falling in love. When it happens it just happens, Kore assumed.

On her part, Maria had given no any valid reason for not loving him. He believed that when she was not sure about how much he loved her, the feelings of love she had been having for him was guaranteed. However, the moment she realised how much he loved her, her love for him went out of the window. It is as though he had ceased to be a challenge to her, and that she needed to challenge herself to find out if she was worth someone else's love.

What will he do, like the priest, if his marriage should hit a bump or he becomes redundant, prematurely? Will he commit suicide? To this question he had no answer. All he could do now was keep his fingers crossed and hope for the best.

# Chapter Eight

# *Solidarity*

It was several years now since Kore saw his wife and children. When he saw them last, it was on a day when he was sent to jail in his country on charges of treason. Now aware of the Swedish Government's plan to get his family to join him in Sweden, he bought gifts for his wife and his two children, out from the money he had managed to save working on a summer job, recommended by Augustine, in one of the city's major cemeteries, removing fallen leaves off the graves, as well as keeping pathways between them clean. As he did so, he kept note of the time each of the deceased person had spent in this world and realized how short life is. This had a sobering effect on him, because it had the unexpected benefit of reminding him about the state of his mortality that he was likely to forget, as he racked up his mind for ways and means to overcome the everyday problems.

One day, quite unexpectedly, he received from immigration authorities a letter about his family, informing him that they had been detained by his home government, and that they were never going to join him in Sweden, any time soon.

From that day on, it was not his mortality which had become a major concern of his life, but his family's. The fear for the lives of his family members, whose fate it was in the hands of a cruel, insensitive and dishonest government, was by far more real to him than anything else.

This sense of fear could not be allayed; not even when the immigration authorities had written him a letter, reminding him of the efforts that were underway to have his family get reunited with him in Sweden, did the fear go away. The letter read as follows,

> Dear Kore;
>
> On behalf of the Swedish Department of Immigration, and myself, allow me to convey my greatest sympathies to you in this your moment of sorrow. We wish to assure you that we shall do everything within our means to help solve the problems your family is facing. We are hoping to start a dialogue with your home government to enable us to have your family members get reunited with you here in Sweden.
>
> Sincerely yours,
>
> (Signed)
>
> Helen Von Rochdale
>
> Principal Director,
>
> Department of Immigration,
>
> Sweden.

Not many days later, he discovered how the plight of his family members had affected people in Sweden, who held demonstrations throughout the country, calling for their immediate release. Not to be left out, politicians made speeches from the podium of every single city-square, whenever the weather allowed it, as well as on TV, condemning Kore's home government for violating the human-rights of its citizens. They also called for the government to do everything possible to have the family get reunited in Sweden. The media also played well its role.

By shading light on the plight facing his family, the media had further succeeded in generating a widespread sympathy for them, throughout the country. Kore was invited by the media to speak to the nation.

Since the spirit of solidarity, demonstrated by people in Sweden, had stirred his emotions quite so deeply, he was forced to shade tears of gratitude for the support shown by the nation to his family. In his radio speech to the nation, this is what he said:

"My family members have always meant much to me. Whenever I felt desperate, their memories have given me strength. However, today, it is their life that is at stake. Do I feel desperate? Thank God, I am not. I am quite confident that those who hound my family members would discover to their shame that it is beyond any reproach.

In my struggle to win their freedom, however, I am not standing alone. Therefore, let those who hold my family against their wish take note of the fact that I have the full support and the sympathy of the people of this glorious nation, to which now I am one of its humble members. This nation would not tolerate any further acts of humiliation directed against any of my family members.

The campaign to free the family from captivity grew in volume with each passing day. Thanks to scores of committees that had mushroomed throughout the country; their task was to keep the momentum of the struggle going on.

What nobody knew was that Klaus Magnusson, the Prime Minister, had been biding his time, waiting for the right moment to make his move. Klaus Magnusson had been recently spending sleepless nights, thinking whether a bill he was going to present to the house would be passed.

When the bill gets to become a law, it is expected that it would introduce some economic austerity measures, much to the detriment of the already marginalised groups, such as old people, students, single parents, disabled people etc. He knew quite well, however, if he had to succeed in his plan, first he must explore to the fullest the political benefit present in the hostage issue.

Having this in mind, and on behalf of the government, he requested Mikael Holmberg, a senior-most member of the Social Democratic Party, whose party had lost power in a recently contested national political election, to undertake a trip to Africa, to help negotiate the release of the captive family, which the latter accepted rather quite reluctantly.

And so, to the joy of the nation, a day came when the government dispatched a delegation that was composed of two men to Africa.

Throughout Third World countries, as well as among many revolutionary groups elsewhere in the world, Mikael, Holmberg was an iconic figure. Two pictures of him, in one showing, alongside Olof Palmer, Holmberg leading a demonstration in Stockholm against the American presence in Vietnam, and in another depicting him giving speech at the UN General Assembly, calling the Americans to respect the sovereignty of Cuba, had been taken to be a testimony of his commitment to universal justice, sovereignty of nations and freedom of people everywhere. He had also been instrumental in formulating a policy allowing

American soldiers that never wished to fight in Vietnam, in the 1960s and 1970s, to gain political asylum in Sweden.

Chapter Nine

# Donkey-Carts and Rickety-Vehicles

The East African coastal city had been basking under a splendid mid-April afternoon sunshine, following a shower of rain the morning, when the two-man delegation arrived at the airport.

There were two senior officials, from the ministry of foreign affairs, at the airport, dressed in black suits, waiting to receive them. Their job, they told the two-men delegation, was to navigate them across the sea of humanity that had swarmed the airport area, before letting them to meet with a Swedish diplomat, waiting inside a hotel-lounge, outside the airport gates. The protocol officers did their job well.

The two-man delegation, together with their host from the embassy, soon was on its way to a white washed five-star beach hotel, built in a Moorish style, complete with beautiful horse shoe arches. In this hotel, the Swedish Embassy had booked rooms for them.

On their way to the hotel, Holmberg was quite surprised to witness the dilapidated appearance of the buildings, lined up on either side of the road, whose general appearance had never agreed with any style or pattern of architectural design known to him.

As the car speeded on a highway teeming with people, donkey-carts and rickety vehicles, leaving a plume of smoke behind, the two men became quite impressed with the tenacity by which the people of this African city seemed to carry on their difficult lives with quite an unimaginable ease and grace.

Faced with a fear that in Africa nothing works out well, Mikael Holmberg could never tell what to expect in a hotel that he was booked in. That fear was happily dispelled after he found out water tapes in the bathroom had both cold and warm water running quite smoothly.

The bed was large enough to accommodate more than two people; bed sheets were spotless clean and clear white; packed in a small fridge there were bottles of all kinds of drinks. Modern looking telephone apparatus, from which one can make distant call, was kept on a small stool, beside the bed. From the wide opened glass windows, facing a beautiful garden, in a middle of which was a water fountain, he got the sweet smell of tropical flowers. He felt refreshed.

After he unpacked his suitcase, he took a short rest as he lay down on his bed. Later he took shower, and then changed into a clean short sleeved white shirt and trousers.

Soon it was five o'clock; both men were in a relaxed mood but felt somewhat hungry. From their five-star hotel rooms, they made up their mind to visit the hotel restaurant, in order to see if they could have a dinner of sort. At the restaurant, situated on the first floor of the hotel building, they went and occupied a table next to a window, with a view to the blue expanse that is the Indian Ocean.

From this strategic position, they could hear the soft soothing lapping-sounds of the waves breaking into the sand and the rocks. Far off the horizon was a glowing red sun, its rays shimmering brightly on the tiny fishing boats appeared to

Holmberg as if they were popping up from the bowels of the sea or descending from the heavens.

Holmberg was so impressed with the view he barely noticed the waiter, in a hotel uniform of white short sleeved shirt and black trousers, holding a pad in his right hand, waiting for them to give their order.

At last, when both men turned their attention to focus on the waiter, they faced the figure of a young polite man with a bright smile. For a moment, they hesitated; the two men were now faced with a moment calling for a practical solution to what is a simple human routine: to eat or not to eat.

In any other circumstances, such a simple human concern would not have needed a moment of their contemplation; now since the two men had no trust for the sanitary conditions of this hotel, or any other hotel in the country of their visit, it was not that simple.

They had a mortal fear of food poisoning; they had a fear of many other things besides, such as malaria, diarrhoea, snakebites, road accidents, muggers, beggars, heat etc. Come to think of it, they had a fear of anything, and everything else, which they assumed could either impair their state of health or render them actually dead. Notwithstanding the fact that the lady from the Swedish Embassy had vouched for this hotel's good sanitary conditions, they found hard to change their minds.

Before their trip to Africa took place, the two men had had enough time to imagine the sort of dangers they would be made to face in Africa. Perhaps, this should help explain the reason for fortifying themselves with pills against all forms of imaginable diseases, and also the reason for carrying in their health kits important information materials they assumed could help them deal effectively with health problems of all kinds.

However, the situation was quite different then from now. Now they were being faced with a moment requiring them to live out their fears. They had thought of this moment many times before, but they had found reason to conveniently brush aside their concern, each with the following ready-made statement: "I shall cross the bridge when I get there."

Facing the bridge of their wisdom now, they discovered the enormous challenge it presented them with. After a long pause, stretching to eternity, finally they took a glimpse of other fellow diners to enable them to assess the situation correctly.

A scene giving them a feeling of reassurance greeted their eyes. Here and there, they saw a group of white people enjoying their dinner. The sight of white men and women enjoying their meals raised their confidence to a point of assuaging their fears, and soon felt free to place their order.

Meanwhile, they waited patiently, anticipating the surprise the kitchen of Africana Hotel might have in store for them. When, at last the food was delivered, and once having tested it, they were not disappointed. But perhaps what they liked most about the food was the taste of freshness that one savoured, long after it has been consumed.

It was now close to nine o'clock in the evening. The two men had finished their supper; they were talking to each other over a cup of coffee when suddenly the man from the Swedish Ministry of Foreign Affairs decided to leave for his room. However, before leaving the table, he told his colleague, "I am having a bad headache. I am retiring for the night; see you in the morning."

Mikael Holmberg looked at the time in his watch, which read 9 p.m. It was a little too early to get to bed, he thought. For quite a moment, tomorrow's impending meeting crossed his mind. He never allowed his mind to dwell on the issue, since his attention was drawn to a sound of music reaching him from somewhere, beyond the hotel lobby. He beckoned at a waiter. The waiter came and then handed him the bill to sign.

As the waiter was about to turn and leave, Mikael Holmberg drew his attention. Thereafter, dipping his right hand in his trousers pockets, he took out his wallet. He opened the wallet; from inside the wallet, he drew out several crispy US dollar notes that he gave as a tip to the waiter.

It pleased Holmberg to discover how simple it was to have another human being glow with happiness, out of a simple gesture that to him had seemed effortless. He stood up, pushed the chair behind him, and then slowly started heading in the direction from where the music was coming. He felt quite tired; his leg-joints felt stiff. He preferred to attribute the feelings to a jet lag and a sudden change of weather.

Somewhere along the corridor, on his way to the music hall, he noticed rows of mirrors hanging on light-blue painted walls. On catching his own reflection in one of them, he hesitated before approaching those set of mirrors slowly; lingering there, he stared at his reflection, in one of the mirrors; making use of his right hand fingers he slowly traced the wrinkles on his face that looked like thin galleys running deep on the surface of a mountain; his wrinkled face, which had given him a rugged appearance, had the effect of enhancing his good looks.

For a short while, he just stood before the mirror looking at his own reflection. But in the mirror, he caught the reflection of other people, on their way to the dancing hall, stealing glances at him.

At the sight of people watching him, he took a step back. He believed nothing could be far more embarrassing than getting caught in a process of vainly admiring one's physical qualities in public; yet, in the private chambers of their homes, most people do a similar thing, on a regular basis, he was aware.

The music hall was a cross between a disco and a public dancing hall. It was large, but not so large as to let the audience lose that physical proximity quite essential for establishing and keeping human contact. Now he walked into this hall, feeling somewhat tense. He located a table, surrounded by chairs, placed quite adjacent to a wall, and laying between the bar and at a point from where the band played the music.

He sat on one of the chairs, placed against the wall, facing the dancing hall. In the hall, the multi-coloured lights shined dimly. There were many people inside the dancing hall, including a group of white men and women. Some of the people in the dancing hall were quite young; others were not so young.

The atmosphere in the hall, charged with excitement, had a pleasant contagious effect upon his mood; he felt relaxed and quite alive. He had never felt that way for quite some time now. Mikael Holmberg was not a habitual drinker of liquor except when the atmosphere was right. He ordered for drinks.

From his vantage position, he watched with great interest as men and women danced with abandoned care. While taking his beer, he allowed the heaving bosoms of the dancing girls to tantalise his libido.

Though he had never told anyone, not even his closest friends, those heavy bosoms and the ample rounded rears that are so much characteristic of some of the African women physical anatomy, which his friends had called monstrous, had held a special appeal for him.

For quite a while now, he had his eyes fixed on a girl that looked exceptionally black; she was tall and had a tight pair of jeans, revealing exceptionally well-rounded curves of her body; she had worn her hair in a natural form; the tight fitting t shirt that she had put on had the words I CARE ABOUT YOU, in red letters, inscribed at the back and in front.

As he sat alone, watching the girls dancing, he allowed his mind to reflect on women in general, and how their beauty has been a subject of great interest to people of all generations, and of every walk of life.

He imagined how poets have spoken eloquently of their physical virtues; how statesmen soldiers have fought to win their love, and how painters and artists have spent many sleepless nights to capture their beauty. Didn't the subtle smile on the face of Mona Lisa bewitch Leonardo da Vinci, and did he not immortalise it for posterity?

Directing his gaze at the tall girl, dancing alone, not far from his table, he observed how the heavy rounded shiny-pearls of sweat had been spread out on her face. Her eyelids were half-closed, and from under the long shade of her eyelashes she was staring at him, he thought.

"What could there be in me to make such an attractive young girl turn her head for me," he told himself.

"Stop it," he admonished himself.

The band had just finished playing ABBA'S "Dancing Queen," and Mikael Holmberg was pouring another glass of beer when he sensed someone standing next to him, at his table. He raised his head up and was forced to hold his breath. Standing before him was the girl in person, her large clear eyes staring at him.

"Hello old man," making use of broken English that she picked up in the streets, she uttered the words in a husky voice, followed with a smile, revealing a perfect set of white teeth.

"Ought she to remind me of my age?" He told himself.

He was about to get real annoyed with the girl for what he had considered to be a callous and rude behaviour when using a tender voice, almost bordering a state of meekness, she said, "May I sit with you, please?"

He searched for words in his mind that could befit the occasion; a moment later, in an amiable voice, he said, "Yes, do so." As an afterthought, he remembered to add hurriedly, "Please."

Despite a fleeting moment of displeasure he had felt for the girl, a moment ago, now he was quite tickled by her presence, in his table, sitting so very close to him.

She sat next to him so that both faced the hall. Now that the girl was there with him, many were thoughts that crossed his mind. He wondered what brought the girl to his table.

As if she had read his mind, she said to him, "Do you like me?"

The question threw him off balance; however, he quickly regained his composure. For want of saying something meaningful in a reply, he said, "What do you mean?"

This time the girl was quite direct in her speech.

"How would you like me to meet you alone, in your room? I have not seen you before. I guess you are new here," she said.

"Are you often here, young woman?" He inquired, brushing aside her question.

"Yes, I like dancing. Besides, I find opportunity to meet with many nice people, like you," she said.

Once again, she gave him one of her broad smiles, which had caused his heart to wildly beat in his chest.

"Why don't you buy me a drink?" She said and pushed closer to him, so that he could feel her warm breath on his face.

Since he never appreciated the idea of buying a drink to a minor, he asked for her age, which she said was twenty-three. At such age, any one was free in his country to take a drink; and so, he beckoned at a waiter, who came to take their order. The girl asked for a beer; to replenish his stock, he ordered more beer for himself.

"What do you do for a living?" He asked her.

"Nothing special," she replied graciously, and then she said further, "My father had me married to an old rich man, who had two other wives, who both made a habit of beating me out of jealousy. I left him."

"Why did your father have to give you to an old man for marriage?" He asked.

"He wanted me to have some sort of security. My father is poor," she said.

Mikael Holmberg felt he had said enough; he was obliged, however, to ask the girl one last question. But before he could utter the words, he felt a sudden touch between his legs. Responding to his reflexes he was going to shout at the girl, but stayed quiet, instead. The girl gave him a broad smile.

Under the table, the girl's hand kept moving, further and further up, until finally it rested on his crotch. With eyes half-closed, he stared at the girl saying something that he never wished to know anything about; instead, he wished she let her hand stay where she had kept it.

As if she had read his mind, for a moment, she did that, before finally withdrawing the hand. Immediately, afterwards, she said, "Well, is daddy willing to take care of his baby now"?

He licked his lips and nodded his head vigorously. He wanted to say yes, but felt he was unable to do so. He discovered, to his surprise, his voice had got stuck deep into a dry throat; it would not come out.

He swallowed, and with much effort he brought himself to finally say, "Yes."

But even then, the voice did not sound quite real to him; it never seemed to belong to him. Having regained the use of his voice completely, a moment later, he told the girl, "My room No is 42. Come up there; come alone." He added excitedly, "Hurry up."

He called the waiter, signed the bill, and went for his keys at the reception desk, heart beating wildly in his chest. The thrill caused by the dream of meeting the girl alone in a room was a bit too much for his imagination.

In the room, he took a quick shower, and changed into white fresh silk-pyjamas, which had the following slogan in red: "Let the Good Times Roll."

He bought the garment when he was on an official visit to the Far East; he liked the words portrayed there.

He sat on the edge of the bed, his mind thinking about the girl.

The thing he intended to do, by any definition, could be considered as an abomination by some people. But had such people ever been tempted, like him, and had they managed to come out clean? He reasoned.

By now he was convinced he knew what his heart desired most. The girl had brought forth in him a kind of feeling he thought he was incapable of having. Nevertheless, he pictured himself with the girl alone in his room. This was as far as he could imagine the situation; there was a thick wall of moral issues separating him from the girl, he found out.

He wanted to touch the girl; he wanted to feel her firm body against his. But could he do it without feeling a sense of strong moral indignation against himself? He wondered.

On the other hand, could he deny the girl and still be true to his feelings? Caught between a rock and a hard place, Mikael Holmberg faced a great dilemma, as he was required to make a choice between principle and passion.

Suddenly, there was a knocking sound on the door. He stood up in a hurry. On the way to the door, he tripped on the mat. After regaining his composure, he straightened his pyjamas, passed both hands through his hair that had become dishevelled, and then went to open the door to the smiling girl, who immediately fell into his arms.

For a moment, they held each other in a tight embrace. Later, the girl went to stand in the middle of the room; using the forefinger of her left hand, she beckoned at him. As he approached her, she took a step back; she smiled and dared him to follow her.

"Come to me," she said in a jovial mood, "Come; catch me if you can," she added joyously.

They went round and round; both were in a hilarious mood; they pushed and pulled, laughing all the time. Suddenly, the girl stopped; without much fan-fare, one by one, she started removing her clothes till she became completely nude.

If Mikael Holmberg once had marvelled at the beautiful shape of the girl, now he was totally engrossed in the beauty of her naked body. The girl approached him, took his hand, and with tender care led him towards the bed.

At this point, far from being concerned with the moral aspects of his intended action, he cared mostly about whether he was going to be equal to the task facing him. Without taking eyes off the girl's naked body, he took off his pyjamas in one swipe.

Now completely naked, a look of doubt spreading throughout his face, he approached the bed slowly and cautiously. He was afraid the girl would embarrass him by saying nasty thing about his aged-body. But to his happy surprise, the girl did nothing of the sort; instead she kept smiling at him. This favourable response had put his fears to rest.

As he lay down beside the girl, Mikael Holmberg almost forgot the cares of the world; tomorrow was aeons of light years away; as for the past, it was merely a moment lost in a world of distant hazy dreams. He felt quite strange how he could easily undergo such a metamorphosis within so short a span of time; it was a form of change, nevertheless, that he felt he wanted to make it last longer, if not forever.

As a result, he thought he knew well what it feels to be a hedonist; like a true hedonist, he cared of only the here and now.

At last, after he had had his feeling sated, his mind became the focus of conflicting emotional currents. He was glad that his fears of an impending failure, at a crucial moment, had been dispelled. Yet, somewhere, deep in the recesses of his being, a feeling of a foreboding nature had started forming. It was as though the consummation of the physical act had brought forth in him the reality of his life, all in full force.

Subsequently, he questioned the morality of his action. He had been tempted and had succumbed to the temptation; was he the first person to have been tempted and had succumbed to temptation? No; not likely. Had not Adam got tempted, and for his punishment did he not fall from grace?

What is his punishment? Is a sense of guilt a serious enough punishment for him to live with? Why should he feel guilty for doing something that had caused no one any harm? The girl he had consorted with was 23 years old, after all; he didn't force himself on her; he had not betrayed anyone; not his Dear wife Angelika, who had been dead, all these years.

God knows how much of a woman's warmth he needed to feel. He should be grateful to the girl for providing him with the warmth of her body. The girl that had shared the warmth of her body shouldn't become an object against whom he could measure his moral rectitude, and should neither be the basis for him to hate himself nor the girl for the thing which had transpired between them, he believed.

The girl, meanwhile, keeping to her side of the bed, had remained quiet. However, she ventured to look at him every now and then, her happy looking face presenting a great contrast to the deep frowns showing up in his face. He caught the girl looking at him, but had pretended not to notice. He wondered if the girl had any kind of feelings in her. Was she capable of having guilt feelings, for example?

With anxious mind, he recollected having read somewhere how for societies with lower level of development, unlike those in the developed world, it is not the feeling of guilt that matters most to them but shame. He wondered of the two feelings which one was an easier burden to bear.

He looked at his watch; it read 2 a.m. He realised he had very few hours left for sleeping. From inside the wardrobe, he reached for his trousers from which he retrieved from its pockets a handful of American dollars. He held the money in his hands, sitting on his bed, feeling somewhat awkward. Should he offer the money to the girl just like that? Would it not look like he had bought some sexual favours from her? And how would she react to the offer? The entire set of questions had crossed his mind, all at once.

Lost in what to do, he mechanically extended his arm in the direction of the girl; the girl snatched the money away. It seemed to him that the girl had no any qualms accepting the money.

By now the girl had left the bed and was putting on her clothes. She looked at him and said in a challenging tone, "How did you like the night, daddy?"

"Thanks God, I have survived the night," he said hastily.

She had finished dressing; while approaching the door now, she turned abruptly to look at him, and for the final time said, "Goodbye, daddy."

As soon as she left the room, a sense of relief dawned on him. While there with him in the room, the girl had reminded him of what they had gone through together, as well as all the other things he was eager to forget about. But could he ever forget? He lay down to sleep, mixed feelings going through his mind. That night, however, he slept his deepest sleep in years.

Chapter Ten

# *Face to Face with Bobe Haigan*

At 6 a.m. he woke up to the sound of the alarm clock. The extraordinary feelings of joy, made possible by the erotic experiences of the previous night, had convinced Mikael Holmberg that he had every reason to feel quite rejuvenated, this morning, if he chooses to forget the moral concerns of his action, which he was happy to do.

He went to the bathroom to shave and to take a morning shower. Afterwards, he changed into a light brown suit he had bought for the occasion. Before going out, ready to face the challenge of the day, he took a long look at himself in the mirror. He was pleased with his reflection; he always had been. Despite his advanced age, Mikael Holmberg was flattered by his thick crop of hair that gave him a youthful look.

On his way out to the dining room, he carried his briefcase. There, he met his colleague having breakfast of buttered bread, omelettes, fresh orange juice and coffee. He placed a similar order for himself. The aroma of coffee in the morning hours had always given Mikael Holmberg a pleasant feeling; it added zest to his life.

And as he watched the calm azure blue waters of the Indian Ocean, out the window of the dining hall, sipping coffee, he felt quite pleased with himself, so much that he believed he had every reason to celebrate in advance the anticipated twist and turns the day was going to usher into his life.

While thinking of the task waiting to be done, he took a look at his colleague who was a man of few words.

Referring to the assignment before them, he told his colleague, "Are you ready for the fight?"

"With due respect for your opinion, I am sorry to disagree with you. But I don't anticipate any such thing," the man said awkwardly. He never took the eyes off his breakfast.

After a short pause, he added abruptly, "The matter is quite simple and clear. We shall ask them to release the family to our charge, and that should bring the matter to the end."

This statement had caused Mikael Holmberg to wince. He wondered at his colleague's self-conceited mind. If the account held in the dossier that had been presented to them by the woman from the embassy, regarding the people they were going to meet with, was anything to go by, they should in fact be prepared for an uphill task.

In the dossier, the people they were expected to meet have been depicted as ruthless, cunning, careless, proud, cruel, vain etc. Unfortunately, his colleague would not be swayed. They had just finished taking their breakfast when the woman from the embassy came to convey them to the meeting-place.

As they drove in the morning traffic, past dilapidated buildings, large and small ones, Mikael Holmberg considered in the drama that was about to unfold how his role was going to affect differently the fortunes of various groups of people in Sweden, at political, ideological and personal levels.

For example, in case of any success of his mission, he was sure that Klaus Magnusson would expect his political fortunes to rise. On the other hand, the Swedish public is hoping to show to the world how the triumph of human right issues is a matter of great concern to them, and Kore would be hoping to have his family get reunited in Sweden.

As for himself, he wondered whether he had any special concern in the matter to the extent of it having somewhat a bearing on his dreams. And what are his dreams, anyway? Like someone digging a pit, hoping that one day he would be rewarded for his efforts, he was filled with anticipation. But like the digger of a pit, who expects to benefit from what he had set to gain - say either gold or diamond - he could not tell what kind of reward to expect.

Crammed inside the car with two other people, on a steamy hot day, Mikael Holmberg felt quite uncomfortable; he opened the car window to let the stream of cold air get inside the car, hoping to beat the heat.

As the car speeded away from the city centre, his memory hacked back to a time when he was young - a time when he was willing to accept any challenge to enable him to win a place in the sun. That was a long time ago now. It was a time, together with people of his generation, he was shot through and through with a great sense of idealism.

But at his advanced age when he should be sitting on his laurels, counting his achievements, he couldn't understand why he should oblige Klaus Magnusson by risking his neck in these distant shores, where the rule of the game was quite different from what he had been used to.

In the past, he believed, no amount of sacrifice was greater, and no mountain of responsibility insurmountable, but he was afraid there were changes in the horizon, affecting his country's future political situation, which do not auger well for politics based on the ideals of solidarity. Even though the old generation still had a role to play in the political life of the nation, yet it is a fact of life that they were not left with much time to live on.

When the old generation passes away as they will surely do, and younger men and women who had been reared on an easy time take over the reins of all political parties, what would then happen to his beloved nation? Would the new generation of politicians honour the spirit of solidarity as nurtured in a deep sense of Swedish political idealism?

What will happen to the ideology of the Social Democratic Party - his party? Would the ideals of the party be kept and honoured, or would they be sacrificed at the altar of some malevolent thing?

All these thoughts had crossed his mind as he headed for a meeting he was not sure how it would end up. The people with whom he was on his way to negotiate with, after all, were not only strangers to him, as he was to them, but their way of life, their attitude to issues of human rights, their culture, had always looked to him strange.

He had always been in his best element when conducting diplomatic forays in Europe and America among people he shared a common civilisation. With the Africans, it was going to be a different story. And yet, he was ready for any eventuality, he felt.

They drove through large fields of sugar-cane and tobacco plantations, extending far off into the horizon. The landscape reminded him of the island of Cuba that he liked to visit whenever he could. Their car was now approaching a large building surrounded with thick walls; on top of those thick walls there were armed sentries, holding menacing-looking guns. The compound inside, Holmberg found out, contained large buildings, surrounded by tanks, as well as armoured personnel carriers of the Russian model.

The compound, which had the appearance of a besieged army fortress, was in fact a home to a president of the country, who currently was on a state visit to Russia. Naturally, this formidable looking-scene had caused Mikael Holmberg, along with his entourage of two people, to develop a feeling of anxiety.

From a short distance of about twenty meters away, Mikael Holmberg saw a figure approaching them. The figure turned out to be that of a tall, youthful looking man; he wore a well pressed khaki pair of trousers, and had a white short-sleeved shirt that hanged out; he had leather sandals, worn without socks; he had a thick bushy set of hair on a head that was long; the dark glasses on his face had given his overall countenance a picture of someone in a conspiracy to cause damage to someone, or something. Since the eyes are said to be a window into the secrets of the soul, the man must have had his own reasons for wanting to hide behind dark glasses, Holmberg must have imagined.

As soon as he stood before them, the man smiled, and in a happy tone said, "Mr Mikael Holmberg; it is an honour for us to have you in my country; you, who is a champion of freedom and justice, are welcome here with open arms."

To hear someone pronounce his name quite so correctly, with such a superb finesse, and in such unlikely surroundings, had greatly pleased Mikael Holmberg, who took a step forward to meet his elegant looking host half-way. When the two men got quite close to each other, they hesitated before hugging with such a warm feeling that someone watching them from the side would have been forgiven for imagining that the men were long lost friends, happy to meet at last. In fact, they were not friends, nor would they ever become friends.

After giving Holmberg a warm welcome, the man took the task of introducing himself. He let his smiling eyes, hidden behind the dark glasses, rest on Holmberg's face and then said, "I am Bobe Haigan. I am Minister for National Security in the President Office. Financial Adviser: President Office. Director General: National Bank for International Investment. Secretary General: Committee for the Promotion of International Affairs." By now Holmberg had lost count of his host's many portfolios. His last portfolio, he said was, "Supreme Custodian: Mother's Welfare and Children Development Office."

While introducing his portfolios, at the same time, he was leading everybody towards a pavilion, in a garden with large trees, far removed from the scene that had cars and other instrument of war. A few steps before reaching the conference venue, at the pavilion, inside a garden, he stopped abruptly, turned around to look at Holmberg, and acting as someone who was exceedingly proud of his achievements, he said, "I carry great responsibility over my shoulder Mr Holmberg."

Holmberg waited eagerly to hear him speak again. What is it going to be? He wondered. He wouldn't be surprised if he came up with a statement that is far more fabricated than anything he had ever said.

"I dedicate all my efforts, my dear Holmberg," he said with a poise, "to improve and protect the rights of women and children. A nation can ignore them at its own peril."

As Haigan was stating the concern he claimed to have for the welfare of women and children, Holmberg felt anger welling in his chest. He was angered at the shameless and hypocritical nature of his host's naked lies.

"What a liar," he said to himself about the man. "He restricts the family's freedom of movement, and now pretends to act as their champion. Who knows, he might have thrown the family into a dungeon," Holmberg seemed to think.

Haigan might have noticed changes in Holmberg's facial expression; hence, in an affable manner, he said, "Is something wrong Mr Holmberg? Are you not feeling well?"

Of course, he was not feeling well, but what did he care? He chose to stay quiet, nevertheless. About Haigan, he believed the man was a pathological liar and a megalomaniac to boot. He believed he is one of those people that tend to lie and lie until they end up believing in their own lies.

"Oh yes. I almost forgot," Haigan said in a hurry."

Holmberg was quite certain that his host was warming up to a certain subject; he felt anxious.

Haigan sat on the edge of his chair, leaned forward, looked straight at Holmberg and then spoke slowly, using a leisurely tone.

Still on the subject of women, he offered, "Mr Holmberg, my government is seriously considering the need to draw the attention of international human right organisations to the plight of women forced into prostitution everywhere in the world."

Although Haigan was a learned man, having a B.A degree from one of the most prestigious universities in America, he never hesitated to benefit from the ancient folk wisdom of his people, whenever it suited his purpose. For example, looking for signs of any emotional distress in Holmberg's face, following what he had just said to him, and having failed to find any, he decided instead to quite keenly observe his guest's ears.

This act was intended to determine if they had somewhat changed colour to become reddish, which, according to the wisdom of his people, is a sign of anguish, fear or anger in a non-black person.

About prostitution, he said, "Mr Holmberg, I am afraid to say prostitution is a widely spread institution here in my country. But while poverty is the reason, I strongly deplore the despicable and repugnant behaviours of well-to-do people of this country, as well as foreigners, who take advantage of poverty to corrupt children into a life of moral decay."

To Holmberg, it seemed as if Haigan had uttered the sentence quite forcefully to see nothing in it should escape his attention.

Listening to his host placing himself and his cruel government on a moral high ground had made Holmberg feel sick. He thought of the previous night with the girl in the hotel, wondering if Haigan knew something about it. Somehow, he was convinced Haigan knew everything. He assumed that the long winding speech on prostitution Haigan had just given was a way of saying to him, "I know what you did last night."

Hence, far from feeling confident as suggested by the calm look on his face, Holmberg felt a cold shiver passing through the back of his neck, engulfing the rest of his body with a large dose of cold anxiety. That made him to hate Haigan, whom he considered to be a wily operator, with all his heart. Nevertheless, he made a point to handle him with a begrudging respect and care.

By now every single chair in the room had been occupied and Haigan had finished introducing his team of five people, who sat opposite from across the table. As soon as the introduction was over, Haigan stayed quiet, but gave Holmberg a curious look. Evidently, he was enjoying himself. He seemed to be saying to Holmberg, "I have said what needs to be said. Now the ball is in your court; let us see what you can give."

Holmberg took the opportunity of the silence to give a short speech. He started by saying, "It gives me pleasure to know that your government has adopted a correct moral stand on the question of prostitution. I condemn, in no uncertain terms, irrespective of their nationalities, people who force women of all colour and age into prostitution. Furthermore, I agree with you that poverty should not be the reason for sexual exploitation of children in any country of the world, poor or rich."

He took a short pose and then went on with his speech. "I am glad," he said, "my colleague and I are here on a visit to your beautiful country, where we have had the opportunity to meet with people like you (pointing to Haigan) whose concern for the right of the weak is a highly commendable act of statesmanship."

This last statement had forced Holmberg to confirm what a notable writer of international politics had said about diplomacy being the art of lying for one's nation, and therefore regretted saying what he had just said.

Did he not lie by attributing the spirit of statesmanship to Hagan? What does the man who causes suffering to women and children know anything about statesmanship? He seemed to think.

As he went on with the speech, Holmberg started to regain his lost confidence. He could now afford to look Haigan straight in the face.

"I wish to propose a toast here," he said in a tone full of confidence. "I wish to say," he added, "let the spirit of magnanimity act as the corner stone of our talk."

He took a short pause, and then said further, "We are meeting here today for reasons known to us all. However, before proceeding on with the business at hand, allow me to introduce my colleagues to you."

He looked at Johansson, his colleague, looking every inch his brooding self. Pointing to him he said, "Please, meet Mr Joel Johansson of the Ministry of Foreign Affairs of the Government of Sweden." Johansson nodded his head vaguely. "To my left," Holmberg went on, "is Ms Anna-Marie; most of you here know her." She nodded her head and gave a nervous smile; finally, he introduced himself.

He posed, afterwards, to have a drink of water and said further, "Let me remind you that my team has the official mandate, from my home government, to conduct the negotiations and accept and respect as binding any decision that would be reached here today." He kept silent after that, signalling the end of his speech.

As he declared the meeting open, a moment later, Haigan said, "I wish to thank you for the short but a splendid speech. And now to the task at hand; I say, let the talks begin."

Chapter Eleven

# *Ransom*

The discussions that followed could be considered as frank and honest. It was frank in a sense that each of the negotiating team had made its terms of reference clear. As to whether the talks were honest, this was to be found in the details. While, for example, Holmberg said that his request was motivated by a need to uphold the principle of human rights, on his part, Haigan said that the family was being treated well, but that it was wanted for insurance.

"To give the issue a proper context," he said easily, "the family is held by my government as a sort of collateral against a three-million-dollar loan that Kore, who is a fugitive from justice, owes my government."

He added after a moment of silence, "I can understand how awful and improper this must look to you. Unfortunately, we are left with no option, especially, in this case, when the debtor is nowhere to account for his action. As you know it well, he has since absconded; we have learnt that he lives in your country now, virtually at the expense of your tax payers' account."

As Haigan went on with his speech, Holmberg couldn't help developing a feeling of disgust and deep hatred for him.

Warming up to the subject further, Haigan said, "Mr Holmberg, tell me, how do you deal with people in your country that incur loans, but fail to pay them on time? If I may assume correctly, I think you deal with them in a most correct manner; this is to say, they are made to pay promptly, in which case, if they don't, their property is impounded. I believe this to be a proper banking procedure that your country meticulously follows."

Holmberg saw some logic in the statement, but failed to envision a situation in which his country would be forced to resort to policy procedures requiring human-beings to be used as collateral. This, as an idea, seemed outright repugnant to him. Nevertheless, he refrained from arguing with his host, since he was convinced there were no finer aspects in the point on which to argue about. He believed, for whatsoever reason, human beings shouldn't be held as collateral in any sort of business transactions.

Although this much had been obvious to him, nevertheless, for the record, he wanted his host to clearly spell out for him the position of his government, on the issue. And therefore, he asked Haigan, "What does my government have to do to have the family released to our charge?"

The question must have taken Haigan by surprise, for it could never occur to him that Holmberg would ask such straight forward question.

He searched for the right words before finally saying, "Seeing that you have sacrificed energy and time to travel all the way from Europe to come here, would you object to making payment to us, let us say, of three million dollars in an exchange for the release of the family?

He added, "After all, let us not forget that the family belongs to a man who has embezzled the money belonging to my government."

Holmberg was not surprised. He had all along been expecting that it would finally come to this end. Holmberg hated Haigan with all his heart. He looked at his colleagues, who stared at him with empty looks in their faces. In his mind, he kept thinking about Haigan, and failed to understand how a man could be so proper and charming, but quite brutish, at the same time. He became aware that Haigan was staring at him. He decided to pull himself out of his emotional doldrums.

"Mr Haigan," he said, "I was not given a mandate to discuss ransom, because this is what it amounts to. However, I believe, this is a matter I would like to take up with my government."

There was a smile on the face of his host that he thought had denoted a sense of triumph. Holmberg cursed his luck. He looked at his colleagues, once again; this time, however, as if to ask for their contribution. They remained quiet.

Looking at Johansson, it became quite obvious to Holmberg that Johansson wasn't going to easily agree with what he had just said. Holmberg knew Johansson to be someone for whom the act of compromising means a sign of weakness. Whenever he had to speak in public, however, Johansson looked clumsy. Johansson was inarticulate; it was a weakness that rendered him unable to air his views quite effectively in public.

Luckily enough, what Johansson had been lacking in fluency, he made up for by having impeccable bureaucratic skills. He was busy taking notes of the meeting with his characteristic meticulous nature when he was forced to listen to Holmberg's next suggestion. He stopped writing in order to listen to his colleague.

"Before taking up the issue of ransom with my government," he said, "my colleagues and I would like to meet with the family to get to know them well, and to also assess the state of their health."

What Holmberg had just said must have made Haigan feel happy. He chuckled and looking quite confident said, "Ah! I can understand your concern. I am sure this could be arranged."

He added enthusiastically, "When do you want us to pay the family a visit?"

By now Holmberg was more than eager to end the meeting - at least for the day. Therefore, he never hesitated to give his reply.

Now," he said.

Haigan had been anticipating this moment for quite a long time. He had long determined that he was not going to be caught with his pants down.

"The family," he said proudly, "is in good hands." He stayed quiet for a moment and then said abruptly, "The head of the family is a fugitive from justice. The family shouldn't be made to suffer his sins. We are a just society, Mr Holmberg."

About Haigan, Holmberg was convinced that he was happy at how things had turned out for him. He was not however going to change his mind about Haigan, whom he thought, apart from being cruel, was a liar. He had made up his mind to not let Haigan's flowery words change his opinion of him.

Chapter Twelve

# *A Well anticipated visit*

As soon as he received information about the coming visit of a two-man-delegation from Sweden, Haigan had made official arrangements for receiving it. To this end, he had arranged for the family to be moved to a comfortable house, in a most affluent district of the city, away from the slum area that he had relegated the family to. He had also employed a maid to help the family with its household chores. He had told the family to expect a visit by some white people who would inquire about their wellbeing, and had warned them against giving any kind of information that would suggest anything other than a life marked with a state of blissful tranquillity.

He had organised rehearsals to teach the family how to conduct themselves. He had made a promise to Hadio that the family would be reunited in Sweden with Kore, but only if they would remember to play their assigned roles well. Furthermore, he had warned Kore's wife against any kind of failure which would mean a relocation to her former home, at the city slum area, and hence an endless separation with her beloved husband, now living in Sweden.

Kore's family was composed of his wife and their two children, a boy and a girl, five and six years old, respectively. The family members had been assembled in the kitchen, having their lunch, when they heard the motor car engine in the front porch of their house. Kore's wife became curious. She approached the window and pushed the curtain aside.

At the sight of Haigan, accompanied by three white people, she became paralysed with fear. She ran back to the dining table. She ordered the children to hurry up to their room; she asked the maid to help getting them dressed up. Meanwhile, she kept herself ready to welcome the three-white people. She surveyed herself in a mirror that was kept beside the door, at the entrance to the room, and was not quite disappointed with her reflection, although she seemed to regret a lack of make-up touch to her face.

Waiting for the team to give a knock, she prayed to overcome any form of obstacle she could face in this moment of her greatest need.

Suddenly, a loud knocking sound on the door jolted her from her prayer thoughts. She opened the door to let Haigan, accompanied by three white people, get inside the room. For a moment, she hesitated; she was lost about what to do; suddenly she remembered those lessons Haigan had taught her. As she opened the door, she put up on one of her most pleasant smiles, then she said, "Welcome to my home."

The team of three white persons – two men and one woman – entered the sitting room that had a well arranged beautiful set of furniture, which managed to impress Holmberg's keen eyes. Holmberg faced Kore's wife, greeted her in English, only then did he remember to ask if she spoke English.

Feeling shy, Hadio said she could speak some English. He asked for her name, which she said was Hadio. He observed the food on the table. Curiously, he approached the table and said, "Is this your launch for today?"

She nodded her head in agreement. The lunch was made of rice and chicken; on the table there was a jug of juice; there was also a basket of bananas on the table.

"Do you eat like this every day?" He enquired. He thought the family ate well.

"Some days we eat better" she replied.

She remembered the second lesson she had been taught.

Haigan had told her, "When addressing a group of white people who might one day pay you a visit, do not forget to look them straight in the face. If you show signs of shyness by looking down on the floor, as women often do here, while addressing strangers, this would be taken by them to mean you are not being sincere."

From that moment of recollection on, she did what she had been advised to do.

Holmberg was attracted to framed photographs in one of the walls. There was this one photograph of black and white that particularly seemed to have caught his attention most; this was a family portrait of Kore and members of his family taken in a studio. The photograph was old; by now the children in it probably would look much older. Holmberg strolled from one section of the room to the other; the rest of the team sat down on the sofa-sets to rest; only Haigan hovered close to him.

Holmberg's thoughts, meanwhile, went to the children; consequently, he inquired about them. No sooner had he asked about them, accompanied by a maid, the children strolled into the room. All looked quite resplendent in their new colourful attires that Haigan had bought for each of the family members, including the maid, for them to wear on this occasion.

With their backs straight, a smile on their lips, the children faced Holmberg. They offered their small hands for him to shake.

Holmberg was formulating some sentence with which to cheer up the children when, to the utter surprise of Holmberg, the boy managed to ask him a question. "How is my father?" He said in a sad note. "Mummy says he lives in your country," he added in a similar manner.

That too was part of the act that in the rehearsals the child had been taught how to perform well. He said it all in his native language, which his mother translated it into halting English.

Haigan, standing a few meters away from the scene, must have become happy to note that the message had struck the chord.

In the room, everyone noticed how Holmberg had got moved by the boy seeking information about his missing father, and anticipated what more he was going to do.

Haigan had never spoken a word to Hadio. He pretended as if he had never met her before.

In fact, just a week earlier, Hadio had been at his office to plead with him to allow the children to have a place in school. Besides, she had requested him to let them have their house back, which the government had confiscated. He had rejected her pleas, on both counts, and had threatened to put her in jail if she ever returned to his office.

Holmberg took the boy by the hand and led him into a vacant space, in one of the sofa sets, and then let the boy sit down next to him. At that moment, he felt a sudden sense of sadness for the boy building up in him. This had the effect of making his feelings of hatred against Haigan to reach it's a highest level; he suspected that Haigan was someone who would have no qualms using innocent little children as pawns to suit his political game. Looking at the little boy and his sister, he felt pity for them.

Thinking of what might happen to the children, and their mother, if left under the mercy of people like Haigan, had made Holmberg want to do something for them - to change their fate.

From that moment on he felt he had found a moral reason to justify his mission. All eyes were turned in his direction, anticipating his next action. Instead of addressing the child, Holmberg looked at Hadio's face, and there he read signs of desperation.

"What is the name of your son?"

"Atosh is his name," she said briefly.

In a voice filled with a sense of purpose, Holmberg addressed the boy. "Son," he said, "your mother is right. Your father lives in my country; there you will join him soon; what do you say?"

Hadio let the boy know what Bjorkman had just said; the boy gave a smile; so did everybody in the room, including Hadio and Haigan. For Haigan, it seemed, the game had been won in his favour. His government was going to get its ransom of three million dollars, and the family would be allowed to subsequently leave the country.

At this point, Haigan must have felt like hugging the little boy, who had made it all into a success. Furthermore, the feeling of trepidation in the room, which everyone had been experiencing, disappeared suddenly against the background of a room filled with sighs of relief. Holmberg had seen all he had wanted to see; it was time to leave; and so, promising to meet again, the two teams each got into their vehicles and drove away.

Holmberg and his colleagues left for their country's embassy, in the city centre, where a working lunch awaited them. At the embassy, both Holmberg and Johansson were introduced to junior and middle-ranking members of the diplomatic staff, who felt quite honoured to get to meet with Holmberg, for the first time. Ambassador Bertil was out of station, on a diplomatic assignment.

Once lunch was over, a special arrangement was made for Holmberg to communicate with Klaus Magnuson through a distant call.

Chapter Thirteen

# A Parliament in Full Session

In Stockholm, it was three in the afternoon. The Parliament was in full session. Klaus Magnuson, the Prime Minister, was about to get embroiled in one of the most difficult political challenges in his whole political carrier. Klaus Magnusson approached the podium to address the house while conscious of how hard his heart was beating against his chest.

In the past, Magnusson never shied away at a hard battle; however, the battle facing him now was unlike any other one, since the Parliament was expected to discuss a bill, which could negatively affect the economic prospects of elderly people, students, as well as large family units, if passed. Party policy makers hoped that the law would enable the nation to promote savings, and hence assure a long-term economic prosperity for the nation.

This, in brief, was going to be a major point in Magnusson's drive to win a majority vote in the Parliament. He was placing his notes in order of their importance when he noticed one of his aides heading in his direction.

He paused to give him an anxious look. The man approached the podium, and then whispered into his ears. There was a sudden look of concern in Magnusson's face. He turned his attention abruptly toward the now equally anxious members of the house; then he said, "Ladies and Gentlemen, I have just received a long distant call from Holmberg. It is urgent, he pleads."

Thereafter, followed behind by his aide, he took off in a great hurry.

Meanwhile, holding the line open, Holmberg could hear the approaching distant sound of Magnusson's footsteps.

Magnusson picked up the phone and said, "Hello old man. How are you?"

He uttered the words in his usual soft voice, leading anyone to believe that the voice belonged to a weakling. The impression apart, Magnusson was feared for his high intellect that he often put to good use, whenever he debated against his opponents.

"I am fine," Holmberg gave a cool reply.

He decided to ignore the high sounding emotional tone reaching him from the other end of the line. Nevertheless, he decided to get on straight with the subject-matter.

"We are required to pay a sum of money to win the release of the family," he said, avoiding giving further details,"

"How much money are we talking about?" Magnusson said, sounding quite adamant.

Holmberg thought it was quite odd for Magnusson not wanting to know the reason for which money must be paid.

"Pay them," he added quickly.

Where is Magnusson going to obtain such a large sum of money? If at all he was going to be Magnusson's paymaster, Holmberg decided to ask him the question.

To Holmberg's query, Magnusson said, "Money is not a problem. If it takes money to succeed, then we will have no other option but to pay money. We can't be seen to fail in our dealings with the tin-pot dictators of Africa, who, apart from being eaters of bananas, are as dark as the tropical-night! The most surprising thing about them is they are so dark, in a room full of them, they are not visible; that is how black they can get, these good for nothing banana eaters. We have set about achieving a noble goal, which we hope to achieve, despite the high price tag attached to it."

"Mind your tongue," Holmberg castigated Magnusson. "I am not someone you could easily impress with either your verbosity or pomposity. You, of all people, ought to know it," Holmberg added, still feeling annoyed with Magnusson.

"I didn't mean it," Magnusson said, sounding sheepish.

"Do you often say what you don't mean, and mean what you don't say?" said Holmberg, fuming at Magnusson.

"Forget it, and let us pay them," said Magnusson.

"You don't seem to understand," said Holmberg impatiently. "You have not answered my question. Let me ask you the question. Where do you hope to obtain three million dollars?"

For effect, this time, he had decided to let the sum get known to Magnusson.

There was a long pause at the other end, and then Magnusson spoke in an unusual haste, as if to compensate for the lost time.

"Well, I was thinking about the loan that we have promised that could help the government in Africa to manage its rural development projects."

This statement was followed with yet another pause. But before he could go on any further, Holmberg told him in an aggressive tone, "What is in your mind regarding the aid money?"

"We need to raise the rate of interest on the loan to regain the three million dollars," he replied in a cautious manner.

"What?" Holmberg said, sounding shocked.

In his next sentence, Magnusson was determined to soothe Holmberg's sense of fair play; hence, he said, "I know how cruel this sounds to you, but what more can we afford to do, my dear Holmberg?"

Holmberg liked neither the tone used by his colleague nor the content of his statement. But knowing quite well that he had no better alternative to what his colleague had to offer, for the sake of the children, he decided to go along with his proposition.

From the other end, Magnusson could not fail to notice the sound of reluctance in Holmberg's voice. Hence, to assuage Holmberg's dark feelings, he said, "My dear Holmberg, you must know, in a world we are living in, nothing seems to be what it is. Besides, all things are not clearly divided into black and white."

For a moment he stayed quiet and then he said abruptly, "You lose some and win some."

Holmberg hated Magnusson, as a politician, when he also doubled as a philosopher.

This last statement had brought their conversation to an abrupt end. Both men had reasons for not wanting to prolong their conversation, unnecessarily. Magnusson had a house to address, while in Holmberg's mouth the conversations had left a bitter taste.

Whoever said there were no openly cynically-minded people in this world? Holmberg thought.

While thinking of Magnusson and Haigan as two most cynically mined people, Holmberg was approaching the coffee room, situated at the inner-most section of the embassy building. He chose, from among several available seats, the most comfortable one; then he sat down and took a glance at the fax messages made available to him by the embassy personnel when his eyes fell on a caption that read, "The Parliament is ready to discuss a controversial bill which could result in austerity economic measures taken by the government."

In Stockholm, at this moment, Magnusson had reached the dais. However, the dais had suddenly ceased to have that forbidding and intimidating appearance that it seemed to possess, just a while ago. Facing the Parliament, Magnusson kept his composer, as he got ready for the task confronting him. Magnusson surveyed the House with a singularly determined glance. It pleased him to discover how tense it looked. For a short while he remained quiet, which kept the House in a state of a further suspended animation?

Once again, he laid down his papers on the dais, and then removed his eye glasses from its place on the upper left-hand pocket of his jacket, before putting them on.

"Ladies and Gentlemen, I have good news for you," he said.

He started his speech with a confidence that he had just acquired following the conversation he has had with Holmberg.

He recounted the outcome of a conversation with Holmberg, but made quite certain to keep secret that part of the deal concerning the money.

"Today," sounding quite euphoric, he proceeded on with his speech, "our nation has rededicated its commitments to the fundamental principles of human rights. None of us here could feel free if elsewhere people's rights are not respected. Ladies and Gentlemen, the captive family is free, at last; it is on their way here."

Magnusson received a resounding applause. He introduced the austerity bill for discussion, shortly after. It sailed through the house without any opposition.

It was now five in the evening. Holmberg had returned to his hotel room, where he took shower and had changed into a well pressed pair of shorts and a t-shirt; he had sandals on his feet. In the hotel lounge, he sat next to a window, from where he had a perfect view of the ocean and felt the sea breeze on his face.

Somehow, he felt quite relaxed; he was pleased with himself and his surroundings. Holmberg was more than certain that come tomorrow and he would have the deal clinched. Soon his mission would be accomplished, and he would have achieved the objective for which he had been dispatched into these distant foreign shores.

On the following day, the two teams met once again to finalise the deal. Holmberg informed his counterpart of his government's willingness to pay the ransom in exchange for the freedom of the family. Haigan, on his part, reminded Holmberg that the family would be released as soon as a confirmation that the money had been deposited to an account number in England, which he had made available to him, had been confirmed.

Three days later, a confirmation was made. The family members were subsequently released to the charge of the embassy staff, which started making preparation for their onward journey to Sweden.

Chapter Fourteen

# *Ambassador Kenneth Bertil*

A day before his journey back to Sweden took place Ambassador Bertil welcomed Holmberg to his residence for dinner. Bertil was a dark, chubby-looking middle-aged man. He had a thick moustache, on a rotund face that didn't fit the look of a polished and eloquent diplomat that he was. Instead, he had a look of a 19[th]Century clerical officer, stationed somewhere in a Central European mid-way train station.

On the day Holmberg arrived for his mission, in this coastal African city, Bertil had been on a countrywide tour that he undertook once a year. It was for this reason that Bertil had not been at the airport to officially receive Holmberg.

Now he invited Holmberg to his hill-side residence where they took dinner while sitting on a wooden balcony, from where they watched as the waves rise and fall gently in the calm blue sea-waters of the Indian Ocean.

Bertil had kept the invitation private; none of the other embassy staff were present at dinner table. Holmberg was accompanied by Johansson.

More than any other foreign accredited diplomats to this African country, Bertil was someone held in highest esteem. He had the respect of intellectuals, members of civil societies, students, as well as members of women organisations. Instead of staying barricaded behind the embassy walls, like other diplomats, Bertil often went out to meet with people, unaccompanied by body-guards.

"I believe in face to face method of diplomacy," he told those who had offered criticism of his unorthodox diplomatic method.

The intellectuals, who respected and admired him for his honesty, engaged him in all sorts of debates; they lovingly called him, "philosopher-diplomat."

This was an informal dinner invitation, and Bertil had kept it that way; both Holmberg and his colleague were dressed informally in short-sleeved cotton shirts and long trousers. As he sampled the full course-dinner, made of spaghetti, fish and fruit salad, Holmberg said, "It is a pity that, in the last held election, the Social Democrats had lost the election. One call from the Prime Minister would have done the miracle."

"I know how much our nation is appreciated in Africa. Our impeccable commitment, made for the struggle of Africa's decolonisation efforts, is one thing for which Africans will always remain thankful to us," Bertil said.

"Indeed; I learnt that the enormous progress our country has made, in such a short period of time, which people in Africa prefer to attribute to socialist policies, has greatly endeared us to the people of Africa," Holmberg said.

"When countries are as poor as those in Africa are, socialism becomes a highly appreciated political doctrine," Bertil said in quite a sincere tone. "However, as you know it well," he added, "socialism has many shades; what perhaps many Africans are unaware of is that the kind of socialism we are practising in our country happens at the level of the distribution of wealth; at the level of the production of wealth, our economy is privately held."

"What kind of socialism do they practise here," Holmberg asked in a sincere tone, seemingly eager to learn something new.

"I believe here is where we have failed African countries," Bertil said. "I believe," he added, "in order to encourage African countries to keep away from Stalinist form of socialism, which currently is causing havoc to economies of the African countries, we ought to have made a concerted effort to promote the form of socialism in Africa that we practise in our country, i.e. social democracy."

During their conversation, when Bertil mentioned the word corruption, Holmberg said eagerly, "Hold on there."

Holmberg whose mind was far from being in a state of tranquillity, despite an outward appearance of calmness, gave Bertil a hesitant smile, while also giving thought to the idea if he should be open with Bertil.

"I paid Haigan a sum of money to secure the release of the family," Finally Holmberg said, looking sad.

Bertil was not someone who was eager to be a privy to other people's secrets, but this was not a personal matter that Holmberg was talking to him about; it was something that touches upon the national interest of Sweden; he felt it was his duty to give ear to what Holmberg was going to talk to him about.

Bertil gave Holmberg a keen look, while remaining quiet.

"Until recently," Holmberg said looking Bertil straight in the face, "the word corruption, as far as I am concerned, was something I could think of quite subjectively about; it was something I looked at from an intellectual and ethical perspective."

"Has anything changed in your understanding of the word, so far?" Bertil asked in a curious tone.

"A lot have changed, my dear Bertil. Now, I know well what the word corruption means," Holmberg confessed.

"What do you mean?" Bertil asked, looking worried.

"When I accepted to pay ransom to gain the release of the family, I had based that decision on a need to secure the safety of the children and their mother, which at that point had mattered to me most. Now, however, each day that goes by, the morality of my action seems to weigh heavily on my mind.

Don't get me wrong. Of course, it is still important to me that I had managed to secure the release of the family, but could I not have done it differently and still achieve the same result? I feel that in my haste to conclude my mission here, I have failed to search for an alternative choice that might have been available to me.

In taking part in the corruption, the word corruption ceases to have a subjective meaning to you. You become corrupt; you are an embodiment of corruption, and I am afraid this is what I have become," Holmberg said, looking tired.

Not knowing exactly what to make of the confession that Holmberg had made about himself, Bertil said, "I don't understand."

Yet knowing Holmberg well, it was quite hard for Bertil to imagine Holmberg could have anything to do with corruption. Thus, overcome by a desire to ease the feelings of guilt in Holmberg, Bertil said in a sincere tone, "No one, not even you, can make me believe you could have anything to do with corruption."

Holmberg, aware of Bertil's desire to help assuage the feelings of guilt in him said honestly, "Those are generous thoughts for which I thank you."

He remained quiet afterwards, as if he was lost in his own thoughts.

Aware of the quagmire Holmberg had got stuck into and wishing not to complicate matters further, Bertil chose to stay quiet.

A moment later, as if he had suddenly come upon an idea that he had been following in his mind, but was in danger of getting lost to him, Holmberg sat upright in his chair and said in a hurried manner, "I am afraid to say I don't foresee any change in my situation; I am guilty of corruption, as charged."

Bertil felt sympathy for Holmberg; he felt that Holmberg was getting unnecessarily harsh on himself; hence, in a tone full of concern for Holmberg's troubled feelings, he said, "You are here on a mission; the mission has been accomplished; the family is free from the clutches of Haigan."

"I know you mean well; however, with all due respect for you," Holmberg said in a polite tone, "I don't believe that the end should justify the means; one has to be a Machiavellian to have to believe in such kind of thinking, and, by implication, I don't mean to say that you do so. It is a bad philosophy, nevertheless; it is selfish and cruel. However, I guess I will have to live with feelings of guilt for the rest of my days."

That statement brought the subject that had been agitating Holmberg's mind quite so deeply to a closing end; both men, it seemed, had seen no any meaningful reason for wanting to pursue the subject further.

Holmberg took a sudden look at his watch that read nine.

"It is getting late," he said. "We have got a plane to catch in the morning," he added.

"The car is waiting outside; the driver is ready, whenever you say so," Bertil said.

Holmberg got up from the chair; he looked up and saw how dark the night-sky has become; from a long distance, he could hear successive booming sounds of thunder.

Bertil noticed how Holmberg was taken by sight and sound of nature, in its majestic display of power. "It is going to rain soon. We are in the midst of the rainy season," he said.

"Night-time in Africa has a way of making you conjure up the primeval world of our ancestors; it makes you wonder whether they had fended off well against those mighty dangerous marauding predators, out there to get them. One can't help wondering about it, sometimes," Holmberg said.

"They have outmanoeuvred them; no doubt about it; we are here to tell the story; aren't we," Bertil said, giving Holmberg a reassuring look.

"Kudos to homo-sapiens," Holmberg said. He was getting ready to leave when suddenly he changed his mind; he resumed his seat, to the surprise of Bertil. And without wasting time, he took up the subject he had been wishing to discuss with Bertil but had almost eluded his focus.

"Africa's political situation," he said, "is one subject I don't have much knowledge about. The continent had stirred my imagination, even as a child. When independence came to Africa, some of us in Sweden finally became happy, and hoped independence will bring development, progress and peace to the continent. Well, that hasn't become the case. As someone who has spent much time in Africa, you are well conversant with African politics; tell me, what has wrong here?" He asked.

"Different countries have different kinds of problems to grapple with," Bertil said readily. He added, "Moreover, I have also come to realise that problems come and go; they are not permanent."

Holmberg's face lit up with anticipation, as he hoped to have more valuable information from Bertil.

"There is, however, a problem unique to Africa," Bertil said, a sad look overshadowing what, otherwise, is a happy and open face.

"Like the West," he said, "African countries do not have democratic rule, comparable to western form of democracies, and like the East, they are not under the rule of a party dictatorship that has a clearly defined ideology. Not withstanding democratic trappings of elected offices, there is a one-man rule in most African countries. In such a rule the ruler and his cronies will rule the state; they brook no opposition; they are robbers, human right is violated with impunity under this kind of rule, the so-called rulers fan the flames of ethnic tensions; they are cruel, vindictive and they are bullies."

Holmberg winced at the seriousness of the accusations Bertil has levelled against these rulers.

"One such obnoxious ruler's name that comes readily to my mind is Sese Seko Mobutu of Zaire," he added.

"Aren't you being hard on these rulers?" He said.

Bertil smiled lavishly while puffing on his cigar; He often enjoys a cigar or two after a hearty meal. "If you think I am being hard on them, talk to a citizen of any one of the African countries where you have these rulers, and hear what they will tell you," he said afterwards.

"So, the rule of cronyism is the bane of Africa's development prospects, you say" said Holmberg.

"Oh, yes; that is right," Bertil gave a wholehearted reply

Holmberg stayed quiet, but gave deep thoughts to everything that Bertil had spoken to him about; after a while he said, "Our Social Democratic party has no clear-cut policy on how to deal with Africa. What would you recommend?"

"I don't know really," Bertil said.

"You are being modest. Believe me, if there is someone who could help us chart the way, that person is you."

"I have never made any effort to give Africa's current political and economic situation an in-depth analysis; however, giving the subject a quick thinking, I should mention the following to you:

We mustn't, at any time, interfere with the internal affairs of African countries.

Our volume of trade with the African countries is not big enough. Therefore, we must expand our volume of trade with the African countries, despite international trade conventions we have signed, placing African countries at a disadvantageous position; if possible we must lobby the developed countries to give Africa a break, by opening up their markets to goods and services from the continent.

We must review our aid policies; we need to design policies that are beneficial to African countries. Aid forms which keep African countries in perpetual state of poverty should be voided.

While there is a need to influence African countries to promote democracy, we must be careful not to foster democratic tradition of Western countries that are seen as alien in Africa. It is well to bear in mind that democratic traditions have had different trajectories, even in the West. If democracy means a rule by consensus, such concept is not strange to Africans.

Civil societies must have our full support; however, civil societies, if they are run, managed and funded from abroad, they will not be effective. We must encourage the growth of those civil societies that are deep rooted in the cultural traditions of the countries within which they operate. Our civil societies in Sweden, for example, are deeply rooted in our traditions and culture. They have independence of their own, too; they don't rely on any one for their survival.

Civil societies that are run by women must have our full support. African women are hard-working people, endure great hardships, and hence deserve a break. My wife, Helena, who is away for medical check-ups in Sweden, is aware of this reality; she is working closely with various women organisations, trying to help them improve their living conditions by finding markets in Sweden, in which they could sell their handcraft-wares.

Looking quite exhausted, following a long speech he had just given, Bertil gave Holmberg a tired look, and said, "I hope I have said something worth listening to."

"Thanks for the information," Holmberg said, feeling quite pleased with Bertil.

"I will try," he added, "to get the central committee of our party to elaborate on your points further, and from such an endeavour determine whether we could have a guideline policy to help us develop a meaningful relationship with African countries, as a party, and to eventually transfer that experience to the level of the state."

"Until then, it is going to be business as usual with the likes of Bobe Haigan, unfortunately," Bertil said.

"Oh; yes," Holmberg jumped at the mentioning of the name Bobe Haigan and said. "By the way, who is this man? What is he? I think he is quite a fascinating man."

"In Bobe Haigan," Bertil said, "you have a face of the African crony."

During all the time the conversation between the two men was taking place, Johansson sat down quietly, looking quite inconspicuous; occasionally, however, he nodded his head and smiled to indicate his presence.

"If one is to ignore his many portfolios, as a measure of his importance, what one can't afford to overlook about Haigan is the kind of relationship he is having with the president of the country. Haigan is the first cousin of the president; the two have been married to two blood sisters, whose father is the head of the army; he has a nephew who is a head of the national security apparatus. Thus, seen from this perspective, in this country, Haigan is a power to be reckoned with."

He concluded his exposition by telling Holmberg, "Don't be deceived by his charming smile and nice words; Haigan is a scoundrel."

That discussion brought their meeting to the end.

On the morning of the following day, accompanied by members of Kore's family, the two-man delegation left for Sweden. A day later, the whole group was at Arlanda Airport, where they received a warm welcome. From the airport, Kore's family were dispatched to Uppsala, where Kore received them.

On meeting his family, for the first time, after several years, Kore shaded tears of happiness. His wife had also wept, but the spectacle had looked quite funny to the children.

The country's major media outlet, in the following days, focused on Holmberg's exploits in Africa. The headlines in the country's dailies were feast for the eyes, all in praise of the nation for upholding the principles of human-rights. Congratulatory notes received from various international humanitarian agencies were also published, which further swelled the spirit of the nation with pride.

Numerous interviews were held with Holmberg, who was able to explain his successes in a lucid language. However, none of Kore's family members were requested to tell the nation about their past ordeals. And anticipating an invitation to speak to the nation, like he did once before, Kore was not asked to give his opinion.

As the nation continued to take note of the successes made by Holmberg, meanwhile, groups opposed to Kore's home government had let the financial secret-deal, which took place in Africa, get known to the world. This surprising twist of fate had happened in a form of a short story published in the famous "Corriere Della Sera" of Italy, later published in one of the Swedish influential dailies.

The story related how the Swedish Government had paid a ransom of three million dollars to win the freedom of the family.

The same paper stated further that the African Government in question had used the money to pay salaries of White Rhodesians mercenary pilots, whose task it had been to bombard positions held by insurgent-groups, opposing their government.

Those air-strafing, the paper claimed, had caused deaths to many people, including women and children. The military campaign, which constitutes an act of barbarism, if not contained in time, it would cause a significant rise in the numbers of refugees seeking asylum in Europe, the paper claimed.

When confronted with such incriminating piece of information, however, Magnusson brushed aside such claims as being somewhat "spurious, baseless and lacking in any kind of factual meaning."

Anyone else would have brushed aside the information, and instead move on with life. But not Holmberg, who reviewed his place in the drama that made him to feel sad. Consequently, he considered many options that would make him able to atone for his sin of omission. The one option that had appeared most appealing to him was to tender his resignation from party politics, citing ill health as a reason.

Happily, Holmberg kept his promise of finding a way to assist African coutries in their development efforts, by establishing an institute to be run through a foundation he had set up. The institute which came to be known as Scandinavian Institute for the Review of Resource Development in Africa was run on guide-line principles laid down by Ambassador Kenneth Bertil who, after resigning from his diplomatic post, became the Institute's first Director.

As for Kore and members of his family, this was to be the beginning of a long struggle to settle down into a life-style of a people fighting to survive in an environment that was strange to them as they were to it.

Chapter Fifteen

# *Make the Best of It*

On the day that his family arrived in Uppsala, Kore took the family out in the evening, to have a dinner of pizza that Hadio and the children liked very much. At the pizzeria, the children went to meet Swedish children that they saw there.

"My name is Atosh. What is your name?" Atosh, without any inhibitions, introduced himself to other children in the pizzeria. He spoke in a simple English language that he had learnt at school, in his homeland. Shifo did the same thing. The children were dressed up in sweaters and jackets Kore had bought from a second hand market, long before the children had arrived from Africa. The clothes suited them well in this spring season, which seemed too cold for them.

When they failed to get the children to respond to them they went back to their table, looking sad.

"Don't worry, you will have friends to play with at school," Kore reassured the children.

"Why don't they want to play with us? Atosh asked.

"Because they don't know you well; but they will play with you when they get to know you well," Kore said, not sure what he had just said would make any sense to them. After all, where they come from children don't need to know each other well enough for them to initiate contacts. He remembered a similar thing happening to him when he was new in Sweden.

"When I was new here," he told Hadio, "I saluted people in the street that I didn't know. In the end, I stopped when I met with strange looks."

"I thought all children were like puppies; they run to each other," Hadio said.

"No; not here my dear; that may sound strange to you, but they will learn, bye and bye; this applies to you too" Kore said.

From the pizzeria, they went back to a newly acquired apartment that the authority had allocated it to them. The apartment had two rooms and a sitting room, on a fifth floor, in one of the high-rising buildings, in Gottsunda – an area in Uppsala, occupied mostly by immigrants. The apartment had a modest set of furniture, which Kore had bought from a dealer of second-hand furniture.

In the evening, the family sat down together in front of the TV to watch several recorded episodes of Pippi Langstromp films in the video that the children liked very much.

By eight, the children who felt tired were ready to go to sleep in a room they shared. At nine, Kore and Hadio retired to their own room to sit and talk; Hadio looked beautiful in her night gown; Kore was in his light blue pyjamas.

"Why did you go away from us? We suffered at the hands of cruel people" Hadio said looking straight at Kore.

They were sitting and talking in a room with a single bed and two sets of chairs only.

"I had no alternative but to do what I did," he said, looking at her with pleading eyes.

"Did you give thought to what consequences your action could have on the children and me?" she said.

"There has never been a day that went by I didn't think of you or the children. I am sorry," he said.

"After you left, they came and kicked us out from the house; after that, they removed the children out from the school," she said.

"How could they do that to you and the children?" he said.

"They did it to get to you. When I pleaded with Haigan, in his office, to show mercy, he said I must do everything to get you to come back home, in order, as he had put it, for you to serve time in jail, for embezzling funds, belonging to the government," she said.

"If I could be guaranteed justice, I would not have hesitated to go back, and fight the case in the court of law," he said earnestly.

"We were lucky; without my aunt, who had provided for us, we would have been begging for alms, out in the streets," she said.

"I wish that didn't happen to both you and the children. I wish we were home, living our lives the way we did before. But the fact is we are not at home; we are in a new country now; let us make the best of it," he said.

"Yes," she obediently said.

"What do you do for a living now?" She said.

For a second he remained quiet; later he said, "I am doing studies at the university."

She sat straight on the bed, and repeating the words "studying at the university", she said almost in a mocking tone, "Aren't you a bit too old for that? Besides, you are well educated."

"I don't sit in a class room to follow instructions given by a teacher - if that is what you might be imagining to be the case. I do research work. I have my own office, and I get stipend from which I pay tax to the government. I am an employee of a different kind," Kore said.

"Why don't you get the right kind of employment?" She asked.

"I have realised that I have little chance achieving anything in my new home country, unless I acquire a Swedish academic qualification. Here they place more emphasis on credentials obtained from their academic institutions for jobs. In a sense, I have decided to pursue higher education to better my chances for becoming successful in this my new home country," he said, looking at Hadio to see if she would find any sense in what he just said to her.

"Do you like what you are doing?" She asked.

"I like doing research work," he said.

Suddenly he felt an irresistible urge to touch Hadio. He touched her face and said, "Considering the difficulties and challenges that have gone through, you still retain your good physical looks."

"I am glad you said so," she said, keeping his hands off her face.

"The sufferings," she added, "were real; I want to forget about them."

Despite the ordeals that she had gone through, in her home country, Hadio still retained her beauty, which consisting of long limbs, narrow waist and a long neck, resting on a not too thin pair of shoulders, had been the source of attraction to Kore, and continues to be the case now. From her special demeanour, it was clear to him that she still maintained the level of confidence that she had always had in herself. At twenty-five, she looked younger than what her real age was.

While sitting in their bedroom, talking to each other, Kore had an overwhelming desire to do more than just to touch her face. He hadn't seen her for some time, and tonight she was more beautiful than he had imagined her. He deliberately edged closer to her, held her face between his hands and said, "I missed you."

"I missed you, too," she said, as she stifled a yawn.

Obviously, this must have caused her to feel quite embarrassed; hence she said, "I am sorry."

"You must be feeling tired; you have had a long trip," he said. "Besides," he added, "it is quite late; we have to catch up with some sleep; we have much to do tomorrow."

She remained quiet. Moments later, Kore turned the lights out, and then got into the bed; shortly after, one could hear giggles and laughter coming from the darkness of the room.

Early in the morning, Hadio visited the kitchen to determine the kind of breakfast to make for the family. Kore, who stood close by, tried to familiarise her with the kitchen and its items. It was 8 a.m.; the two had an appointment to keep at 9.30, at the social welfare office.

As Hadio set to make breakfast, Kore made sure that the children wake up, have their teeth brushed, take shower and get ready for breakfast. At 9 a.m. sharp, the family were on a bus, on a journey that took them to their destination.

By 9.25, they were inside Social Welfare Office, where they met with an official who was a slightly built dark hardy looking woman who was in her early fifties; she had a deep-set pair of eyes that could render any attempt at reading the emotion passing through them quite difficult to fathom. She had a long chin that gave her face an elongated shape.

In the past she never married, nor was she married now; she valued her work more than anything. Ever since she took the job, at the age of twenty-five, she never knew anything else in her life. She spoke slowly and carefully as she weighed in her mind what to say.

She meant many things to many people; some thought she was vindictive and cruel, while others considered her to be helpful; she liked to think of herself, however, as someone who was dedicated to her work, and was determined to make sure no one should benefit from the loopholes present in the system, at the expense of society.

Few people knew that the woman herself had once been a refugee from Hungary. She belonged to a group of people whose lives had been saved by Raoul Wallenberg - the famous Swedish diplomat. Other members from her family were not as lucky.

She had remained thankful to Raoul Wallenberg for saving her life; in her apartment, she kept a shrine; there she made prayers, asking God to keep him safe, where ever he may be.

On the table, in her office, she had a framed black and white portrait of Raoul. To her few closest friends, in relation to Raoul, she was often fond of telling them, "While God gave me life, Raoul Wallenberg made sure I keep it."

She lived for the day when correct and reliable information about the fate of Raoul would be known to the rest of the world. She had no reason to trust the Soviet Union a bit, who, in connection to the fate of Raoul, would say one thing one day, but say another thing another day.

She had dedicated her life to his memory by serving humanity selflessly – an ideal that Raoul had fought for. The best way to do it, she realised, was to assist the poor to obtain education; and so, to her credit, she had at different times paid school fees of more than twenty school children from the three continents of South America, Africa and Asia, all of whom today call her mother.

"Welcome to Sweden. My name is Ingrid," she said in English, offering to shake hands with both Hadio and Kore, while remaining seated. Afterwards, with reference to the children, she said, "And these two-young people must be your children."

"Yes," Hadio and Kore said quite at the same time.

"Please sit down," she said.

They sat on chairs, facing Ingrid across from the table.

"I am aware," Ingrid said as she addressed Hadio, "you don't speak any Swedish. I will address you in Swedish, nevertheless. Your husband will act as an interpreter for you.

Hadio nodded her head, and gave a shy smile.

"First and foremost," Ingrid said, "I wish to welcome you to Sweden."

Kore interpreted what Ingrid had said, just as he will continue to also do so with the rest of their conversation.

"Thank you," Hadio said.

Our meeting is taking place here today in order to make sure that, being a newcomer to this country, your initial entry into the society is quite smooth. Keeping this in mind, this office has made sure that your current accommodation is suitable to the needs of your family members. For this reason, we took your husband away from his student accommodations to your current home, at Gottsunda.

Today, you will have a cheque written in your name, to enable you to buy new set of furniture, as well as clothes for you and your two children. Arrangement had already been made for the children to attend a school near you.

A sum of money to cover the cost of living for you, during this current month, will be given to you. You will visit this office, once a month, until when finding some work to do your fortune would have changed for the better.

Another important course of action this office has undertaken, in relation to your current legal status in this country, is to get you to take lessons in Swedish language. I am advising you to take your studies seriously, as fluency in the Swedish language will be a key for enabling you to find your way into the Swedish society.

It is the duty of this office to make sure that you and your family members do not suffer any needs. However, it is important for you to know that your needs are met for by the tax payers of this country. It is my hope that, one day, you will earn a decent living to enable you to pay your share of the tax that will be used to help others that may need assistance.

Finally, I will talk to you about two sets of values that are important to us in this country; these are the values of equality and freedom. While we acknowledge that all people are not equal, in every sense of the words, given that some are more gifted than others, yet we hold dear the truth that all people are born equal; we strive therefore to make effort to provide equal opportunity to everyone in the society, irrespective of their colour, gender, ethnicity or religion.

Perhaps, as a new comer, it is essential for you to understand what does equality stands for at the household level. Mind you, between you and your husband, no one is superior to the other. A better household is built on a framework of sharing everything on an equal basis, from rearing children to household chores, including the household economy.

Freedom is yet another value much cherished in this society. It is important to bear in mind that in pursuing your freedom, you need to respect the freedom of other people. At the personal level, the free decision-making process is a product of freewill. Hence, in a household relationship, like yours, where you are a wife to your husband, this means that you should be able to say yes when you mean yes, and say no when you mean no.

Your body belongs to you; and although your husband has a conjugal right to your body, yet he must take into consideration the fact that you are free to accept or reject any proposition made to you by him on matters entailing physical relationships.

Finally, I wish you good luck and hope that you will enjoy your stay in this country.

"Thank you," Hadio said and offered a shy smile.

Just as they were getting ready to leave, after she handed the cheque, Ingrid drew their attention.

"By the way," she told them, "I need to remind you to keep the following in mind: under no any circumstances is wife or child beating practices allowed here in Sweden; female genital mutilation is forbidden in Sweden; both are punishable crimes."

In just six months, Hadio had mastered the language so well that her instructors were quite pleased with her achievements, and within a year she assumed work as Assistant Nurse at Uppsala's Akademiska Hospital. The children had settled down well into their studies, and had acquired many friends; by now they were fluent in Swedish.

Hadio loved and admired almost everything about her new country; however, there was one thing that had been bothering her mind most. Sitting and talking to Kore over a cup of coffee, at an IKEA Restaurant, one fine Saturday morning, as the children left to look for games to play, she told Kore, "Why do people here hard to approach? Don't misunderstand me. Perhaps hard to approach is not exactly the right phrase to describe what I wish to say. Maybe they just mind their own business."

They were on a visit to IKEA shopping centre, to replenish their household stock of utensils, cover sheets, bed sheets, cups and glasses.

The IKEA visit that the family undertook twice a month was not only for buying household items, but it was an opportunity for the family to socialise together in a way they were unable to do in their home. Because of Hadio's irregular working hours, the family have not always been together, at any given time, at their home, to sit and talk together.

"That could well be the case. But again, in this country," Kore said, making reference to Hadio's statement, "people don't need each other's goodwill to survive. Where we come from cooperation is a strategy to survive in an environment of scarcity and poverty."

"I have never looked at it that way, but now you have said it, it makes some sense to me. No wonder, I haven't seen any of our neighbours coming into our home, asking to be replenished with a salt, for cooking food, that they may have run short of," Hadio said.

"In this country, people have their supply of "salt," enough to last throughout the eternity," Kore said. "Mind you," he added, "there is no virtue involved in either one of the cases. Here, in this country, there was a time when communities cooperated to an extent of farming their plots together; they went as far as keeping doors to their houses wide open for anyone wishing to get in to do so. Apparently, those days are now long gone. Now some people live alone, and sometimes they die alone in their apartments," Kore said solemnly.

"It is a pity that it should happen here," Hadio said.

"If poverty is what makes us to cooperate with one another, it also makes our society a dangerous place to live in. In Sweden, you do not live in fear of someone cutting your throat, to pick your pockets," Kore said.

"At any rate, we can't afford to get judgemental," he added.

"Agree," Hadio said.

Chapter Sixteen

# *Sarah*
# (1945)

It is quite in the nature of things for one to have less appreciation for the activity that determines one's immediate life. As such, man will either hanker for an uncertain future and feels nostalgic for the past. As he pursued higher education in the university, life was far from being an ideal one for Kore. Hence, he constantly dreamt of a day when he would leave all that behind him.

While at the university, well before his family came out of Africa to join him in Sweden, he had acquired a friendship of one Peter Welles. The two had lived at Student Staden, in a building facing the university campus, in rooms separated by a long corridor. Whenever they had a free time they would visit the city's various pubs together, where they had taken their drinks, and sought the company of girls.

After his family arrived from Africa, the two continued with their friendship. In fact, Peter became a family-friend; he attended birthday celebrations held for various members of

Kore's family; both children and Hadio had shown a liking for him; to show their appreciation for him, the children called him, "Uncle Peter."

From the moment Kore met Peter, and the two became acquaintances, Kore had never ceased to feel uncomfortable in the presence of the man. This is not to say Peter had an intimidating personality; far from it. Peter had a special knack for endearing himself to people when he needed them most, but he was not the type to sustain friendship. If he got into any sort of hot discussion with someone, he was not the kind of person who would be able to sustain the discussion to its logical conclusion. He would often concede defeat, withdraw to himself, and then sit down quietly in a corner, looking at people around him with suspicious eyes. Many times, after he had had discussions with people, Kore had come upon him shading tears of frustration, in secret.

Peter was slight in build; whenever he talked to a person, he had a habit of looking sideways and behind; he acted as if he feared for his life; when he spoke, words came out of his mouth with a speed of a machinegun.

There was one subject that brought Peter's emotions to rise to a boiling point; it was his mother.

With reference to his mother, he would tell Kore whenever he got drunk, "You may probably think that I am being mischievous, or unnecessarily difficult. It is only that I can't bring myself to love her; you reap what you sow!"

Peter talked so much about his mother, in his conversation with Kore, that having conversation with him was boring, Kore thought. It is his mother, after all, Kore reasoned. What does the man wish him to do? Psychoanalyse him? Cuddle him? Or give him the impossible love his mother had missed giving him? Sometimes Kore was not sure what Peter had missed having in his relationship with his mother. Was he longing for his mother's love, or a sense of identity he claimed she had denied him?

In future, Kore would regret knowing Peter so quite closely.

But who is Peter? Since to know Peter is to know his mother, Sarah, and the circumstances that had led to his birth, perhaps a most pertinent question, regarding who Peter is, is to ask the question, who is Sarah?

Sarah, Peter's mother, was born and brought up well. She came from a family that traced its origin from a time in the past when it had ardently offered its support to various Swedish monarchs in their military campaigns, to conquer, to pacify and to rule. For its priceless contribution, the Bissell family, through royal edicts, had been rewarded with titles, tracts of land, as well as other means of wealth, which it invested in the industrial sector of the Swedish economy, to generate a fabulous wealth for its various members.

Hence, at the turn of the twentieth century, it had become the single richest family in the whole country. It interests in the world of business had encompassed a whole world of enterprises, ranging from mining, to banking, engineering, manufacturing, communication and real estate.

When Sarah was born, Martin, her father, who represented her side of the family's branch, had been acting as an Executive Director for the conglomerate. Sarah was brought up in a sheltered life. She had everything that she coveted for in life. For her early education, a governess had been sent from England to be her tutor of the English language.

When she was in her early teens, her father had sent her to a high school, reserved exclusively for children of the elite class. After graduating from high school, Sarah pursued a university education in Stockholm University.

It was during this time when she was still pursuing her first degree in economics, under the tutorship of Gunnar Myrdal, that the Second World War broke out in Europe. Luckily, her country's neutral position would make it possible for her to finish her studies, well in time. It is well to bear in mind, however, although the condition of neutrality in Sweden was to guarantee its people a measure of peace, yet many were people in the country who had felt betrayed. To such people, as a concept, neutrality was a by-word for capitulation, cooperation and concession.

And despite peaceful atmosphere that people had been enjoying, throughout the country, there was a general fear that the war might possibly acquire quite a different face, thereby dragging the nation into its vortex.

When the war ended, the jubilation that took place in the country knew no bounds. However, at the Bissell family's estate, situated on an off-shore island, close to Stockholm, is where the largest party of them all was held.

Anyone who was somebody in the society got invited to this party. Apart from celebrating the allied victory, the dinner party was also intended to be a confidence-building exercise for members of the business fraternity; it was also expected to provide an opportunity for political leaders to renew their pledge to uphold principles of social democracy.

To Martin, Sarah's father, however, the party had a personal significance for him. In holding the party, he had Sarah's welfare at his heart; as his only child, he wanted happiness for her; it did not feel right, at twenty years of age, she should be locking herself up inside her room, doing what no one knows.

Moreover, with a genuine measure of sadness in his heart, he realised how the once rosy-colour of his daughter's skin had drastically changed to look quite pale, due to long hours she had been spending inside her room. Martin knew well that a pale look that had an aesthetic quality much admired by members of the European upper classes, during the Victorian era, was no longer considered fashionable in the days of his daughter. She would have to improve on her appearance, he thought.

Whenever Martin brought himself to think of his daughter, he often wondered if it was indeed his daughter's welfare, and not his own personal welfare, he cared most about! Of course, Martin had a deep love for his daughter.

Nevertheless, it was not lost on Martin, as his only child, Sarah alone was the person who could give him an heir. For this reason, he wished the dinner party would be a forum to provide the opportunity for Sarah to meet with other people of her age. He knew the party was not going to be short of such a possibility.

The dinner party, whose guest of honour was the prime minister, started quite early in the evening; it was a prestigious affair; the list of people attending the party read like who is who in the world of business, industry, commerce, education, politics etc. After dinner, at seven sharp, speeches followed.

Once speeches were given, in a brightly lit hall, the guest started to gradually do away with their stiff postures, in favour of easy-going manners, holding cocktail in their hands and chatting with each other against the background sound of classical music.

Just as he had expected, the dinner party turned out to be what Martin had dreamt about.

"But wait! Where is Sarah?" He asked himself.

At the dinner-table, Sarah had been nabbing on her food, sitting next to him, watching people with lazy eyes. Martin thought she looked beautiful, even though he wished she had dressed to match the occasion. When he couldn't locate her in the hall, he became a little frantic in his manner. He decided to look for her elsewhere. He did not have to go far.

There, in the adjoining hall, on a deserted balcony, he saw Sarah nestled against a gangly-looking young man of about her own age. He lingered at the spot; he kept looking at the pair before he went away, to join the guests at the hall.

The boy in the balcony with Sarah, like herself, was from the university; the two had had a platonic relationship, once before; this had been quite clear to whoever had kept note of their friendship. Like Sarah's family, his family was one of the richest in the country, too.

At a time when intimate relationships among many of their peers had been blossoming into a love affair, the two had remained unattached. However, both had had previous relationships with other partners that had not lasted long.

Hence, at the dinner party, the presence of James Moreno (for that was the boy's name) came as a pleasant surprise for Sarah, who had been showing signs of boredom. Sarah had given him a warm lingering peck to his cheek. Immediately, thereafter, she had dragged him out to a place in the balcony, where Martin had seen them together.

There was a kind of energy displayed by the two youngsters on this evening, which had been a marking feature of their every single movement. For example, on their way to the adjoining balcony, the two youths looked as if they were gliding on a pair of roller skates.

Once there, short and delicate-looking, Sarah smiled as she stood on her toes to give the tall and thin Moreno a kiss in the mouth. For a moment, the kiss had a disorienting effect on both. They pulled away from each other, only to come together, once again.

When they kissed, once more, this time, it was an intimate long-lingering kiss. During the long following hours that they had spent together, thereafter, they were able to reveal the feelings of love they had for each other, which neither had been aware of until now.

"How is it possible for one to have a feeling of love and yet not knowing it?" Sarah asked, looking imploringly into Moreno's dark eyes.

This was a difficult question, even for Moreno, who was a student of human-psychology. He made a doubtful face and then said in a reply, "These are difficult times; let us blame it on the war." He bent and whispered into Sarah's ears, "It is enough that we have found each other, at last"

Without uttering a single word, Sarah nodded her head in agreement.

A month later, both Sarah and Moreno finished their education. Moreno would find employment in his family's media industry. Sarah would assume the post of a private secretary in her father's office.

It was soon getting close to three years since the end of the war; consequently, people began to settle down into a life that looked normal again. To Moreno, however, his media job had demanded so much time from him that he could not spend enough time to be with Sarah. Sarah, on her part, couldn't find any valid reason whatsoever why Moreno wouldn't spare time to be with her!

One day, at a short moment notice, Sarah asked Moreno to meet her at Bergius Botanic Garden; the haste with which she asked for a meeting made him feel worried. Sarah had never displayed such urgency before; their meeting had always followed a careful planning. Merino knew how meticulous Sarah was in everything she did. He felt worried. He left his place of work in a hurry. At the garden, he found Sarah seated on a stone bench, looking anxious, waiting for him to arrive.

The day was bright despite the chill in the air. Moreno joined Sarah on the bench. A short distant away was a young couple; the girl's left arm was wrapped around her partner's neck while he fed birds bread crumps.

Dispensing with formality of exchanging greetings with Moreno, Sarah gave Moreno a straight look; in a business-like manner, she said, "What do you value most? Do you value your work more than you value me?"

Moreno was stunned. Moreno was one of those people who never read any meanings into everything that people say or do; but, if he did, he would have been careful with Sarah.

"Of course, I value both my work and you, and not necessarily in the same order," he said mildly.

Whenever Sarah was in a state of agitation, she had a habit of not sitting still. Now, suddenly, she stood up, and then started pacing the ground in silence, a look of tortured concentration showing in her face. Finally, she stopped pacing the ground. Hiding a sign of agitation, she said with determination, "You know how much I have been looking forward to a holiday?"

Moreno nodded his head and remained silent. He was anticipating what more she was going to say. She was probably going to ask him to accompany her to Paris. She had spoken to him about the issue previously. There was nothing in life however he would love to do more than to accompany Sarah on her journey to Paris. Yet, it pained him to know that, given all the backlog of assignment waiting to be finished, there was no way he could agree to travel with her to Paris.

Still on the same subject, Sarah said, "Would you like to come with me to Paris?" Then she threw the bait to entice him; "We shall have a good time together," she said.

This last statement had held such an appeal for him that he almost changed his mind. He pulled himself together, nevertheless, and uttered his reply that had made Sarah to give a nervous smile. Moreno flinched at his own reply; he avoided looking Sarah in the face. For a short while, the two had remained silent. Moreno felt he had to do something to soothe

Sarah's injured feelings. As he approached her, arms stretched out, he offered her a gentle smile.

Knowing well what his intentions were, Sarah said, "No; you don't have to do this; you have made your choice and I have made mine." She added, "I shall be leaving for Paris, the day after tomorrow, from where I will be in touch with you."

This last sentence brought blood flowing back into Moreno's pale face. Consequently, he forced a smile that Sarah didn't reciprocate. She turned and left in a hurry. She never wished Moreno to see tears now freely flowing down her face.

Chapter Seventeen

# Sarah in Paris
# 1948

Although the train trip to Paris was a long and tedious affair, yet Sarah had enjoyed every bit of it. Occasionally, the train passed through hamlets and towns that reminded her of the war. Sarah imagined how real the war might have been to people who had lived in those hamlets and towns, where nearly all buildings in them had been scarred by marks of bombshells, their streets torn to shreds, and felt quite sad. However, since a beehive of activity was taking place everywhere to reclaim the lost glory of life, Sarah ceased to feel sad shortly after. After a long and gruesome journey, through several countries, the train finally pulled into the major Paris train station.

It was late in the evening of an early spring day when the train pulled into the main Paris Railway Station, Gare Du Nord. The slight cold breeze of wind blowing relentlessly across her face brought memories of Moreno flowing into Sarah's mind with such an intense force she got surprised. Up till now, Sarah didn't realise how much she was missing Moreno.

Before embarking on her long-awaited journey to Paris, Sarah had made arrangements that had included booking for a room in a hostel, on the Right Bank, at Arrondissement 4th, from where she thought she would have a true glimpse of Paris, both past and present. Had she wanted, Sarah would have stayed in one of her father's many owned chateaus. The reason she hadn't done such a thing it was because she knew such course of action would cut her off from the hassle and bustle of Paris life. But, perhaps, what she relished most of all was the idea of having a chance to walk in the cobblestoned streets of Paris that she assumed some past French men and women of great historical stature could have stepped on. The name Robespierre and Alexander Dumas came readily into her mind. Such prospect gave her goose bumps, which, having started from the back of her slender arms ended at the base of her neck.

On the way to the hostel, Sarah marvelled at the architectural beauty of the buildings. Indeed, Sarah was thrilled to be in Paris, "The city of lights." She was pleased that the war had spared Paris from facing the destruction, which, unfortunately, had been the lot of some of the other European great cities.

A special fascination the city of Paris had been holding for Sarah was that it had offered her the opportunity to practise French language that she had studied privately under a French tutor.

As it turned out, there were some guests already in the hostel; many, like her, were young people. Because she was determined to improve her spoken French, therefore she distanced herself from the other guests that spoke in English.

Apart from having a pleasant atmosphere, the hostel turned out to be exactly what she had imagined in her mind to be; placed on the first floor of the building, the hostel had broad rooms and low-lying windows, from where one could catch a glimpse of life outside.

On her first evening in the hostel, after she took a shower and had changed into new skirt and a short-sleeved cotton blouse of brown colour, Sarah ate a simple meal of cheese sandwich in a small dining hall, at the end of a long corridor. Afterwards, she retired to her thinly-furnished room to make plans for the following day.

While in her room, contemplating her presence in Paris, she thought of places she wished to visit, all at once, but soon realised the dangers of having to bit more than the mouth can chew.

An affable and bubbly middle-aged plump Corsican lady by the name of Lesia became Sarah's friend in the hostel. From her association with Lesia Sarah hoped to practise her French.

Lesia had been employed to manage the affairs of the hostel by a Parisian law firm. She cleaned floors in the sleeping rooms, made sure that bathrooms were clean and changed bed sheets. The law firm that paid her salary had been commissioned to take care of both the financial and legal aspects of the business by its French owners, who lived in the Comoro Island – a French island colony - situated off the coast of East Africa, where they owned a large farming estate, growing plants from which vanilla are harvested.

Every evening, after her working day was over, Lesia would spend some time talking to Sarah before going to sleep, in her own quarters.

Lesia was in her early forties; she was short and vivacious by temperament. She still retained the beauty that once had attracted her former husband to her. Lesia had thick rich black glossy hair that she parted in the middle.

Soon after they came to know each other well, the two women engaged in talks, mainly comparing notes of their love affairs.

Sarah spoke about her boyfriend, Moreno, and Lesia talked to Sarah about Mario, her absent husband.

"Mario," Lesia told Sarah animatedly "was a ruffian and a rascal." "He brought me to Paris," she added, "when I was seventeen years old, only to go away, a year after that; he left for Algeria; there he joined the French Foreign Legionnaires; I never saw him again."

This discussion, as usual, was taking place inside Sarah's room. Sarah had a hectic day; she had just taken a shower and had changed into clean pyjamas; she was reposing in her bed, a book she was about to read in her hand, when Lesia paid her a visit.

The revelations that Lesia had made about her missing husband made Sarah feel sad, and so she was forced to say, "Do you think he had any feelings of love for you"?

"I guess he liked me the way one likes Corsican orange: plump, sweet and juicy." She said in a determined tone. "Unfortunately, soon after he had squeezed the juice, all out of me, he abandoned me. I never saw him again," she said.

"Oh, poor Lesia," Sarah said feeling genuinely sad; however, detecting a note of admiration for him in Lesia's voice, Sarah said, "Do you still like him?"

"Of course, I want him. As a woman, you must know well how often we women are attracted to man like Mario. Mario was quite devious, silly and cruel; he could also be caring, warm and considerate, quite at the same time," she said, showing no sign of bitterness. "As a person," she added quite dramatically, "Mario was unpredictable; he offered challenge; he was exciting; a predictable man is a boring man; he is not for me."

At the end of that brief exposition about strange attraction some women find in men that could well be considered rude as well as cruel to them, both women laughed heartily.

Sarah was able to visit places in the city of Paris that she had always wanted to see. She saw and admired Palace Granite - home of the Paris Opera; she visited Eiffel Tower and the Cathedral of Notre Dame, as well as Paris famous museum, the Louvre. She had been to Le Lido where, at last, she realised her long-life dream of watching the Moulin Rouge perform their famous cancan dance.

Accompanied by Lesia, she had also sampled nightlife at Le Caveau de la Huchette, in the Latin Quarter, where she witnessed Black musicians from America playing magic jazz music, to the wonderment and enjoyment of Parisians.

From Paris, Sarah wrote letters to Moreno, telling him how much she missed him. With the arrival of a man in her life, however, who told her that his name was Laurent Bacchus, all that would change.

Back from a visit to the Catacombs, one day, two weeks from the day she arrived in Paris, Sarah looked for a convenient café to sit, have a rest and take a cup of coffee. She sat down at Café du Dome's sidewalk, in Montparnasse, on the Left Bank, in a table, under a tarpaulin.

While there, sitting and sipping coffee, enjoying watching people, her eyes fell suddenly on two tall African men, dressed in light blue flowing robes, taking a walk on a pavement, a few meters away from her. They were talking to each other, laughing, revealing exceptionally white set of teeth.

Behind came a man she assumed to be from the Far East. He was dressed in a pale brown suit, a white shirt and a tie to match the colour of the suit. On reaching a point parallel to where she was seating, he stopped, turned around and then walked toward the direction that he came from. It appeared to Sarah as if the man had forgotten something home that needed retrieving.

Across the road, a French woman in a grey trench coat and a maroon coloured hat, slightly tilting to the left, was taking a walk in high heel shoes that had made a peculiar sound on the cobblestones. Accompanying the woman was a slightly built child-girl, trying to catch up with the fast-pace taken by the woman.

At a junction, two blocks away, two teenage girls took turn to sing. These were the same girls Sarah had seen a few days earlier. On that day, Sarah had stopped briefly to listen and to marvel at their angelic voices, as they sang their beautiful songs.

About the girls, who had been dressed in a shabbily looking pink frocks and large-sized boots, Sarah had thought it wouldn't take long before someone discovers their talents, and, thereafter, makes it possible for them to find their way as performers, in one of the great French cabarets.

Watching the world go by, from her position at Café's sidewalk, Sarah admired Paris for the multitudes of people, belonging to different nationalities, who had made this great city their home. Sarah prayed for a similar thing to take roots in her homeland, to add colour to its grey and drab Swedish surroundings.

Presently, she retrieved a book from the handbag and started reading it. The book was about how to spend time in Paris, at a much lesser cost. It was a handbook favoured by younger generations of tourists visiting Paris.

Sarah was casually dressed in light blue blouse, a brown woollen gown, and had a pullover on. While her mind was filled with images of death, in a form of heaps and heaps of human bones, which she had witnessed at the Catacombs, suddenly her eyes fell on someone staring at her, sitting not far from her table.

In the beginning, she never believed the man was looking at her; it could have been her imagination; she was flattered, nevertheless. It was not as though she was about to fall in love with him. But is there a woman, she had imagined, who would not be delighted by a look of admiration from a male admirer - even if that admirer was a man of no larger presence than the one facing her, from the opposite table, now seemingly engrossed in reading from a paper she thought to be Le Monde?

As she kept on reading the book, a moment later, she felt she had a company in her table. As curious as she might have been, she was determined not to look. At last, however, overcome with curiosity, she turned her attention away from the book, and was forced to hold her breath.

There, sitting in her table, she saw the man who had been starring at her across from her table. He smiled at her, revealing a set of teeth that seemed too large for his small rounded face, with a receding chin. The man had a crop of thin straight hair on a head that was round, but which appeared to be rather small. A tiny nose adorned his face; his light blue eyes were set close to each other, and the colour of his skin was a shade lighter when compared to that of most people in the café; he was slight in build. He had a wind jacket worn over a brown polo shirt.

"Hello!" the man said to her. He added, "I hope I am not causing you any inconveniences."

She wanted to reply in the negative, but remained silent instead; she never knew why! Perhaps it could have been either because of the way the man had looked at her or maybe something about his voice. In the end, to oblige the stranger in her table, she said, "Hello," in return, and then she remained quiet. He nodded his head and waited patiently. Sarah was anticipating what more he was going to say. It would be either something about the weather or whether she liked Paris, she guessed.

To her surprise, when he spoke to her it was on a quite different subject altogether. The man spoke in perfect French to her, using a kind of accent that was not easy to place.

"You are beautiful," he said. After that, he remained silent.

Sarah was lost on how to react to the compliment. It was not often people said she was beautiful. And even though she had been a recipient of such a compliment, a few times before, some conversations of sort had always preceded those moments. And although Sarah was pretending as though she was reading from the book, whose pages remained open, she was no longer concentrating on the contents of the book. Instead, sitting next to her, the man had become a certain preoccupation in her mind.

Could it be that he wanted to say something but felt shy? Did he mean what he had just said to her? Who and what is he? Why is he quiet? Sarah felt the situation quite challenging.

While all sorts of thoughts went on in her mind, the man sat quietly. He waited patiently; he wanted to keep her guessing at his next step. His silence was, therefore, quite deliberate and well planned. From his previous experiences with women, he knew that one must be careful how to approach them. If you take a hasty move, women would see that as sign of desperation in you. Keeping them waiting, while savouring each moment, is the surest way to hold their attention. This approach, he believed, had paid dividends in the past, and the girl before him was not going to be any different, he assumed.

He caught her stealing glances at him several times; he pretended, however, not to notice anything. He kept the situation to draw a little longer before finally speaking to her. When Sarah mentioned the name Bissell to him, he almost bolted from his seat.

As soon as he recovered from the shock, in a voice drained of any kind of emotion, he said, "You are not by any chance related to the Bissell family of Sweden?"

"Yes, as a matter fact I do," Sarah said.

"It is quite strange that the two of us are meeting here without any prior arrangement! If it is not a coincidence, what else could it be?" He said seriously.

"I don't understand," Sarah said in reply, not knowing exactly what else to say.

Sarah felt often impatient with people, whose speeches are glorified with metaphors or symbolism.

"You see, I happen to know the Bissell family counts as one of the richest families in Sweden, so too is my family here in France - the Bacchus family," he said cautiously.

After a brief silence, he said, "Does it not surprise you to know that each of our families was involved on the wrong side of the war?

Mine was the most important element in the Vichy Government, whose relationship with Nazis is a well-documented fact of history." he said.

One of the paradoxes of the outcome of the Second World War in Europe had been, on one hand, to clarify, to confirm and to rigidify borders, while keeping the movement of refugees in a state of flux, on the other hand. In this post-war demographic sea of changes taking place all throughout Europe, it was not quite hard for someone, like Bacchus, to claim any kind of identity and make it look real.

His favourite identity was based on a claim he had been making about belonging to an ancient Hungarian aristocratic family, which had lost their property, following the communist takeover of Hungary, but had since fallen into hard times. It suited his interest today, however, to claim ties of family relationship with the Bacchus family of France - one of the richest families in the country.

Sarah had all along been aware of her family's alleged ties to the Third Reich; she could even remember one of her favourite aunts that had been married to one of the most powerful members of the Nazi regime. However, that never bothered her much. A person is free to marry anyhow he or she wants to; she had always conceded this point to herself.

Furthermore, she didn't bother herself to verify the point made by people about her country's historic cooperation with the Nazis, both for strategic and economic reasons, and so she didn't let herself get affected by rumours, even though some could be quite scathing by nature.

Take, for example, the claim made about how the atmosphere of peace in her country, during Second World War, had a direct link to the suffering of its Norwegian neighbours. However, because of her acute sense of perception, about things and situations, Sarah felt she could understand Bacchus's feelings well, especially the feeling of hatred that he had been having for his family.

On the other hand, before she mentioned her name to him, his interest in her was quite normal. Whenever he was broke, which often had been the case, he would look for any tourist girl to whom he could apply his charms, by making use of his social pretensions, to enable him to have his simple needs for food and sex-drive served. In time, he developed this art of living to perfection. For example, to bring under his control a girl he might have set his eyes on, depending on circumstances, he would praise, shame, humiliate, ridicule and even flatter her.

Only ten days before meeting Sarah, he parted ways with an American girl with whom he had been living, for five long months, in an apartment rented by her. In America, the girl's father was highly valued as a writer. Bacchus belittled his achievement, however, by claiming that his writings were too simple and obvious in their meaning; not the stuff meant for any serious reader of books, he had told her

Chapter Eighteen

# Meet Laurent Bacchus

Over the past centuries, Paris has become a Mecca of sort for people who have found in its warm bosom the satisfaction of life they have missed having in their homes of origin, for reasons of religious, political and cultural persecution, or merely for lack of opportunity in personal advancement. Hence, it has always acted as a hub of foreign intellectuals, politicians, entrepreneurs, revolutionaries, pimps and petty thieves who, in pursuing their daily lives in the streets of Paris, brushed shoulders freely with one another and with original Parisians.

In 1948, Laurent Bacchus whose name no one knew was one such individual connected to this legion of people for whom Paris became a home.

His home that was located somewhere in the territories that once had belonged to the Austro-Hungarian Empire, from which he fled, following the execution of his parents by nationalists, allegedly for conspiring with the state agents, when he was fifteen years old, he had very little memory of. Since then he had spent most of the twenty-five adult years of his lifetime shifting and moving from place to place.

The history of that movement had left an indelible mark in his ability to speak several languages with an ease of a native speaker of any of the countries to which he claimed to belong. For example, as he sat there talking to Sarah, he genuinely felt to be a French man. Naturally, he also believed the claims he was going to make about himself to be true.

"You see," pushing his chair closer to Sarah, while leaning forward, he said, "for their sins of co-operating with the Vichy Government, and by extension the army of occupation, I had to forsake my family to join the underground movement to fight the Germans."

He paused to check if his story was having any impact on Sarah. Sarah could not wait; she urged him to go on with the story. She beckoned at a waiter who came and took order from her. Sarah asked for more coffee and a bottle of mineral water. She told Bacchus to have something. It was 11 a.m. in Paris. Bacchus, who never had breakfast this morning, asked for couple of tuna sandwiches and a cup of coffee with plenty of cream.

While imagining the taste that the breakfast would have in his already watering-mouth, he warmed up to the subject further. "Within the underground movement," he said eagerly, "I was placed in a section dealing with information and communication."

He stayed quiet afterwards. "One of my duties," he added suddenly, "had involved a dangerous task of having to convey vital information, from one point to the other, often from the city centre to the countryside, and vice versa. The Germans were eager to break this conveying belt of information they knew had been keeping the momentum of the struggle going on. Many times, by dint of my imagination, I had escaped the many traps laid out by the Germans. Hence, the Germans had referred to me as "The Elusive Jack."

Sarah had read all about the French Partisans, who she had come to admire a lot. However, the possibility that she would have the honour of having to meet with one of them, one day, and even pay for his breakfast, was far removed from her mind. As she sat there in the café, mesmerized by the revelation made by Bacchus about himself, in her mind he acquired the stature of demigod. No longer was he the little man with small-rounded head, and large set of teeth, she had imagined him to be, just a few moments ago.

As for Bacchus, he felt he had one crucial statement to make, which he didn't know how to do it. While he was grappling in his mind with the issue, suddenly he heard Sarah saying, "Are you, by any chance, keeping contact with any members of your family?"

That question gave him an opportunity to say what he had wanted to say all along, but didn't know how to do it.

"I parted ways with my family, Dear Sarah, not over their close working relationship with the Vichy Government only," he said, "but also because of a very fundamental principle involving their role in the destinies of millions of people, who today lead a wretched life merely because the rich must get richer."

When he uttered her name, for the first time, Sarah felt happy and proud. The subsequent preoccupation in her mind with that happy realisation had made her almost miss what he was saying. She decided she would concentrate.

"While the wretched life I have made reference to is to me quite real," he was saying, "yet, by going back home to my family, I could leave all that behind me. This wouldn't mean much, because people that do not have the same luxury of choice which I have would still continue to suffer indignities, caused by poverty."

Listening to Bacchus making his point, Sarah became convinced that Bacchus was someone that had an appointment with the destiny to keep.

"Thus, I have dedicated my remaining days to a life-long political struggle to restore the dignity of the disinherited, and for that reason I have joined the Communist Party of France," he amiably conceded.

If asked to give her opinion about Bacchus, Sarah would have probably said he was selfless for having once put his life on the line to fight against the enemies of France, not to mention his current struggles against the forces of capitalism.

While sipping coffee, enjoying mid-April morning sunshine, Sarah had a strong urge to say something to impress Bacchus, for whom she had developed a great respect. But how could she do such a thing without appearing to him that she was patronising him? She was tense! She must find something to say. Suddenly, a great relief dawned on her. Sarah had found the right words with which to compliment him. She repeated the words in her mind, to determine if they would have the impact she wished them to have on him.

"You have made a great deal of sacrifice for France. France must be proud of you!" she said, finally.

Bacchus looked at Sarah; his face was blank of any sign of emotion. She expected him to say something. The moments drew a little longer, and then Sarah was relieved by a smile on his face, followed by what he had to say in connection to her comments.

"France is my home," he said; "I owe my life to her," he added.

He remembered to say, shortly after, "Thanks all the same."

The two stared at each other but remained quiet. In his silence, Bacchus savoured what he considered to be his moment of triumph.

By now Bacchus had finished eating his breakfast that he had consumed with much gusto. Having seen the way that he had wolfed down his breakfast, Sarah realised how every single moment of his life had constituted an act of sacrifice made for the good of France. Perhaps, one thing that she had found most appealing of all his actions was that he was calm and composed in his manners.

Now that he had Sarah where he wanted, Bacchus felt free to talk to her about other things. Yes, she had already been to places of historical, cultural and political importance, she said in reply to one of his questions.

"You still have one important thing to do. You need to get to know people, whose vast contributions to the fields of arts, philosophy, literature, psychology and politics have made Paris what it is today: the world nerve-centre of intellectual ideas," he enthusiastically told her.

As he spoke to her, he offered a smile and waived at a middle-aged man who had just walked into the café. Pointing to the man, who by now had found a place to sit down, in a table, not far from their place, he told Sarah, "See that man there? That is Simone. Simone is currently the most celebrated French poet." He added, "We are good friends; one day I will introduce you to him,"

Sarah welcomed the invitation warmly. She was convinced if his friends were going to be anything like him, in terms of experience, she would have much to benefit from them. In future, she wouldn't be disappointed in her expectation, since among his friends Bacchus counted people of all types, including, men of letters, journalists, academicians, musicians, philosophers etc. Indeed, Sarah would feel much inspired whenever she would spend time among his friends at Sorbonne University campus, or elsewhere in the city of Paris.

However, what Sarah didn't know about Bacchus, in his association with people he called his friends, is that he had found a way to flatter their egos, so that he could cheat them, steal from them and pretend to love them when he hated them; when he fell out with them, he scandalised them, blackmailed them, and abused them in every conceivable way.

At home, in the evening, she told Lesia about a man she was attracted to, whom she had met at Café du Dome.

Lesia let a cautious smile cross her lips, and said, "Be careful, who you offer your love to. To someone, on a vacation to Paris, like you, feelings of love do come easily. Good luck."

To give her stay in Paris a sense of purpose, a few days later, Sarah decided to enrol at the university to continue with her economic studies. Afterwards, she wrote to her father a letter, asking him to send money to her, in a form of a stipend, on a regular basis.

By now Sarah had been away from home for three long weeks. She was not planning to get back home any moment now, either. To Moreno, she had sent a short note, in which she briefly mentioned about Bacchus, upon whom she showered much praise, as well as using the occasion to terminate their relationships.

Moreno who hadn't received any message from Paris, for quite a while, and was beginning to feel worried, the note had confirmed his worst fears; the note had a devastating effect on him. Naturally, he felt compelled to write a note of his own to Sarah, in which he requested her to reconsider her decision. Sarah wrote back to say she would treasure memories of their relationships, but that she was now in love with someone else. She ended her brief note by saying that it was time for her to move on.

Chapter Nineteen

# *Brilliant Small Ideas*

After bidding a warm farewell to Lesia, her friend, a few days later, Sarah left the hostel to rent a small apartment of a single room, containing a small kitchenette and a bathroom, situated on the Left Bank, at Arrondisement 6th. Here, she invited Bacchus to move in with her. By now, the two had become lovers. Bacchus had introduced Sarah into different aspects of lovemaking, the type of which she had read in THE PERFUMED GARDEN, (an Arabic sex manual) written in the fifteenth century by Muhammad ibn Muhammad al – Nefzawi, and translated into English from French by Sir Richard Francis Burton.

For the introduction into this world of erotic bliss, which made her to value her body more than ever before, Sarah gave thanks to Bacchus, whom she also gave credit for making her into what she called, "a complete woman."

Life, as far as Sarah was concerned, had constituted a moment of great joy. However, two months from day she arrived in Paris, Sarah missed having her menstrual period.

Since she had been constantly using some sort of preventive measures, she counted out the prospect of pregnancy.

"It must have something to do with my state of health," she reassured herself.

And so, one windy and cold morning day, she left the apartment in a great hurry to consult with a doctor that Bacchus had introduced her to, after she suffered from fever, a few days earlier. To her surprise, from the test that he took, he confirmed the state of her pregnancy to her.

She left the clinic in brisk steps, while mindful of the elevated beat of her heart, which she was unable to relate to. Was the elevation of the heart-beat a sign of a happy emotion, or one based on worrisome thoughts?

At home, she found Bacchus at the breakfast table. He looked up at her face and could read trouble. He smiled nervously; she returned the smile and then she said, "I have good news for you Mon Cherie."

Lately, Sarah had started peppering her sentences with French words, evoking sentiments of a loving relationship.

"Fire it. I am all ears," he said.

"I am pregnant, Mon Cherie. Is it not wonderful?" Sarah carefully said.

"Yes, indeed," he said; afterwards, he added somewhat nervously, "have you said you are pregnant? Don't tell me you have once again come upon one of those brilliant small ideas of yours. Come; tell me; what is it going to be, this time?"

Sarah smiled briefly; then she said in a half-joking manner, "Not ideas, you stupid little thing. I am pregnant with a baby. It is your baby and mine."

Bacchus had just had a spoon full of porridge. When the news hit him, he swallowed the porridge which felt like a fist full of nails. He almost choked; he coughed, again and again. After a while, he stopped coughing.

"Are you not feeling well Mon Cherie?" Sarah said anxiously.

Finally, after regaining his composure, he said, "Oh, nothing serious," he forced a nervous smile.

"I am fine," he said lying to her. Because he wasn't prepared for the news, it hit him hard.

"Never mind; just play it along; there is no point in raising hell," he reassured himself.

A moment later, acting like someone who had just awoken from a deep sleep, he said in a hazy manner, "Oh, what were you saying? Yes, it was about a baby! Wasn't it? It is yours and mine, you said? Wonderful!"

Then for the sake of clarity, he told her, "What are your plans?"

In a great haste to correct him, Sarah said determinedly, "You mean our plans Mon Cherrie, our plans!"

"Yes, of course; our plans, I am sorry," he said sheepishly.

Encouraged by what she had imagined to be a positive response from Bacchus, she said, "I propose that we have the child."

She threw a nervous glance at him before saying, "What do you say?

"I say, let us have the baby," Bacchus said eagerly.

At this response, Sarah threw her arms round his neck and covered his whole face with kisses. Bacchus mind was far away.

A few days later, something happened. However, whether it was a case of coincidence, it was quite impossible for Sarah to tell. After learning about Sarah's pregnancy, Bacchus took to coming home late at night – something that he never did before.

Most of the times, he came home accompanied by strange-looking people. Sarah could swear that she heard them speak in a language that was not French. As they spoke to each other in a whisper they gave Sarah a conspiratorial look. She didn't feel comfortable in their presence. When she raised the issue with

Bacchus, he cut her short. They are his friends, he told her, not her friends, and advised her not to raise the issue with him again.

One day, quite suddenly and unexpectedly, Bacchus stopped coming home. Sarah could not get a wink of sleep that night, and had to inspire herself with encouraging feelings, just to pull through the night. In the afternoon, of the following day, she went to the police station to report Bacchus missing.

At 78, rue Bonaparte, the police station had many visitors, this Saturday afternoon; most were women, who had made a point of shouting at the police on duty, and at each other. Leaning against the counter was a policeman to whom a woman in a red-dress was talking. As she talked to the policeman, the woman gesticulated with her hands.

The policeman had a wide black thick ledger that lay open in front of him. It seemed he was trying to say something to the woman, who kept shouting at him, instead of listening. The policeman went around the counter, held the woman lightly by the shoulder, and then led her out of the police station. Two other women went in; they too had spent time shouting at the police officer, and at each other, before leaving the police station.

Soon it was Sarah's turn to face the police officer; she gave thought to what she was going to say. She was there to report the case of a missing man, of course. What kind of man was he to her? Was he a husband? Was he a boyfriend? What was this man to her?

As she was contemplating what to say, she was jolted from following her thought by the policeman who said, "Come in Mademoiselle."

The policeman, a tall young-looking man, with cherubic cheeks, wide bright eyes, a patch of red in the rims, which could be a sign that he had had a long night spent on a drinking spree said, "Yes, what can I do for you, mademoiselle?"

"I want to report the case of a missing man," she said cautiously. She tried to look cheerful.

"Let us have your particulars first," he told her.

Sarah gave her name as well the physical address of her home.

After he finished writing down the information, he said in a guarded tone, "You mentioned something about a man missing. Who is he?"

My boyfriend," she said.

"Do you have anything of the missing man here with you for identification purposes? A photograph of him, let us say?" He asked.

Sarah who had remembered to pick up her handbag rummaged through it for anything that she could use to identify Bacchus, but failed.

"Can you remember anything about him, other than his name?" He impatiently said.

"No; I have nothing," she said in a feeble voice. She added in a meek tone "but I could find something home."

"Yes, do so," he said.

She left after that, feeling demoralised and quite foolish.

At home, she ransacked the apartment in a desperate search for any photographs of Bacchus, but to no avail. Then suddenly she remembered! She admonished herself for not coming up with this important piece of information, at the police station. Subsequently, she called the police officer who easily recognised her voice on the phone, just as she recognised his.

She said elatedly, "Officer, I have a very important piece of information about the identity of my boyfriend, Bacchus, I want to share it with you."

It was quiet on the other end of the line. After a while, the officer said, "You can pass the information, please."

She posed briefly to savour the moment; in her mind, she believed, the information was going to impress the police officer; she anticipated how the police officer would react to the information and felt both excited and proud.

She pursed her lips, and, addressing the officer, said hurriedly, "Bacchus, my missing boyfriend, is the eldest son of Monsieur Thierry of the Bacchus family."

That piece of information elicited a response from the police officer. However, he was not impressed; he laughed, instead. Her cheeks felt warm. Sarah suspected that she was going to undergo yet another round of embarrassment, only this time, she imagined, it might be a bigger embarrassment, and hence more humiliating.

The officer stopped laughing. He knew he should not have laughed, it was a reflex action; he could not help it. To his knowledge, this was not the first time this sort of thing was happening to a foreign girl. It often happens to innocent girls taken for a ride by such people as the imaginary Monsieur Bacchus. He could not understand why some girls are willing to believe people who will lie to them.

The police officer felt pity for the girl, but thought he should tell the truth. At last he gathered courage, and said, "Mademoiselle, Monsieur Dennis Thierry of the Bacchus family had only one son; he died in the recent war. You have met an impostor, I am afraid."

He took a pause and said, "Since you do not have any kind of information about the missing man, we shall have to visit your apartment tomorrow in order to lift some fingerprints that could assist us in our investigation and identification purposes."

Sarah did not hear the last part of the officer's speech. The telephone slipped through her fingers and fell down. Her legs gave under her; she fell on the bed, and made no any attempt to get up. She closed her eyes, wishing she would fall asleep, never to wake up to see another day. She fell asleep and dreamt of her mother. Every time she got in one form of distress or another, Sarah had a vivid dream of her mother drowning up in a sea.

When that incident took place, Sarah was a five-year old baby, sitting on a sea shore, watching the wind effortlessly on the sea's grey surface, on an early summer's afternoon day. Her mother had left her under the care of one of the housemaids. From her position, Sarah had been able to follow every single movement made by her mother, and then suddenly it happened.

Even though Sarah was a child, nevertheless, she had been able to sense the danger facing her mother from the way she had been frantically splashing about in the sea, crying for help, at the same time. Instinctively, Sarah had responded by crying desperately. She had seen her mother one more time before she disappeared. Thereafter, she had never seen her mother again.

After his wife's death, Martin, Sarah's father, had never married again. Single handily, he brought up Sarah, relying on an English tutor and a governess for her early education.

She awoke up from her sleep covered in tears. It was dark in the room. It took several more seconds for her to realise where she was. She was hungry, made herself some sandwiches that she felt she was unable to eat. She went back to sleep.

Two policemen, on the following morning, called at her apartment. She immediately recognised one of them to be the same officer who she had spoken to, at the police station. She offered to give the men some coffee; they politely declined the offer. One of the two policemen, the older looking one, went to lift some fingerprints from the teacups, glasses and everything of significance in the room.

Meanwhile, the officer who she had met at the police station stayed with her, and pleaded with Sarah not to worry; he reassured Sarah by telling her, with the fingerprints at their disposals, they were bound to solve the riddle of the missing man. A half-an-hour later, the duo of the police officers left the apartment, promising they would be heard from soon.

A month had gone by, and there was no word from the police and no sign of Bacchus either. Then one day, the phone rang. It was the police calling; they phoned to tell Sarah that the fingerprints they had lifted from her apartments had matched those of a man caught trying to steal the work of art at Le Louvre Museum.

Furthermore, they told her that the man and his accomplices would be arraigned before the court of law to answer charges of attempted theft. She was invited to the court to give her testimony, a request she declined to undertake, since she avoided getting into a situation where she would be forced to come face to face with Bacchus.

Sitting alone in her room, without a friend to console her, Sarah recalled circumstances that led to her situation, and felt quite sad. She looked at her role to critically determine if she could have been, in anyway, responsible for her current misfortunes.

She had trusted Bacchus totally to a point that she believed everything he had told her about himself. But had she been a little inquisitive she probably would have discovered his true identity. Bacchus had been glued to her for most of the time; he would never let her go out of his sight by hovering close to her. She had taken this as a sign that she was dear to him. However, with a benefit of hindsight she could see things quite clearly now. He must have been afraid, she assumed, if she stayed with someone alone, his true identity could have been revealed to her.

Bacchus lied to her and she had not hesitated to fall in love with him! But did she fall in love with the man or the stories that he had told her about himself? Would she have fallen in love with him had he told her the truth about himself?

Inevitably, she was forced to accept the truth: she had fallen in love not with the man, but the stories he had told her about himself.

She thought of the child in her stomach; a child conceived out of lies and out wedlock. She was close to six months pregnant now. For reasons of both physical and ethical nature, the question of terminating the pregnancy couldn't arise in her mind.

# Chapter Twenty

# *Peter*

Sarah left Paris to give birth to a baby boy in Sweden, for whom she had maintained an ambivalent attitude. After the Paris love misadventure, Sarah could never let herself trust anyone with her love. In fact, Sarah had developed a mortal fear and a deeper hatred for all men, even though in her outward appearance she seemed quite accommodating to men.

Many years later, much water had passed under the bridge, as far as Sarah's life was concerned. From the day she left Paris, Sarah had made a success out of her life; she had become one of the most highly respected personalities in the country's political circles.

Within the party, she was responsible for its foreign affairs. She had held several portfolios, including the position of a minister, on several occasions.

After she got back home from Paris, Sarah had settled down a few kilometres in an area south of Knivsta, where she bought a property that had been up for sale. The property consisted of a two-hectare piece of land that had two large buildings on it;

one of the buildings, which was in a state of disrepair, Sarah had managed to fix it.

Luckily, the two structures went for the price of one. She had paid half the cost of the buildings from out of the money she had saved working in her father's office, the other half she paid from the loan she took from the bank.

As she sat in her office now, inside a building that acts as a seat of the government in Stockholm old quarters, observing movements of sea-going vessels from the widow of her office, she thought of the day when she came back home from Paris. She thought, on learning that she was pregnant, how her father had gone into such a great state of shock that he had managed to only utter the word, "Ugh" in response.

He looked comical, she had thought and laughed.

"Why laugh? Do you think it is funny that you are pregnant?" He had said in an annoying tone.

"No. I think you are funny." She had said in reply. Then she had added, "I mean the way you look at me!"

That statement must have raised his anger a notch higher. His eyes burning with anger, he had told her, "How dare you pull the good name of Bissell family into the mud?"

Sarah could not recollect seeing her father in such a state of agitation before.

"I did not; I simply got pregnant," she had said in a scornful manner.

Whereupon, in an irritated voice, he had said, "Who made you pregnant? Was not he a mere thief in Paris, of all people?"

From her father, Sarah had been expecting some sort of understanding; perhaps even a certain measure of pity; what she had never expected from him is a dressing down. She had become ragingly mad at him, subsequently. She remembered telling him, "I am sick, tired and lost about what to do; meanwhile, all that you care for is the good name of the family. Well, I do not care about your good name, especially, if this would mean to you that I would have to act as an incubator for you to determine whose male seeds should be kept inside me, and when to deliver; I refuse to play the role; go find someone else to do it for you."

Thereafter, she had bolted through the front door of her father's apartment.

Martin had made a feverish attempt to restrain her from getting away; she never obliged him.

Sarah left the family home, but had retained the name Bissell.

Initially, Sarah had never visited her family, not even during the happy season of Christmas did she visit her family. Before he died of cerebral palsy, her father had requested Sarah to return home, but each time she refused to oblige him. Then one Christmas day, accompanied by her son, Peter Wells, fifteen now, she unexpectedly turned up at the family's home. Sarah had decided to pay the family a visit on a Christmas day, for it was a time of the year members of her family came to celebrate Christmas together; it was also an occasion for the family members to take stock of their achievements and failures.

From the day she left her family's home, a great deal of change had taken place in the Bissell family's affairs. Her father, including her aunt, as well as other family members belonging to her father's generation, had passed away. The Bissell family business had passed into the hands of members of the family belonging to Sarah's generation.

Sarah's visit had provided joy to members of the family, who believed Sarah had been forever lost to them. Members of the younger generation of the family had never seen her in person; they had seen her pictures in newspapers or when giving interviews on TV; they thought she was smart, and nearly everyone in the family had been proud of her achievements.

Sarah introduced her son to members of the family, who behaved nicely to Peter.

The name Peter - her son's name - had a special meaning for Sarah. She thought the name belonged to people who had made their mark in history; St Peter, Peter the Great and Peter Martyr are just a few examples of people she wanted her son to emulate. As for the surname, Wells, she had made up a story about the name belonging to a man, from a prominent American family, who she had met in Paris, to whom she had been engaged before dying in a motor accident.

Her family members talked to her about many things on that Christmas day, except one thing: they didn't wish to know anything to do with the identity of her son's father. Of course, some senior members of the family knew circumstances of his birth very well. A long time ago, following a report made by a senior Paris Cosmopolitan Police officer to the Swedish Embassy, the latter sent a letter to Martin, informing him about everything that he had wished to know about his daughter, and her involvement with the man who had called himself Bacchus.

Peter became the centre of attraction on that Christmas day. Some of her family members had gone as far as calling her son "a cute looking boy." Sarah, however, took such compliments with some inner feelings of reservation. She thought, "Whose legs are you trying to pull? Anyone with perfect pairs of eyes could see from a long distance that Peter is anything but "a cute looking boy."

Peter, who had a cunning physical resemblance to his father, had been a constant reminder to Sarah about a man she had always wanted out of her thought system. That, perhaps, should help explain the reason for enrolling him in a boarding school, at an early age; she had managed, in this way, to keep him away from home and out of her sight.

Despite having little feelings of love for her son, otherwise, Sarah did everything to make sure that Peter never suffered any need. She could not, however, offer him one very important thing; she couldn't bestow on him the honour of carrying her family's name; she could not give him an identity to make him proud, so to speak.

As time went by, Peter realised that there was a feeling of intimacy missing in his relationship with the rest of the family members. He suspected that there was deliberate attempt to have him excluded from all kinds of situation, such as when the family members had exchanged feelings of intimacy.

He remembered how, on more than one occasion, when the rest of the family members had paid a visit to the family graveyard, to pay homage to the soul of their dead ones, he wasn't there. Whenever the family members exchanged presents he had received almost none, or had received them late. He wanted to know from his mother the reason; his mother would not initially commit herself.

One day, when he was twenty years old, Sarah told him everything he had wanted to know about himself. Not surprisingly, soon after the secret of his life had been revealed to him, he became visibly angry with his mother, and the world around him. He believed his mother was guilty of a heinous crime, of which he had become its hapless victim.

As strange as it may seem, Sarah felt no any inner compulsion to woo her son to herself. If anything, after she told him the truth, she was able to achieve from her confession a peace of mind. Peter had dealt with the situation, on the other hand, by finding reasons to blame his mother whenever things didn't work out well for him.

Responding to her son's increasingly hostile attitude, Sarah would tell him, "Be reasonable Peter. If I had abandoned you, matters would have gone awfully wrong for you."

In response to that remarks that made him hate his mother, more than anything, he would ask her the following disturbing question: "Why didn't you do it? It was not out of love for me that you did not do it; you lacked the courage to do it. It would not have been a moral thing for you to do, you would say. But what do you know about morality, mother?"

"You can never make me undo," she would say, sounding quite agitated, "what has been done? For how long are you going to hold me responsible for every little thing that goes wrong in your life? Don't be silly like your father?" The last part had always come from a slip of the tongue

"If he was such a silly man," he would say aggressively in reply, "why did you fall for him and let him sleep with you?"

The association with a father he had never seen, and hated by everyone, had made Peter hate his mother with all his heart, and had also made him hate with passion everyone around him.

Despite everything, Sarah had felt morally compelled to do something for Peter, now that he was about to finish his higher education. Sarah had long realised, being an average student, her son had no special gifts worth mentioning; as such, she was convinced, he would need her assistant to find his way in life.

To have to succeed in life, Sarah believed, it is not important that one should be extremely intelligent. Highly intelligent people are bound to fail in their endeavours, if they are not well connected, socially. Having convinced herself that the course of action she intended to take, in relation to her son's future, was a right thing to do, she introduced Peter's case to close friends - to people who mattered in the society; people who could secure for him a niche in the society; people for whom she had done favours in the past, and felt it was their duty to do the same for her now.

Peter and Kore graduated almost about the same time; Kore graduated a month earlier. On the morning of the day Peter

Wells was defending his Ph.D. thesis, within the premises of the old Uppsala University building, something took place there that would make Kore live to regret.

The examining professor, a thin looking man of middle age, considered to have expert knowledge concerning the subject of Peter's thesis, had asked Peter important questions. When he was left with no more questions to ask, members of the audience were welcomed to ask Peter questions of their own, if they had any. Kore had stood up and asked a question that he was convinced the professor had overlooked.

"Why is it that the theory you have adapted to guide your thesis is nowhere reflected in the general body of your work?" He had said.

To this question, Peter had no satisfactory reply to offer in his defence. He uttered some sort of a reply that had made no sense.

At the end of the discussion, lasting a little less than two hours, the five-men evaluation panel had to retire to a private place, to enable them to discuss the merit of the thesis, and hence the fate of its author. The five men evaluation panel, by conceding the point made by Kore, had found Peter's thesis quite weak. Luckily, however, Peter was declared passed by a slim margin of three votes to two.

As soon as he was declared passed, Peter approached Kore, sitting in a canteen along with many other people, waiting for a final word to come from the evaluation panel, and told him in a hysterical voice, "I would never forgive you for asking the question. You wanted to stop me from succeeding, but your nefarious designs have failed. It is my turn now; you wait and see."

"You have misconstrued my intention," Kore said in an anxious tone.

He wanted to say more, but by then Peter had already stormed out of the canteen.

# BOOK TWO

# Chapter Twenty One

# *Bureaucracy*
# 1987

Kore obtained a job to work as a researcher in Uppsala, at a newly established institute for international studies. The institute was placed inside a 19th Century old looking building, overlooking Uppsala's major thoroughfare, known as Kungsgatan. The employees, who worked as researchers, were no more than five in number altogether including Kore. One could surmise, from its appearance, the institute was run on a shoestring budget.

Kore got this job because of a negotiated settlement that had taken place between the Labour Office and his employer. The employer didn't advertise for the job, and neither did Kore applied for it. Therefore, since his employment was not in line with the market logic of supply and demand, Kore was afraid that his position in the institute was not going to last long.

As he hadn't been party to an agreement that took place between the Labour Office and his employer, he also had no information about the actual terms of his employment.

Apparently, Kore had been a beneficiary of a programme recently introduced by the government.

To fight unemployment, which had been on the rise, throughout the country, the government had made a point of entering into a sort of agreement with prospective employers, promising to pay a large percentage of the salary of every person they would chose to employ.

The idea behind the project being that, after putting an employee to a trial-period of nine months, and once having determined their worthiness, the employers might wish to retain their services, by paying a full salary of a person they employed.

One of the aims of the institute had been to undertake research work on developing countries, hoping to contribute to development initiatives made there.

On his first day at the institute, the director, a middle-aged burly-built woman by the name of Madeleine, introduced Kore to the rest of the employees. At the end of her speech, a round of applause and smiles followed, before the employees could beat a hasty retreat to their office rooms.

Kore stayed behind while Director Madeleine made strenuous efforts to collect numerous pieces of papers that lay on the table. Later, she told Kore in a commanding voice, "Follow me; I shall take you to your office." She took off in such a great speed that Kore was forced to trail behind in a futile attempt to catch up with her. For a woman of her size - her mid-section bulging out in all directions - she was quite swift in her strides, Kore had noticed.

From a bunch of the keys that she carried in her right plump hand, she used one to open the door of a room, situated at the end of a short corridor.

"Well, here we are. This here is your office," she told Kore in her heavily accented Swedish English.

As an afterthought, in a manner of someone asking a question rather than affirming a point, she added, "You will like it?"

Kore had to take a single look at the place to realise the cubicle that the director had called the office was anything but an office.

He also realised, from its appearance, the place was a halfway-stop for papers and other odd things waiting to be discarded. As he explored the room with his eyes, he heard her saying, "Good, yes?

He remained quiet. The director, it seemed, didn't wait for him to give his opinion for she took off swiftly, leaving him to stand in the middle of the room, looking bewildered.

Not far from where he stood, he saw a single chair and a table pressed against the wall; on top of the table there were old looking books, pamphlets and magazines that belonged to another age. As they had exceeded the use for which they were intended, these items had filled every single space in the room.

Except for the single old-looking telephone apparatus, and an ancient looking silver-coloured Remington typewriter, otherwise, all other office accessories required for efficient working were absent. Kore sat on a chair, facing the old telephone and the Remington typing apparatus. For a moment, he wished to believe the director had opened a wrong door and that she would get back any moment soon, to set things right. At the end, he realised how mistaken he must have been in his expectation. Indeed, as the director had put it, the room was intended to be his actual place of work.

"Take the challenge and never relent," he told himself.

At home, in the evening, he met Hadio getting the family dinner ready on the table; it seemed she was in a happy mood; she was humming her favourite song from her country. In the kitchen, at the washbasin, he approached her from behind, and did something he never did before: he made her face him and kissed her.

"What is wrong with you Kore?" She asked, her face showing signs of astonishment.

"Nothing is wrong; I simply kissed you," he said smiling.

"When did we ever kiss? She said, not to protest the kiss, but to show that the kiss had come to her as a surprise.

"There is a first time for everything," he said as he held her chin in one of his hands, the way a Hollywood actor does when kissing a leading lady, and kissed her, once again.

This time, Hadio managed to free herself from his embrace, took two steps back, and gave him a worried look.

"Are you drunk Kore," Hadio said; she took off the apron, picked a towel from the kitchen table and dried her hands.

"Kore smiled; took a deep look at Hadio and said, "I am drunk with happiness."

Hadio remained quiet; she didn't know what to say.

Kore took her in his arms; this time, she didn't resist him; he looked her into her eyes. "I have been offered a job," he said.

Before he could speak again, Hadio gave him a kiss. "It is my turn to get drunk with happiness," she said."

"Why didn't we kiss before, the way we are doing it now? Kore thought to himself.

They had never kissed before because each must have assumed that such a thing was unacceptable, or unknown in their culture. Yet from the way they kissed, it seemed to Kore that kissing was not a strange thing to either of them - certainly not to him. The strange thing about the kiss – if at all any - was that it took place between them, which never happened before.

"May be, we should be doing this more often," he said in between those kisses

Hadio nodded, as she continued kissing him.

Soon after recovering from their overwhelming state of happiness, they went to the sitting room. For a while, it seemed they forgot about the food; in the sitting room, they talked about the job, and what having a job would mean to the family's fortunes.

'From now on, buying a house and a car on a mortgage basis will cease to be a dream for us," Kore said.

'A journey abroad, accompanied by our children, on a holiday, will be a possible thing for us now," Hadio said.

"Besides, we could afford buying all sorts of things for our children,' Kore said.

"Having dinner outside will be a common thing, every weekend," Hadio said.

"Talking of having dinner, why not go out now and celebrate this happy occasion? Keep the food for tomorrow." He said.

The news had made Hadio feel so happy she feared that she might be in a midst of a fine dream.

"You mean right now? She asked.

"Why not," He said. "Are the children not home from school? He added.

"They are here," Hadio said.

"Go, tell them; we are going to have dinner at a Chinese restaurant," Kore said.

Several minutes later, the whole family was on their way to the city centre, on bus NO. 7, and not to the Chinese restaurant, as had earlier been envisaged by them; they were on their way to MacDonald's– children favourites eating place.

If by kissing Hadio Kore had caused a surprise in her, Hadio matched his action with one of her own by letting the lights on in the room, for the first time, as they got physically intimate, at night.

The job was a new revelation that proved to be a blessing to both, as it added spice to their marriage-life.

What no one knew was that their state of happiness was not going to last long. Nevertheless, the time that Kore had spent working in the institute, it would be the most memorable period of his life in Sweden.

It was during this time that he took his family on a trip to Egypt, to see the pyramids of Egypt. This was the time also when he paid for Hadio's driving licence and had paid for Atosh to start taking training in tennis, his favourite spot.

Less than two months from the day when his employment took place, the Institute employed someone from outside Sweden and let him acquire the title of Senior Program Coordinator. From then on, Kore's presence in there ceased to have any meaning.

Director Madeline, one fine morning, several months later, held a brief conversation with Kore, sitting in the kitchen, sipping tea, reading from a morning newspaper. As she had nothing special to talk to him about, it soon became clear to Kore that by talking of such a mundane subject as the weather, she was forcing the discussion.

The director, he believed, hadn't shown any signs of hostility towards him, but she was not on a friendly term with him, either; she was someone that had kept relationship with him at arm's length distance. So why was the she now acting in such a friendly manner towards him?

On the same day, in the afternoon, Kore got the answer to a question that had been agitating his mind, throughout the day. During afternoon tea, Director Madeline told the employees about a decision which had been made by European Union, in relation to the Institute's work.

"The European Union," she told the employees," has given 1 million euros in assistance to the Institute, to help with its research work."

Immediately after this, Victoria, the Secretary, left for the kitchen; when she returned she held in her right hand a well decorated cake, made to look like the continent of Africa; in her left hand, she held a bouquet of flower.

Laying both the cake and the bouquet of flower on the table, side by side, she said, "This calls for celebration."

Kore was proud to learn that the cake was given in honour of Africa. He felt extremely proud for getting selected to cut the cake, which he did with great respect and care. This was not the first time he had an opportunity to cut a cake, this or any other one. He did it in his house to celebrate the occasion, although none of his parents had ever done such thing before. Celebrations had been done with food and drinks, instead.

His father had never cut a cake to celebrate anything, and neither had his mother. No one that he knew from the older generations had anything to do with cutting a cake to celebrate something - birthday, particularly.

It not hard for people who are strange to traditional cultures to assume that for a society that never relies on a calendar, to keep records of events, a celebration such as birthday celebration should be unthinkable to them. They, on the other hand, find it quite strange that someone should want to celebrate a day that brings a person closer to a dying day.

Soon the employees, including Kore, were enjoying eating their cake, while anticipating a change that one million euros could bring to their lives. As the party progressed, the director stood up to give a short speech. That he would partially form the subject of the speech about to be delivered Kore had no way of knowing it.

Suffering from poor-eyesight, the director put on a pair of reading glasses, which looked quite small for her large beefy-face, still holding traces of beauty from her younger days.

From a file that lay on the table, she drew out a small piece of paper containing a note that she read in a halting manner, "We are meeting here today to celebrate a happy occasion," she said. "It is an occasion," she added, "in which our institute has received a large sum of money given by the European Union, as a token of appreciation for the contribution our Institute has been making towards the development of peace research in Africa. The money, I am sure, would enable us to redouble our efforts to achieve the pinnacle of excellence, in all our future endeavours."

There was a resounding applause after the brief speech.

"However," the director went on (and here is when it came to the crunch) "as we are celebrating this occasion with a spirit of happiness, it is also an occasion calling for sadness."

As though she was officiating at the funeral of a dear departed friend of hers, a moment later, in a solemn tone, she said, "Today, we are sorry to announce the departure of Kore, our dear and beloved colleague, from the Institute."

She posed to take a short breath, gave Kore what had amounted to a pitiful look, and said, "This Institute regrets losing you. However, we wish to assure you that we will treasure your memory with care and respect here. We have been hoping, all along, that you could remain here with us; poor financial circumstances, unfortunately, would not allow it. We wish you good luck in your future endeavours."

She picked up the bouquet of flower from the table and gave it to Kore. "Please," she said, using a grave tone, "accept this as a token of our appreciation for your excellent work."

A round of applause followed the brief speech. The employees beat a hasty retreat to their office rooms, saying nothing to Kore, whom they left sitting alone.

Since the news had caught him by surprise, Kore never knew what to make of the situation. From time to time, he had a premonition that he was not going to last long in his new employment; now when that fear had become real, he was overwhelmed with shock. Like an ambushed soldier who feels confused, on coming under an enemy fire, Kore had a similar feeling.

He had lasted only nine months in his work. After recovering from the state of shock, and once having acquired a level of sobriety enough to enable him to think straight, Kore gave thought to a reason that could have led for his sacking and was met with further confusion.

In the Bible, Christians are told that the Lord works in mysterious ways. Working in a far more mysterious ways than one can imagine is bureaucracy. Because there is no language appropriate enough for addressing a bureaucratic entity, dim-witted though it may not be, but it is hard to convince, has fewer feelings, fear no one, and it is cruel by nature, Kore stopped raking up his mind, thinking of the director and the reason for not letting him to carry on with his work, at the Institute.

Chapter Twenty Two

# Heading Home to Gottsunda

From his place of work, he crossed Kungsgatan, turned left and walked straight on until he came at interjections of Kungsgatan and Drotninsgatan, and then turned right and walked straight, past Stora Torget, (city main square) aiming to get to his home in Gottsunda, on foot. He crossed Fyrstorgatan, then he crossed Östra Ågatan; he crossed Trådgardsgatan, and crossed Nedre Slostgatan.

As he climbed up the steep hill, approaching Karolina Library, walking on a narrow path, running parallel to Drotningsgatan, he carried in his left hand the bouquet of flower which the Institute had given it to him. He felt as though his movement was taking place in the space, where silence reigns supreme; the movement of his feet seemed not to touch the ground-surface, and no sound coming from his footsteps, or any other form of sound reached his ears. He was impervious even to the motorcades whizzing sound.

He crossed Överslotsgatan and took a small path at the far-end corner of Karolina Library that led him to the graveyard. He entered the graveyard through a tiny iron gate. This century-old grave yard, surrounded by a short stone wall, is famous for its serene-atmosphere as well as its beautiful tomb-stones. Shaped from out of white marble stone are figurines of angles with spread-out wings, their curly looking hair well-kept, and their baby-looking faces turned sideways and upwards, to give heavens a blissful stare. Tall trees cast shadows on the bed of flowers in their full bloom.

Sitting on one of the stone-benches to rest his tired legs, Kore gave thought to a position he was occupying in the world around him and felt lost. Beneath the ground, there is the eerie world of the dead; above it, there is the world of the living. Where between the two worlds does he fit into? It occurred to him.

Though he was alive, yet, like the former, he felt he was not able to celebrate the miracles of life; and although he wasn't dead, yet he felt dead to feelings of joy and happiness. Can anyone in his position be happy? How can he be happy when he has just lost a job?

Presently, his eyes fell on the bouquet of flower in his lap. For the first time, he became aware of the flower in a way that he hadn't been aware of it until now.

Apart from its beauty, one thing about the flower that had intrigued his mind most was its symbolism. When given, for example, to a newly married couple, the flower is made to be a symbol of prosperity, love, happiness or even fertility. Now, as a jobless person, what should the flower mean to him?

He saw no sense in bringing the flower with him back to his home; what was he supposed to tell Hadio, his wife? "I have been kicked out of my job, and now I have this flower, let us celebrate." He took a last look at the flower and then deposited it into a nearest dustbin. He left afterwards.

From the premises of the grave-yard, he was on his way back to the city centre, not to his home in Gottsunda, as he had envisaged earlier; he strolled along St Olofsgatan, running parallel to the old university building.

It was five o'clock, on a Friday evening; had it not been a summer day, the city's street and its numerous lanes would have been overflowing with cars, pedestrians and cyclists. All throughout major shopping-centres, people would have been making their shopping, anticipating a lively Friday evening dinner with family members and friends.

However, with such a few people in the streets, on a summer day, the city of Uppsala often acquires the look of a ghost city. This dismal picture of Uppsala, happily, is a short-lived thing.

Summer will soon be over; once again, Uppsala would have its population of students flocking into the city, in order for it to reflect what ought to have been its true epithet: "The City of Eternal Youth."

For many past centuries, after all, this city has been a destination-point for many young students wishing to pursue studies at the prestigious University of Uppsala.

A bus-load of German tourists, on its way to a parking lot, at the premises of the old university building, had just passed him.

Of great attraction for the tourists visiting this part of the city is the century old Cathedral, known as Domkyrkan. The Cathedral, apart from holding the remains of Gustav Vasa and St Erik, as well as other Swedish important historical figures, royal coronations had once taken place here.

A few meters away to the west of the Cathedral are the old university building, dating back to 14th Century.

To the north, a block away from St Olofsgatan, across from the old university building, is an old university student quarters. Here, in one of those student buildings, there is a room August

Strindberg - the Swedish literary genius - is said to have occupied, during his days, as a student of Uppsala University.

As he left the grave-yard, on his way to the city centre, Kore had no place in mind he wished to visit; now, he knew exactly where he was heading to. He had reached an interjection of St Olofgatan and Syslomansgatan.

From opposite side of the road, across from Syslomansgatan, is the famous Café Avandahl, known throughout Uppsala for the quality of its products and for its history. Here, it is said, at Café Avandahl, August Strindberg took an occasional cup of coffee.

On his right, across St Olof Gatan, painted in red colour, is a four-storey building; this is Church House – the headquarters of the Swedish Church.

In the same block, as the Church House, across a small road, is St Erik Square. The square has been named after a Swedish King, who in the 11ᵗʰ Century died in a war his army fought against the Danes. St Erik's square is a place of paradox. While the name of the place has a religious connotation, it is not associated with sacredness. Instead, it is an inconspicuous ground for parking cars.

Kore crossed Sysslomansgatan, turned left, walked parallel to Sysslomansgatan, until he reached his destination point, which was a little cosy bar. He knew the bar when it had been owned by a man called Mehrab.

Mehrab, in his fifties, had been on friendly terms with his African clients. He knew how to keep his African clients committed to his bar; oftentimes, he had let them take their drinks on credit.

They, on the other hand, had sat there quietly, showing their sympathy, as he cried his heart out, recounting how the rule of the clergy had ruined his country. His intense disliking for the clergy had not been limited to their role in politics alone, but had also included the religion they professed to practise and preach.

Kore remembered the day he befriended Ndelo who had been among the few people he had first met in Uppsala In the small community of the Africans that lived in Uppsala, who knew each other well, Ndelo had been well known for his inexhaustible talents for making ludicrous jokes about people and things.

On the occasion when Kore and others had met at the pub to say their farewell to Lamine, after finishing his medical studies successfully, and had been heading back home to the Gambia, Ndelo had told Kore to be careful not to mistake the nationality of Mehrab, the pub-owner, with something he was not.

"When I did that mistake, it had almost cost our friendship to Mehrab," Ndelo had told Kore.

"I can still remember," he had added, "the tantrums he threw against me for making that mistake."

"What did he do," Kore had asked.

"I am of Aryan stock," he had shouted. "Where I come from, my people are the only Aryans in a sea of strange people. Get that through your thick head," he had added in a hysterical tone.

"What did you do?" Kore had asked.

"Why, I stayed quiet. If it could make him happy, I would have gladly conceded Hitler himself to be his cousin. I could have probably thrown in Doctor Joseph Mengele's atrocious name for a good measure, just to keep our mutual gainful relationship in place," Ndelo had said, which caused the men to laugh at the jock.

The instant he got inside the bar, Kore realised that the place had changed hands. The bar, inside, no longer had those numerous baseball caps and hats and mugs that once had adorned its walls. Mehrab had been fond of all things American.

This should explain the reason why the walls in his bar had all sorts of American memorabilia.

Mehrab, who had never been to America, had such stupendous knowledge of the American geography, history and political economy that it was a quite mind-boggling thing to hear him speak about America.

When Kore couldn't find Mehrab there, he got disappointed; a little chit chat with him would have done him a lot of good. On the other hand, he prayed that Mehrab realised his life-long dream of finding his way to California - San Diego - to be more precise.

Kore had always wondered what is it that had made Mehrab fall in love with San Diego – a place he had never seen.

In the bar, in place of the American memorabilia, all walls were adorned with framed pictures of world's largest cities, ranging from London and San Francisco to Lagos and Bombay.

Kore was contemplating where to sit when his eyes fell on someone waving and smiling at him, quite at the same time. This was someone he had met inside a lecture hall, at Nordiska Afrika Institutet, in Uppsala, where the man was giving a lecture. Mikael worked as a university lecturer, at a southern university campus. The two had been introduced briefly to each other by a common friend.

Mikael from Ethiopia was a short wiry-looking man; he kept a long goatee, which had the effect of exaggerating the length of his face; he had a bushy hair, turning grey.

"Hey, Kore, come join me, please," Mikael shouted.

Kore was flattered to hear someone that he scarcely knew well remembering his name.

Kore obliged Mikael; he went to join him.

Kore ordered for a drink of beer that Mikael insisted on paying for; Kore hadn't been drinking for quite some time now; he was even under the impression he had quit drinking; however, he had made up his mind that today it was going to be an exceptional case.

Couple of drinks later, the two men took to each other well. They began their conversation by talking about African politics that both felt leaves much to be desired.

When the subject of Mikael's lecture, "Africa and Environmental Destruction," came into focus, Mikael told Kore, "African countries are solely responsible for the destruction of Africa's environment. Their failure to come up with a source of fuel, other than charcoal, which people use to cook food with, has consequences far beyond imagination.

"We are living in an interdependent world," Kore said seriously. "The future of Africa's environment," he added, "in terms of environmental issues shouldn't be seen in a total isolation from that of the rest of the world. If Africa should come face to face with apocalypse so will the rest of the world."

"You are quite right. However, the rest of the world is making efforts to deal with the mess they are responsible for. What is Africa doing?" Mikael asked sincerely.

"Progress in Africa," he said further, "must be measured not in terms of GDP growth, but whether African countries can find an alternative source of fuel energy for cooking food with. At a rate we are cutting down trees to satisfy this insatiable need, the whole continent will soon become a desert."

"No amount of efforts made to save Africa's environment will succeed, I believe, unless the fundamental underlying cause of environmental destruction is tackled worldwide," Kore said.

He didn't want to appear as if he was contesting Mikael's views, and so he thought he was going to say no more, when Mikael told him,

"What, in your opinion, is the fundamental underlying cause of environmental destruction?"

Kore threw caution to the wind, and decided to answer the question as honestly as he could possibly do.

"The twin evils of capitalism consisting of burning fossil fuel for gaining energy and the depletion of the world resources for consumption purposes are the fundamental underlying cause of environmental destructions," Kore said.

"Can you elaborate further your point for me, please," Mikael said.

"Talking about managing carbon emission, by finding an alternative clean source of energy, will prove useless so long as profit is a formidable engine driving the world economy. To gain profit, corporate and central banks must undertake trading activities; traded for profits are the world natural resources turned into goods and services, and everything else in between." Kore said.

He took a pose and put down on the table the glass of beer he had been holding in his hand before proceeding on with his speech. "The world resources," he said, "is not infinite; at a rate in which countries in the world are exploiting world resources for economic benefits, the world would soon cease to exist as we know it today; it would collapse under its own weight." Kore said.

For a moment, Kore stayed quiet; he picked up his glass of beer and took a sip from it as he let his eyes sit on Mikael and said, "When the world is left with nothing more to offer, in terms of natural resource, what would happen then?"

Looking depressed Mikael said, "It is quite a frightening prospect, but there is logic to what you are saying. Yet this shouldn't stop us from finding a way to avert the catastrophe. I thought the same way after I had read your articles in a newsletter you had helped to edit. I mean, "Resource Development Review.""

"That was then. Now I am jobless," Kore said.

"You are joking," Mikael said, looking genuinely shocked.

"It is true," Kore said.

"When did it happen?" Mikael asked.

"Two hours ago, to be precise," Kore said.

"And three months since the journal that you had helped to edit came out," Mikael said.

"Exactly," Kore concurred.

They were quiet, as if each was contemplating what to say next when quite abruptly Mikael said, "I remember going through the newsletter when I came across several of the articles with your name on them. I had never thought I would meet you. I think they were three or two articles. Were they not?"

"They were three," Kore said.

"I had mixed feelings after I finished reading those articles. Don't get me wrong; they were all excellent articles; however, the sheer number of articles in a single newsletter, all of them written by you, is what made me sit up and think" Mikael said.

"I don't understand," Kore said.

"I don't know how to put this to you. You see; such stupendous intellectual effort that went into writing those articles would probably have won you an accolade anywhere else; here, in Sweden, it is different," Mikael said.

"How is that different?" Kore asked.

"It pays sometimes to give impression you know less than you do," Mikael said.

"Do we know less than others?" Kore asked.

"This has nothing to do with you and me," Mikael said.

"Standing out from the rest of the crowd, for whatever reason," he added, "is something in Sweden people look with distaste."

"Conforming is what you are talking about, something which traditional societies are good at. I thought Sweden is an advance society," Kore said.

"Viewed from a Swedish perspective, I am talking of a team player. If you are perceived differently - sorry for the metaphor

- you would find your life rearranged in the same way as when a set of old furniture in a room is made to give way for a new one; you would find, like an old furniture, you are a disposable thing," Mikael said, sounding sad.

"How can anyone guard against other people's perception and yet succeed," Kore said, and then remained silent.

"It is a hard world we are living in" he said, finally.

"Of course, it is; it is hard for me with a job, just as it is hard for you without one; it is hard for everyone, rich or poor, including the royals of this country," Mikael said. "No one," he added, "can escape from this aspect of human nature,"

"I wish someone had told me what to do?" Kore said.

"Perhaps someone wanted you to learn in the hardest way possible, by bearing the consequences of your action - if you know what I mean. I am sorry," Mikael said.

"Life must go on," Kore said.

"Yes. It must.'

They took their drinks together until it was a little past midnight when they left the pub; Michael offered Kore a lift in a taxi he had hired. Kore gave the taxi driver the direction to his home.

Fifteen minutes later, he was at his home address. He thanked Mikael for the good evening, and bade him farewell, wondering if they will ever meet again.

He hadn't had time to knock when the door opened, and there behind the door stood Hadio in a sleeping gown, her hair looking quite dishevelled. Hadio was shocked to see Kore, looking drunk, staggering and unable to stand on his feet.

"I have been kicked hard at my skinny backside." He repeated the same words, several times, sounding like someone who was in a great physical pain.

"Why are you drunk? She shouted at him.

"I have lost the job," he said lazily.

"I don't believe you; why have you lost the job," she said in disbelief.

"I don't know," Kore said; he was tired; all he wanted to do was to go and sleep.

"I have every right to know. I am your wife," Hadio shouted at him, yet again.

"Let us talk about it tomorrow; I don't feel well now," Kore said in almost pleading tone.

"I need to know the reason; why can't you tell me the reason?" She insisted, sounding hysterical.

"I don't know; why don't you go and ask them?" Kore asked feeling irritated.

"You must have done something wrong; why should they offer you a job, only to take it away, less than nine month later?" She asked in exasperation.

"Go ask them," he said in a tired voice.

Since he knew that that he wasn't going to win in an argument with her, especially as drunk as he was, he stayed quiet, afterwards.

As he tried to make his way to the couch, placed in the middle of the seating room, he tripped on the carpet and fell on the couch; he made no attempt to get up; he lay down, intending to go to sleep.

"You can't go to sleep with your clothes on," Hadio said, as she set out to help him get off his clothes; she tucked him up; later, she turned the lights out, and left him to sleep on the couch.

# Chapter Twenty Three

# *Labour Office*

Kore went to the Labour Office, a few days later, in order to register himself as a person seeking a job. Jakobsson, the official in charge at the Labour Office was a middle-aged man. His clean-shaven face had a deep tan that Kore associated it with the Swedish middle-class tourists, coming back from one of those cheaply packaged chartered holidays, on Spanish holiday resorts.

Whether foul temper was part of his nature, it was quite hard to tell. However, from the way the man addressed him, Kore had a feeling that he was far from being friendly.

Kore had interpreted the look of unfriendliness in his face to be a sign of warning to his clients that said, "I am here not to socialise, but to do business. Hence, keep your distance."

A few days later, through his own personal initiative, Kore was called to appear for an interview at a research institute for policy management.

"Thanks God; once again, you are going to get employment; we shall be secured in our economy," Hadio said when he told her about the job-interview.

She was quite delirious with happiness, it seemed. From the day when Kore lost his job, Hadio had assumed the responsibility for paying loans that the family had been owing different financial institutions, as well as taking care of the family's other household expenses.

Inside the bus, on his way to the interview, Kore imagined the kind of questions he might be expected to give answers to, and thought he was ready. His mind was so much fixated on the interview that he couldn't allow anything to distract his attention, not even the rain that had just started pouring down hard could do it.

Some of the questions he had been imagining in his mind were the following: Why do you wish to have this job? Apart from academic qualifications, what more do you have that will get you this job? What are your strengths and weaknesses? Give three of each kind.

He had rehearsed answers to each one of these questions, and many more others, that he felt he was ready for the challenge. The interview, he was sure, would be carried in Swedish. He was not the best speaker of the language, but it was not the language examination he was going to appear for; he felt a little worried, but got over the fear soon; they advertised for a researcher; after all, all work on research are carried out in English.

"Let my experience and education speak for me to the interviewer(s)," he reassured himself.

The office where the interview took place was located a long distance away from the city centre, in a building surrounded by maple and oak trees. The Institute for Policy Management found in this rustic environment, was intended to give those working there the serenity they need to produce the best they could from the research work they have been entrusted to do.

As he approached the building he imagined what a wonderful opportunity it would be should he secure a job there. Getting a job there was a dream of his life.

In the interview that took place in small room Kore sat nervously facing the interviewers, sitting across the table from him. Greetings were exchanged, followed by introduction before the interview got underway.

Kore was shocked to find out, among the three interviewers – all men - one had found fault with his Swedish accent. The man's rounded looking face had been made to look less rounded by a thin pointed jaw; he had a wild looking pair of eyes popping out from their sockets; the overall facial appearance of the man gave impression of someone that was extremely angry. Kore decided he would be careful with him.

When Kore wished to know more from him, without any hesitation, the man said sharply in reply, "Your Swedish accent leaves much to be desired; therefore, we are left with no option, but to disqualify you from further contesting this post, Mr Kore."

He followed this short but harsh statement with the following intimidating statement: "I am surprised by people, like you, who can't speak the language, using a correct accent."

"There are as many Swedish accents in Sweden as there are regions," Kore said, angered by the man's haughty and aggressive demeanour. He posed briefly to consider whether he should go on or stay quiet. He was getting interviewed for a job, after all. Wouldn't be wiser for him to stay quiet, instead of antagonising the interviewers by saying something that might not go down well with them?

"What are you trying to say?" the man asked in a razor-sharp tone, as Kore was contemplating what to do.

"Why is the man acting in such a devilish manner? Is the man quite so emotionally insecure that he can't control his anger? What is he? Is he insane? Or, has he awoken up on the wrong side of the bed? Perhaps, it is my sight that had caused such anger to rise in him?" Each of these possibilities had crossed Kore's mind, as he gave the interviewer a keen look.

Since he had been quiet, for a while, the people making up the panel gave him a sort of look that Kore took to mean they were beginning to lose patience with him. In his case, he too has had enough, and wanted out.

"I was not socially conditioned, like you, to speak Swedish, using accents known to you," he said forcefully."

At this point Kore didn't care much about the job; he had a feeling that the job had been lost to him before he could even get it. He was angry. Addressing the man further, hoping to make his point clear to him, he said, "You are speaking in a Gothenburg accent, which, unfortunately, I am unable to do, because, unlike you, I was born and brought up abroad."

One of the men, doing the interview, told him in a menacing tone "Well, that is enough, Mr. Kore. The interview is over. You can go now."

Some people, for some reason, according to the Hindu spirituality, exude an aura that gives a bad vibration; the man who had commented on his accent in the interview could have such a quality in him, he was convinced. If some people exude a bad vibration, it is quite logical to assume other people exude good vibrations. As far as Kore was concerned, there is a clear meaning in this later assumption; how, otherwise, can he explain to himself the feeling of serenity which engulfs him every time he comes across Mandela's portrait. Others might get similar feelings on coming upon the portrait of Jesus Christ.

In his case, he would never know the sort of vibration his aura exudes; just like no one will tell a truth to a person whose mouth emits a foul odour, similarly no one could tell him anything about a vibration that his aura emits, assuming they know something about auras, and how people exude good or bad vibrations.

At home, in the evening, he found Hadio in the kitchen, holding a long wooden spoon stuck inside a cooking pot of meat stew. The moment she saw him she left what she was doing; instead, she wished to know from him something about the interview.

"Have you been offered the job?" Hadio lasked the moment he got inside the kitchen.

Kore laughed, but realising it was a foolish thing to laugh, he said, "I am sorry."

Annoyed with Kore for laughing, Hadio said, "It is not a laughing matter. Why are you laughing?"

"I am sorry to disappoint you. I have not been offered the job" he said, feeling genuinely sad for not getting offered the job.

"What happened? What went wrong?" She asked, looking stressed.

At that moment, he wished he had good news to tell; however, since he had no such news, and couldn't lie to her, he told the truth; he told what had taken place during the interview.

"Why," she shouted almost hysterically, "did you have to argue with them? If they said something you didn't like, instead of initiating shouting contests with them, you should have stayed quiet."

"Hadio, please cool down," he told her politely. "There is nothing," he added, "I could have done to convince them to offer me the job."

"Yes, you could," she said in a determined voice.

"You seem to think that the problem is me; well, it is not true," he said, hoping that Hadio would understand him.

"What is the problem?" She offered a challenge.

"The problem, Dear Hadio," he said in a slow but measured tone, "is in my accent. No amount of responsible behaviour, on my part, could have made them change their mind."

"I don't know about that;" she said.

After a moment of silence, she added, "You have a knack for rubbing people the wrong way; you need to change."

There it was, Kore jumped at the words Hadio had used to describe him. Does rubbing people the wrong way, in its meaning, convey the same thing as having an aura that exudes a bad vibration?

He approached her, held her up in his arms and told her, "I will make efforts to change. However," he added, "if I fail, don't get cross with me. Remember the adage, 'You can't teach old dog new tricks' Well, I am the old dog."

They both laughed.

On a visit to the Labour Office, several days later, Kore met Jakobsson in a happy mood; he had never met Jakobson in such a mood before. Jakobsson waved a piece of paper that he handed it to him. He told Kore, "Go to the given address." He added, "Be there by 9.00, tomorrow. If you are lucky, you will have a job."

Kore was happy to have a shot at a job. He didn't know what kind of job, but he trusted Jakobsson to make a right choice for him. He kept awake all throughout the night, contemplating what having a job would mean for him. This time, he didn't let Hadio know anything about the interview. He didn't want to tell her about the job interview, because he was afraid she would start building castles up in the air. He didn't want her to be full of hope and to then start to imagine things that would be quite hard to materialise.

He, himself, had built such castles up in the air when he was called to appear for the interview, only to feel quite empty inside, when no job had come his way.

In the morning of the following day, after the family members had finished taking breakfast that he had prepared for them, Kore washed the dishes before taking a shower. He needed to look quite presentable, and so he decided to put on his brown pair of suit - the only pair that he owned; the collar had started to fray on his jacket suit; in general the suit looked old and worn out.

It was eight by the time he was ready to leave. Dipping his hand in his old trousers pockets, to reassure himself that he had enough money to pay for the bus ticket, he was shocked to discover that he had none. Ten minutes had already gone by; he panicked; he searched every nook and corner of the house to see if he could find money laying idle somewhere, just enough to cover the cost of the bus ticket. He found nothing.

Once, not a long time ago, he had been the owner of a bicycle that had since been stolen. For one to steal, or to have a bicycle stolen from, had been a rite of passage that a student must be prepared to undergo in Uppsala – an exercise to which, he remembered, the student community had attached no any moral stigma to it.

He decided he would attend the interview, whatever it takes. He walked; he trotted, and ran against the blowing wind of October month; he passed through numerous city lanes, went across bridges and walked on narrow forest paths; he ran between trees and around trees, trudging on a ground covered with wet grasses.

Half way there, he broke the run; he was soaked in sweat; he took off his jacket and the tie; he placed the tie in the jacket pocket; holding the jacket in his left hand, he resumed his run.

As he continued running, he felt ill at ease; he was afraid someone might mistake him either for a mad person or a criminal. Whereas running is a Swedish national past time, people in Sweden do not run dressed up in their best suit.

To his shock, moments later, he came upon a police car parked on a shoulder of a road, on a deserted ground, facing the direction to which he was heading. As he went past the car, still running, a policeman got out of the car; he shouted for him to stop.

As the policeman approached him in his lazy strides, giving him a grim look, Kore's fear of not getting to the interview on time preoccupied his mind.

The policeman, tall and lean, addressed Kore in a not-so-friendly tone. "What are you running away from?" He said.

In his struggle to sound audible, catching his breath, while attempting to sound convincing, Kore said, "I am in a hurry. I have an interview to attend."

"Are you serious?" the policeman asked in disbelief.

"Oh; yes," Kore said briefly. He didn't want to say any more than what he had already said; he saw no reason to explain things to the policeman that didn't concern him.

The policeman gave him a doubtful look and said, "Why don't you hire a taxi?"

Kore thought the question was lacking in logic. Why take a chance of getting late to the interview if he could afford hiring a taxi? It was either the policeman had no sense of logic, or perhaps he didn't trust him. Kore assumed.

On the second thought, however, it occurred to Kore that the police officer might be sincere in his statement, because, in this officer's world, a taxi fare is within any one's economic reach. Such being the case, there was no way the police officer could bring himself to believe Kore was not able to afford a bus ticket, let alone taking a taxi to any place.

The police officer reminded him of Marie-Antoinette - the Queen of France - who couldn't understand the reason if bread was not available for the protesting masses in the street, why not give them cake.

The policeman gave Kore a suspicious look, but in one word said, "Go,"

Kore was glad to be free, to resume his run; this time, he raised the pace. He was determined to do his best. "It is now or never. I can't let this chance slip through my fingers," he reassured himself.

He arrived on time in a hall with more than twenty people, both male and female, all individuals with foreign background, waiting nervously, sitting on white plastic chairs, standing in rows of straight lines.

He had run a five-kilometre race, covering an area extending from one section of the city to another one. He should have felt tired, but he was not; he was too anxious to feel tired.

Presently, two men came strolling into the hall; one of the men, an ethnic Swede, was tall and had broad shoulders; he seemed to be in his forties; the other man, unlike his Swedish colleague, was short and had a potbelly; the later looked older of the two.

The Swedish man, facing an anxious crowd in the hall, said in a heavy voice, "Good morning, Ladies and Gentlemen. My name is Ulf Johansson. I am happy you have shown a strong desire to want to do work for this company. Unfortunately, we have a single position of a cleaner, which will go to a most qualified person from among you.

However, to determine who is best qualified, from among you, we will test you for the skills required for you to do the job, effectively. Brushes, buckets, vacuum cleaners, dusters, floor mops - all of which are articles of your trade - have been kept in the next room, to be used by you."

He posed briefly, turned to have a look at his companion, and in a hurry said, "Magid, the Chief Cleaner, will supervise the exercise. A letter will be sent to a successful candidate, as soon as the results of your performances come out."

He concluded his short-speech by saying, "Good luck to you." In a cheerful tone, afterwards, he told his colleague, "They are all yours, Magid." The moment Johansson left, Magid said in a commanding tone, "Follow me."

There was a commotion in the hall, as people left their position to run towards the direction taken by Magid, and started lining up for the test. One by one, Magid followed them inside the room where the test took place.

When Kore's time came up, Magid looked at the list of names he had on a paper he carried in his right hand.

"What is your name? He asked Kore.

Kore told him his name.

"You are over qualified for this job" he said. "This interview is not for you," he added.

"Next," he called another candidate.

Kore left feeling sad, thinking what good was his life if he can't even work as a cleaner?

He was ready to do any kind of job if it would enable him to put food on the table. He was aware that Hadio was the one doing it. Magid had refused him the chance to do the test, even as Kore pleaded with him to let him have the test, promising the man that he was willing to forgo his qualification, to just be able to do the test.

When Kore insisted on getting the chance to do the test, in reply Magid told him that by allowing him do the interview, he would be doing disservice to those who are best qualified for the job.

A few days later, Jakobsson sent him for another interview. This time, once again, it was a cleaning job at the Akademiska Hospital, where Hadio worked as an Asistant Nurse.

To his surprise, he met the same duo of Magid and Ulf; once again, he didn't get the chance to do the test, and the reason was the same as the one given before: he was too qualified for the job.

The third time Jakobsson proposed an interview, Kore refused to oblige him.

"Why do I have to go for an interview that I can't have? He told Jakobson.

"All interviews are not the same. If you persist, you are bound to get one," he said.

"Why," Kore asked Jakobsson, "does it always have to be an interview for a cleaning job that you have been sending me to do."

"What is wrong with cleaning?' Jakobsson asked.

"Nothing is wrong with a cleaning job," Kore said. "Have I said there is something wrong with cleaning? He added.

"Why don't you go and do the interview, in this case?" Jakobsson asked.

"You are not sending me to do the interview; goose chasing is what you are asking me to do," Kore said.

"You can't reject doing interview" Jakobsson said.

"I haven't," Kore said. "You don't listen. With you, it is either my way or the highway," Kore said; he stood up and went away, leaving Jakobsson sitting alone.

As soon as Kore left the office, Jakobsson took out his diary from the drawers of his desk. He had set up his mind to write down his impression of Kore. He removed the pen from an upper left-hand pocket of his trendy-looking blue jacket.

After that, he wrote down the date and the subject matter, to which he gave the title, "My view of Kore." He sighed and took a pause.

The note that he wrote down afterwards was brief; whatever its face value, he congratulated himself for establishing what he thought to be Kore's true psychological profile - a quality, initially, he believed, until now, he had not been endowed with.

The exercise would encourage him to do more of the same thing with his other clients. The note read:

"I have met with Kore this morning. I do this, at the end of every month, in order to assess the state of his joblessness. I have discovered, with each of Kore's visit to this office, our meetings have increasingly acquired a hostile posture. Kore, who seems to have no trust for the state system, chooses to see me as a representative of the system, for which he seems to have a deep-rooted hatred; that makes him project his hostility on me. He picks and chooses the job to do; he will only do the job he is qualified to do. I intend to let this matter get known to the relevant authorities, including the Social Welfare Office.

I find Kore to be quite intelligent, but I think he has a very high-exaggerated sense of himself. If I could be allowed to quote the famous quote, I would say, 'Kore is suffering from the delusion of grandeur.' He could be a danger to both himself and the society, if not properly managed."

He went through the note and smiled; he closed the diary and kept it in its original place. Writing that note had an obvious therapeutic effect on him, for now he was quite pleased with himself.

Suddenly, he felt an urge to have a cup of coffee. On his way to the kitchen, he whistled his favourite tune. His colleagues who saw him were surprised, as they never could imagine that Jakobsson whose state of gloomy nature was part of his personality can scale the heights to reach such a blissful state of joy.

# Chapter Twenty Four

# *Do You Have Something to Declare?*

For quite some time now Kore was out of job; hence, the signs of pressure taking its toll on him were there for anyone to see. Having worked at the institute for a period of less than one year, he discovered that he was not entitled to a benefit from anywhere, and, therefore, the Social Welfare Office was the only source left for him to draw the benefit from.

When confronted with such a preposition, he found the idea quite displeasing as well as repugnant. He would not do it, because it was not morally correct for him to live on a hand-out, he believed.

For a long time Hadio had been insisting that he should get in touch with the Social Welfare Office. Whenever she told him to do so, he told her it was not a moral thing for him to live on a hand-out.

One day, when he used this line of argument on Hadio, she told him, "I don't see moral issues having anything to do with it. Since you are out of job, you should seek assistance from the relevant authority; it is their moral duty to help you."

"I am not a beggar," he said.

"I can understand your situation. Don't think that I don't sympathise with you," she said. "However," she added quite passionately, "when you let pride take control of your action, it is when I begin to have doubts about you,"

"What do you mean?" He asked, looking quite astonished.

"As you know it well, mine is the only income that keeps the family together. Unless we get another income to supplement what I get, we are going to end up in a gutter," she said.

He was convinced that because of the job that gave her an upper hand, she could afford to give him such a hard talk.

Tired of arguing with Hadio, he said, "You keep talking to me as if I am your child; I am your husband, for God's sake."

"Then be a real husband, I say," she said diligently.

To avoid getting into further argument with Hadio, he went out; he wanted to breathe a fresh air and think.

When he returned from taking a walk, he placed a call to the Social Welfare Office, to book a time. A few days later, he was on his way there, his head bowed down in a total shame; he was going to meet face to face with a moment he had been dreading to think about, let alone facing it.

On his way to the Social Welfare Office, the cold air in the atmosphere and the grey skies common in the autumn season were not enough to make him feel miserable. What had caused such a feeling in him was that he knew he was going somewhere to beg for his upkeep. Hadio, his wife, had taken the whole thing quite different from him.

Whereas Hadio believed that the state had a moral duty to extend support to him, Kore thought it was not a moral thing for him to ask for assistance. These were two diametrically different points of views, which could not be reconciled without one losing ground, and thereby losing face. In Kore's estimation, he emerged out the loser for going to Social Welfare Office, to ask for assistance.

At this point, he hated himself and hated Hadio too.

On his way to the Social Welfare Office, he stopped at a railway crossing-line, waiting for the northern-bound train to pass; for a moment he wished he was on the train, to avoid going to the Social Welfare Office.

Once he was there, he came face to face with a scene that staggered his imagination. There was an assortment of cars, new as well as old ones, parked in front of the major entrance, foreign sounding music blaring out from them. The owners of those cars were men in black suits, their hair greased, looking shiny and well kept, leading young women, old women and children to a waiting room, large enough to hold more than sixty people, at a time.

Everyone seemed to be in a jovial mood as if they were getting ready to take part in a carnival. Some revealed a mouthful of golden teeth when they laughed. Kore seemed to think a vault in a bank it is where gold should be kept, not in the mouths of people seeking assistance from the Social Welfare Office.

There were other group of people composed mainly of women in large black garments that covered their bodies, from head to toe; they pushed prams with children in them; they spoke to each other in loud voices, oblivious of their surrounding; they laid down prayer-mats in the waiting hall; there, they purported to say their Muslim noon prayers.

When his turn came up, Kore got inside one of the office rooms in the corridor; the office room with its single desk and a single chair had a forbidding look of an interrogation room. On entering the room, he surveyed the room as though he was anticipating some sort of a surprise to come his way. True to his anticipation, there was surprise for him inside the room, waiting, in the person of Ingrid.

"Come in; sit down. My name is Ingrid," she said in a commanding voice.

As soon as he got inside the room, and caught sight of Ingrid, Kore recognised her, but said nothing. On her part, she did nothing to indicate that she knew him. Both acted as if they never met before.

Kore sat on a chair, facing Ingrid across from the desk.

"Do you have something to declare?" She asked in a sharp tone.

For a moment, Kore thought he came to a wrong office.

As he was considering what answer to give, Ingrid said to him abruptly, "Do you have a car?"

"No, I don't have a car," he replied automatically, as he would do with the rest of all the other questions.

Do you own an apartment?"

"No, I don't own an apartment,"

"Do you hold any bank account?"

"No, I don't hold any bank account."

"Do you hold shares in any company - be it here or abroad?

"No, I don't hold shares anywhere,"

"Do you receive royalties from somewhere?"

"No, I don't receive royalties

"What do you have?"

He wondered what kind of questions she was asking him. Just because he didn't have any material wealth to speak of, it does not mean he has nothing. He has his wife and children; he has his friends, or at least he had had them once before. He decided not to give the kind of answer she was hoping to have, which he thought was, "I have nothing." Instead he said, "I beg your pardon."

"In case," she said, "you are wondering about the kind of questions I have just been asking you, you should know well, in this office, it is a standard procedure for us to ask such questions. Our aim is to make sure that you are destitute enough to warrant getting assistance from us; the questions also help us in deciding how much support you should get from this office. Is it clear?"

"Yes," Kore said.

"For your upkeep, you are required to report to this office every end of the month. You need to prove that you are seeking job seriously; mind you, through channels that are available to us, we will keep track of everything you do or don't," she said in a forceful tone.

Afterwards, she handed him the cheque for his upkeep. Kore left the office, feeling far more demoralised than when he got there.

# Chapter Twenty Five

# *Library*

From the Social Welfare Office, Kore went to Karolina Library, which he regarded to be his informal place of work. Like many other jobless academicians, the library authorities had offered him a table. Apart from using the table for reading and writing purposes, the library had also been a convenient place for hiding himself. He had told his children that he held an employment in the university.

One day, when by sheer accident the truth came out, he felt a colossal amount of shame.

While making effort to find a misplaced piece of paper, on which he had made his mathematical calculations, his son came upon a note from Ingrid of the Social Welfare Office, addressed to his father. Kore had guarded such correspondence with religious fervour. This one note had fallen, evading his attention.

Initially, when the boy came upon the note, he never wished to believe his eyes. Even after witnessing the name of his father, on the document, still he never wished to face the truth. Indeed, the letter was from the social welfare office, for it had the logo of the institution clearly inscribed there.

Finally, when he was convinced of the truth, he fell effortlessly on the chair. In the kitchen, sitting in the chair, facing a table, the images of his father preoccupied his mind. What should he make of his father? Would his father ever look the same again to him? The father who had taught him to value truth, for the sake of truth, had committed the cardinal sin of telling lies.

"No matter what consequences, speak the truth," his father had told him.

Atosh loved his father dearly. However, like all feelings of love that people have for one another, the love for his father was based on a respect he had been having for him. The new discovery that he had made now about his father made him loose that respect, and with it also went away his love. He wept silently to himself.

As he kept thinking about his father, he heard the opening sound of the door to the apartment. He stood up and walked through the corridor, all the way to the doorway. Standing close to the door, he saw his father taking off his jacket and kept it on a hanger by the side of the door. With tears in his eyes, Atosh faced his father. Kore looked at his son and noticed that he was angry.

Cautiously, he asked him, "Is something wrong?"

The boy never bothered to answer him; instead he asked a question of his own.

"Where are you coming from?" He said; he never waited for a reply.

"Don't tell me you are coming from your work place in the University," he added peevishly.

Kore put two and two together and came to a conclusion that his son had managed to somehow come upon his lies. He felt angry; his son had no reason prying, he thought; and so, he never indulged the boy in his quest for the truth. Instead, he kept silent as he went on shading off the garments and kept them on a hanger.

It was a gloomy winter day. Kore was tired, hungry and feeling cold. Lately, due to a poor economic situation, Kore had been taking a single meal, in the evening; He was glad, however, the children had enough to eat at school.

"Never mind; go do your homework," he told his son in a tired voice. Instead of obeying him, Atosh tormented his father with one last disturbing question.

"Why did lie to me, father? Are you a liar?" He said in a horrid tone.

The insult was too much for Kore to bear. He approached his son and slapped him twice, on the face. The boy was not intimidated; he kept looking at his father; he was about to say something, but thought the better of it; he went to his room, instead. Later Kore would be overwhelmed with feelings of regret, especially, because he could not get over what he considered to be a look of disgust that his son had given him.

On the table, in the dining room, Kore found three letters; two of which had been addressed to him. His son, Atosh, had kept the letters on the table. Kore looked at the envelopes bearing his name to determine the source of origin and realised that one of the letters came from the government research-funding agency, known as Swedish Institute for Research Development, (SIRD) and the other came from another government agency, known as Swedish International Resource Development Agency (SIRDA).

Soliciting research-funding from SIRD had been providing some sort of stopgap measures for unemployed academicians, like him.

He realised, as he opened the letter from SIRD, how fast and hard his heart beat against his chest; wet with sweat, his hands trembled, and in the heat of the room he shook with cold. When the letter finally lay open in front of him, he hesitated.

"What if it carried a negative reply?" He asked himself.

"Have I not placed all my hopes on the outcome of this application?" He reasoned further.

Once a year, applicants were encouraged to forward their research proposals to this agency for funding consideration. This was his fifth attempt. Kore had no alternative but to go through it.

The note inside was brief. It started by acknowledging the worthiness of the proposed subject of study, and had ended with a discouraging note, which stated that since the project proposal hadn't been well formulated, it couldn't therefore be approved. It ended with the signature of Peter Welles, for he was responsible for applications dealing with development research,

When he finished reading the letter from SIRD, he took a look at the other envelope, and with a heavy heart opened it. SIRDA is an agency through which Swedish Government channel its aid to Third World countries. It offered job-opportunities to people with expert knowledge on issues dealing with social, economic and political development of Third World countries.

As a rural sociologist, Kore had previously applied for various jobs. A month ago, he had applied for an advertised post of Advisor. He had previously sent more than twenty different applications in response to various advertised jobs. He received negative replies for each one of his applications. Now he received the letter that sealed off his fate. It read:

Dear Kore,

This is to acknowledge the receipt of your application for a post of Advisor in Zambia. We are sorry to inform you that you are too old to apply for this post, which is meant for candidates under the age of thirty-five. While you may wish to apply for other future openings for seniors, you are also free to appeal this decision, as our organisation believes in the concept of equal opportunity.

Good Luck in your future endeavours.

Martin Isakson.


Section Director. Swedish International Resource Development Agency (SIRDA)

"In Sweden, why do all negative notifications on job applications have to be sent on a Friday?" Kore asked himself. This reminded him of the rumour suggesting that such notifications had the intention of spoiling the applicant's weekend mood.

Although he couldn't bring himself to believe the rumour had any authenticity, still he preferred to give the issue the benefit of the doubt, knowing well that human beings are capable of things more heinous in nature than sending candidates negative notifications on their job applications, on a weekend's eve.

Every time he received a letter of reply to one of his applications bearing the sentence, "Good luck in your future endeavours," Kore questioned the respect that he had been having for a society which had a place of premium reserved for the quality of honesty in its value-system.

He wondered whether words such as, "Good luck in your endeavours," are not part of elaborate and sophisticated set of ruses which, like the flower he received after getting sacked from a job, society has devised to avoid coming face to face with hypocritical and cruel side of its nature.

For quite a long time now, Kore had been counting on the possibility of getting some sort of employment, and had dreamt of what it would have meant for him and his family. Getting a job would have made him to do in Sweden many things he had been unable to do.

A job would have enabled him to pay grocery bills; buy his children little things that children like; take his family to watch movies every week-end; have dinner outside with his wife; take the children and his wife to a theatre for them to watch artists perform plays. In short, he yearned for those ordinary things that most people take for granted.

Most of all, a job would have made him a provider for his family, and thus make him a real husband to his wife, and a father worthy of his children.

The letters that he had just read made his spirit sink to its lowest point of desperation. He made a cup of tea, sat down in a chair and sobbed silently.

From his room, Atosh entered the kitchen to try to get some water to drink; while there, he came across his father sobbing.

Slowly, he approached his father; addressing him carefully, he said, "What makes you cry, Abo?"

Atosh could have been convinced that his father was weeping because of what he had called him; a liar.

"Forgive me for making you feel sad. I promise I will never do it again," Atosh said in a regretful tone.

Kore looked at his son through wet eyes. He got hold of his son's right arm and then directed him to a chair, so that his son could sit there next to him. By now, Atosh was holding tears back.

Looking straight into his son's eyes, he said, "Son, never put that kind of thought in your mind. I am weeping not because of what you called me; sometimes the burden of life becomes quite so unbearable that one must weep because of the pain one feels."

After this conversation, both stayed quiet. Finally, Kore stood up; he approached Atosh, held his son in his arms, and then son and father hugged. From that moment, all negative impressions Atosh had been harbouring in his mind about his father disappeared.

# Chapter Twenty Six

# *Martians*

While still recovering from the shock, following the news he had just received, the telephone rang. Kore strolled along the corridor to answer the call. He picked up the phone and said,

"Hello."

There was a moment of hesitation on the other end. Finally, a voice that he immediately realised belonged to Peter said, "Can I speak to Hadio?" Peter didn't bother to say a word of greetings to Kore. He acted as if he was talking to someone who was a total stranger to him.

Since Hadio was not yet home, he let Peter know it. Peter asked if he could leave a message for Hadio. Kore remained silent. It seemed a lack of enthusiasm in Kore had not discouraged Peter. Addressing Kore further, Peter said, "When she comes home, tell her to phone me. She has my home telephone number."

Kore ran back to the kitchen; he let his eyes scan the items on the table; there he saw a letter bearing his wife's name. He picked it up, gave the sealed envelope bearing his wife's name a closer look, and discovered that it bore the insignia of the medical department that Peter had connections with.

He became fired with curiosity; he wondered what was in Peter's mind that had made him wish to share it with Hadio! To Kore's family, apparently, Peter was no stranger; the family knew him from his university days. Even though, on one or two occasions, he had called during Christmas to wish the family "Greetings of the Season," after his graduation Peter had never visited the family again.

Nevertheless, he had kept a sporadic telephone contact with Hadio. Whatever the two of them had been talking to each other about, Hadio had never said to Kore anything about it, and Kore had never bothered asking.

Kore was tempted to read the letter, but thought the better of it. It was seven years since the family arrived from Africa; since then much water had passed under the bridge. Atosh and Shifo were gaining in years; both were doing well in school. Hadio had mastered the language quite well; now she was working as an Assistant Nurse. Each day that went by, his wife gained more friends; in his case, he gained fewer friends, and lost old friends.

Kore assumed the modest success his wife had been achieving in her profession, working as an Assistant Nurse, had made her to become more assertive in her dealings with him. This situation, he believed, had resulted in a misunderstanding between them, so that they ended up shouting at each other every time they failed to agree on any issue. On her part, Hadio accused him of making unnecessary and unending complains about his life. Kore believed that Hadio had cared less about him and his affairs.

And yet whenever they quarrelled Kore had never failed to sympathise with his wife, who toiled hard to keep the family together. While in such a conciliatory frame of mind, an inner voice would speak to him. That voice would be saying to him, "It is in keeping with your generous character to think positively about your wife. However, does she have the same feelings for you? Is she really kind to you?"

The flow of such questions in his mind would go on, and on, until he would feel a throbbing pain in his head.

Just three days before receiving the letter now in his hand, he had quarrelled with his wife again. He had been to the city centre, on the morning of the same day, to buy a pair of trousers, to add to two other worn-out pairs that he owned.

Given the nature of the new pair of trousers, which was of high quality, he thought he had got the pair for a bargain price. Consequently, he had wanted to impress Hadio with his luck. In the evening, after supper, he remembered the pair of trousers, and so off he dashed to the wardrobe to retrieve it.

Strange, how a trivial looking thing, such as a pair of trousers, could sometimes make a big difference in one's state of emotion. His joy did not last long; Hadio had decided to remain quiet the moment he had displayed the pair of trousers for her to see it; she would not share in his enthusiasm.

"Well, why are you quiet?" Kore had asked.

"I am tired. I had a lot of work to do, today. I can't do or say anything," she had said in reply.

"Why should your job be an excuse every time you choose not to talk to me?" Kore had asked exasperatingly.

"What do you want me to say to you? Do you wish me to say anything just to please you?" She had said. Venom was in her speech.

Seconds later, she changed her mind abruptly; she snatched the pair of trousers from his hands and stared at it; pointing at the pair of the trousers, she had said, "Is it this thing that makes you feel proud of yourself? What is this?"

"What does it look like to you? It is a pair of trousers, of course; that is what it is; in case you don't know it," he had said.

"It is a new pair of trousers," she had shouted back. "Given the high price you have paid for it," she had added in a scornful tone, "you could have bought several hand-me-down pair of trousers, using the same amount of money you have paid for this piece of rag. It is a bad business you have conducted, and you want me to feel impressed."

For your information, I don't fancy putting on hand-me-down clothes that you so much admire. I would rather put on what you call rugs than to have the type of clothes you want to impose on me," he had said. He posed briefly and had said, "It is a question of maintaining my dignity."

"You are being quite unrealistic; you are out of job; you don't earn anything, and yet you are feeling ashamed of having to put on second-hand clothes, while I, who earn something, choose to have them," she had said effortlessly.

"You have made a personal choice which I respect. But, please, let me be free to choose what I want," he had said almost in a pleading tone.

"You are inconsiderate," she had said in a malicious tone.

"No, not at all," he had said in a hurry. "I am aware," he had added, making effort to sound convincing, "there is not enough money in this household of ours to cover all our individual needs, but have I ever let my needs to interfere with the needs of the family? Do you still think I am inconsiderate? I love my children," he had said.

"Do you love me?" She had said swiftly.

He realised that Hadio had never put that sort of question to him before.

"Why do you ask?" he had said for a lack of something better to say.

"Just answer the question, please," she had said, looking adamant.

He sighed and remained silent for a while, and then said, "I love you,"

"I don't believe you," she had said, giving him a suspicious look.

"Suite yourself," he had said.

Short of coming to blows, the two had kept arguing with each other until they retired to their own separate beds. Because they had been living in a two-room apartment, Kore had to retire to the sitting room to spend the rest of the night in a couch that was so small he was unable to stretch out his legs properly. For quite some time now, let alone their bed, he and his wife had not been sharing their room.

Kore was about to open the letter when he heard a sound of footsteps in the hallway. It was Hadio back from work. Sitting in the kitchen, a half-empty cup of tea on the table, he held the letter in his right-hand, and considered what to say to her, as she approached him. The two had become further estranged, following the quarrel of the past two days. He offered the letter to her, and quite unceremoniously said, "This is for you."

He remembered to add, "It is from Peter."

She accepted the letter, but said nothing. She sank down into one of the chairs, opened the letter, and started reading it. Kore studied her facial expression to see if there was a sign of change in her face. Suddenly he noticed a slight change. What had been a mere twinkle in her eyes soon proved to be more than what it is.

She let a smile to spread throughout her face. This sudden change in his wife's state of emotion had caused him to feel curious and anxious, quite at the same time. As soon as she finished reading the letter, she gave the letter for him to go through it. He welcomed the gesture with much enthusiasm. The letter read,

Dear Hadio,

The Government of Sweden has been following with utmost concern the issue of female genital mutilation, and the way it is being practised by a segment of the immigrant population of this country. Since the government is convinced that female genital mutilation is dangerous to health of young girls and women, therefore, the government has decided to organise an awareness campaign, and now it is looking for someone to help coordinate the campaign work.

As an Advisor for the institution co-sponsoring the project I have taken the liberty of recommending you for the job, knowing full well that you have all those qualities required to do the job effectively.

If you are willing, let me know so that I could formally let the government medical department responsible for the project know about you.

Sincerely yours,

Peter Wells.


He gave the letter back, and didn't make any comment.

From the kitchen, she took the corridor; there, the phone was kept on a little wooden table that stood against the wall. Kore heard Hadio saying, "Hello." This was followed with a quick barrage of excited words from her.

"Yes,' she said.

There was a brief silence, and then Hadio said, "I would be more than happy to meet you."

That statement was followed with a sound of laughter from Hadio, yet again. It was a long time since Kore heard his wife laugh with such abandon care. She hung up and went back to the kitchen.

"I have accepted the offer; I have let Peter know it," she told Kore. She looked at him and told him, "What do you say?"

"Seeing that you have already accepted the offer, my opinion is of less significance to you now," he said, using a sharp tone. He added, "By the way, regarding your present assignment, what are you intending to do about it?"

"I am going to resign and take the new offer, which I find spiritually and ethically to be much more rewarding to me than anything else," she said.

"Good luck to you," he said sarcastically.

She gave him a jaundiced look; she was about to say something to him, but remained quiet. She made a cup of tea and sat down, facing Kore across from the kitchen table. Because of excitement over the job offer, she had forgotten to ask him about the children.

He volunteered the information, nonetheless. He told her that while Atosh was in his room, back from school, Shifo was not yet home. After a brief moment of silence, he added, "I fear Atosh is angry at me."

Suddenly, she stood up; in a great haste, she left in the direction of her son's room. She remained there briefly before getting back to the kitchen, looking angry.

"Why did you hit my son?" She said,

"You stand corrected. Our son, I suppose, should have been a better proposition" he said with less effort.

"Never mind; I simply want to know why you have to hit him," she said in a determined tone.

As she addressed him further, she became increasingly mad at him. Lately Hadio had taken to shouting at him, whenever the two had failed to agree on any subject. He felt that her level of tolerance had shrunk down to a minimum level possible; she too would have probably thought the same way about him.

He kept silent, but considered in his mind what to say. At last, he decided to tell what happened. He mentioned the word liar to her that he said his son had called him.

She looked at him as though he was a total stranger to her. She tightened her lips that gave her face a menacing look; using a voice that had denoted a serious intention, she told him, "But you have lied to him. Haven't you? However, when reminded of your lies, you wish to punish whoever speaks the truth to you."

"What is the truth? He asked.

"You are out of job; that is the truth. However, you have decided to lie to your children by telling them that you are gainfully employed," she said.

"It is all for good purpose; it is all for good purpose." Kore repeated the sentence, as if it would convey the exact meaning that he may wish her to have.

"And pray, what is it?" She challenged him.

"Imagine, if the children were to see me fast asleep in my bed, on their way to school, every morning; what would they think of me? That, as their father, perhaps I don't want to do any work," he said in a voice full of anguish. "What kind of signals," he added despairingly, "would such message send to their young mind? What would be the outcome of such impressions upon their character? What kind of father figure do you wish for the children to have in me?"

Kore never believed himself to be a liar by telling his children he was employed at the university. His only sin was that he had internalised societal values that put emphasis on work ethics, which he had then preached to his children.

Unfortunately, he could not have envisaged a situation where he would not be presented with the opportunity to practice one of those societal values. And so, having belatedly discovered the futility of preaching to his children what he could not practise, his dilemma became real.

"If having a job is important for the upbringing of your children, why don't you accept any job offer?" She challenged him

"I have searched for all kinds of job and couldn't get one; you know it well," he said quite doggedly. "Out of four hundred applications that I had made not a single one had yielded an interview. You know everything, yet, like everyone else, you choose not to believe me," he added despairingly, knowing well that everything he had said would fall into deaf ears.

"You have been choosing jobs; no wonder you can't get any job? She challenged him.

"Here we go again," Kore said in frustration. "Time and again, have I not told you," he added, "there is no job I haven't looked for; I couldn't get even a cleaning job, because I am over qualified for it, they said"

"What is wrong with cleaning, if I may ask you?" She said.

'Nothing; what is wrong with you?" He said, looking frustrated. "Have I said there is something wrong with cleaning job? Please don't put words in my mouth," he chastised her

'I don't think you are serious. You would do only the job for which you are qualified to do, but nothing else"

"I am aware that one job is not better than another one," he said. "However," he added, "when through sheer hard work and determination one has managed to gain enough skills and knowledge to become a sociologist, a doctor, an agronomist or a lawyer, one's calling lies in pursuing any of the above-mentioned professions, not waiting tables or cleaning toilets in some lousy person's lousy office."

At this point, Hadio stood up and said, "It is enough." She added, "I don't have time to argue with you."

"Sit down," he shouted, fuming at her. "You have started this conversation; whether you like it or not, you will hear me," he added.

He paused to give her a sharp look; in that look, Hadio could have noticed a sign of extreme anger. Since she had never seen Kore getting so angry, she was gripped by fear of Kore. Hadio did as ordered; she sat.

Before proceeding on with his speech, he posed to give what had amounted to a spiteful look at her.

"When you have been trained to drive a train," he told her, "it is the train driving that you must do, not becoming a pilot of a plane. It is for this reason that different kinds of educational institutions are here for; they are here to train people to become productive members of society, through practising what they have been trained to do.

What do you think would have happened to this country, in case those who have been trained to do one thing are made to do something else? This country, I assure you, would have long ceased to exist. That is why, it will not happen to people like Peter Welles, but to a selected group of people to who people like me belong.

In a sense, it is a case of pure discrimination, and I am reacting against it," he said vehemently.

"Oh, stop it. You are being sensitive. I know immigrants, like you and me, who are holding important positions in this society," she said in a challenging manner, as she gradually started to recover from the fear of Kore.

"Yes, but how many are they?" He said disdainfully. "You could count them," he added, "at the tip of your fingers. For everyone immigrant that has landed a responsible job, there are a thousand more others that are jobless, or in a job beneath their skills."

"You are a bitter man, Kore. You need a change of attitude; be positive," she said.

"It is you, not me, who need to have a change of attitude. The sooner this takes place, the better it is going to be for everyone," he said.

"Suppose you don't get the kind of job you wish to have; what do you do?" She said. "It is this family," she added feverishly, "that pays the price every time you refuse a job offer. You know what Kore?"

"What?" he said.

"You are an idealist of a worst kind," she said.

"What do you mean?" He said.

"The problem with you is that you want to have a family, but you also want to keep your idealism," she said.

"Is it wrong to be an idealist?" He said.

"True idealist, such as Buddha, Gandhi, or even Mandela, never mixed the two things," she said. "In your case," she added furiously, "you want to eat up your cake and keep it. I can't put up with your idealism, anymore. You will have to choose one or the other. It is because of the misplaced sense of your idealism the children and I had suffered in Africa. Thank God, we have a life here. Next time, where would the misplaced sense of your idealism take us to? To the hell, I guess; No Kore; I am afraid, this time, you wiould have to go it, all alone."

"What you choose to call idealism, it is a set of principles which give a meaning to my life," he said, sounding tired.

"Principles that are rigid can't be true principles," she shouted back in reply.

Kore was about to say something when he thought he heard footsteps in the corridor. It was Shifo, back from school. He went to meet his daughter; after a brief exchange of warm greetings between them, he took his daughter's hand, and the two went to the sitting room to talk. Meanwhile, in the kitchen, Hadio was getting ready to make dinner; tomorrow it would be Kore's turn.

At twelve years of age, Shifo had grown up to become a beautiful girl, but also intelligent. Somehow, more than anyone else in his family, she was the person most closet to him. When his moods were at their lowest point, he had always found joy in her presence.

Shifo inspired in him the wish to live. Unlike Atosh, her brother, she was not withdrawn to herself; she was a happy outgoing child, but like her brother, she too was doing well in school.

Seeing his daughter nestled against him in the couch had made him to think of her future, and felt worried for her. He imagined, like all children of her age, Shifo in her mind possesses a rosy image of the world. That image offered to her young mind a world of infinite possibilities; it is a world where everything is made available to everyone in a society; it is a world where friendship is a cherished value, and it is a world in which people are co-operating to build a better world.

Shifo spoke to her father about this world now. She spoke to him about the world that had no social boundaries; where friendly people lived in impressive looking houses, and where everybody is happy and full of smiles.

"Do you know where I have been today, after school, dad?" She spoke to him in her characteristic happy innocent tone. She never waited for her father's reply.

"I went to Kerstin Lundin's home, at the other end of the town, in Sunnersta," she eagerly told her father.

Sunnersta is an area where well-to-do people lived in larger-than-life-size homes.

"We spent hours in Kerstin's room, where we played all sorts of games," she said, her face shining with excitement. "Kerstin," she added, "has a huge television set in her room. What a beautifully decorated room Kerstin lives in dad! She has all the room to herself. I wish I could have a similar room. From her room, we went out to the courtyard. Guess what I have seen there? You will not believe it. They have a lawn tennis court and a swimming pool for all sorts of weather."

Shifo was growing up fast. At the speed with which she was growing up, Shifo would soon be required to have her own room, separate from the one she shared with her brother; the other remaining room in the apartment belonged to her mother, and Kore had the sitting room.

The question is, given the family's humble economic situation, where is that extra room going to come from. Neither Kore nor Hadio had ever brought up the subject for discussion between them; it was a reality none of them wanted to face, but which they knew they would have to face it, sooner or later.

The more she talked, the more she warmed up to the subject and the more she became excited.

"I spoke also to Mr Lundin; he is Kerstin's father. What a friendly man he is. I want you to meet him. I wish we had a similar house. When do you think we could have one?" She asked her father, giving him an honest look.

One very important aspect of any child's innocent mind, Kore knew well, is the capacity to attribute to either one of its parents some qualities of heroic nature. However, knowing well his inability to achieve his daughter's dream for her, he cursed his luck.

He wanted to tell his daughter to relinquish her ambition, which under the prevailing circumstances was far from being attainable. He wanted to tell her that the world of Kerstin Lundin can't belong to her, and that that world would remain to her what it has always been: the shimmer of mirage.

He wanted to tell her that her friend Kerstin was only a temporary friend; that their friendship was bound to end once they were grown up and have entered the labour market. Furthermore, he wanted to tell her that since they were living in a socially different world, any prospect of him meeting Kerstin's father was as remote as it was for human beings meeting with Martians.

And finally, he wanted to tell her that unless he wins millions of dollars in a lottery game, there was no way they could move away from their two-room apartment, with a separate kitchen attached to it, in one of the high-rise project buildings in Gottsunda. He could not, however, express those dismal views to his daughter because of a fear that it would destroy the rosy-tinted image of the world that she had kept it in her young innocent mind. He kept quiet, and so did Shifo.

# Chapter Twenty Seven

## *Female Genital Mutilation*

Two weeks after receiving Peter's letter, it was time for both Hadio and Peter to have a long discussion with senior officials, at the headquarters of the Swedish National Health Centre in Stockholm. Together, they were expected to draw up plans on how to generate information on female circumcision, as well as how to disseminate that information to the public. Hadio was happy with her luck. She decided to make the best of the opportunity by working hard.

To celebrate the first-phase of the project, at the end of three months period, a party was held at the famous Uppsala's Clarion Hotel Gillet. People attending the party came from all professions, as well as party dignitaries, and representatives of various civic organisations. The opportunity was also used as an occasion for launching the project formally. The whole episode was viewed on television, where Hadio was introduced to the nation. Her graceful manner, beauty, and eloquence, were able to charm everybody. "Say No to Female Genital Mutilation Now," became the name of the project.

246

"One of the objectives for which the project had been initiated" Hadio said to the generous applause of the audience that she addressed from a podium, in the hotel's chandelier lit conference room, "was to save the coming generation of would be genitally mutilated girls from the horrors of the practice, which is not only outdated but also cruel."

Another well-known personality to appear on the TV, alongside Hadio, was Gudrun Helmut Waldorf - a spokesperson for an organisation known as United Women Association against Cruelty to Girls and Women. Gudrun was in her mid-thirties; she was of medium height; she had a smooth fair complexion; although in appearance she looked fat, yet she was quite agile in her bodily movement; she had a commanding voice, which she had always put to good use, whenever she addressed people.

In her speech given on the same podium taken earlier by Hadio, she expressed a feeling of deep concern that she said she was having for the plight of women that had been made to undergo female genital mutilation. "The practice of Female Genital Mutilation is one area in which my organisation," she said, "is working to eradicate from Sweden. Female genital mutilation is the greatest act of atrocity committed against women."

She took a pause; shouting to be heard over jeering supporters, she said, "Women are victims of male chauvinistic behavioural tendencies common especially in Third World countries; this must not be tolerated here. Let me remind you that no amount of campaign to improve the lot of women is going to bear any fruitful results unless policy measures meant for empowering women, in all spheres of life, are put in place.

There is also a need for the project to initiate a research-study to consider ways and means to achieve the above-mentioned objectives. Finally, I wish to give my congratulations to Hadio for the good work."

The project, for the first time, was able to unite people from across ideological spectrum. Even those right-wing groups which in the past had accused members of left-wing organisations of blindly supporting cultural practices of various immigrant groups, for reasons of maintaining political correctness, gave their wholehearted support to the project.

Not quite surprisingly, however, the project had caused a large-scale amount of anger coming from groups of Africans, who forwarded letters of protest to Hadio's office, condemning the aims as well as the activities of the project. Hadio, particularly, became the object of their scorn and wrath; they called her all sorts of abominable names, and had also threatened her with dire consequences.

When a documentary film secretly shot somewhere in Africa depicting on the TV a graphic image of what the circumcision ritual looks like, it brought racial and human right issues into focus.

"Why," the detractors of the documentary shouted, "have the producers of the TV programme felt free to temper with a sacred-body of the little girl, who knew nothing of what was taking place in her life? Or was it the girl's racial makeup which had given cause for the producers to act with such unwarranted alacrity?" They asked.

Over time, the project came to receive much praise for doing its job well. One day, however, following an incident that was to become a topic of emotive discussion, throughout the country, this favourable sentiment was shattered to pieces.

It was a singularly pleasant Saturday evening of a warm summer day; the family had just returned home, after a rare outing together, when suddenly the telephone rang. Kore went to answer the call.

"Can I speak to Hadio?" Someone, sounding hysterical, asked.

Before Kore could say a word, Hadio took the phone away from him and in her sociable tone that she had recently acquired said, "Hadio speaking." For a long time, afterwards, she uttered only the word 'Yes' in a grim tone.

"I am on my way. I won't take long," she said in the end. She hung up the phone, went to her room, changed into some easy-to-wear clothes and left.

On the way, she remembered to take her handbag, and had conveyed the urgency of her action to family members by shouting, "Something serious has come up. I am on my way to the hospital."

Meanwhile, at home, she left Kore and the children guessing at the nature of the problem that had made her to swiftly take off to the hospital. Kore felt let down, because he had wanted to take advantage of the outing, to help bring understanding between Hadio and himself.

On her way to the hospital, Hadio could not think properly. The news she had just received convinced her that all her past efforts were in danger of ending in vain. A few minutes later, she found herself at the hospital gates; she parked the car in one of the hospital parking lots; afterwards, she proceeded to the emergency room where she met a colleague and a lady doctor waiting for her to arrive; both were in a gloomy mood.

After short greetings, followed with introduction, a sorrowful look in her face, a stethoscope around her neck, looking shocked, the lady doctor gave Hadio a detailed account of what had taken place. She spoke to Hadio about a case that had involved a secret female circumcision ritual which had gone awfully wrong, and had now resulted in the victim losing a great deal of blood.

"The fortune of the victim is wavering between life and death," she said. "Every effort," she added, "is made to make sure that the patient recovers as soon as possible." On that note, the doctor went away, leaving Hadio feeling quite demoralised.'

# Chapter Twenty Eight

# *One Point Out of Ten*

As soon as this unfortunate incident became widely known to the public, through the media, it attracted the attention of a vocal section of society that subsequently asked the government to take serious steps to pre-empt any such similar action from taking place, in future.

A case was consequently registered at Uppsala's District Court, where the state brought criminal charges against the parents of the girl. The parents, in utter disregard for the consequences that their action would have, on the poor little girl of fourteen, had taken the responsibility of carrying out the operation in a privacy of their home, making use of crude instruments to do so. They did this to avoid detection by the authority, which persecute parents who allow girl-children to undergo such operation.

Apart from relying on legal and academic institutions for expert opinion, the state had also benefited greatly from information given out by individual citizens that are well versed about the subject of female circumcision. Hadio gave interviews widely to the media. In those interviews, she had made her stand quite clear on the subject of female circumcision; she called the accused parents of the girl "criminals." She also said that they must face the full weight of the criminal justice.

"Hadio, the country's foremost activist, on issues associated with female genital mutilation, is calling for the parents of the girl to face the wrath of the law," read a headline in Dagens Nyheter, which is one of the country's daily newspapers with one of the widest range of circulation in the country. From Hadio's statement, the country's most well-known social commentators drew their own conclusion.

"Given Hadio's position on the issue," they said, "there is no way the parents of the girl would not end up in prison.

Because the incident had aroused a great deal of interest, throughout the nation, hence efforts were made to inform the public about the subject of female circumcision on the nation TV.

Several panel discussions, dealing with the subject of female circumcision, became quite an important component feature of TV programmes. Members of the public who wished to contribute to the debate were invited to make calls to the studio.

One such programme was aired at a prime-time of eight in the evening. Out of three individuals constituting the panel, Hadio was one of them. At the end of a brief introduction, the moderator, a woman in her early thirties, exhibiting an unusual charm and grace asked questions.

She directed the first question to a woman panellist who was dressed in a very conservative style. Indeed, the lady's attire, as well as her composed manners, had matched both her teaching profession and her marital status as a mother of two fully grown up children. Addressing the lady in her name, the moderator said,

"Tell us, Maja, in your opinion, what are the impacts of female genital mutilations on women sexual feelings?

Marja spoke at great length about female reproductive organ; she concluded her remarks by saying, "A woman that has been genitally mutilated is denied a chance to enjoy sex."

The moderator directed the same question to the second panellist, Astrid, who said she agreed with Mariana.

Next the moderator directed the same question at Hadio.

"Well, Hadio," she said, "you are a Programme Manager for the project "Stop Genital Mutilation Now." You are also hailing from a culture and a society practising Female genital mutilation (FGM). What are your views on the subject? What are your sexual experiences as someone whose genitals have been mutilated?"

In his apartment, sitting with his children, Kore was curious; he wanted to hear what reply she would give.

Hadio gave a nervous smile before she could gather courage, and then she said, "Women genital mutilation is excruciatingly painful; it leaves behind both body and mental scars on its victims."

There was an evident look of sadness etched into the faces of the panellists.

After a short pause which gave her enough time to contemplate what she was going to do, Hadio said, "However, in relation to your question regarding my sexual experience, as someone whose genitals have been mutilated, if it were possible for me to measure in a scale the level of sexual pleasure that I feel every time I have sex, I should give myself one point out of ten."

That reply made fellow panellists laugh slightly. Kore winced. He felt insulted; he was embarrassed to have the children listen to their mother speaking callously and without any feeling of shame about her genitals, and how little of sexual pleasure she had been getting out of her love making with him. She made him feel angry for opening a window to their bedroom for the public to peep through.

"What a silly thing to say in public," he said to himself. He took the wireless telephone set to the next room in order to make call to the studio, away from the children.

After giving her thanks to Maja, Astrid and Hadio, the moderator requested members of the public to contribute to the discussion, through telephone calls, which they did in large numbers.

Kore was one of those people who called the studio.

"I want to extend my thanks to the initiators of the programme for proposing such an insightful means and ways to enlighten the public on a subject which is quite sensitive, but of which little is known about," he said nervously when he got the chance to speak.

As he kept on speaking, he took advantage of the state of anonymity the call to the studio had afforded him, and decided he would be anything he wished to be. He decided he would be any of the following: critical, provocative, daring, sarcastic, cynical, ironical, pedagogic etc.

"However," he said after a short pause, "I wish to register my disappointment over the way the panellists have handled the subject. It seems to me that everyone had considered the problem from only one angle, which is women circumcision and the impact it has on their sexual life. Be that as it may, I am determined to follow the same approach to shade light on the subject.

Let me remind your viewers," he added in a hurry, "the knowledge that we have regarding this sensitive subject is not much. Hence, I wish to take this opportunity to give credit to Mr Alfred Kinsey for doing everything possible to enrich our knowledge of this subject.

In his seminal work, dealing with women sexuality, Mr Alfred Kinsey has made several crucial discoveries known to us. One of these discoveries clearly points out how a large percentage of women respondents, in the study conducted by him, could not define orgasm. His finding becomes quite intrinsically curious when one takes into considerations that Kinsey's respondents were American, for whom the culture of circumcision is an alien thing."

At this point he took a detour from his speech in order to remind the listeners, who might have been interested in having more information on the subject, to read Sexual Behaviour in Human Male and Sexual Behaviour in Human Female.

If the viewers of the programme had been a little observant, they would have discovered the change in Hadio; she looked quite upset, and the reason for this was not hard to find. Hadio had recognised Kore in the voice of the speaker.

At this point, the moderator said, "What is your position on the issue?" There was a touch of anger in her voice that didn't escape the attention of Kore.

The question threw Kore off balance; he was not expecting the moderator to interfere with the flow of his ideas; for a second, he lost his sense of concentration. He searched in the recesses of his mind for any information that he could retrieve for him to make use of.

Luckily, his efforts were rewarded easily. Not so long time ago, he had the opportunity of reading series of articles in a journal that had enriched his knowledge on the subject.

As he had been quiet for some time, while the line remained open, the moderator never knew what to think. Acting under the impression that Kore might have gone off the line, the moderator said carefully," Are you still there?" to which Kore replied, "Yes," in a haste.

"Well then, do you have something you want to say?" the moderator asked.

"Yes," Kore said.

"Well, go ahead," the moderator said.

He coughed slightly and then started giving his speech in a halting manner. As he went on with his speech, he gradually gained confidence.

"First and foremost," he said, "I wish to propose to the authorities concerned a need to show kindness to the parents of the girl, now in prison, by setting them free and have them reunite with their daughter.

When referring to people, things and events, our choice of words is not free of biases; hence, I wish to say Female Genital Mutilation – having FGM as its acronym - has been wrongly applied to circumcision. You do not mutilate someone that you love; after all, parents of circumcised daughters, like all other parents, have deep love for their daughters.

We must avoid giving ready-made answers to complicated issues of sexual nature. Since sexual needs of male and female are met differently, hence sexual partners must discuss their needs candidly for them to have a meaningful sexual life.

Furthermore - and this one is directed to the lady-panellist - I wish to remind her that if it is due to a lack of clitoris that she fails to get sexual pleasure, perhaps, together with her husband, she may want to explore that part in a woman's reproductive organ called G point, which is believed to offer an alternative to clitoris as a source of sexual pleasure in women.

I can understand the desire to empower women alone as a way of offering solution to the problem. Empowering the whole society, nevertheless, is where the real answer to the problem lies. Remember: there is neither a villain nor a hero in this human drama that has been enacted for millennia of centuries within the African continent. In this case, everyone is either a hero or a villain.

Finally, I wish to conclude by saying women circumcision is a deeply rooted practice in certain African cultures, pre-dating the introduction of foreign forms of religions within the African continent.

It is a harmful practice, of course, but everywhere people continue to carry on with it. Thus, we need to ask ourselves the following question: why despite all efforts made to eradicate the practice, it has not been abandoned? What makes this cultural practice so versatile to the extent that it proves quite hard to fight against?

Once we have got answers to these questions, we will know where to go from there.

He concluded by saying, "Thank you."

There was a sign of wonder in the faces of the panellists who whispered to each other. The camera focused on the moderator; the moderator looked at her watch, which indicated to her that time was up. She thanked the panellists, subsequently, for the contribution they had made, and reminded the public to direct their enquiries at Hadio's office, whose addresses she had let the audience have.

The statement Hadio had made on TV about her sexual feelings and the subsequent response by Kore became a straw that broke the camel's back. Hadio didn't think there was any logical connection between Kinsey's findings and the practice of women genital mutilation.

"Do you believe," she said angrily, "because there are women in America who couldn't define orgasm, as documented in Kinsey's report, this will affect the status of the genitally mutilated women here and elsewhere, by making them suffer less from their physical injuries?

"I am not the one who brought up the correlation between the two. I am following your argument to its logical conclusion," Kore said.

"What do you mean?" Hadio said.

"Did you not attribute the absence of sexual desire in you to a lack of clitoris?

"What I am saying is that women with clitoris do not suffer the physical harm, which is the fate of those who have been genitally mutilated"

They were having dinner; the children sat with them, and listened as the two parents kept arguing with each other; such heated argument between them had become so common the children were bound to hear them argue.

If the public gave Hadio their wholehearted support for holding such hawkish views on the issue, a repudiation of her views by Kore was what awaited her at home.

One day, back home from giving her latest interviews, oozing confidence, Hadio came across Kore in the kitchen, reading from a newspaper. The moment he caught sight of Hadio, Kore stopped reading the paper. Pointing at the caption underneath her photograph, on the front page of the paper, where she had called for stern measures to be taken against the accused parents of the girl, he told her, "What do you hope to achieve by this?"

"Why, of course, justice is what I hope to achieve. As a criminal act, this should not go unpunished," she said easily.

"If every cultural practice is considered to constitute an act of crime, where do we draw the line?" He asked.

"This is not any cultural practice; this is female genital mutilation, which put to jeopardy people's lives," she replied forcefully.

"If you attribute a criminal intention for every act of female circumcision, are you not saying our forefathers were criminals too? He asked furiously.

"It doesn't matter what I think; the most important thing is that this awful practice should end," she said in an impatient tone.

"Making reference to the discussion that took place on the TV, a few days earlier, he told her, "How you could bring yourself to sit quietly as you listened to the moderator commenting on your body, in a most disrespectful manner, is quite beyond my comprehension."

Looking straight at Kore, Hadio nodded her head but stayed quiet. A moment later, giving the appearance of someone confronted by an unpleasant task of having to put an unwanted conversation to an end, she said, "Say what you want; to me, circumcision and genital mutilation are words that are intended to merely give an objective meaning to a barbaric practice. Whether you like it or not, nothing will stop me from fighting this horrible criminal act that is committed, with impunity, against women."

"You are not seeking justice; you are after revenge. Since you can't punish people who have caused you to be circumcised, you are now taking revenge on people doing similar thing to women and girls of today," he said.

Hadio didn't know what to think of Kore; she failed to understand the reason for Kore behaving in such a crude manner; she knew him as someone who abhorred social conservatism.

"I pity you, Kore," she said finally as she gave him a disdainful look. "Like most men," she added in a solemn tone "there is no way you could feel both physical and psychological pains that generations of circumcised females have gone through. Yet, the least I have been expecting to come from you, and many other men, is to have a grain of sympathy for women that suffer enormous pain, due to this barbaric cultural practice."

"I beg your pardon," Kore said, sounding as if the statement has offended him.

"What did you say?" he said. "I warn you," he said shouting at her, "not to put blame on men for actions you women are responsible for."

"What action are you talking about," she said, challenging him.

"It is an open secret that no men would stoop so low as to allow a girl child to undergo the ritual; this is a job done by you women, which you do it well," he said in a haughty manner; convinced that he had put Hadio in her place, he emitted a kind of laughter that Hadio didn't like.

Hadio looked at Kore and in a spirited manner said, "Yes; we women do it, but when we do it, we do it to satisfy men's insatiable desire for virgins. All men have something for virgins. You wish to have a virgin here, and hope for more others when you die.

She had more to say but stopped halfway when the telephone rang. She went to get the call, which brought their conversation to an end.

In the court-house, a few days later, following a series of postponements, the defendants were found guilty of the offence, and sentenced to serve a jail term of five years, to be followed by a permanent expulsion from the country, after their release.

Meanwhile, the court had made a special provision for the girl, who had since recovered, to live in Sweden, under the care of foster parents.

From that day on, their relationship entered a turbulent wave of deep moral crises. Kore was especially hurt by the confession Hadio had made on TV about her sexual life. Hadio felt the same way about him. The quarrel that followed between them became so intense that whenever they hurled verbal insults at each other, those insults were no longer guided through any moral code of conduct. Kore called his wife all sorts of names. He accused her of immodesty, of lying to the public, and of being a master of fabrication. On her part, she called him a spoiler, a failure in life, and that he was jealous of her successes.

The situation deteriorated further because of the constant trips Hadio had been making every time she had to attend a seminar or a conference, away from Uppsala. She came home and went away as she pleased; she stopped consulting Kore on any of her itineraries. Many times when she came home late accompanied by friends, whom she would invite in for coffee, she never bothered to introduce Kore to them.

On one or two occasions, Hadio came home accompanied by Peter, who said nothing to Kore. Peter and Hadio took a seat in the dining room, and talked to each other with a burning enthusiasm about a conference on circumcision that was due to be held in Cairo soon.

Then the day for the departure to Cairo came, finally. That day Hadio was highly excited. She was scheduled to take a flight bound for Cairo at six in the evening. On the same day, she took the whole family including Kore out to launch. To the children, she spoke animatedly, and promised a present in a form of a miniature replica of the Pyramid of Giza to them. Kore felt quite relaxed; however, he never said much.

Moment before leaving for the airport, Peter called in to offer Hadio a lift. Seconds after kissing the children goodbye, Hadio pulled Kore aside. The gesture had made him feel elated. He anticipated a word of affection, but was taken aback when instead she offered him a sealed envelope; without saying a word, she took the elevator to the ground floor.

As soon as she left, Kore got into such a great hurry to read the letter that he skipped words on it. He had to re-read the letter, several times, before the letter could make sense to him. It happened that the letter was quite brief and to the point. Clearly stated in the letter was the objective for which it had been written. Hadio had made her intention clear in the letter, which was to terminate her marriage contract to him. The letter referred to quarrels taking place between them as a burden weighing heavily on their capacity to forge ties of friendship and love, based on respect for each other's needs.

For a moment, after finishing reading the letter, he felt as if he had lost all sense of feelings in his body; his whole body had gone numb. He was in the same state when someone coming off the elevator shouted his name.

This was Kristina, a Swedish old lady with an apartment next to his. The lady could be in her eighties, but was quite adamant about keeping her apartment against demands made to her by social welfare authorities, wishing to place her at the elderly people's home. She was short and thin, and seemed to be always in a lighter mood.

Unlike other people from her generation and ethnicity that had left the area in large numbers, following an influx of new tenants, who were immigrants, she chose to stay put in her apartment. She was not going to be intimidated by anyone.

At the beginning, she was cautious when dealing with these immigrants; then she was slow in interacting with them, but once she came to know them well, she never regretted her decision to stay put in her apartment.

They were mostly generous to her; during their festivities, they offered her to share with them their meals. What she liked most about the neighbourhood was its gregarious atmosphere; the children, who other people would probably consider them to be cheeky and rowdy, were the apple of her eye.

Kristina had one peculiar habit; she talked about her cats to anyone that cared to listen to her. To some of her cats, she gave them names of famous actresses of her time. Brigit Bardot, Sophia Loren, Elizabeth Taylor, were some of the names she gave her cats

"If feline qualities could be associated with women, in terms of the way they walk, and the lithe form of their bodies, why not give names of actresses to my cats?" She reasoned.

On this day, however, Kore was not willing to listen to any cat-stories; his mind, after all, was engaged in something far more serious than any cat-story can ever be. As the old lady was getting ready to engage him in a conversation, he opened the door to the elevator and pressed the button to the ground floor. The old woman shook her head in a sign of astonishment, and had absentmindedly said, "Poor man; he has become rudderless."

Kore never felt like getting back to his apartment; he wanted to have to breathe fresh air, and so he decided to go out for a walk. Outside, it was wet, damp, grey and cold. Kore was not someone whose state of emotion had fluctuated with seasonal changes. Furthermore, he had been previously hard put to understand how changes in the weather could possibly affect the way people feel.

Now, the formidable grey-looking clouds of april month, drifting lazily up in the sky, had evoked a feeling of melancholy in him. He drifted past green meadows, into forests, across the city's many bridges, and through the city lanes. Finally, he found himself at the heart of Uppsala.

The clock at the city-square read seven; it was deathly silent.

He had covered several kilometres. Since his mind was engaged on the subject of a separation from his wife, he didn't feel tired. He believed that despite difficulties he had been facing in life, his life was a bearable one, considering that at the end of the day he had a home to go back to.

While there, he enjoyed watching his children as they joke with each other and laughed. He couldn't bear to think, sooner or later, he would live by himself. Does he have enough fortitude left in him to enable him to carry on with such a life, and still keep his sanity intact? He imagined.

He took a bus home, where he prepared evening meal for his children. Afterwards, it was time to retire for the night. That night he did not sleep well; his mind was heavily engaged in thoughts, each one more ominous than the other. After a long tossing and turning, finally he fell asleep.

# Chapter Twenty Nine

# *Beginning of the End*

In the following day, in the evening, Mr Fawzi Abedeen, the Egyptian Minister for Health, declared the conference on circumcision in Cairo formally opened. The conference attracted delegates from all across the world. When not inside the conference hall, delegates took opportunity of getting to know each other well.

On their final day, a resolution calling for a need to promote educational awareness on the dangers inherent in the practice of circumcision was adopted. Finally, a day before their departure, a tour of the city was organised to the joy of the participants, who were looking forward to visiting museums and important monuments of ancient Egypt.

Apart from gains made in the conference, in terms of knowledge, Hadio and Peter used the opportunity in Cairo to broaden their newly found- friendship. Every evening, they ate their supper together; later, they spent the rest of the evening in either's room, talking and watching television.

On their last day, sitting and watching the television together, Peter approached Hadio, and then held her up in his arms. She offered no resistance. Softly and quite gently, he pulled her toward himself. The two gazed at each other's eyes, as if to determine the kind of expression each had for the other. They hesitated before kissing. What followed took neither by surprise.

Hadio responded with a dignified patience to Peter's feverish attempts to explore the well-defined contours of her body. As she let him accommodate himself into her, she thought of her action. She had the same feeling when they had met at Peter's apartment, several times before. She wondered each time what had made her wish to do what she was doing. Was she doing it because of lack of any feelings of love for her husband, or for the love she was having for the man in bed with her?

Hadio was not allowed to follow her thoughts any further. She woke up soon to Peter's desperate panting and ranting sounds coming from his throat, as he reached the climax. A moment later, he asked the same question that he had asked her once.

"What was it like for you?" He told her. He added, "I have enjoyed myself."

"I don't know what to say Peter," she said. After a brief silence, she added, "You are the first person to express such feelings to me, after all."

"I wish you could do more to reveal the feelings of love you have for me," he said. "That is," he added disappointingly, "in case you have any feelings for me."

Hadio remained silent.

Each time she had some sort of physical relationship with Peter, and had gone home shortly after, Hadio had tried to avoid having much to do with Kore. Oftentimes, she had become impatient with him. Little things about him had irritated her. If she thought he had stayed in the bath-room much longer than necessary, she had found enough justification in that to shout at him. If he made a joke, she had never laughed.

Although she had long reached a decision to leave Kore, she was not sure if moving in with Peter was a right thing to do. There was something about Peter that made her have a fear of him. His way of looking at her, or cutting her short in the middle of a speech, or shouting at her unnecessarily after losing an argument to her, had made her to feel quite vulnerable, in his presence.

And even though she was convinced that leaving Kore for another man was not quite a right thing to do, there was little she could do to alter the course of events, as they were unfolding before her eyes. She found her situation to be quite like a person in a canoe, carried by a strong current, heading for the falls.

They spent the rest of the evening in the balcony of their hotel room, from where they observed the city going about the business of closing down for the night. It was getting quite late, and so they thought it was time to sleep.

In the afternoon, of the following day, they left Cairo and arrived home late in the evening; they parted at the airport, promising to get in touch with each other soon.

It was little past six, on a Sunday evening, when Hadio arrived home. Except Kore, who was doing the laundry at the basement, the rest of the family members were inside the apartment. A half an hour later, carrying a basket-load of clothes, Kore got inside the apartment.

He was beginning to unpack in the bathroom when he heard Hadio's voice.

"Is it you Hadio?" He asked loudly but received no answer.

Instead, his daughter, Shifo went to meet him. In her hand, she held a miniature pyramid of Giza that her mother had remembered to give it to her, as a present.

Hadio's presence had made Kore feel anxious; he was lost on how to greet Hadio. Should he display warm feelings of affection? What if she refused to reciprocate the gesture?

He washed his hands in the washbasin; from there he went to meet his wife, who looked quite dignified in her beige green brown suit. She wore her hair short; with a slight touch of make-up to her face, she looked smashingly beautiful.

As he approached Hadio, seeping tea in the kitchen, Kore had an irresistible urge to hug and kiss her. If he was planning to take such a chance with her, Hadio offered her hand for him to shake, instead.

"I am hot; I need to take a shower and relax; I am exhausted," she told him.

Kore could not help feeling humiliated. Here is his wife who had been away for seven long days, and now she wouldn't speak to him. She spoke to the children before she went to her room.

Suddenly, the telephone rang. Kore went to answer the call. It was Peter. Peter told him he wished to speak to Hadio; Kore hung up on him without saying a word.

There was no doubt that the frequent calls made to his house by Peter had caused him to feel irritated. This, however, was not enough to explain the reason for feeling furious and antagonistic towards Peter, quite at the same time.

The disregard that he had been having for the social etiquettes was one thing that had made Kore hate Peter. He was in his home, for God's sake, not somewhere in a telephone exchange room, in a seedy hotel, serving anxious clients. Why can't he understand such a simple thing, and behave himself.

He was jolted from following his thoughts, when the telephone rang with a piercing and annoying shrill. Kore ignored the call until Hadio went to get it. The two spoke briefly before Hadio left for her room. On her way there, she remembered to let Kore know that she would like to have a meeting with him.

Strange how authority and responsibility could change some people so thoroughly that they would not recognise themselves, even if it were possible to rewind their life, and show to them what that life had once looked like, he assumed.

Whenever he let some unkind thoughts about Hadio to enter his mind, Kore reflected on his role, in the family affairs, to determine if the bad blood between Hadio and him had anything to do with him.

He often acknowledged to himself that he had become ill tempered, easily irritable and suspicious of everyone. He believed this to be a natural reaction to his waning fortune that he was convinced had been forced upon him by circumstances beyond his control.

He expected, of all people, his wife to understand his situation and hence sympathise with him, not adding to his misery by asking for a divorce.

"Yes, I sympathise with you Kore," Hadio who had just had a rest in her room, of twenty minutes, told him in response to his statement about her alleged lack of sympathy.

They were sitting and talking in Hadio's room.

"But on the second thought," she added, "what you need is not sympathy; you need to face the truth. You know how much I have been trying - at least, during this phase of our life together here in Sweden - to have to know you well. Yet, you do not seem to appreciate my efforts."

As she kept speaking to him, she lowered her voice, which had the effect of touching Kore, because in that gesture he saw a sign that she cared for his feelings.

"In this case, why do you wish to divorce me now?" Encouraged by what he took to be a sign of respect, he said in a pleading tone. "Have you ever thought of what a divorce could do to our children?" He added.

Hadio was determined not to give in to that kind of sentiment. She believed, in his own way, Kore was a kind person, and a loving father to his children, but she wasn't going to let that sentiment to influence her decision. She looked at him and said, "I agree that the children belong with their two parents. If, however, the parents are at each other's throat, as often as we are doing, would not this spell doom for them?"

"What do you mean?" Kore said, not knowing what to think about Hadio.

"You have not been the luckiest of people Kore. This has caused a lot of pain in you," she said.

She stopped briefly, took a short breath and then said, "This situation, I am afraid to say, has blinded you to many good things that you have been blessed with. Unfortunately, your hatred for a system that you think has let you down has had an adverse effect on us."

"You know it is not true what you are saying. Say it is not true! You know how much the children love me!" Kore said, holding tears back.

Seeing Kore in such a desperate state of mind had made Hadio almost feel pity for him; nevertheless, she would not let this to interfere with what she was about to say to him.

"The quarrel between us," she said, "has removed all feelings of love that I have been having for you. I can't pretend that this is not the case. I am afraid, if we should continue in this way, nothing but a feeling of hatred would develop between us. I wouldn't want this to happen to us."

Lately Kore had found hard to understand Hadio. At one moment, she sounds kind and understanding; the next moment she is indifferent.

Kore treated the statement made by Hadio as a height of impertinence. Hence, he told her in an angry sounding voice, "You act and behave as if you are not who you are. You have been cheated into believing that you have a control over your life. You are merely a puppet. Whoever is pulling the rope, sooner or later, he or she would bring the show to the end; that would be the end of you, believe me. They can't let you talk of circumcision forever. They will soon find some other "worthy cause" for them to espouse, which you would not fit into. When they will choose to fight for the cause of the Bushmen of Kalahari - as I assume this is what they are going to do next – what will you do? I wish you luck."

# Chapter Thirty

# *Imam*

To add a measure of sanity to his marriage life, Kore had to seek help from a third party. He invited, subsequently, someone whose title of Imam refers to his position in his community as a religious leader. He had been introduced to him by someone with whom he had been friendly, but somehow had lost contact with him. He hadn't seen him for some time, and was given to believe that he had left the country. So, when he ran into him in a shopping centre, not far from the main city square, he couldn't keep quiet about his marriage life. It was then that this friend recommended that he summons the help of Imam which Kore did; it would be a decision that he would live to regret.

Unlike other people in his profession that Kore knew from his childhood days, this Imam looked quite different, both in terms of the way he was dressed and in his manners.

His head was covered in checked black and white coloured garment, favoured by Arabs. He wore a Punjabi type of dress - a long-brown shirt coming down to his knees, and a pair of baggy trousers. He looked gloomy, and was far from being friendly. He had a big beard that didn't sit well on his narrow-shaped face.

Though he was not an Arab, he had a peculiar Arabic name; he called himself Abu Hamza. He was accompanied by two male-assistants, both dressed like him. The two men were of the same age as the Imam's; they were in their early forties.

Hadio served tea and pastries before the meeting got underway. After gulping down copious amounts of tea, and had eaten loads of pastries, the Imam didn't waste time. The team had assembled in the sitting room, which looked too small to hold the number of the people inside the room. The two assistants sat in one of the sofa set, leaving the other sofa set free for Kore and the Imam to sit in. Hadio sat on a chair, set apart from the crowd.

It was a Saturday afternoon. The children, who saw their sitting room getting crowded by strange looking men, left the room begrudgingly. They had been waiting to watch their favourite wildlife show on the TV.

"What has brought us here today," the Imam said, as he addressed both Kore and Hadio, "is a need to discuss your marriage problems."

Now directing his gaze specifically at Kore, he said, "Considering your wife's desperate desire to have a divorce, I shall not waste my time in asking her to change her mind."

He posed briefly, took a long look at Kore as if to determine the impact his statement has had on him. A moment later, as he went on with his speech, he said, "You are young enough to raise another family of your own, if you wish."

That statement has had quite a demoralising effect on Kore; hence, from that moment on, Kore had started having doubts about the man's intentions. The Imam, on his part, it seemed, was not bothered with a look of disappointment in Kore's face, which he must have assumed to be a normal reaction, coming from someone not willing to face the truth.

"In case your wife decides to leave, you will have no one to blame but yourself" he told Kore in a disparaging tone. He added, "You did let her get away with everything. Look at how she is dressed up. By not putting on an Islamic garment, she is walking almost half-naked, and by not admonishing her, you thought that you were doing the right thing. Well, you are wrong. Deep in the recesses of your mind, you have always known yourself to be wrong. Unfortunately, you have been lacking the courage to act."

He stopped, took a short pose and then went on with his speech. "You would probably like to say in your defence that you had no other alternative except to act in the way that you did, but I would beg to differ with you. I believe you had a choice that you deliberately let it to slip through your fingers; today, as a result, you are overwhelmed with a feeling of both regret and remorse."

Though Kore felt somewhat furious, he decided to remain calm; after all, was not he who had invited the man to his apartment? The Imam had not forced himself into his sitting room.

Filled with a sense of conviction, the Imam went on with his speech. Addressing Kore further, he told him, "You are not a coward, but your actions seem like that of a coward. Like a coward, you seem to easily resign to your fate, whose seemingly awesome disposition disarms your ability to act positively. Do not forget that your future lies in the Hands of Almighty God, you seem to have forsaken lately."

Following that statement, his assistants shouted in Arabic, "Allahu Akbar" (God is great in English.) He gave his assistants a triumphant smile, took a short breath afterwards, and then went on with his speech.

He said, "I have been noticing with much regret that none of your family members, including yourself, has ever visited the mosque, from where you could draw some spiritual benefits. Come to the mosque, and do not forget to bring the children along with you. In saying your prayers at the mosque, you will not be alone; you will be in a company of other people, who will help to lighten the burden of disappointment that you are carrying in your heart and mind. You can't afford to stand outside the community of people, and still manage to survive in this God-forsaken harsh social environment. Try us, and you will never regret."

Then as he kept on speaking, his eyes fell on a large-sized golden frame bearing Kore's PhD, embossed in golden letters, hanging in one of the walls in the room. He got up and approached the wall slowly to have a closer look at the certificate. He let his eyes rest on the certificate; for a moment, he stayed quiet; he looked at the certificate as if he meant to assess its worthiness.

Addressing Kore, finally, while pointing to the certificate, he said, "Here is the badge of your shame. How dare you display this despicable object for everybody to see it openly? To me, it seems that you are proud of that certificate, which is nothing but a mere piece of paper.

What, if I may ask you, do you have to show for it? Though I don't have fancy looking papers in the walls of my home, yet I live better than you will ever do. See how miserable your apartment looks. I live in a house, a real house; not anything like this shack that you are living in.

He took a brief pause, but later went on with his speech that Kore considered to be a malicious speech.

"For your information," he said, "I have more personal cars than I know what to do with them. Do you have any car? No, you don't. Do you want to know why I have everything while you have nothing? Well, I have them all because I am not like you; I am different.

In your case, you want to be like them; in fact, you die to be like them; but you know what? They won't let you. Knowing how much you want to be like them, they had created an illusion for you to pursue. They had told you to go get their education, believe in what they believe in, dress up like them, eat like them, think like them, and speak like them.

As he spoke, he never kept to one place. He paced the ground in the little room, back and forth, which had the effect of irritating Kore. He could tell him to stop pacing the ground and would have pushed him out of his apartment, but realised doing such a thing would make him look silly.

He invited the man to come to his house, after all; what this man is doing, he had been doing it to other people, who gave value to his speech; it seems he is used to giving such malevolent form of speeches, it occurred to Kore; he enjoyed tormenting people while hiding behind his title of Imam.

To think he can do all of this, and still get paid for it, made him to believe he could do anything he wants to people; it is obvious that he had little respect for people he has been dealing with. Kore decided he was not going to be among the people he disrespects, but for today, and only today, he would let him have a field day; from that moment, Kore closed his mind to what the man was saying; to Kore he was as good as dead; he didn't exist. He let him go on with his idiocy.

"They promised," he went on with his speech, "to let you join their society if you will succeed in any one of them. You have succeeded in all of them, contrary to their expectations. However, have they allowed you to join their society? No; they haven't. Have they given an office for you to hang your Ph.D. certificate? No; they haven't. Have they give you a job to enable you to take care of your family and become a proud man? No. they haven't.

Moreover, what is quite sad about this whole sordid state of affairs is that it matters to them little that you have succeeded in gaining what to them is a highest level of education one can acquire. In this way, what they had intended to be an illusion for you to pursue forever, it is no longer an illusion, because you have managed to transform that sense of illusion into a reality; after all, now you have a "nice piece of paper" to show what you are capable of.

Besides, you are as good in their language as any of them can be. Like them, you eat potatoes more than you eat rice and mutton, which is the staple diet of your people; ice hockey is your favourite game now, not football. Do you drink beer? Yes, why not? Hell, you are more Swedish than the Swedish themselves.

Despite all the above-mentioned achievements you have to your credit, no one has given you a recognition that is due to you. If you still wonder why this has happened to you, you will do well to remember that illusion by any other name remains what it is. You see, my friend, as far as the people to whom you have been addressing yourself are concerned, there is a thin line dividing what is illusion from what is not.

Now that you have called their bluff, what is it going to be next; tell me? You may wish to try again, but you will fail, once more. Mark my words: it is not you, but they who determine when the rule of the game needs changing. They are past masters in the art of POLE SHIFTING. People like you often are caught up on the wrong side of the game. I pity you. If I were you, I would throw that piece of paper into the dustbin, or else post it to its source of origin."

He briefly stayed quiet, which made Kore to believe that the man had run out of steam. What Kore didn't know was that the pose was meant to give him a chance to take a breath and to plan his next step.

"Let me add by reminding you," he suddenly said to the disappointment of Kore, "although your present circumstances may seem quite pitiful, yet all is not lost to you. See; you have children that you can save from falling into the same trap that you have fallen into. Bring the children to us in the mosque; they need instructions in the way of Allah; they will receive their instruction in Arabic; once they are qualified enough, they will receive further instructions in one of the Muslim world's most prestigious universities in any Muslim Arabia country. Think, the choice is yours"

For the first time, he asked his assistant to get him some water to drink, from the tap. He said he didn't trust the food habit of the family. If so, Kore wondered, why he didn't have any objection to consuming several gallons of tea and tons of pastries when it had been offered to him?

"The problem with you is that you never could grasp the reality, even if it was shown to you. Here is the thing." he said with full vigour, as if he drew nourishment from the water he just drank. "We are living," he went on, "in a multicultural society, with all the benefits this entails. But you, you have failed to take advantage of living a multicultural life. You have crossed the cultural boundary line; you left your side of the boundary, hoping you will benefit from the grass you assume is greener on the other side of your boundary line.

Me, on the other hand, I keep to my side of the cultural boundary line. My kids go to a school, paid for by the government, which we independently run, where we teach our children something about their religion; they cover up, and everything is taught to them in absolute terms; they never argue whether God exists or not; he exists; a man knows his place in a society, so does the woman, boys and girls are taught not to mix on any occasion.

You, on the other hand, have been taught to believe that a woman is equal to a man except, in your case, it is not true. In your case, your wife, earning a living for the family, is better than you without a job. What do you have to say? Nothing, I guess. Everything means nothing to you, because you have been blinded by following a falsified knowledge that you have been taught to believe in, which you have internalised, and it has led you to a dead end now. There you are. For you, there is no help coming; soon everything will be lost to you – your wife, your children and maybe even your life."

The taunting was too much for Kore to bear. Hence, he told him, "You have said enough, now go."

The Imam chuckled and said, "I know what goes inside your mind. You wish you could do something to hurt me for telling the truth, but you can't, because you are afraid to get into the police book of record.

Just like a newly born baby, you have no any criminal record: yes, you have never cheated any one; you have never stolen from any one, you didn't fight with any one; you have never defrauded any bank of its money. You are the epitome of good citizen. The question is: what has that made you? You have been caught in a web of lies fed to you by those who you admire, but for you they have no admiration; in fact, they despise you."

After a short pause, he went on with his speech that seems not to have an end. "If you wonder why I am brutal in my speech, it is because I want to be truthful to you, and because I follow the dictate of my religion that exhorts me to preach the truth, even if that truth is a bitter to those upon whom the truth is told."

With a tired look on his face, Kore stared at the man. He had nothing to say to him; by claiming that they were different, the man had closed all avenues for carrying out any meaningful conversation between them; Kore felt that having a conversation with him would be like a conversation taking place between a deaf and a dumb. He wished he would get over with it, and leave him to his misery.

No sooner had he finished addressing Kore then the Imam set his focus on Hadio

Addressing Hadio he said, "You are not the only woman in this community of ours wishing to have a divorce. Others before you did the same thing. However, in your case, because of what you wish to do after the divorce, you are different. I do understand, after divorcing your husband you wish in the name of love to cross religious, racial and cultural borderlines to unite with a man you wish to be with."

As he was getting ready to go on with his speech, Hadio told him in relation to what he just said to her, "What I wish to do with my life is my own business. Furthermore, I do not take kindly to your insinuations about my intentions regarding who I wish to be associated with."

Coming from a woman, the statement caused a shockwave among those present in the meeting. As a result, one of the Imam's assistants requested Hadio to remain calm, and show some respect for the Imam who had her interest at heart, he said.

The aggressive Imam wasn't going to let his zealous spirit to be subdued by the brief tumult that he would soon brush aside as an incident of lesser meaning to him; and so, he went on with his speech.

"Should someone listen to me speaking," he said, "he or she could easily accuse me of arrogance against people of other religious and cultural beliefs; however, nothing could be far from the truth, for I have great respect for all religions, races and cultures of the world. In fact, I have so much respect for each of them that I sing in praise of the God, who has created them and kept them that way i.e. different."

He had a habit of blinking his eyes, which drove Hadio mad each time he did it.

She found the respect that initially she had been having for him diminishing in her, just as her hatred for him grew in volume, with each single time that he blinked his eyes. She felt like telling him to stop blinking his damn eyes or get out of her apartment, which she had a feeling she was going to do it, given his speech that was devoid of any respect.

"With reference to what I have just said about God's creative mind, who are you to try change the order of things, as pronounced by God?" He told Hadio. A brief moment of silence followed, at which point he took a look at his assistance to assess their reaction; afterwards, he said, "Is this not what you wish to do? You have a dream of crossing cultural and religious borderline in search of a strange love? Repent, and you will have the blessings of God," he said with poise.

That statement was too much for Hadio to bear. Consequently, she stood up, ready to leave.

As she moved away from the sitting room, the voice of the Imam followed her.

"Don't take the leap." He was saying. "Stick with your own kind," he added.

He took a short breath, turned once again to look at his assistants, blinked as usual, and then went on with his speech.

"Your husband, as a jobless person," he shouted, "has never been taking good care of you. As such, according to the Sharia law, you could set yourself free from the marriage contract that binds you to him. If you could come to the mosque, we would arrange a marriage for you to join in a holy matrimony with someone - someone who can take good care of you."

At this point, Hadio quite abruptly turned around, took brisk steps towards him, and gave him a contemptuous look. She was no longer exhibiting a sign of anger. She approached him slowly; her lips had a slight twist that appeared like a frozen smile.

"You act more like a pimp that you are," she told him, "than a religious leader you are claiming to be. What a hypocrite you are! It is well and good for you personally, as well as your family members, to cross the so-called religious and cultural borderline to seek a living in this country, whose people you hate and despise. Why are you here then, if I may ask you? Why do you wish our young ones to be sent away from home, while it is no secret your children are somewhere here?

You said that you have a big house and many cars. Who gave them to you? Tell me. Since you are not skilled in anything, and have no job worth talking of, all that I know is that you might have cheated someone into giving you what you have. I fear you are one of those people, having got married to four women in secret, live off their income.

Take a look at yourself. See how you are dressed. You are a confused man. You seek power over other people. You are worse than a fascist. I doubt if you are a truly religious man you are claiming to be. From what institution of learning have you qualified to bear the title you are claiming to have?

The community needs to wake up to your destructive and wicked ways. If what you are claiming is true about yourself, where is a sense of compassion, understanding, humility and kindness in you? You are the type of a person spreading poison in the name of religion and culture. I don't want to see you here. Get out of my house." This heated discussion, which had sent emotions soaring high, brought the meeting to the end.

Meanwhile, as the Imam was contemplating leaving the room, his eyes fell on the pastries on the table; with unbridled enthusiasm, he ordered one of his assistants to pick them up for him.

"Moreover," he said, "while you are at it, don't forget to break the crockery. It is a small price she must pay for insulting me."

The Imam noticed in his assistant a sign of hesitation and forcefully told him, "Do it."

The assistant did what he had been ordered to do. Soon the three men were on their way out, laughing their heart out.

While this shameful spectacle was taking place, not knowing what else to do, Kore stayed quiet.

# Chapter Thirty One

# *A Change of Circumstances*

Every morning Hadio went to her office, at downtown Uppsala, to work; she never returned home before six in the evening. To her, it seemed, the office was the only place she could have a peace of mind. He, on the other hand, had mixed feelings about their marriage. Such was their marriage-life that their separation had seemed quite inevitable. However, Kore was taken by surprise when the separation took place.

One evening day, accompanied by Shifo, Hadio came from work looking quite tired. Following a brief exchange of greetings with Kore, daughter and mother went in the bathroom to refresh, changed into new clothes, and thereafter went to join Kore for the dinner that he had prepared. At the dinner table, between Hadio and Kore, one of them would say something, not to address each other, but their daughter.

Quite abruptly, and to the surprise of both Hadio and Shifo, Kore banged his fist on the table, and said, "I am tired of everything in this country."

Throwing what amounted to a wicked glance at Hadio, he said, "I am tired of you; I am tired of this town; I am tired of people pretending they are nice to me, when I know they are not. I am tired of eating potatoes every single day of my life." He used so much energy to express himself that he got out of breath, and so he remained quiet.

Hadio took a look at Kore; slowly, in a measured tone, she told him, "You know what? All the shouting you are making about this and that ever since the family arrived here, it is all because you have failed to get a special recognition you had been accustomed to getting at home."

A look of surprise showing in his face, Kore managed to say in reply, "What do you mean?

"I mean, in this country, you can't be the same person that you had been once, back home. Can't you see it?" She said.

"I don't understand," Kore said.

"Circumstances have changed; you need to change with circumstances. By complaining as often as you have been doing, it is not going to change anything; if anything, it would make only matters look worse for you," she told him.

"What do you propose that I should do? Take a heavy load and stay quiet? I am not a donkey," he said.

"I didn't say you are one," she said.

"You don't need to say anything. Action, they say, speak louder than words. You need to stop finding fault with me. In your opinion, I am always saying and doing thing that are not right. Oh! Wait. I know what your answer is going to be," he said.

"What?" Hadio asked

"A change of circumstances is obviously what you are having in your mind. Don't you?"

"Indeed. I wish you could change," she said.

"I am not a larva that changes into a caterpillar; I am a human being. I don't change; I adapt," he shouted back.

"You are quite ridiculous. You play with words. I have had enough," she said and prepared to leave. She reminded Shifo, her daughter, not to forget to do her homework. The food remained on the table, almost untouched. With a kind of quarrelling taking place, at the dinner table, none of the family members had any appetite for the food left in them.

As soon as her mother left, not speaking a word to her father, Shifo left.

Kore was left sitting alone in the dining room, feeling miserable. A moment later, he took the dishes to the washbasin, cleaned them and then kept them inside the cupboard; the food he kept inside the fridge.

From the kitchen he went to the sitting room, which also had acted as a sleeping room for him; there he sat down to read one of the four Vilhem Moberg's books on migration that he had started reading.

From the time in the history of mankind when a few people took first steps out of Africa, the history of humanity has become one of migration, he believed. Kore felt that in telling the story of Swedish mass migration to the USA, which took place in mid-nineteenth century, Moberg, the most prominent of all Swedish writers on migration, had succeeded in capturing one such episode in the annals of human history of migration. He wondered whether any of the people that left for America ever had managed to return to Sweden.

At this point, he let his mind to focus on the migrants currently living in Sweden, and had a similar thought crossing his mind about them. Just a few days ago, he had helped bury a friend; before that he had been to a marriage ceremony, and before that he had been to a hospital, where his friend's wife gave birth to a baby boy. He tried to imagine what significance those three events could have on his understanding of life, and had realised those events represented the circle of life taking place right in front of his eyes.

When such a circle of life becomes a common thing in the lives of the migrants, it could imply only one thing to the migrants; it means their current home has ceased to be a place of sojourn, to be abandoned at will. It has become a permanent home - for good or worse.

The possibility that he was going to stay in Sweden for good made him sit up; a shudder went through him; he found hard to imagine what life would be like for him in Sweden without Hadio.

Although he had given Hadio all his respects, other than sharing a physical intimacy with her, he didn't share any of his other intimate feelings with her - his fears, his dreams or his love for her - those he had kept to himself.

"You don't appreciate what you have until it is gone," is one maxim that had made sense to him now, when he could do little to change his fate, as far as his relationship with Hadio is concerned. He wished he had done more to reveal his feelings to her.

It is strange how people fail to benefit from such treasure-trove of wisdom available in all maxims until it is too late, he thought. His fear was that it was too late already for him to alter the course of events in his favour. He couldn't forget the look of hatred Hadio had given him, as she left to go to her room, a moment ago.

He had read several pages from one of Moberg's books, but found that he wasn't concentrating enough on the contents of the book to make heads or tails of what he was reading; and so, he shut the book, and gave a sigh of despair. For a long time, he just sat on a chair, thinking of nothing else but his wife, Hadio.

On the table, in front of him, in a wooden frame, was Hadio's photograph, taken on their wedding day. Hadio, in a white wedding dress, waving her arms, looking at him with loving eyes, a Mona Lisa's type of smile crossing her face, now seemed like a dream.

One thought of Hadio had led to another one until he could think of nothing else. He thought of many delightful moments the two of them had spent together, sharing a physical intimacy quite so passionate in nature that both felt the act was not devoid of a meaningful spiritual significance to them.

However, as he sat in his study room thinking of Hadio, matters of a spiritual nature now were off his mind. He thought, instead, of Hadio's physical attributes - tall, dark-brown complexioned, long proportional limbs and a large bust; Hadio was a sight to behold.

With thoughts of Hadio deepening in his mind, the cravings for her physical intimacy also grew in him. At that moment, the image that he had been having of her, in his mind, was of Hadio dressed in a white silky sleeping-gown, as she lay on her stomach, clutching at the pillow, sleeping a blissful sleep. That thought caused the rate of his heart-beat to raise a notch higher in his chest-cavity. He admonished himself, consequently, for feeding his mind such intimate thoughts about Hadio that would never materialise.

Nevertheless, he recollected a time when reconciliation had seemed impossible, following a quarrel between them, yet there was nothing even then which could stop them from getting intimate - physically. In the past, they had soothed each other's feelings with kisses after they quarrelled, to be followed by an act of lovemaking, the intensity of which had never failed to surprise them both. The possibility that, after all, such prospect was not a staff made up of a dream gave fillip to the resolve in him to visit Hadio's room.

Once he got there, he carefully pushed the door to the room wide open. Despite the dim light shining in the room, it took five brisk steps for him to get to Hadio's bed, where he witnessed Hadio's sleeping figure, silhouetted against the dim-light of the room. He sat on the edge of the bed, next to Hadio, thinking of what to do. Now that he was there in the room, Hadio asleep, the reality of the situation that he got himself into dawned in his mind, in all its force.

It was clear to him that getting into Hadio's room, at the dead of night, was tantamount to committing a crime; in the legal parlance that crime is known as "invasion of privacy." Going a step further by touching her body without her permission is yet another crime, known as "attempted rape." Does he want any of these charges brought against him?

He stood up, thinking of sneaking away, when he heard Hadio's voice. "What are you doing in my room?" She was saying.

Kore felt like a child caught with his hand in a cookie jar. He felt ashamed; he had nothing intelligent to say, and so he offered a sheepish smile that failed to impress Hadio.

"You haven't been inside this room, all of these past months. I think you have no reason to be here now." Hadio said; she half raised herself, leaned on her right elbow and gave him a serious look.

"I wanted to let you know how much I miss you. I wish to be close to you again," Kore said sincerely.

"Despite all the quarrels taking place between us," Hadio said in her usual measured tone, "I have not lost my respect for you. But that is quite another issue, altogether. The fact is I have reached a point that you and I cannot stay as a wife and a husband."

If Kore had a dream of one day getting reconciled with Hadio, that statement had confirmed the worst in his mind. He panicked; for a second, he almost lost his sense of concentration, but recovered soon after.

Throwing pride to the wind, he said, "But I love you with all my heart. Would you not give me a second chance? I could correct my mistake. It is not impossible, you know."

"No, Kore; you are not in love with me; you are in love with yourself. Ever since the day we arrived here, you have been talking about yourself; you have been making constant complaints about one subject after another - all of them having something to do with you.

You never had time to sit and talk with me about us; to me, you have never uttered before the word, 'I love you.' You have been taking me for granted, I am afraid. I don't think there is anything which is substantial enough for you and me to discuss about. Please, go away," Hadio said almost angrily.

Taking cue from what Hadio had said, Kore left the room quietly; he entered his room and went straight to his bed to lie down, thinking of nothing special. The feeling of hopelessness was so overwhelming that he could not make sense out of anything.

At sunset of the following evening, Kore waited eagerly for Hadio and the children to get back home. To his surprise, no one turned up home. Later at night, he discovered a piece of note on the night-table, left by his wife, stating that she had decided to leave him, and that steps were underway to formalise their separation, after Christmas holidays.

What Kore didn't know was that Hadio had moved in with Peter and had taken the children away. After reading the note, he went to drink his sorrows in a pub; later, when it was late at night, he went back home.

A week later, he received a letter from the housing agency asking him to vacate the premises. The Social Welfare Office found him a single room, in a building with long corridor, where youths considered to be juvenile delinquents also had their rooms there.

# Chapter Thirty Two

# 1993
## *Ombudsman and Labour Office*

A month later, Kore received a letter requesting him to visit Uppsala District Court. The court, he was informed in a letter he received, would determine between him and Hadio who should have the custody of the children. Kore was so much overwhelmed with joy that tears lingered in his eyes when he met his children, at the premises of the courtroom, and had the opportunity to hug them.

Dressed in a splendid looking green skirt, a blouse, a black leather jacket reaching down to her waist, Hadio looked beautiful. Hadio took a look at Kore and then nodded at him. Accompanying her was Peter in a grey corduroy suit; he had a grave look on his face; his round small face presented a great contrast to the rest of his burgeoning body.

Hadio asked the children to get back to her; the children obeyed her rather reluctantly. The damp grey weather had added to Kore's feelings of distress that had been compounded by a lack of sleep; he felt weak.

The courtroom, to his relief, Kore discovered, lacked some of the most forbidding looks of a normal courtroom. There was a long table at the middle of the room, at the head of which sat the judge. Kore and his lawyer sat on one side of the table. Hadio and Peter, accompanied by their lawyer, sat on the other side of the table. The children sat in separate chairs; both looked nervous.

Ingrid, from the Social Welfare Office, was also present in the court-room.

Presently, the court was declared open by a judge who seemed to be in her thirties; she was slightly-built, but had an energetic look; she reminded the court the reason for which the court was taking place, which was to determine between the contending parties (she mentioned their names) who should have the right to the custody of the children. Afterwards, she invited lawyers representing both sides of the case to put their case forward.

After spending a long period of time, resting his case, finally the young-looking lawyer representing Kore, whose lack of vigour in his body and action gave impression of someone with health impairment, said in a weak voice, "Your honour, my client is a good citizen; he has a deep respect for the laws of this country. His lack of gainful employment, therefore, should not be used as a reason for denying him the custody of his children; his present circumstances, after all, are not one of his own making. Besides, he has a deep love for his children; he loves them dearly, and they love him too. The children will miss him, if taken away from him."

At this point, Shifo stood up and ran to her father, hugged him and started crying.

"Let no one, Your Honour, break this bond of love," the lawyer shouted, pointing to Shifo clinging to her father.

Meanwhile, facing Shifo, the court guard requested her to return to her sit; tears falling down her face, she returned to her seat reluctantly.

Hadio's lawyer, a middle-aged man, tall, with a pronounced stoop, said as he addressed the court, "Your Honour, let no one in this court get influenced by the argument presented here by my colleague." He posed to give a look at Kore's lawyer before going on with his speech.

"That argument," he said, "was nothing short of a ploy, meant to mix facts with fiction."

He made a shifting movement as if he was intending to get up but then suddenly settled firmly in his chair.

"Your Honour," he said confidently, "it doesn't matter under what circumstances the father of the children has been rendered jobless. The fact remains that he is jobless. This is a court of law; the facts count more than anything else, here. In the case before us, the facts presented here do not favour giving to the father the custody of the children due to his position of joblessness, which I am afraid to say would render him unable to take care of his children well.

As a matter of fact, if it was not for the support he is getting from the Social Welfare Office, this poor man would have lived quite a miserable life. As for the question concerning circumstances under which he has become jobless, that is an issue to be addressed either to the Labour Office or the office of the Ombudsman for Discrimination, both of which offices have no bearing on what is going on here, at this moment."

That statement had made Kore feel quite angry. Subsequently, he abruptly stood up, and while repeating the words Ombudsman and Labour Office, in a mocking shouting tone, he gave the lawyer a sharp disgusting look. Everybody in the courtroom remained silent. His lawyer tried to plead with him to get seated, but to no avail.

In an anguished voice, albeit full of contempt for Hadio's lawyer, he said, "What do you know about either one of the agencies you have just mentioned? You know nothing, because you have had no reason, whatsoever, to set your legs in either one of them. Having your little certificate from the school of law tucked into your brief case, you were immediately sent to the courtroom; while there, you were made to fight cases with no any sort of impediments placed in your way.

You see, Mr Lawyer, there was no any reason, whatsoever, for you to have to waste your precious time by running to the Labour Office in search of a job. As for the so-called office of Ombudsman for discrimination is concerned, it has nothing to do with people like you, for whom the word Ombudsman is a mere concept; its finer points being merely a subject of theoretical speculations."

Now he was breathing heavily. He felt sharp pain in his chest; he was sweating profusely, and his head felt heavy. It was quiet in the room; for a short while, he remained quiet. Hadio's lawyer, fidgeting with papers in his hands, pretended he was unaware of what was going on in the court room.

Kore continued with his speech.

"Moreover, the idea that a country should have the office of Ombudsman for Discrimination is quite a commendable feat," he said sharply. "Yet, in this country," he added, "I doubt whether it measures up to its declared intention. Allow me to refresh your minds, ladies and gentlemen. Do you know, just last year alone, there were more than one thousand two hundred and ninety cases of discrimination that had been forwarded to this office for action? How many of them had resulted in a remedial action taken? I don't know; you tell me."

He would have gone on, and on, with his diatribe, had he not been dissuaded by his daughter's face that was soaked in tears. He sat down after that.

The judge requested Ingrid from the Social Welfare Office, who was present in the courtroom, to say a few words. She stood up and thanked the judge; she gave Kore a nasty look and started to address the court.

Kore was not expecting Ingrid to be in the court house. He didn't expect Ingrid to put a nice word for him now; if anything, from the way she had been dealing with him, he felt he had every reason to expect the worse to happen. In the courtroom, she cast unfriendly look at him, after every while.

"Your Honour," she said, "I have known this family from the day they arrived here. I have been privileged to know Hadio better than her husband. Hadio is known to most of us here as someone who has made much to improve knowledge in our society, for which act most of us are grateful. Unfortunately, she has had a bad luck of having a husband who refused to cooperate with her, to build a viable happy family.

As a father, Kore has never been a good-role model for his children; for not giving support to his wife, he has brought misery to his family; and for refusing to do an honest day-work, he has become a parasite, living as he does on social welfare benefits.

While there is no any law in this country that can force someone to take up a job other than the one for which one is qualified to do, this society doesn't like when someone decides to pick and choose jobs. Here we don't do cherry-pickings with jobs. Here, society takes care of those who care for it; unfortunately, in Kore's case, he has placed himself outside the perimeters of society; and for that reason, he should bear the consequences of his actions."

For a moment she stayed quiet, but continued giving Kore a hostile look. Pointing to Kore, she said finally, "No amount of blame that he puts on the Labour Office, or the office of

Ombudsman for Discrimination, will improve his situation, which only he can do it by himself."

She finished her speech by thanking the judge, gave Kore the same nasty look and said, "Due to his irresponsible behaviour, I am asking the court to deny him the right to the custody of the children." She gave Kore one of her nasty looks again, and then resumed her seat.

As soon as she sat down, the judge made her ruling on the case.

"This court," she said, "feels that the mother of the children is the most appropriate person on whom to bestow to her the custody of the children, and this is also the opinion of the social welfare officials. She has the means and the resources at her disposals to guarantee to her children the material comfort required for their proper upbringing. The court, however, will like to recommend the right of visitation, at least once a month, if the father will choose to have his children with him."

There was smile on the face of Hadio. The children ran to their father and challenged their mother to go away without them.

# Chapter Thirty Three

# *Cave Man*

From the court-room in Kungsgatan, a pain in his heart, Kore walked alongside other people on his way to the river bank. Whenever he felt miserable, he had a habit of sitting on a stone-bench by a river side, to rest and reflect on life. Today, as usual, it was cold, damp and grey, yet Kore wouldn't allow the weather to discourage him from his intention.

People have a way of finding in something a solace to help ease the feelings of suffering in them. For some, it means watching a film show - in fact, there are two cinema-houses, standing just opposite where he was sitting, across from the river and the road; to achieve the same objective, other people would listen to music or read a book; still others find solace in either taking a drink, or, at worst, a drug.

Less than two weeks ago, sitting on the same stone-bench, by the same river-bank, Kore had given thought to the idea that if there was a single object binding him in what could be a possible common shared human experience with both present and past inhabitants of this city, that object is Fyris Ån river that cuts through Uppsala.

From his river-bank reflections, Kore was able to have a better understanding of the Vikings; not the Vikings who fought and won multitudes of victories against their enemies; not the Vikings who established trading centres in far off places; not even the Vikings who discovered new continents, but the Vikings who did things that other ordinary human being could do, such as making song in praise of this river; fish in it; swim in it; set sail through it; drink from it; use its water to cook food and even die in it, all of which things the Vikings did with the river, during their time.

Sitting on the same stone bench, by the same river bank, today, two weeks later, Kore had let his mind to focus on those features that a river and a human being share in common, and was stunned by what he discovered. The river, it occurred to him, like a human being, has the beginning and the end. Whereas a river comes to life from out of mother-earth womb, from out of a woman-womb comes a human child. During a life-long journey to its destination, like a human being, a river goes through different stages. When a river is young, like a young person, it is known for its agility and speed; in its middle passage, like a middle-aged person, it is strong and full of energy, and toward the end of its life, like an old person, the river becomes large - its movements cumbersome, ponderous and slow. While the river flows toward its destination, becoming one with the sea, thus achieving nirvana, how does the human being achieve nirvana?

Today, Kore was not willing to contemplate the fate of humanity, since the nature of his problems had overwhelmed his capacity to feel at one with other human beings.

He felt drops of sweat forming in his brows, despite the cold wind blowing relentlessly across him. He felt strange how he could feel warm and feel cold quite at the same time. It was quite a strange feeling, one that he never had before. He stood up and started taking a walk, but feeling tired, he felt he should rest by sitting down somewhere. He thought of a restaurant, and decided to get into a nearest one for a cup of coffee.

At the entrance to the restaurant, emblazoned in a neon light, he saw the name of the restaurant that read, "Meal at Nadir's." He needed to check for money in the pocket of his jacket to see if he had enough money to buy him a cup of coffee; he felt cold. Whether the feeling was due to the cold weather or the hunger pangs he couldn't tell. It was launch time.

The restaurant was filled with the noise of customers; some were busy placing their orders, while others were enjoying meals with their friends. As he was approaching a vacant seat in the restaurant, he had a cunning feeling that he had been there once before, and then suddenly he remembered.

He remembered the short man with hair painted blond, his eyes looking blue from wearing contact lenses. Despite the camouflage, Kore had been able to tell from his facial features that he was a non-ethnic Swede; he was an immigrant, who was trying to pass for a Swedish person. He recollected how the man became agitated the moment that he asked to be served a cup of coffee.

"What is wrong with you black donkeys? Don't you have eyes? Can't you see we are serving lunch now?" The man had told him, looking quite agitated.

He had said the words, "black donkey," in a language which Kore knew something about.

"If I am a black donkey, what does that makes you? A brown donkey, should we say?" Kore had said sarcastically in reply.

That response had forced the man to look down - a gesture which Kore had interpreted to mean that he had felt embarrassed, knowing that the secret had come out.

It didn't take long, however, before the man recovered from his state of embarrassment, after which he had said aggressively, "I am Nadir, the owner. I can call you anything I want."

The quarrel taking place between the two men must have attracted the attention of some of the diners who watched the spectacle secretly, from their positions.

"You know what; you remind me of the pot calling the kettle black, if you know what I mean," Kore had shouted.

" What do you mean," the man had said, looking lost.

"Oh, forget it. Remember, here in Sweden, you are not allowed to speak from both sides of your mouth. You, and your kind, often complain about racial discrimination that you are alleging have been directed at you, here in this country, yet you wish to practice the same discrimination on me. In this country, you are nothing. This is Sweden. Go back to your home country, and feel free to be a racist that you are," Kore had shouted, a morbid feeling of hatred for the man building up in him. "And by the way," he added after a moment of reflection, "Don't come to me for solidarity when the racists turn up heat on you."

"I am not going to soil my arms fighting you. I am calling the police," the man had said.

Kore had given the man a single look and had felt pity for him. To avoid having further altercation with the man, he had left the premises, shortly after.

This time around, however, he was met by someone who seemed quite friendly. The man took great pain to personally offer Kore the service he needed. Kore took his cup of tea and then left.

It was the end of the autumn season. Outside, it was cold, and the skies were overcast. Kore didn't know what else to do, and so he went to sleep in his little room, and woke up late in the evening, feeling hungry. Lately, because of a tight budget, he was not eating well.

Apart from the room rent separately paid for by the Social Welfare Office, a mere two hundred and fifty dollars, equivalent in Swedish Kronas, meant to cover the cost of food and other expenses, paid through the same office, required that he used the money quite judiciously. This had meant that he could ill-afford to consume nourishing foods, such as meat, milk and fruits.

Whenever the subject of food entered his mind, Kore could not help thinking of the large amounts of foods that once had been available to him, at his former refugee camp, and how little of it he had eaten. Also, for some unknown reason, every time he reflected on his former life, at the camp, his mind would never fail to conjure up the image of a big Pole who had a prodigious appetite for food; the big Pole's single major dream had been to be a bus driver, one day. Did he succeed in his dream? He could; who knows?

Kore walked through the corridor aiming to get to the kitchen; in the kitchen, he brushed shoulders with young people of different nationalities. He was living in a hostel reserved for youths with immigrant background. All were considered to be juvenile delinquents.

In a symbolic way, that trip to the kitchen had spoken volume to him about his life. At his age, he looked too old when compared to people around him, whose lives were at the stage of a take-off. To them he must have looked as ancient as a dinosaur; he thought that was how they judged him to be until he overheard them speak about him, unaware of his presence.

There were two boys (aged no more than 25), on this occasion, talking to each other. One of them had said about him, "The old man is a funny man. I don't like him."

"Why don't you like him?" the other boy had asked.

"He ignores people; he doesn't talk to anyone; he doesn't greet anyone; it is as if we don't exist in the same world as his," he had said.

The other boy chuckled and had said in reply, "You got it right. We are not living in his world. He is living in old people's world. He is a cave man." After that they laughed.

Had they compared him to a dinosaur, he would have perceived their statement to be merely a metaphor, and forget about it; however, in calling him cave man, that had made his age look real old; in his early-forties, he felt that he had become too old.

At that moment, it had occurred to Kore that old-age is one thing quite hard for the young to form a concept about; for the young, old age is only for the old. But for the old, the time-frame separating those two sets of ages is so short that most of them don't believe they have lived through it. If only the young could figure out how short life is, they would look at the world around them with a sober mind and a sense of humility, Kore had imagined.

He opened his little cupboard to retrieve a box containing wheat germ and made porridge. He poured the porridge into a small bowl, and then left for his room; inside his room, he consumed the porridge with great relish. Kore had several more days left before the end of the month, which meant that he needed to go slow on the remaining money, which had also meant more porridge days, by implication.

One day, however, something happened that changed this monotonous food consumption habit of his. As he was sitting in the common kitchen, at the end of a long corridor, with rooms on either side of it, a book by his side, eating porridge, a boy with a room next to his entered the kitchen; it was six in the evening; except the two of them no one else was inside the kitchen.

"Good evening BABA," the boy said.

The boy was polite, and had been so from the very first day he met Kore. He couldn't have been more than twenty years old; he was short and well built; this was obvious from his arms that looked big; his short looking neck was attached to a broad pair of shoulders; his smile revealed an unevenly set of brown teeth

Kore kept the spoon he was using to eat the porridge in the bowl, raised his face up to look at the boy and said in a most polite manner, "Good evening to you."

Perhaps feeling encouraged by the positive response Kore gave him, the boy said, "May I sit with you? He addressed Kore in a simple Swedish he had been in the process of learning, at special classes, meant for foreigners, waiting their application for asylum to get processed.

"Sit, by all means," Kore said.

Before he could sit down, the boy went to retrieve from inside the fridge a plastic container of food. He warmed the food in the microwave. He poured the food on a plate and then sat down, facing Kore across from the table. The scent of the food wafting towards Kore might have raised his palate to a point of wanting to see what the food was made up of. Having noticed how Kore's sense of curiosity had been heightened by the sight of the food may have induced in the boy the need to invite Kore to share the food with him. The food made up of roasted chicken served with rice, brown source and eaten with salad had an enticing quality to it that Kore didn't know how to react to the invitation. If he accepted the food readily, how would the boy feel about it? Kore thought.

The boy who had seen in Kore's facial expression a sense of hesitation insisted that Kore should share the food with him.

Kore had just a split of a second to decide what he wanted to do. He hadn't had the chance to come across such food which he had been dreaming of; he threw care to the wind subsequently; he decided not to let the chance pass him; the boy can think what he wants.

The two enjoyed their meal that they shared from the single plate. When they finished eating the food, Kore took the plate to the wash basin with the intention in mind of wanting to do the washing, but the boy would not let him; he did the washing, instead. The boy made tea afterwards that they drank together.

Kore thanked the boy and left for his room, leaving the boy to sit alone in the kitchen. While inside the room, Kore thought about the boy and found him to be someone special; he was selfless, which, as a character, was hard thing to come by, in a world that Kore had lately been living in. About the boy, Kore assumed, here is someone who was hard up, like himself, and yet he is willing to share his only meal with him. Such moments had made Kore's hope for humanity rise. He got curious about the boy. Who is he? What is his name? Where is he from? Why is he in Sweden? He wanted to have answers to these questions, and thought he would talk to the boy when they next meet again.

On the following evening, the boy invited Kore to share the meal with him, once again. The one additional thing Kore had noticed about the food, this time, was the portion had become larger than the one of the previous day.

"You don't know me, and yet you have been kind to me. Why?" Kore asked the boy who he had invited him to his room.

"You are old enough to be my father," the boy answered. "Older people deserve respects, according to my culture," the boy added.

"What is your culture?" Kore asked.

"I am a Kurd from Syria. My name is Avan," the boy answered readily.

"Mine is Kore," Kore said. "I am happy to meet you, Avan," Kore said.

The boy smiled.

Further discussion had made them to reveal about themselves to each other. The boy's story about himself was no less formidable, given his young age. He told Kore that he had been born to a family of farmers. He was the last child in a family of four boys.

Like his brothers, he too had been to school, but had cut short his education to assist his father with the work in the farm. Life, he said, had been hard for his family; thanks, he said, to his uncle that had been working as a seaman in a Greek ship, who had sent them money on a regular basis, and had therefore served the family from suffering. When this uncle had finally come back home to get married, and later had left for Sweden, the fortune of his family changed for the better, he told Kore. After he had established himself in Sweden, his uncle had sent for him, he told Kore. His uncle, he said, was the owner of a hotel in Uppsala.

Less than ten months ago, while in a camp for refugees (he had applied for asylum) on a visit to a city centre, one day, he got attacked by two skin head boys that he had fought against and had resulted in one of them get badly hurt. The incident had led the authority to remove him from the refugee camp and had instead placed him there with other boys considered to be juvenile delinquents. Twice his application for political asylum had been rejected, he told Kore. Currently, he was working for his uncle, several hours a week, to avoid being in the streets, he said.

Kore saw the opportunity in this discussion to inquire from the boy if he could arrange a meeting with his uncle.

"I would like to talk to your uncle about getting me a job to do," he said. "Can you please arrange meeting for us?" Kore pleaded with the boy.

"Yes, I will do the first thing when I meet him tomorrow," the boy said.

On the following day, the boy came back in the evening with news that pleased Kore a lot.

"Azad, my uncle," the boy told Kore, "would be pleased to meet with you, early in the morning, tomorrow.

Here is a chance for him to have little extra money to buy things that he felt were going to be essential for his life. There were new books in the market that he would like to lay his hands on. His only two pairs of trousers were progressively getting worn out. His worn out pair of suit he had long discarded. Besides, winter was soon here; he couldn't rely on his old pair of jacket to see him through the winter, not to talk of his old shoes. If he could secure a job, he would tend to these needs easily, he imagined. With much enthusiasm, he looked forward to a meeting with the boy's uncle.

At eight, on the following morning, the two left for their destination. The bus they took was full of people who looked gloomy, which was not unusual for people reporting on duty on a Monday morning, anticipating a week long period of hard work, waiting for them to do. No wonder, Kore assumed, people refer to Monday as "Blue Monday." When the two reached their destination, to his utter surprise, Kore met the boy's uncle standing, waiting in the middle of the hotel foyer. As soon as the two passed through the hotel entrance, the boy's uncle moved forward to meet Kore, and offered to shake hands with him while smiling.

"I am Azad," he said.

"You are Kore," my nephew had told me about you; he said afterwards.

"Your nephew is a fine kid," Kore said.

"He better be, if he wants to remain in my good books," Azad said. The way he uttered the words while giving the boy a compassionate look, at the same time, suggested to Kore that Azad had a deep love for the boy.

If you were someone who might have seen Omar Sharif"s picture (the famous Egyptian actor) you would think, by looking at Azad, you are standing in front of a long lost twin of Omar Sharif, complete with the thick moustache and those large eyes that had the quality of mesmerising young ladies.

A moment later, placing his right arm on Kore's shoulder, Azad led the way into an office, in a place not far from the hotel foyer. Meanwhile, the boy went to attend to his business in the hotel kitchen.

"What would you like to drink," Azad asked. "I have always enjoyed a good cup of Kilimanjaro Coffee in the morning hours; I take mine black; the coffee has an excellent taste," he said with enthusiasm.

"Tea for me, please," Kore said.

Azad rang the bell and a waiter came to take their order.

The office was a small place: it had simple look. A table that stood in the middle of the room had files placed on top of it; two chairs were placed on either side of the table. On the table, there was a framed portraits of two people in a black and white colour- a man and a woman – both looking old, which made Kore to assume that they were probably Azad's parents. The light in the room shined dimly. To one side of the room, there was a single sofa that Azad and Kore went to sit in; in front of the sofa was a long wooden table.

"Avan told me much about you," Azad said. "I am sorry about everything that happened to you," he added, "Such things," he continued, "do happen often to highly educated immigrants,. I have never had the education you have. The Swedish Government knows how to deal with people like me; when dealing with you, they are lost." He took a sip from his drink and waited Kore to say something. Kore stayed quiet. He put the cup on the table and resumed his speech. "You probably know that the first immigrants to this country were industrial workers who came from the Balkan, Greece and Turkey. But since late 70's, more and more educated people from Third World Countries have found their way here, trying to escape despots out to get them. How to deal with this group of people has presented this country with great dilemma. Today in early nineties, no wonder, Sweden has the largest number of doctors, teachers and engineers working as taxi drivers in its cities.

At this point, Kore interjected and said, "I too have thought of becoming a taxi driver, but no taxi company would hire someone who has no driving license: In my case, I couldn't raise money to get me a license."

And now, Azad changed the subject and instead talked about Kore. "Avan," he said, "told me you were looking for a job to do here. I don't know what kind of job would fit your profile, and even if there was one to fit your profile I wouldn't be able to hire you. In order to hire you, I would be required, according to the rules that regulate labour laws, to satisfy many requirements that I am unable to do. But since I can't hire you officially, I would like to offer assistance to you."

Kore recoiled in horror at the word assistance; he didn't come to look for assistance; he came to look for job; he came to offer services in exchange for a pay. "What does he mean by assistance?" Kore asked himself. "Am I so helpless that the man thinks all I deserve is getting assistance from him?" He reasoned.

"I didn't come to ask for assistance," he said. "I have come to look for a job to do," Kore added.

Azad smiled and said, "While charity is not in my mind, assistance is the drive engine of individual progress. We need assistance to make headway in life." It seemed that Azad was not put off by a belligerent stance taken by Kore on the subject of assistance.

"I want you to know without getting assistance from someone I wouldn't have achieved anything," he said. "You will be surprised to know," he added, "it was a person from Africa, like you, from whom I got this assistance, and to whom I would remain indebted, throughout my life." He took a sip from his coffee and looking Kore straight in the face said, "Let me briefly tell you how I secured this assistance." Azad's statement rose a sense of anticipation in Kore, similar to one he felt when sitting around a camp fire in his village, as his grandmother prepared to tell stories.

His family's fortune had met a dramatic turn, mainly for the worse, he told Kore, the day when the loan sharks had come to reclaim the land the family had been owning, for failing to pay their debts. For the Kurdish Syrian farmers to be squeezed out from the lands they owned had been a regular thing, since they rarely had access to a bank credit that the majority of the Arab Syrians had. With no place to call home, his family, made up of his mother and father, went to live with his eldest brother, Behat, in another part of the country. Being a sharecropper, his brother had economic problems of his own; he had a wife and three children; the fourth child became Avan.

To help take the burden off Behat's shoulders, his father had looked for job at construction sites, accompanied by him. What they had earned together they had shared with the rest of the family members of his brother. His father had been grateful for having a roof over their head.

One afternoon day, a group of five elders, belonging to his clan, had sat down to discuss his future, and had reached a conclusion, in 1967, at 20 years old, he must take the burden off the family by emigrating to somewhere; Germany had been mentioned as a possible destination point. One thing however, had stood in the way of that proposition becoming a reality. He must have a passport; given his ethnicity that wasn't a Syrian Arab, getting a passport wasn't going to be easy. At the point when they had almost given up hope finding solution to the problem, someone had come up with a suggestion that had steered a hot debate in the meeting. He had mentioned Afrin, - a clan member - who had made it big in Damascus. Afrin had acted as a Chief Editor of a newspaper considered to be the mouth piece of the Syrian Government that had been under the rule of the Baath Party, led by Nureddin al Atassi.

Someone in the meeting whose name was Arman had got so agitated that he had to stand up from the chair to drive his point home. He had objected to the name Afrin, whom he had called a back-stabber.

A man in a meeting had asked Arman to sit down. This was a middle aged man in a black suit. His mode of dressing had differed from the rest of those in the meeting who had worn their male traditional costume of baggy trousers and shirts; while some had jackets over their shirts, others had vests, and all had sash tied around the waist.

Asid - this was the man's name – had directed his focus at those in the meeting; they, in turn, had looked at him, waited patiently, while anticipating what more Asid had to say to them.

Asid had told the meeting he knew Afrin well. He said he had been to University in Damascus with him. Before Asid could resume his speech, Arman had wished to know why that information should matter to them.

Someone in the meeting had asked Arman to be patient.

Asid had said in a composed manner that Afrin had not been the only soul working for the government. He too had been working for the government occupying a senior position in the city's municipality, and had he not given them assistance when required? He had asked them.

Asid had told the meeting that Afrin had come to the conclusion that his people could be served better by becoming part of the establishment. He had believed there had been nothing to gain by staying out of the system.

Asid had reminded those in the meeting that Afrin had managed to convince the rulers of Syria that instead of impoverishing the whole community of people, thus risk a large scale revolution taking place, there had been a need to have some of the Kurds feel they had a stake in the wellbeing of the state, and so the government had agreed with him. In this way, Afrin had opened up many avenues of opportunity for our people. He was a good example, he had said.

He had informed the meeting that he had been planning a journey to Damascus for the following day, and had asked Avan to accompany him. In Damascus he had said he would get Afrin to get a passport for Avan.

He had secured his passport not long after, and with it a contribution of three hundred dollar notes from Asid. The rest of the clan members had also made their contribution of five hundred dollars.

A week later, after bidding farewell to his family, from his home in Al Hassakah, he had started his journey. After a journey that had taken him through several Syrian and Turkish villages, at last, the first leg of his journey had come to end in Ankara. At a ramshackle hotel, in the Ankara old quarters, he had the chance to meet with two youngsters of his age. They had become his friend, and had spoken to him in a form of Arabic that had looked strange to him. They had given him a tour of the city, and for the first time he had enjoyed a fresh breath of freedom. Beautiful looking white women tourists, in short skate with their hair reaching down their back swinging wildly, mesmerised him.

He had developed a deep feeling of love for his friends; most of all, he had loved them for their generosity; they had been so generous that they had offered to buy him his meals. And so when they had proposed to him that Piraeus, Greece, should be a point of destination for their journey together, not Germany, he had not hesitated to agree with them. They had told him of the numerous job opportunities available on merchant ships in Piraeus port.

The proposition made to him by the boys had seemed appealing to him. He had thought of problems that he could face in Germany, looking for jobs and a place to sleep that may not be there and had despaired. Getting employment in a ship would have guaranteed both things, he had imagined.

Finally, when the time to buy the ticket had come, the boys had told him that they had bought theirs in advance, but had been ready to accompany him to buy his ticket for a journey to Piraeus that would take them via Izmir and then on to Athens and finally to Piraeus. After he had bought his ticket, the boys had convinced him to change his money into a Greek currency, and had offered to do it for him - a proposition that he had accepted without any hesitation. They had advised him to keep fifty American dollars for emergency sake. Out of the fifty dollars that he had used for his journey to Ankara, and another thirty dollars he had spent while in Ankara, as well as the fifty dollars that he had kept in his pocket, he had given Abdulla, which was the name of one of the boys, the rest of the remaining dollars to go and change them into a Greek currency.

Meanwhile he and the other boy had stayed behind, waiting inside a restaurant, at the bus station, sipping tea while they had enjoyed talking to each other about a bright future in Piraeus, which the boy had told him it was theirs to have.

The other boy, several minutes later, having excused himself, had to leave for the toilet, letting him to sit alone. Half an hour had gone by, and neither of the boys had appeared. When another half an hour had gone by and still neither of them had shown up he was convinced that he had been swindled of his money. It had been getting to be five, in the evening, and the departure time at six had been approaching precariously. Either he had to break his journey, to go after the boys, thus risk losing the chance to travel, since the departure time had been approaching fast, or accept the loss and go on with his journey. He had opted for the latter of the two possibilities.

He had taken the bus with a heavy heart, and had feared for his future. In Izmir, he had changed bus, and by a miracle he had ended up in Athens, from where he had proceeded on with his journey to Piraeus. By the time he had reached Piraeus he had not a single dollar left in his pocket. Consequently, he had gone without a single meal for two long days. On a third day, he had had enough. He had walked into a restaurant and had ordered for a lunch that in its appearance had looked similar to one at his home; the food had been made up of grilled lamb, vegetables and eaten with pita bread. The food, he had realised, hadn't differed much from that of his homeland.

He had taken his time resting in his chair, contemplating what to do, after he had finished eating the food. He could try to sneak out or present himself to the manager. He had opted for the latter. The manager, a short potbellied man, had been contemplating calling the police when a man left his table. He had spoken to the manager. That man was tall man and heavily built; he had an extra black complexion; he had been accompanied by other two black men. The tall black men had spoken to the manager in fluent Greek. As they had kept speaking to each other, the manager had fidgeted with his apron; at other times, he had used his right hand to touch the temple of his head. Azad said he had interpreted the act to mean that the manager had been accusing him of lack of sense. What the manager had no way of knowing, Azad had told Kore, was that there is no way on earth you can deny a hungry person a chance to eat, when he or she sees food.

He had not come across many black people in his life; however, Azad had heard stories told by his people who had called black people cannibals.

Finally, at the end of a long dialogue between the manager and the big man, the latter had turned his attention on him, and had spoken to him in English. When the big man had failed to elicit any kind of response from him - since he couldn't speak English - he had addressed him in Arabic; the big man and his companions were from Sudan. Later, he had spoken to his friends in a whisper, after which his friend had nodded their heads. Thereafter, the big man had dipped his hands in the pocket of his trousers and had come out with some money that he had given it to the manager. The manager had counted the money and had returned some amount of money that had been paid in access of the cost of the food.

Afterwards, the three men, accompanied by him, had resumed their position in the table; the big man had asked about his plans. He had been looking for a job, he had told them. The big main had told him that they were seamen and that their ship had just docked at the port for the purpose of loading and unloading some items. They had been scheduled to leave soon, he had told him. He had become happy when the man had told him of a vacant post in the engine room of a wiper. He could have the job, if he wished, the big man had told him. As a Chief Mechanic, he could speak for him to the Captain, if he wished to have the job, he had said. The other two men had worked as oilers. He had taken the job, which had required no prior experience. As a wiper, he had been responsible for cleaning engine room and various tools and equipments.

The three men had become more than his friends; they had taken him under their wings and had offered him protection in many ways. The big man in fact had become his guardian. Every step he had taken, he had made sure to consult with him.

After five years, the three men had retired from work and had gone back to their country, leaving him alone, but richer in experience and matured in mind.

He had gained a promotion to work as an oiler and had held the job for another five years before he too had to retire.

He had his many year's savings, amounting to thousands of English Pounds, given to him by the Captain of the ship. It was 1977 when he had set his foot back in his home, by which time he had found his father had passed away. With the money he had earned from working in the ship he had bought his eldest brother, Behat, a family house and a farm. He had got married to his first cousin, Aran, and had left his home; this time he had left for Sweden. Two years later, he had sent for his wife and together they had worked as cleaners at Akademiska Hospital.

A pizzeria was going on sale because of bankruptcy; he had bought the pizzeria which he had run it well; in due course of time, he had bought another pizzeria and another one until he had a chain of pizzerias in and around Uppsala. Once he discovered the love that the Swedes had for pizza had been waning, he had sold all his pizzerias and had branched into hotel business. Now he was the owner of a hotel in Uppsala.

Azad took a look at Kore and told him, "I had gone through the pain of telling you the story of my life to prove to you that sometimes, we need to not only give but accept assistance, just to make this world a better place to live in." He posed to take a short breath and said, "You see, I have been where you are, and so I know how you feel."

Azad kept his promise of assisting Kore. Every Friday evening Kore received a sealed envelope; kept inside was three hundred Swedish Kronas. In due course, Kore became a family friend.

# Chapter Thirty Four

# *Showdown*

Kore was grateful for the support he was getting from Azad, and didn't know how to think him enough. However, his side of the emotional problems, arising from a separation from his family, had stayed with him. He was not feeling well; he had been feeling quite weak these past few days. A throbbing headache, made worse by nagging thoughts of Hadio and the children, hadn't allowed him to have a goodnight rest.

From the day his wife had left him for another man, and had also taken the children away from him, Kore had become a changed man; he had lost faith in public institutions. He believed that the institution responsible for employment had let him down; the one responsible for legal justice had let him down, too; now he was going to the Social Welfare Office. Should he expect anything other than the usual let down?

At the end of every month, he went to keep appointment with Ingrid of the Social Welfare Office. Kore approached the office with the usual sense of trepidation. Besides the usual monthly sum for his upkeep that took him there, once every month, this time he had made up his mind to talk to Ingrid about another subject, altogether

At the Social Welfare Office, he met Ingrid waiting for him. The moment that he got inside the office, from the way Ingrid looked at him, he could tell that Ingrid was in a foul mood.

"Come, sit down," she told him.

He sat down, facing Ingrid across from the table, and then he remembered to say, "Good Morning."

She ignored his remarks; instead she said in a hurry, "Yes; what can I do for you,"

Kore never wished to waste any moment.

"If she wants is to get over with me, as quickly as possible, why deny her the chance," he thought to himself.

"I wish to have a bigger apartment." he said.

She never gave him a chance to say more.

"What do you need a bigger apartment for?" She asked in an intimidating sharp tone.

"I wish to have a bigger apartment to enable me to accommodate my children, whenever they visit me," he said feeling ill at ease.

"And how do you intend to pay for it; tell me;" she challenged him.

"I was hoping to get some assistance from your office," he said, not so convincingly.

"I am sorry to inform you that, except the cheque for your monthly upkeep, you are qualified for nothing else from this office," she said looking quite detached.

"Do you have something more to say, Mr Kore?"

"No," said Kore briefly.

"Well, then, goodbye," she said finally.

He accepted the cheque and left the office. He never wanted to argue with Ingrid. If he couldn't have a large apartment, he would try something else; he would improvise.

He bought a mattress and kept it on the floor to be used by him whenever one of the children came to visit him. It was not a most convenient arrangement, but it was the best arrangement he could think of.

One day, however, for reasons that were far removed from his control, things came to change suddenly and quite drastically.

It had all started with a football match that was to take place in Denmark, at Copenhagen's main football stadium. His son, Atosh, wanted to watch the match. Kore planned the trip, subsequently, to the smallest details. To pay for the trip, Kore had to borrow some money from someone, with high interest charged on the loan.

They were scheduled to leave on a Saturday morning, arriving at their destination in the late afternoon. A close relative of his would pick them up from the train station and take them for sightseeing, before getting them to the stadium to watch the match.

They never took the train, on the following morning, on Sunday. Kore had obliged his cousin, who wanted him to stay, so they could talk. If a day after that, which was Monday, had not been a holiday in Sweden, he would not have allowed the change of schedule to take place; a step that he would live to regret for long time.

On Monday morning, Hadio went to pick up Atosh. This time he was not standing on the pavement, outside the building, waiting for her; she panicked. Hurriedly, she drove the car to a nearby telephone-booth, from where she called Kore's telephone number. When she couldn't receive any reply, the fear of Kore taking the child away from her became real in her mind.

With that fear in her mind, she drove the car to a nearest police station, where she reported her son as missing, and told the police she feared Kore might be planning to take the child away. The police authorities launched an immediate manhunt for Kore that extended to other Scandinavian countries, including Denmark.

She let the police have Kore's and Atosh's passport-sized photos she had retrieved from her handbag.

It was nine in the morning; Kore and his son had just finished taking their breakfast of coffee and cheese sandwiches in a restaurant compartment of the train. He was on the way back to his seat (his son had left before him) when Kore thought he heard his name getting mentioned in the TV, at the restaurant's compartment. The anchor-man had just finished presenting international news; he was going through local news now. Kore stopped to carefully listen to the news. The news was given in Swedish, since they were in Swedish territory.

Kore listened carefully to the anchor man saying, "Displayed on the screen is the photograph of Kore and Atosh. Hadio, his ex-wife, fears that Kore is planning to leave the country, taking his son with him. If any one of you sees him, kindly get in touch with the police near you, immediately."

He couldn't understand what had made Hadio want to take such a drastic step; he had never given her any reason to suspect him of such a foul play. He didn't conceive such a dreadful plan and never would he ever do such a thing. He had no particular place in mind to take his son, even if he had wanted to; had she forgotten that, in his homeland, he was a fugitive from a government that was baying for his blood? He asked himself.

He looked out the window of the fast moving train and saw the sleeping hamlets, blanketed in a heavy morning mist, their lamp posts shining dimly. The empty-looking paved streets gave to the scene a ghostly appearance.

Looking at the scenery, with its grim looking features, Kore got an eerie feeling. Hollywood needs to make horror movies there, depicting a bunch of zombies chasing their victim with nowhere to hide. Kore imagined.

Back in his seat, he took a look at his son; he wanted to talk to him but thought the better of it; he let him to pursue his thoughts freely, whatever they may be.

As he was going through pages of morning newspaper, he heard someone call his name. Before he could offer any response, three large-bodied men, who turned out to be policemen, pounced on him. They bent his head, and used a large amount of force to handcuff him; the boy tried in vain to shield his father from the police by holding on to him.

Kore was taken to court, a few days later; he was charged with a crime of making attempt to kidnap his son. The slightly built judge with a shiny bold head, presiding over the case, after making a thorough review of the case, using a florid language to express his point, dismissed the case for a lack of credible evidence.

Referring to various incidents, however, in which a great number of male immigrant parents had taken their children to their original homelands, he acknowledged Hadio's fear as justifiable.

When delivering judgement, this is what he said; "While I see no evidence to suggest a crime has been committed, I am going to recommend the case to be forwarded to the family court, which has the competence and the jurisdiction to deal with such cases."

To Kore's utter shock and surprise, the case took quite a new dramatic turn after getting referred to the family court for a hearing. Incorporating the social welfare's view of Kore that referred to him as, 'compulsive, reckless and hardly responsible as a parent,' the judge overturned the court-decision, which earlier had enabled Kore to have the children with him, once every month.

In his new ruling, the judge stated the following: "Since Kore is deemed to be compulsive, reckless and unreliable, among other things, I am forbidding him to have contact with any of his children for a period of two years."

Life without his family had become a burden quite hard for Kore to bear. His daughter, he missed her more than anyone else in his family; her smile, as well as her large clear eyes, full of tender feelings for him, had a way of making him feel at peace with himself. He will miss holding her small hands, looking into her eyes, as he told her stories about himself that she so much liked to listen to.

His wife, Hadio, he missed her in a totally different way. She had never made him to feel at peace with himself, like his daughter did. With Hadio, however, they had shared a common point of reference. Hadio's presence, in his life, had reminded him of a person that he had once been in his homeland – responsible, respectful, productive and creative.

With nothing to look forward to, and the bridge connecting him to his past now severed, he felt he had nothing left for him to live for.

He wanted to visit Hadio in her office, but couldn't bring himself to do such a thing; he saw such act as a way of demeaning himself to her, and yet he couldn't get Hadio's thoughts off his mind. Then, one day, getting off bus number seven, from Gottsunda, on his way to the City Library, he thought he saw Hadio getting inside a bank.

Like many people visiting the library, the library had become an important place for him to visit. He had been visiting the library quite so regularly that about him someone might say he had become a fixture there.

Over the years, the library has performed different functions for different people.

A library is a place, accompanied by their children, parents visit once a week, to borrow or return books. But for others, it is a place where one could sit and craft a world that few can comprehend, understand or even perceive its meaning. One such world is found in DAS KAPITAL, a book Karl Marx wrote, sitting in the library of the British Museum.

To Kore, however, the library had become a place that offered him an opportunity to keep away from the harsh reality of the world, outside.

Now that there was a chance for him to meet Hadio, he didn't know how he should react to the occasion. He recollected a day when she came home, back from a trip to Cairo, how Hadio had given him a cold shoulder when he wanted to embrace her; instead, she had given her hand for him to shake, and had told him, "I am hot, and I need a shower."

While following those portentous thoughts, in his mind, about Hadio, he saw the figure that had just got inside the bank getting out. On seeing Hadio's figure from the front side, his mind was set up.

"I must talk to her, "he decided.

It was an afternoon of a cold winter day; aware of the snow that had hardened into ice, Kore took careful steps. He could not rely on his old battered winter shoes. Hadio had a black overcoat, a thick brown scarf wrapped around her neck and a brown woollen cap that reached down to her ears. She carried a black leather brief case, the type that people use to carry books or documents. From the bank she walked straight, then turned left, and took a walk on a narrow pavement, running parallel to Drotningsgatan.

Looking at her from behind, taking quick steps, her back straight, holding head high up, Kore couldn't help feeling impressed with the way that Hadio carried herself. When he took a careful look at her from behind, however, Hadio appeared to have grown heavier. What could it be? He imagined; it couldn't have been pregnancy; that much he was sure about; ever since she underwent a botched caesarean section in her homeland, Hadio had been rendered barren. Both she and Kore were happy with their two children.

As he got nearer and nearer to her, he faced a challenging dilemma about how to address her. In the past, whenever he addressed her, he used her first name of Hadio. This had been the case, when they had lived as a wife and a husband, and life had the quality of being spontaneous. Now, the simple thing about how to address her had become a great challenge for him.

''How should I address her to suit the new changing relationship? What should I do? How should I greet her? ''

All these thoughts had crossed his mind as he approached her from behind. He never wished Hadio to think that he was endearing himself to her. By now he was two steps behind her; if he were to stretch out his arm, he would have easily touched her. A second later, he was walking beside her, and then he said, "Hey."

The words came automatically tumbling down from his mouth. Hadio swung around to look at Kore; she gave him a short smile.

For a moment, it seemed Hadio looked for words to say; then, giving him a wide smile, she uttered the words, "What a surprise. Oh, it is you. How are you, Kore?"

"I am fine," he said. "I don't mean to bother you, but when I saw you I thought I should talk to you" he added carefully.

"You have done the right thing. I would have done the same thing. I have some minutes to spare; what do you have in mind" she said jovially.

The sight of Hadio, in such expansive mood, had boosted Kore's moral to such a great height that it made him gain enough confidence to make him want to talk to her further.

"Why don't we go somewhere," he told her, "sit down and have coffee?"

"Why not," she said. "Do you have a place in mind?" She added.

The positive response given by Hadio had caused a feeling of elation to rise in Kore, so much so that he felt like he should take her hand and lead her. He felt somewhat embarrassed, however, to imagine that such a feeling had never occurred to him, when the two had lived together as husband and wife.

"There is a place nearby here that I know well. You might have been there. They serve good tea, coffee and excellent pastries," she said, jolting Kore from further following his thoughts.

They were standing at junction of Drotningsgatan and Ostra Agatan, in front of a three-story building, with a largest book shop in town. From there, they turned left and then took a short walk to a nearest building, and got inside a café, facing a river.

Having been in business since 1876, Café Guntherska Hovkonditori & Schwerzeri is one of the oldest cafes in Uppsala. As one enters the café, there is a narrow room beyond which there is a larger one. The counter was kept in the first of the two rooms; from there, one could sample the items one wishes to have and pay from there. It is not an exclusive place and the prices are fair.

It was 11 a.m.; the place looked empty; somewhere close to the entrance, a family made up of a man, a woman and their two children were talking and having coffee. The overwhelming smell of coffee, and the warm atmosphere inside, elicited a sense of wellbeing in Kore.

"What would you like to have," Hadio asked Kore.

"I will have black coffee," he said.

In any other circumstances, Kore would have insisted on footing the bill. That he couldn't do it now, it was because he was broke; this had made him almost hate himself; for some reason that he couldn't explain it to himself, he felt the same way for Hadio.

Hadio took tea with milk, and apple cake; she paid on the counter. They took their order back to their seats, in the larger room, where there were a few young couples talking to each other. Hadio removed her overcoat and placed it on an empty chair, next to her seat. Kore placed his behind the chair.

Hadio took a sip from her tea and a bite from her apple cake; making face to mean she had found the apple cake quite agreeable to her taste, she leaned backwards in her chair and then said, "Heavenly."

Not getting the real meaning behind the remarks, Kore said "What is heavenly?"

Hadio smiled joyfully. "The apple cake is heavenly," she said. "How about your coffee?" she asked Kore. For some inexplicable reason Hadio felt happy to be sitting there, talking to Kore.

"It is not a bad one," he said, in a not-so-enthusiastic tone.

As he sat there facing Hadio, across from the table, Kore's mind took a sudden turn. Now, he started to think about what he was doing there, sitting in a table with a woman who had deserted him, and had even been responsible for him not getting the chance to meet his children. There was such strong emotional sign of anguish showing in Kore's face that led Hadio to say in a hesitant tone, "Are you not feeling well? You look tired."

"I am tired, exhausted and weak. How else do you expect me to feel? I am a human being; I am not a robot. If you cut me, I will bleed, and if you tickle me, I will laugh; that is how much human I can be," he said determinedly and with hatred.

"I care about how you look and feel. I am sorry if you don't feel well; but why are you telling me all this now?" She said, a look of pity for him showing in her face.

Influenced by the emotion of anger, Kore was beginning to loose his sense of decency and propriety.

"You act as if you are innocent when you are the architect for most of the misfortune that has befallen me," he said in a voice sharp with emotion.

"How could I be the architect of the misfortune in your life unless you wish to say I am some sort of a deity," she said, looking frustrated.

"You may not be a deity, but you are everything else that you are; you are selfish, malicious and cruel," he said in a nasty tone.

"That is enough. I am not going to sit here with you while you keep on throwing insults at me," she said. "Have you brought me here just to do that?" She asked in disbelief.

"Let me tell you why I think you are everything that I have said you are. You are selfish because you never cared about my feelings when you left me. You are malicious because, having left me, you went after a man who once was my friend, but he is my sworn enemy now, and you are cruel because you took my children away from me," he said.

Hadio remained silent; she looked as if she was contemplating what to say; with a feeling that lacked any sign of pity for Kore, she said, "Call me anything you wish; however, that will not change anything. Besides, what right do you have to call me selfish? Who between us is selfish? Tell me. You who refused to do any work, or me who had been making sacrifice to keep the family together?"

"In this case, why did you throw away your family for a man you scarcely knew anything about?" Kore said throwing away all sense of decorum.

"I am not going to discuss Peter with you," she said.

"Does he care about our children? He said.

"Stop it, I said, or else I will leave," Hadio said, feeling quite desperate.

The fact that she refused to have any discussion about Peter with him had made Kore quite angry, so much so that he was forced to throw away the residue of modesty in him and said, "Whatever has made you fall for him, that will not last long. I know the man better than you do. He had once been my friend, remember."

At this point, Hadio didn't feel obliged to have any further conversation with Kore. She couldn't bear to sit there and watch Kore make a mockery of himself, in front of everyone in the café. She was embarrassed to be there in a café, getting subjected to a tirade of insults by a man who seemed to care for nothing. She got up abruptly, gathered her handbag, took her overcoat and strode purposefully towards the gate, aiming to get away from Kore.

Hadio's sudden decision to depart from the café, leaving him to sit there alone, had caused a sense of confusion and anger in Kore. He had never expected her to go away, living him to sit there alone.

He stood up; in a full stride, he followed her, and in a most hysterical manner he kept shouting at her. "Come back. Come back, you witch,"

By now Hadio had already gone away; he turned around and saw people staring at him with a look of bewilderment in their faces. Once he realised the awful situation he had got himself into, he left the place in a hurry. He was afraid someone might call the police. He didn't want to have any more trouble with the police.

These were trying moments for Kore. In the past, each time he faced some sort of misfortunes, he would simply conjure up in his mind his image, as a child, when the world had offered him a sense of security, warmth, love and care. He would think of his home where he would hold conversation in his mind with Auntie Safia, his cousin Gure, as well as other members of his family. He would open a widow in his mind – so to speak - which would enable him to watch the dusk falling, in his home village.

Such mental trips had once offered him a great sense of relief from his current state of discontentment with the world that he believed had become increasingly cruel to him.

Unfortunately, however, with ever-increasing incidents of misfortunes in his life, his ability to revisit the past to draw some solace from it had lately started to fail him. On such occasions, he would turn to a book for a comfort; however, this would not last long. This state of restlessness, he discovered, would go away after speaking on phone with Hadio and the children.

Despite the quarrels of the past few days, Hadio did let him speak to her on phone. To his astonishment, one day, she declined to speak to him. Thereafter, every time he attempted to phone the house, Peter answered his calls.

Peter, one day, said to him, "Stop bothering my family with your silly calls, or else I will report you to the police."

That statement made Kore feel deeply angry.

Still in a deep state of anger, he heard Peter's voice sounding in his ears, as if the voice was reaching him from a hole in the ground; that voice was saying to him, "You have thrown your family into a dustbin, from out of where I picked them up; you have no one to blame but yourself."

Later, to Kore's annoyance, he chuckled.

Since Kore wasn't willing to engage in a war of words with Peter, he simply said, "What takes you to the dust bins?"

After that he hanged up on Peter. From that day on, Kore ceased calling the house.

Then one day, overcome with a feeling of frustration for not getting to see any member of his family, he made up his mind to pay the family a visit. He got the address of the family's residence, as well as the school they attended, from his son that he had accidentally met inside a bus.

It was one of those days the windstorm in Uppsala gets so strong that nothing anchored to the ground seems safe from getting uprooted. Trees sway violently, as the wind passing through the leaves and the branches give a frightening hissing sound.

For lack of a bus fare, Kore had to brave the elements to get to his destination. Kore couldn't afford to waste the meagre share of money he got from the social welfare office on a monthly bus ticket.

Once he reached there, he found a major entrance to the building had been locked, and so he was forced to wait on a pavement, on the front side of the building, where he hoped either Hadio or the children would see him. As he stood there alone, under the biting cold wind blowing across him, he anticipated a meeting with either the children or Hadio; he had a feeling of anxiety building up in him.

Suddenly, from a short distance away, he saw a police-car approaching. The car came to a stop a few steps away from him, standing on a narrow pavement that lay between the road and the building the family lived in. From their position, inside the car, the policemen - two altogether - spoke to him. They wished to know what he was doing there. Kore remained silent. He knew the reason, but hadn't felt any need to explain himself to them. Kore's deliberate silence must have offended them; he could notice this reaction from their looks.

One of the two policemen, the oldest looking one spoke to him in a voice that Kore was convinced neither had sympathy nor understanding. He decided he would be careful with him.

"What is your name? He asked.

Kore gave his name.

"Look here, the police said in an angry tone, "you are in a free country where no restriction is placed on your movements. But just as the freedom of your nose ends where your mouth begins, similarly the freedom of your movement ends when you interfere with the freedom of other people."

The police officer took a brief pose, and then said further, "We have received a call from a gentleman living here in this building," he pointed to the building, "accusing you of phoning his family, often at ungodly hours of the night."

Kore remained quiet, but gave the officer the same look of defiance, as the latter addressed him further.

"Besides," he said in an aggressive tone, "you are trespassing on other peoples' property. We ask you to cease from carrying on with this miserable habit of yours, or else stringent measures would be taken against you."

The police officer finally said in his severest and most acrimonious tone, "Do you hear me?"

Kore continued to give him the same look of defiance. The police officer, one more time, repeated the question; once again, he failed to get the meek reply that Kore believed the police officer was hoping to get from him. Finally, he told Kore to go away, but remembered to remind him that they would keep an eye on him. They drove away after that.

As he was contemplating leaving, Kore was shocked and stunned to catch a glimpse of Peter, from behind the window glass, staring, laughing at him.

# Chapter Thirty Five

# *Great Expectation*

From the day Hadio went to live with Peter Wells, she expected much from life. Now that Kore was out of her life, Hadio intended to utilise her energy to benefit herself and her children.

Early in their relationship, Peter's enthusiasm for Hadio had known no bounds. Each evening, whenever he arrived home from his office, Peter brought flowers to Hadio. Several days in a week, he took the whole family for outing, in his car, to have dinner and watch movies together.

He took Hadio, on some weekends, to dance to the tune of jazz and blues music, at Uppsala's famous jazz club - the Katalin. There, for the first time, at his suggestion, Hadio took her first drink of alcohol; she became jovial and light in spirit, and subsequently felt free to talk to everyone.

After that, she looked forward to weekends, so that she could have the opportunity to dance, to the tune of the music, at the Katalin, and have a drink with Peter as well as enjoy the company of other revellers.

Despite such frequent gestures of loving relationship between Hadio and Peter, signs were there - subtle though they may have been - indicating that all was not well. One day, just a few months into their relationship, as Hadio was entertaining a group of women from her country, Peter came home from work, earlier than his usual. In the sitting room, he sneaked at the women; he found the women talking and laughing loudly; they seemed happy. Without a warning, he lashed out at the group of the gossiping women.

"This isn't a market place," he said, addressing them angrily, "where it is free for you to get in, anyway you want to."

Meanwhile, Hadio's guest had got themselves into a frantic state of mind; they picked up their bags in a hurry and left the house, feeling shocked and dismayed at Peter's unwarranted hostile action.

As they were trying to find their way out, they heard Peter shouting at them. He was saying, "Next time, remember to call before you come here, unannounced and uninvited. You are in Europe now; try to behave in a civilised manner."

Hadio shaded tears of frustration. She was sure that she would never live to meet those women again; not only that, but she knew too that they would spread words to others, who would not want to have anything to do with her. With that single act of madness, Peter had managed to cut off all links Hadio had been having with the a few women from her country that she came to know.

Later, Peter tried to appease Hadio's feelings of anger and frustration with sweet words. This was to be the first most acrimonious quarrel to take place between the two of them; it wouldn't be the last one, however.

Peter, one time, planned to have Hadio, accompanied by her two children meet his mother, whom he called, "The hag." Hadio had always been aware of the negative feelings that Peter had been having for his mother; yet, she wouldn't use any form of a moral yardstick to judge him.

What mattered to her most was Sarah's feeling for her. Would Sarah like her? She decided to try not to impress Sarah, out of fear that such action might backfire on her.

On the appointed day Peter arrived home, from his work, quite early. At six in the evening, accompanied by Hadio and the children, they left.

Hadio had put on a long gown, a blouse, a thin turtle neck sweater and a jacket; she combed her hair and wore it in a natural form. Peter, who didn't approve of the way Hadio had kept her hair, told her, "You would look better if you pulled back your hair and then tie them with a ribbon." Hadio knew better not to argue with Peter, and so she obliged him half-heartedly. She dressed the children well. Peter had put on his favourite grey corduroy suit.

Sarah lived in a mansion that stood on a hilltop. To get there, they drove on highway leading southwards; later, they swerved left and then drove on a well-kept gravel road of three kilometres to Sarah's mansion. As the car approached the building, Hadio was struck by an extraordinary atmosphere of solitude that paradoxically enough had been amplified by birds chirping restlessly. Tall oak trees, which seemed to have been forever there, surrounded the house.

Standing on the long veranda was Sarah, waiving at them and smiling. There was chill in the air. Sarah was dressed in a long gown, and had put on a light blue pullover; she had sandals on her feet that were covered in a pink coloured woollen socks. From a point in the veranda of the house, whose elevation had been emphasised by the height of its foundation, Sarah surveyed her guests with a majestic gaze of a queen.

Peter never liked the look on his mother's face. As he approached her, followed behind by Hadio and the children, the look in his mother's face must have chilled him to the bones.

Indeed, there was nothing in life that Peter hated more than paying his mother a visit, he had once told Hadio. Hadio was very much aware of the fact that this was a rare visit that Peter was paying his mother. Peter had told her that each time he had paid his mother a visit, that visit had ended up in a great fiasco. Hadio hoped their current visit wouldn't have the same ending.

One by one, they climbed up the stairs to get to Sarah, a smile on her face, standing on the veranda, waiting for them. Sarah offered a warm handshake to each of the family members; thereafter, she led the way into the sitting room that stood next to a main entrance. "Make yourselves comfortable while I go and fetch some drinks for you." Sarah said in her heavy voice, before she left for the kitchen.

Sarah had retired from public service. Now, Sarah was an active member in a Swedish society for bird watchers. The passion that she had been having for birds was reflected in the way she had the walls of her sitting rooms covered with pictures of colourful birds, taken from all parts of the world.

At her advanced age, Sarah looked young. Her hair and eyes, especially, had the lustre mostly associated with younger people.

For someone of her age, Hadio imagined, Sarah exhibited an unusual level of physical agility. Sarah was soon back, from the kitchen. In her arms, she had a round wooden tray that held glasses and a jug filled up to the brim with chilled lemonade.

Addressing Hadio in an enthusiastic tone, she said, "I have made this for you and the children. I hope you would like it." Then she added, "I know Peter does."

. Peter felt a strong inner impulse to contradict his mother, but kept quiet; instead he offered her a grave face that his mother chose to ignore, as she continued to entertain the rest of the family members.

"Let us have the drinks now," she said. "If you don't mind;" she added politely, "later, we will have dinner."

Peter never had anything good to say about his mother whenever he talked to Hadio about her, which had been quite often. While watching Sarah serving drinks, talking so freely to them, and without any reservations, Hadio was forced to have a second opinion about Sarah. After she finished serving drinks to her guests, Sarah sat next to Hadio.

The children spoke to each other in a whisper, as Peter continued to have the grave look in his face.

"Peter told me about the children. There are several video games I have made available for them in the recreation room," Sarah said.

The room was a place children belonging to members of her family and friends liked to sit and play there, whenever they visited Sarah. The children became excited the moment Sarah mentioned something about the video game. Sarah accompanied them to the recreation room to make sure everything was in place, before joining Hadio and Peter in the sitting room.

Back from the recreation room, Sarah said to Peter, "Are you two working together? I don't mean to pry, but you know well that you haven't mentioned anything about Hadio, apart from stating that you were planning to visit with a friend."

The revelation came as surprise to Hadio; she was shocked to learn that Peter hadn't told his mother anything about her.

"Not quite," Peter said disinterestedly.

Addressing Hadio from out of the blue, Sarah said, "Wait; your face seems familiar. Where could I have seen you?" She added impatiently, "I must have seen you somewhere!"

It was silent. Hadio seemed anxious, while Peter had a gloomy expression in his face.

Suddenly the puzzled look on Sarah's face changed, a hesitant smile crossing her lips, she said, "Why, I must have seen you on television."

Her knowledge of who Hadio was seemed to have evoked a feeling of excitement in Sarah.

"To tell you the truth," she said hastily, "I have always been under the impression that, in your part of the world, women are quite timid and meek. However, you have proved me wrong."

She looked at Peter as if to ask for his contribution; he remained silent.

Eyes gleaming with pride for Hadio's accomplishment, she said further, "Your assignment calls for courage, bearing in mind that the subject of genital mutilation is considered a taboo in your society."

"Thanks for the compliment," Hadio offered her genuine sentiments.

Referring, however, to what Sarah had just said to her, Hadio said eloquently, "Must I shy away from talking about a natural endowment belonging to other half of humanity, caused in a society like mine to lose its natural quality?"

She shot up a look at Peter, sitting quietly, watching the two women sharing a jovial moment. His facial appearance looked combative though; she chose to ignore him.

"I could make effective use of euphemism to express my point, but I have chosen not to do so; hence, the need for calling a spade a spade," Hadio concluded.

Both gave a hilarious laughter.

"Well Peter, my curiosity has not been satisfied yet," Sarah said, as she turned her attention away from Hadio to focus on Peter. "You know quite well," she added carefully, "you haven't still told me anything about you and Hadio."

"Why does it matter to you? I could tell you anything I wish," he uttered the words in his usual adversarial manner

"Well suit yourself." Sarah said resignedly.

To save a bad situation from getting worse, Hadio said, "The government medical department, to which Peter is acting as its consultant, is the sponsor of the project 'Stop Genital Mutilation Now,' of which I am its Project Manager. But Peter and I are also currently living together, hoping to get married soon."

A note of silence followed, and then Sarah managed to utter a single word "Ugh."

There was a sign of disappointment Hadio thought she had recognised in Sarah's brief remark. Apparently, she was not given much time to think. Sarah got up abruptly and said, "Time for dinner."

She headed for the kitchen in her usual brisk steps

A moment later, without offering any excuse to Hadio, Peter followed his mother into the kitchen.

Hadio was left sitting alone, wondering how the evening would turn out. There was tension in the air that she felt with a measure of regret. She tried not to allow herself to get emotionally affected. She retrieved a small mirror from her handbag, took a quick glance at her reflection; convinced of the need to add a touch of makeup to her face, she left for the washroom. On the way there, she could not help overhearing mother and son talking to each other in subdued voices, albeit laden with volatile emotions.

She caught Sarah at the point of saying to Peter, "Are you truly in love with her?"

Hadio posed to listen, while mindful of the dangers of eaves-dropping.

"What are you? Are you a marriage councillor?" He said angrily.

"I am your mother," she replied easily

There was a clinking sound of glasses and spoons, knives and forks on the kitchen board.

"A reluctant mother is what you are," Peter said disparagingly.

"I feel pity for you. I know you Peter. Not only you are incapable of loving, but you believe you are not loveable," Sarah said.

"You can't intimidate me mother. I have my own life to live and so do you. By the way, talking of love mother, what credentials do you have to lecture me about the subject of love and marriage? We are two of the same kind mother, or are we not?" He said vehemently.

"No, we are not. I never cheat innocent people by making them to believe in something that has no real basis for believing in. Let the woman and her children go before you ruin them." Sarah was throwing out a challenge.

It was silent inside the kitchen, which had made Hadio to assume that Peter might come out and catch her. Subsequently, she rushed into the washroom that stood several paces away from the kitchen.

Inside the washroom, she waited undecidedly; her nerves pulsating with the beat of her heart, as the rest of her body shook like injured animal; she also seemed lost about what to do, having momentarily forgotten the reason that had made her wish to visit the washroom, before coming upon the conversation taking place between mother and son.

Should she take to heart everything Sarah had said about Peter? Something that Sarah had said to Peter made her feel quite demoralised. What is more, the serious tone Sarah had used to express her feelings left little room for doubt in Hadio's mind that Sarah meant what she had said. Yet, Hadio could not take everything for granted.

Finally, she decided to give the issue the benefit of the doubt. She washed her hands, cleaned her face, applied a makeup on her face, looked at herself in the mirror and then left.

On her way to the sitting room, she made up her mind to try to look as natural as possible, although deep inside she was feeling tormented by the conversation she couldn't help overhearing.

In the sitting room, she found Peter; she offered him a smile that he never returned.

She went away, feeling somewhat discouraged; she went to see Sarah in the kitchen. Sarah was getting the food on to the table. Hadio offered to assist her. Soon everyone was getting ready to enjoy their meal of beefsteak, potatoes, vegetables and salads, when unexpectedly, and to the surprise of everyone, Peter vented his anger on his mother.

"I refuse to have dinner. It is a price you must pay for the insults you have just heaped on me. I also forbid Hadio and the children to have it," he said looking quite annoyed.

Peter's hostile remarks took everyone by surprise. Sarah gave Peter a contemptuous look and said, "You are free to go Peter. However, you have no right to decide for Hadio and the children. You may have been the cause for their coming here, but they are my guests now."

After making her point clear to Peter, Sarah stayed quiet.

Meanwhile, Hadio found herself in an awkward situation, since Peter was demanding that she should accompany him. Hadio was evidently torn between a desire to respect the wishes of Sarah, to stay and have the dinner, or complying with Peter's unreasonable demands to leave. Reluctantly, she stood up; she gave in to Peter's demands.

Peter left the house, followed reluctantly by Hadio and her children. Out of guilty-feelings, Hadio could not bear to look Sarah straight in the face. Sarah, nevertheless, followed them out to the veranda, to see the family off. When Hadio turned to have last look at Sarah, through the car window, she saw Sarah waiving. Sarah's action had reinvigorated her slackened morale that would soon change.

There was a total silence inside the car. To Hadio, the situation had reflected a state of lull before the storm.

"I have been watching how you two were getting on well," Peter said, a moment later. There was a trace of anger in his voice.

"She is your mother. I think she is wonderful to talk to," Hadio said courteously.

"What do you know about her?" Peter asked.

"I know nothing. But do I have to?" Hadio said.

"Yes, I think wisdom demands it. You don't take people to heart that you hardly know anything about," Peter said.

"How would you I rather dealt with her?" Hadio asked

"How should I know? Why, you should have used your imagination, I suppose," he said.

Detecting a sign of hostility in Peter's remarks, Hadio was lost on what to do and think. She hadn't done anything wrong to purposefully annoy Peter, but that exactly was the impression she gathered from the way he had been talking to her.

"She is your mother. I have nothing against her. Peter, please do not involve me in your quarrels. I do not want any part in it," she said unambiguously.

"I have always suspected that you two were of the same kind; you are obstinate, vain and without any feeling," Peter said in a voice full of hatred for Hadio.

By now it was obvious to Hadio that Peter lacked a reasoning capacity; she felt she had no reason to indulge in further discussion with him.

Peter did not allude to the incident until several days later. He had just got home, back from his work, looking happy and full of excitement, when he met Hadio deep in a sorrowful mood. He approached her from behind and then gave her a light kiss on her lips.

"I know you have every right to think of me as a monster. I had no reason to talk to you in the way I did. Will you please forgive me? Come and have a dinner with me. I have booked a table for us two, at a Chinese restaurant. It is a Friday, and tomorrow is a Saturday; what do you say?"

"What about the children?"

"Damn the children," he uttered the words with such a scathing force that it unsettled Hadio's mood. As soon as he uttered the words, he realised that he had offended Hadio's feelings. And so, he tried to appease her injured feelings with nice words.

Hadio felt that Peter's erratic behaviour had made him quite unpredictable. His mood that alternated between the two emotions of elation and dejection had made her not quite sure about what to think of him.

Not quite a long time ago, she thought she knew what she felt about him. She liked Peter, especially, because of the way she thought he cared for her. However, with a passage of time, she came to realise that he cared for her in a manner that she considered to be selfish. He felt injured, for example, if she did not cuddle him in public, or shower him with praise.

"You have nothing good to say about me Hadio," he said to her, one day, several months later, as they were returning home from a party, at a friend's house.

"I don't understand. What do you mean?" She said.

" Each time I argue with my friends, you never agree with me. Oftentimes, you chose to side with my adversaries," he said.

"I thought the people we visit hardly are anything but your good friends; why, you had just said it, yourself," Hadio said.

"Yes, they are my friends; however, each time I have to argue with any of them I don't see them as my friends, because they conspire to put me down; as my wife, you should not be siding with them."

"Am I your wife? Since when have I become one?" Hadio said.

"Stop it please," Peter said in irritation.

"Why should I do that? I think this is just as a good a time as any to talk about the kind of relationship we want for ourselves," she said forcefully in reply.

Whenever Hadio mentioned the subject of marriage to him, Peter became evasive or hostile, depending on the mood he was in. When they got together, initially, it was on understanding that, in due course of time, they would get married. As time went by, Peter tried to convince Hadio that a marriage contract means nothing to a couple like them.

"It is the mutual feelings of love and not a piece of paper which is important," he argued. In the beginning, before she changed her mind, she thought there was some logic in his statement. However, with a passage of time, Hadio was forced to resign to her fate, having convinced herself that Peter was not intending to marry her.

The children were another sour-point in their relationship. Peter claimed they were disrespectful to him; they called him names, he claimed. One time, unaware of his presence in the house, he had overheard the children call him "an old hen," he had told Hadio. He could never forgive them for comparing him to an old hen, of all creatures of the world, he had told her.

# Chapter Thirty Six

# *Look here Nigger*

Losing a family to another man is an act of great tragedy that could happen to anyone. But poor economic situation had made matters worse for Kore. For example, for lack of bus fare, Kore had to take a five kilometre walk distance to try to get to talk to his erstwhile family. It would take him another five kilometres to walk back. Considering the shifting weather patterns, in the Swedish summer, alternating between windstorm and rain, walking such a long distance, in an almost half-empty empty stomach, must have been a sheer torture.

On his way home, he remembered the police officers that had just spoken to, and thought of other police officers in an incident that had taken place at Stockholm train station, quite a long time ago now.

He had been to Stockholm on a visit. On his way back to Uppsala, he missed the train, and had been forced to wait for the next one inside a bar, at the train station, which, at eight in the evening, had looked deserted. While there, he had ordered for a glass of beer and a sandwich. At the bar, he had seen a Swedish woman that he knew her from Uppsala.

On the way to the bathroom, he had stopped by her table in order to have a brief talk with her. Back in his table, minutes later, he had noticed two bulky looking guards approaching him; the menacing look in their faces, directed at him, had put fear in him.

'What could I have done to warrant such an unfriendly look?" He had thought about them as they approached him.

"You must leave the bar," they had said, fuming at him.

"Why should I do that" Kore had said in reply, looking quite astonished.

As he had been speaking to the men, he had tried to find a reason that could make them act in such a despicable manner. It could be the case of a mistaken identity, he had concluded

"You are drunk," they had said.

"I am not drunk," he had replied, looking angry.

"Yes, you are," They had insisted.

"Don't you have eyes?" he had shouted at them.

"You are drunk. You must live the bar immediately," they had insisted, but went away after that, leaving Kore to wonder what the hullabaloo had been about.

Five minutes later, accompanied by two police officers, they returned.

As soon as the police closed on him, they had grabbed his elbows, one each. The train station had been full of staring people. Kore had never felt such sense of humiliation before. At the main gate to the train station, they had pushed him out. When he had tried to draw the attention of the two policemen to a jacket he had left in the bar, they had never given him any heed.

A Swedish woman who had seen everything had became angry at the police; she had approached the police officers and had said to them, "Leave him alone. Your action is vile and reprehensible, to say the least. Let him go, you pig."

Instead of heeding the words of the woman, they had shouted back at her.

"Get lost, or else we will charge you for interfering with the police duty," they had told the woman.

Shaking her head, the woman had left the scene quietly.

Meanwhile, the two police officers had kept insisting that Kore should go away - jacket or no jacket on. When he had refused to abide by their orders, they had got hold of him and had led him into a police station - a block away from the train station - where they had charged him for drunkenness.

The police on duty, a large-built hot-tempered blond woman, had ordered him to remove all items from inside his pocket trousers; she had asked him to hand over his trousers belts. Afterwards, she had taken him to a cell room in a corridor, pushed him inside the room, before locking the door from outside.

Inside the cell-room, Kore had met with a stream of cold air getting inside the room from somewhere high up on the roof; the cold air stream had been meant to make those accused of misbehaving in public, on account of being drunk, get sober. Inside the room, there was a small concrete slab that one could choose to either lay or sit on it. Kore had sat on it. With no jacket on, he had shivered with cold.

In the walls of the cell-room, Kore's attention had been drawn to graffiti, bearing a message, written in Swedish, directed at the Finnish migrants; the message had reminded them to go home, back to their country of origin. 'Ak hem, javla Finlandlare' they had read in Swedish. Similar graffiti he had seen on empty city walls had carried a similar message.

Due to wide-spread allegations of alcohol misuse, Finnish immigrants had acquired a reputation for violence in Sweden, especially with a knife. Kore couldn't tell if such allegations had been made to rationalise biases, by giving them a factual meaning, or they had held some sort of truths in them.

Most Finnish migrants had been workers, who had kept a sporadic contact with their homeland; others had been students. There was another special group of Finns now in their middle age that had been brought to Sweden, in the 1940s, for safe-keeping - away from the war that had been fought between Finland and the Russia. Much had been written about this group of people.

For Kore it had been a lesson seeing white on white hate displayed on those graffiti. He had always thought that hate between groups of people had existed only across racial line. Hate, like love, is colour blind, he had realised.

In general, Kore had found one or two Finns he had befriended to be a down to earth people; they had been friendly and open-minded individuals. One Finnish friend had been generous enough to invite him to his home in Helsinki, which should be regarded as one of the most beautiful European cities, by any standard.

Any visitor to the city of Helsinki would find the large Russian built church (Finish: Uspenskin Katedraali, Swedish: Uspenskij-katedralen) built on a hill top, not far from Helsinki harbour, to be one of the most magnificent sites to behold.

In Finland, during mid eighties, you could walk the streets in Helsinki and never come across a single African. A handful of African students, however, were found in various university campuses. Most Finns had acted friendly towards Africans they had met.

Despite the gentle reception that Finns had accorded Africans, to Kore that alone had not been enough to make him believe that Finns were born to love Africans. Africans were a rarity in Finland, and since a rare object is often considered exotic, Finns were bound to love Africans for their exotic nature.

Would the Finns have the same feelings for Africans, let us say, if Africans had lived in large numbers in Finland? This thought had crossed Kore's mind, most often.

Close to the church, Kore's friends had his home. On discovering, in one of the buildings, close to the church, the Apartheid State of South Africa had its Embassy Kore didn't know what to think. He couldn't bring himself to believe that such embassy could exist in a country, like Finland, which had been an unequivocal supporter of the South African liberation struggle.

Imagine the shock he got, one day, when he came to discover that the Apartheid State of South Africa not only had its embassy in Stockholm, side by side with one of the Africa National Congress's largest offices in Europe, but for more than three hundred Swedish companies, business with the Apartheid State of South Africa, in mid-eighties had gone on, quite as usual.

Apparently, Swedish policy makers, he would come to learn from a professor of African Studies that he spoke to, had never seen, in this act of political somersaulting, a breach of moral political conduct. The professor said Swedish policy makers had justified their action by resorting to the principle of neutrality, which they claimed had afforded the country the right to play on both sides of opposing political fields.

At around 2 a.m., the police woman let Kore out of the cage, and then ordered him to go away, after returning to him the items that she had taken away. Since no means of transportation was available, at such hour of the night, he requested the police officer to allow him to shelter in the premises till dawn; to his dismay his request was refused. Outside, he faced a great dilemma.

Dressed in a pair of black jeans, a shirt and a light pullover, like a ghost, in a cold late autumn night, he had been forced to walk the deserted streets of Stockholm for the rest of the night, hiding from police cars. He left for Uppsala in the morning, after reclaiming his jacket from the bar.

This was the first serious encounter Kore had ever had with the police. Apparently, it wouldn't be the last one. In future, when he failed to secure a meeting with any member of his family, Kore was tempted to call Hadio on phone. However, each time he remembered his encounter with the police, he was forced to drop the idea as hopeless.

Finally, one day, he came upon what he believed to be a brilliant idea. He made up his mind to visit the school compound in order to meet his children. In the school compound, he watched school children play football in an open field that lay next to the school building; looking at them, he felt envious of their parents, who would take supper with them, and together enjoy watching the 7.30 news bulletin on TV. He had forgotten how it felt to do so.

Twice, he was successful in his mission; however, one day, as he enjoyed a cup of tea with his children, in a school canteen, talking and laughing with them, feeling quite happy, some police officers approached him, sitting in the table with his children. They looked at the children; then, they looked at Kore. Pointing at Kore, while addressing the children, one of the policemen said, "Do you know this man?"

"He is our father," Atosh said in a firm tone.

"What is your name?" The police officer asked Kore

Kore gave his name.

It seems the presence of the police in uniform had attracted the attention of students in the canteen who stopped talking, and with curious eyes watched the policemen talking to Kore and his children.

"What are you doing here?" The police officer asked Kore in an intimidating tone.

"I am seeing my children," Kore said.

The police officer asked to see Kore's identity card that Kore gave it to him. He matched the information on the identity card with the information they had been having on him.

Using an impatient tone to address Kore, he said, "You are not permitted by the law to see your children here. I am afraid you must accompany us to the police station," he added.

"We want our father; please leave him alone," the children pleaded with the police, using an agitated tone.

Kore hesitated; he looked at his children; he wanted to say something, but before he could bring himself to talk to any of his children, one of the police officers said in a commanding tone, "Stand up, come with us; hurry up."

To avoid getting into further trouble with the police officers, Kore let them lead him out of the canteen, into a police car, waiting outside the school compound.

"Leave our father alone; we want our father back," the children kept hysterically shouting at the policemen, who remained oblivious to the cries of the children.

Inside the police station, he was directed to a plain looking room with a single table and two chairs, kept on either side of the table. He was told to sit on one of those chairs and wait. Meanwhile, the two policemen who got him there left him to sit alone in the room.

A moment later, another group made up of three police officers entered the room. One of the police officers, carrying a thick file in his right hand, walked round the table and then sat down, facing Kore across from the table; the other two policemen chose not to sit down.

The three men were heavily built; of those three men, the one facing him from across the table looked quite old. All three men remained quiet for a while, but gave him an intense look.

Sitting there, looking at the three policemen, looking at him, caused an uncanny feeling in Kore; he was in for a big trouble, he suspected.

"What is your name?" The oldest of the three police officers asked.

"Kore," Kore replied easily.

The man looked at the files that lay open on the table, in front of him. "What were you doing at the school yard?" He asked, using a sharp tone.

Kore did not like the tone the man was using to address him.

"Is there any law prohibiting people from visiting school yards?" Kore said harshly.

"No. But there is a law that prohibits you from visiting that particular school yard where your children are," said the police officer.

Later, he added quite mischievously, "And would you keep your mouth shut. Here, you are not in your forest-home; therefore, you must act like a civilised person, even if you are not one, by any stretch of imagination."

Following that statement, his colleagues burst into laughter.

"You are free to have your opinion about me just as I am free to have my opinion about you," Kore replied quite forcefully. He added in a mischievous tone, "I believe you are narrow-minded, cruel, bigoted and lacking self-esteem."

That statement, he knew, would cause a major embarrassment in the three men, and might consequently cause them to act severely against him. Kore was acting like someone courting a disaster of some sort; perhaps he was. He felt he had lost much; he felt except his dignity, which he decided to allow no one to take it away by intimidating him, he had nothing more to lose.

His reply, it seemed, had taken the three men by surprise; as a result, they scarcely knew what to do. However, after they recovered from the shock, one of the policemen went to stand quite close to Kore where he towered over him, and then spoke to Kore in a voice filled with disgust.

He said, "Look here, you foolish man, you are allowed only to give answers to questions we ask. Other than that, no one is interested in your views."

When Kore turned his face up in order to have a closer look at the police officer speaking to him, he was surprised to discover that he was staring right into the eyes of a young-looking police officer, who was an immigrant, like him.

"You are rude and lacking in self-respect," Kore said; "I am afraid," he added, "your despicable behaviour makes a mockery of the people who would like to see more of your kind of people become police officers; with people like you, however, they can't be more wrong; you are worse than a slave driver," Kore said.

"Shut up, old goat," the young policeman retorted.

Kore busted into a hysterical laughter.

"What are you laughing for?" The young policeman shouted in dismay.

"You are nothing to me but a hound dog. I pity you," Kore said in a voice full of contempt for the police officer.

Kore's response steered a burning anger in the oldest of the three police officers, which forced him to get up from his seat and to hysterically shout at Kore.

"Will you shut up *neger*?" He said.

Kore was aware that he has left the threshold behind. From now on anything could happen.

"What kind of satisfaction do such people get when they shout the word *neger*? "No doubt, like the policemen before me, they must be getting a satisfaction of sort; otherwise, why use the word on me," Kore said to himself.

He decided to deny them that sense of satisfaction. He stood up. Because they had never expected Kore to challenge them, they took a step back. He laughed; he dared them to come to him; they stood still, eyes burning with anger, looking at him.

"It is obvious to me that your uniform is a symbol of manhood to you; you are quite insecure without your uniform," he told them.

The insult was a little too harsh and degrading; it taxed their patience. And so, like an angry buffalo, they charged at him. They rained heavy blows on his body; he tried to stop them from hitting him, but failed.

They threw him against the wall so hard that he felt he could hear his skull cracking. This was followed with an overwhelming smell of blood in his mouth. Like a heavy sack full of salt he fell on the ground. While still on the ground, they kicked him some more till they fully worked out their anger.

Blood flowed down from both his head and nose, soaking wet his clothes and the rest of his body. He tried to stand up and failed. Presently, everything took a dramatic change in his mind; a total silence descended over the room; he felt the room had become so small that if he were to stretch out his arms, he would be able to touch the ceilings. At the same time, he felt there was no adequate air in the room for him to breathe.

Finally, when he focused his attention towards the three men before him, their appearances deeply frightened him. The figures before him had fitted well the description of the mythological Nanauner - the dreaded savannah creature of his childhood years – having a part iron and a part human body.

Those figures now were heading in his direction. Kore closed his eyes that were half blinded by blood, flowing down from the gushing wound on his head. As they approached him, he gave forth a loud crying sound, and then everything went dark around him; he passed out and stayed in a comma, for several days.

When he came through, he found himself in a bed, in Akademiska Hospital room. His head, his right arm and his torso were swathed in white plaster. After elaborate operation that had lasted many hours, done by expert doctors on various parts of his body, he slept for long hours before waking up again.

At that moment he thought he could hear people speaking. It was the doctor, accompanied by a nurse.

"How is he doing?" The doctor asked the nurse.

"He is fine," the nurse said.

At this point, Kore opened his eyes and caught sight of a doctor, smiling at him. "Hello there," the doctor said, sounding amiable.

Kore opened his mouth to try to speak, but realising that speaking had become a difficult thing to do, he made use of a sign language to communicate with the doctor; he asked for a pen and a paper; with much difficulty, he wrote down the following questions, using his left hand:

"Where am I? What am I doing here? What has happened to me?

"Never mind, you are in safer hands now. Why don't you take a rest? You need it. We shall talk when you are ready," the doctor said.

On his next round, the doctor satisfied Kore's sense of curiosity.

"According to the statement given by the police," he told Kore, "you had made use of a chair to hit them. When they tried to stop you, you accidentally hit your head against the wall. In a melee that followed the commotion, your arm and three ribs got broken, and so is your hip. The head fracture that you have sustained is a serious one; we would like to give it a closer look."

Kore nodded his head and remained silent. The doctor could have well told him the police had stated that he had got hit by a car. He decided not to contest the statement; it would be their words against his, and the police words prevail, always.

He recollected an incident that had been widely reported in newspapers. In the newspapers, it had been stated that, at a Stockholm's train station, a man who had a quarrel with the police fell from a long staircase and died. When questioned about the incident, the police officers, who had been involved in the case, claimed that the man had purposefully thrown himself to his death.

Similarly, there was another reported incident involving other police officers. After they had shot a man in the back, causing him to die, the police had claimed that they had shot the man in self-defence, because the man had threatened to kill them with a hatchet. In both cases, the victims were individuals with immigrant background.

Akademiska Hospital is a place where doctors gliding through its corridors are in a tremendous hurry to extend help to the sick. Kore was one such soul who came under the kind care of Doctor Andrea. One day, some of the patients will receive a discharge after healing; others whose lives are destined to end up there will not. Kore felt he was prepared for either of the possibilities.

Kore requested the hospital authority to inform Azad of his presence in the hospital, which they did promptly. Azad and his family, including Avan, visited him on a regular basis. They brought with them either flowers or sweets each time they paid him a visit.

# Chapter Thirty Seven

# *Cynical Rejoinder*

At Peter's home, the family was going through a wave of deep moral crises. There was a mutual feeling of antagonism between Peter and the children. Hadio wished Peter would somehow become more accommodating to her children. She wanted to believe that Pater's lack of feelings for the children was just a phase that was bound to pass with time; unfortunately, that never happened. Instead, the family members kept drifting, further and further apart.

The children locked themselves inside their room, as soon as they got back home from school. They were estranged not only from Peter, for whom they had shown no any kind of love and respect whatsoever, but also their mother. They never visited the malls, like other children of their age did, or played games in the video game-halls; they had no friends in the neighbourhood worth-mentioning.

Shifo, on several occasions, had tried to pay Kerstin Lundin a visit- currently a neighbour - but for some unknown reason the thrill she was hoping to get from the visit was not there. The children yearned for their old neighbourhood, which to them had suddenly become far beyond their reach.

As both Hadio and Peter became increasingly busy in their jobs, they found they barely had enough time for each other. To the utter surprise of Hadio, Peter would come to hold her responsible for every little thing that would go wrong in his life including a waning sexual feeling in him.

One day, soon after they had finished making love, Peter said to her, "I wish you would say something, instead of looking stone-cold under me, each time we do this…"

"I don't like the way you are using my body to satisfy your physical urge," she said firmly.

"What do you mean?" he said looking shocked and perplexed. In a tone full of hatred, he said afterwards, "I feel all my effort is wasted on you; you have killed my libido."

Hadio took the insult to heart and said in a mocking tone, "What do you wish me to do? Offer you a medal for a job not well done?"

Hadio's response that amounted to a cynical rejoinder infuriated Peter so much that, in response, he said, "No, I don't need any reward from you as you are incapable of appreciating a good physical act of love making."

Using a wicked tone, eyes bulging with hatred for Hadio, he added, "After all, let us not forget that you have never been endowed with any kind of wherewithal to enable you to have any sexual feelings, at all. Sometimes, I wonder if you have any kind of human feelings in you! Come to think of it, when have you last uttered a single affectionate word of love to make me happy?"

At this point, Hadio decided to keep quiet. Later, alone in her room, she agonised over the fate that had brought her into the life of Peter. Since no amount of regret would be able to bring the past back to her, for the sake of her children, she decided to persevere, against all odds.

Apparently, despite a prevailing state of disharmony in the affairs of the family, to a not-so curious observer of the family affairs, there was an outward expression of tranquillity in their individual lives. Unfortunately, this outward appearance of harmony where none was there would not last forever.

One day, addressing a letter to Hadio and Peter, the school authority requested their presence there. When Hadio and Peter, accompanied by the children, went to face the school committee, made up of three people - two men and a woman - one cold winter evening, they found waiting there was a couple and a boy. The headmaster introduced the couple as the parents of Joel - the boy Atosh had used a knife to threaten him with.

"Your son, Atosh, is accused of drawing a knife on Joel. His action is against all sense of decency and the laws of this country," the headmaster said, addressing both Hadio and Peter.

"What do you have to say in your defence," he asked Atosh, as he directed his attention away from Peter and Hadio.

Atosh remained quiet, but directed his passionate look towards the headmaster, who mistaking the silence for a sign of hard-headedness, on the part of Atosh, shouted, "Answer my question. Have you drawn a knife on Joel?"

"Yes, I did," Atosh said meekly.

"Yes, you did. What did you do?" he asked impatiently.

"I drew a knife on Joel," Atosh said timidly.

Moved by the look of fear in Atosh's facial expression, the headmaster changed his mind about Atosh; he told him politely "Why did you do it, son?"

"I was afraid," Atosh said.

"What were you afraid of?" The headmaster asked curiously.

"There are boys out there who want to beat me up. I thought Joel was one of them," Atosh said in a beseeching tone.

"What do the boys want from you?" The headmaster asked

"I don't know," Atosh replied.

"How many were they?" The headmaster asked in an inquisitive tone.

"They were three or four boys," Atosh said;" I am not sure," he added.

"Is Joel one of them?" The headmaster asked looking at Joel.

"I don't know," Atosh said, looking down

"Why then did you draw the knife on him?" The headmaster hastily asked.

"As I was taking a walk home, alone, I heard from behind me footsteps. I panicked," he said.

"What did you do after that?" The headmaster asked

"I drew the knife."

"What happened then?"

"Joel ran away when he saw me drawing the knife. I was not going to use it,"

"Did you run after Joel?" the headmaster asked.

"I did not run after him. I kept the knife to protect myself."

Atosh held back tears as he spoke to the headmaster. Hadio approached Atosh, held him in her arms, and made attempts to console him with kind words. The sight of Atosh holding tears back, and a mother consoling her son, must have caused feelings of distress to develop in some of the people that were present in the room. Peter seemed detached from what was taking place in the room.

The headmaster looked at Joel, and addressing him, he said, "Do you know Atosh?"

"Yes, I know him," Joel said, looking at Atosh.

"How well do you know him?" the headmaster asked.

"I don't know him well. We attend different classes in school," he said and stayed quiet.

"Have you two ever had a quarrel before?" the headmaster asked.

"No, we didn't," Joel said.

While the headmaster was asking both Atosh and Joel questions, the parents remained silent.

At last, the headmaster focused his attention on his colleagues and asked them if they had something they wished to say. They had nothing, they said. Later, he put the same question to parents of both sides; they too said they had nothing. Joel's father, in a whisper, initiated a talk with his wife, and a smile crossed both their faces.

And so, it came as a great relief to everyone in the room, a moment later, when the headmaster said in his clear voice, "It is all clear to me there was no harm intended when Atosh drew the knife on Joel. This was an act coming from someone, in anticipating harm done to him, had resorted to a desperate action."

He took a pause, took a careful look at the people around him and said, "Despite a fear of attack, nevertheless, this school shouldn't condone such action."

For a moment he kept quiet; people in the room gave him their anxious look.

"Finally," in a happy tone, he said, "I wish to thank Mr and Mrs Sorenson for bringing this case to the notice of the school authority, instead of to the police. This means the public has trust in us. Now, to bring the matter to a happy end, ladies and gentlemen, if you will allow me, I would ask Atosh and Joel to shake hands and promise to be good to each other."

The boys shook hands to the joy of everyone in the room. Moment later, after saying their goodbyes, looking happy and satisfied Mr and Mrs Sorenson's family left.

No sooner had the family left then the headmaster drew the attention of those left in the room to the task ahead.

"Ladies and Gentlemen," the headmaster said, as he addressed those individuals present in the room, including three members of the staff, Peter, Hadio and the children, "while we are happy that we have been able to solve one problem, we still have one more issue to deal with. The issue in question concerns the welfare of Atosh and Shifo, both students in our school.

It is clear from their school record that they have not only ceased to perform in their studies as well as they used to do in the past, but in their dealings with teachers and students they have displayed an overwhelming signs of aggression. Perhaps, as parents, you would like to tell us the reasons for this sad state of affairs."

The two turned to look at each other, and then Peter said in an ambiguous tone, "For quite some time now the children have been living in an environment that is quite new to them."

"What environment are you referring to? Could you be more explicit?" the headmaster said.

"I beg your pardon? I don't understand." Peter said.

The headmaster addressing Peter said, "Well, let us see now; you did mention something about the environment. What environment are you alluding to? Is it the social environment outside your home, or is it your own home-environment that you are referring to?"

"I mean both," Peter said, almost evasively.

"If I may ask you, what did any of you do to alter the situation from getting worse?" he said impatiently.

"We are trying to raise the level of co-operation in the family to the best of our ability," Peter offered a feeble response.

"For how long have the children been living in this environment now?" The headmaster asked the question somewhat in a haste.

"About two years," Peter said resignedly.

"Two years is a long-time to work out 'the level of co-operation,' he repeated the phrase used by Peter deliberately.

There was a long silence in the room. By now Peter was willing to do anything and everything to get away from there. He liked neither the type of questions the headmaster was asking nor the tone that he used in asking them.

The headmaster, a short and a well-built man, who had a head as a large as a block of a building stone, resting on a thick neck with sinews that stood as he spoke said, "I have realised that the matter stands outside of our jurisdiction."

Peter kept an eager look; Hadio made futile guesses about what the headmaster was intending to say next.

After a brief silence, he said, "Unless something positive is done, at home, we are convinced that the level of deterioration in the educational performance of the children will continue to go down, with the same alarming speed, to reach a point of no return. As such, we recommend the case to be forwarded to the office of the social services, which we feel has the expertise as well as the jurisdiction to deal with such cases effectively. Given the natural educational talents of the children, and what was once their excellent behaviour, it would be a great shame indeed if the matter is not tackled in an appropriate time."

He stopped talking briefly; he wanted to judge from the facial appearance of his guest whether what he had just said had been received well by both Hadio and Peter. Afterwards, he said abruptly, "We shall make our official position known to the same office soon."

On that note, everybody stood up; the headmaster offered to shake hands with both Peter and Hadio.

The family left the school compound, and drove home in a dismal mood.

At home, from out of the blue, Peter took the children to task.

"You are a duo of liars, conspirators, leeches, snakes; you have no sense of gratitude whatsoever," he shouted at them to the surprise of Hadio who stood still.

"I have been doing everything to make you people happy here," he said. "However, as if it is not enough," he added, "you still have to conspire with the school authority to destroy my name. I shouldn't have brought you here. Indeed, your place is in the ghetto, from where I picked you up."

Peter was so much overwhelmed with feelings of agitation that he could not keep to one place, as he directed his vituperative attack against the children.

Directing his gaze at Atosh, he said, "You have much to learn from this society; people don't go to war here at a slightest act of provocation. You are not in the bush here, where a slight provocation makes your people run into those dirty little mud-holes that you call home, to retrieve dirty-looking old little rusted spears and knives, and engage in large-scale savageries, afterwards.

The adage, "You can take an African out of the bush, but you can't take the bush out of an African is reflected clearly in your behaviour. You are a little savage that needs taming down."

"Peter, please" Hadio tried to interject in a feeble voice. Peter gave her no chance to say much.

"Stop it, you witch," he said fuming at her. "I don't want to hear anything from you; you are the cause for all the mess that I find myself in," he added furiously.

While Hadio had remained silent, looking quite shocked, the insult was a little too much for her daughter.

Facing Peter, Shifo told him in a menacing tune, "My brother and I have not asked to come and live in this place of doom. Thanks to our mother; she is responsible for everything that went wrong in our lives." Tears were flowing down her face, "We want our father back," she shouted hysterically at her mother.

As the children and Peter continued to constantly trade insults, it helped little if Hadio tried to calm down the situation.

To her dismay, on such occasions, she found not only was Peter rude to her but so were the children.

"Why don't you two show a modicum of respect for Peter who is like a father to you?" She had told the children whenever there had been a quarrel between Peter and them.

She had long ceased to employ that act of persuasion when the children took her advice as an opportunity to repudiate her for conspiring with the man that had been a cause of their miseries, they claimed.

# Chapter Thirty Eight

# *Fair Breeze Rest Home*

Kore had spent several months in the hospital; now he was beginning to feel well again. He had been constantly dreaming of getting a discharge from the hospital, so that he could go on with his life, like he did once before. To his shock, surprise and dismay, his wish never materialised.

One sombre evening day, he was told to put on his clothes. Afterwards, he was taken to parking lot, and was told to get inside a car. When he tried to make enquiries both from the driver and the driver's companion, waiting inside the car, about the intended point of their destination, they remained quiet. Kore closed his eyes, and decided to keep his brain free from all sorts of ominous ideas.

After a long drive, through the city roads, and into small countryside gravel-roads, suddenly the car came to a standstill. Kore opened his eyes, only to be met with a strange looking three-story building, in red bricks. On the field, covered with snow, there were people whose absence of free gaiety in their movements spoke volumes about their poor-state of health.

Looking suspiciously at his surroundings, Kore thought he knew where he was, even though he never wished to admit the fact to himself.

His fears were confirmed the moment he disembarked from the car. A couple of heavily built guards, dressed in white overcoats, approached him carefully; they pleaded with him to be nice. One of them addressing him in a manner of someone suggesting to him that he was about to resist co-operating with them, in a soothing manner meant to induce a friendly spirit of acquiesce in Kore, told him, "Easy now."

Kore was angered at the way these monsters of men cooed over him. As the guards were ominously angling their way towards him, he wanted to tell them that it is not him but they who should take it easy. The two never gave him a chance to speak to them; like a cat would do to a rate, they instantly pounced on him. They carried him, and soon had him tied to a wheel chair that they pushed it hard and fast as if the devil himself was on their heels. The speeding wheel chair made Kore's brain reel.

Seconds later, they took him inside a room, in a corridor, on the ground floor of the building; there they put him in a strait jacket, before leaving the room that they locked from outside.

Inside the room, Kore was forced to reflect on his present fortunes; he had no reason to doubt the state of his mind; he told himself he was not mad, again and again. He found himself to be in such an unbelievable situation he almost convinced himself that he was hallucinating.

Gradually, eyes closed, he let his mind to focus on his grandmother's spirit, which in the past had acted as his guardian angel. The thought of his grandmother brought tears in his eyes, which forced him to address her spirit to come and deliver him from a situation that he compared to hell. He said loudly, "ever since the day that I left home, I have suffered a lot."

He wept and beseeched his grandma's spirit to come and take him with her. "Grandma, I am so tired," he said. He wept some more and wished his grandma's spirit would give him the usual sign of the lavender-scented soap to indicate her presence that never happened.

Kore remained awake for the most part of the night until he fell asleep. In the early hours of the morning, he dreamt that he was in his grandma's laps, feeling the warmth of her thick but otherwise soft thighs; with his head buried deep in her large soft breast, Kore felt safe.

They sat at the front porch of their little hut made of cow dung and sticks. Dusk had just fallen in the village. It was quiet except for the sounds made by crickets as well as a stray dog that barked with repetitive monotony, while scores of fire flies whizzed past; the shooting stars traversed the sky with incredible speed. He was four or five years old

He was in a middle of such a dream when he woke up to the sound of the door getting opened. Presently, a tall man with a huge stomach and wide shoulders of a boxer stepped into the room. The man seemed to be in his fifties. The same guards of the previous day, looking jittery, accompanied him. They let Kore out of the straight jacket and then stood aside.

The tall man stepped forward. "My name is Henrik Olsson. In this institution, I am the most senior doctor responsible for the general health of the patients here. Welcome Mr Kore," he said amicably, as he shook Kore's hand.

Later, the doctor took Kore by the hand, and together they sauntered through the hall, on their way to the doctor's office, situated in a small inconspicuous office building, in red bricks, overlooking a ground covered with snow, showing signs of receding. There was a table right in the middle of the doctor's office; on top of the table were plates of food. The room looked too small to hold large numbers of books and papers scattered all throughout the room; other books and papers were piled up together on the floor.

It was on the same table the doctor sat down to take his breakfast of a large sized bowl of porridge, buttered bread, several poached eggs, coffee and a large glass of apple juice.

Between mouthfuls of food, Doctor Olsson told Kore who by now had found himself a chair, "My apologies for putting you in such inconvenience, last night, but we had to make sure; I hope you understand. I assure you it will not happen again."

Before Kore could digest well that piece of information, Doctor Olsson said further, "Mr Kore, I usually like to cultivate friendly relationship with people that are going to be with me here in this wonderful world of mine. It makes my work seem less cumbersome and quite easy to handle."

Kore clearly objected to the use of the phrase, "wonderful world of mine," that Doctor Olsson, it seemed, had intended to refer to an acute social environment of a mental institution.

Warming up to the subject further, Doctor Olsson said, "You see, here in this world, Mr Kore, normally we are not in a hurry to give assistance to our guests. However, soon after we have gathered all the necessary information about them, only then do we offer our services to our guests."

Instead of relying on metaphors and allegories to embellish his speech with, Kore wished Doctor Olsson would use a much straight forward form of speech to express his point. But then, he decided not to give too much thought to the issue; one must be prepared for anything in the mental institution, he believed.

Speaking to Kore further, Doctor Olsson said, "Mr Kore, from now on, you are not to be made to retire to the place of abode of last night."

Afterwards, Doctor Olsson ordered the two orderlies, on a stand-by, to direct Kore to his room; the room turned out to be a far better place than the one of the previous night.

As Kore would come to know, the institution had three different divisions based on the insight the medical authorities had been having about the mental sanity of the inmates. Kept on the first floor there were people considered to be suffering from mild brain disturbances; half the space, on the first floor, was made up of sleeping rooms; the rest of the floor has a large hall, where patients felt free to walk, or have a rest on benches located at strategic points. Kore was kept on the first floor.

The people that Kore saw outside the hospital-gates, upon his arrival, on the previous day, were kept on the second floor. Besides being mentally disturbed, these people were also physically a wreck; they required a constant physical support to perform the least of any physical activities.

On the third floor there were hardened cases. These were dangerous people who had killed, maimed, raped and had committed all sorts of abominable and outrageous acts of crimes that had shocked people, and had made them feel disgusted with them. They remained locked inside their cell rooms, for almost all the time, where they were kept to themselves.

There was a strict rule in place forbidding patients to visit units other than their own.

After taking breakfast in the dining hall, followed by a short rest in his thinly furnished room, Kore decided to undertake a tour of the place, to familiarise himself with his new environment. The place, he noticed, had never presented to him the formidable image that people have usually been associating with such institutions. Its population looked calm.

Everybody was well dressed, too; except for the orderlies, no one wore a uniform of any kind. And so, unless one had a previous knowledge of the place, there was nothing on earth which could have revealed its true nature to someone who was not a keen observer of things. He saw people of different nationalities, sex and age that adorned the corridors.

Gradually, he lost the feeling of tension that had earlier overwhelmed his sense of personal security. He felt quite at ease; apparently that feeling would not last long.

Coming in his direction, from the other end of the hall, he caught sight of someone that looked exceedingly short; he had a big tummy; the man had a pair of white short trousers and a t-shirt on; the clothes on the man looked a trifle too tight on him. His white socks, bearing Nike label, reached up to his knees. He moved toward Kore in quick steps. Before Kore could decide what action to take, he was right there before him; in his hands, he held a balloon, embossed with a European map.

Kore was about to go past him when he heard a sound of a whistle. Suddenly, addressing the man with the balloon in his hands, a group of men who seemed to have appeared from nowhere shouted, "Well, what are you waiting for Nordberg?" They added, "Show it to him."

Kore backed up in anticipation of a physical struggle. The man called Nordberg threw the balloon on the ground, and started to frantically kick the ball in all directions. Meanwhile, the people who had just emerged from out of the shadows of the building cheered Nordberg on. They asked Kore to do the same thing, which he did quite reluctantly.

One of the men, fat and plumb, drooling from the mouth approached Kore, and then spoke to him quite enthusiastically, albeit in a disjointed form of speech.

"Nordberg," he said, "is Europe's best footballer." He added, "Europe is in his football, and in his football is Europe; only Nordberg can kick Europe and the football, all at once; no one does it better than him."

For nearly five long minutes, Nordberg continued with his antics. A few minutes later, someone blew the whistle again, and the group of men, along with Nordberg, like a thin smoke, receded into the recesses of the building.

As soon as the group went away, it occurred to Kore that he might have met Nordberg somewhere. As hard as he tried to locate in his mind the place he might have met him, he could not come up with an answer; he had almost given up hope when, like a flash in a pan, he got the answer he was looking for.

Nordberg, he realised, was none other than Nadir, the owner of the pizza joint that he had had an altercation with once. Kore never knew what to think of him. He couldn't bring himself to feel sorry for him, without equally having the same feelings for himself, since both were sailing in the same boat.

In future, Kore would come to know circumstances that had lead Nordberg to end up in a Fair Breeze Rest Home, and felt quite sad. Although it could not be proved in the court of law, the story that went around maintained that when Nordberg refused to pay extortion money to a notorious criminal gang of extortionists, the same gang had coerced three girls into accusing Nordberg of rape.

In a testimony they gave in the court, however, the girls insisted that Nordberg had forced himself on them, on his own volition. Angered by the rape allegation, his Swedish wife, Norah, filed for a divorce in a court of law; she also asked the court to extend full custody of the children to her; both cases were ruled in her favour.

Further investigations revealed that Nordberg had avoided paying government tax on his huge wealth, for which crime he was sentenced to three years in prison. As for the rape offence, Nordberg was found guilty, as charged, and was sentenced to five years in prison. The sentences were made to run concurrently.

On the way to prison, he requested for a balloon with a European map imprinted on it. Not many days later, he was taken to Fair Breeze Rest Home and not to the prison as had been earlier envisaged.

Ever since that day, Nordberg had never kept the balloon out of his sight.

Before Nordberg ended up in Fair Breeze Rest Home, he had been the owner of a chain of kebab restaurants. Kore would also come to know that Nordberg had been so successful in his business that the country's highest municipal authority awarded him the honour of bearing the following title: "The Swedish Man of the Year."

As a token of appreciation for the Swedish society that had given him such honour, he changed his name to Nordberg, from Nadir, on the day when he received the award.

A brief meeting with Nordberg might have been a chance encounter with the bizarre; however, it was not going to be the last one. A few steps down the corridor, Kore came across a tall man with a long beard; he had a large saffron-coloured turban on his head, and wore a sarong of the same colour as the turban. The man facing a window was involved in treacherous act of balancing a long spoon in his mouth, its broad side-end holding a plum. He stopped the moment he saw Kore approaching him; he smiled and said, "Hello there."

He addressed Kore in perfect English, using an accent that sounded exotic.

"My name," he said, "is Sinbad." He added quite feverishly, "I am not Sinbad the Sailor, mind you. I am the Sinbad that flies high up in the sky."

He gave Kore an eager look, offered to shake hands with him and said, "As you were heading this way, a moment ago, you have been privileged to witness one of the most rewarding experiments ever made. I was measuring a distance between our planet-earth and planet-mercury to where I intend to fly, using a vehicle currently in a process of getting manufactured." He never waited for Kore to react to his statement; he took off suddenly.

Next to a window, and close to a place where the flying Sinbad had just vacated, there was a bench. Kore decided to sit down, to enjoy a moment of rest. As he sat there, the images of the aggressive orderlies, the gluttonous Doctor Olsson, Nordberg the footballer and the flying Sinbad came entering his mind, all at once. Suddenly, he had a feeling that someone was approaching him. To him it appeared as if people were popping up from a magician's cap to come and meet him.

"It seems to me that you have already made acquaintances with both Sinbad and Nordberg!" the man announced confidently, the moment he stood before Kore, who could not help noticing how the measured tone in his speech had made the man to differ from everyone. Subsequently, Kore took a deep look at him. The man looked back; he offered Kore a warm smile. He sat next to Kore on the bench. Kore stared at the man's eyes; the man returned the stare with a steady focus. Looking closely at the man, he must be different, Kore believed.

"Who are you?" Kore asked the man.

"I am someone who should not be here," he replied cheerfully.

"But you are here, nevertheless," Kore said.

"And so, would you." After a while, he added, "Maybe. Who knows?"

"But I am already here. Am I not?" Kore said impatiently.

"No, you are not; wait until you have been formally institutionalised," the man said casually

Kore thought it was hopeless talking to the man. He stood up; he was about to leave, when the man told him, "Wait; I know what you may be thinking about me; I am not as mad as you may tend to think I am. When I set my eyes on you, I knew from the way you walk and how you observe things around you that you are different."

"Never mind," Kore said. "Just tell me, if you are not mad, what are you? He asked. "And again, what are you doing here?" He added.

"Being here is not a measure of someone's level of mental competence; of all people you should know it," he said in a calm voice. "Are you mad? He asked.

Although the question had made him to feel offended, Kore stayed quiet.

"In these surroundings, it is important what you wish to think of yourself. However, just as important is the institution's opinion of you," he said studiously.

Kore was beginning to suspect the man was mad. However, he soon realised there was some sense in what the man was trying to say. Therefore, since it could not be possible for him to be mad and sane quite at the same time, Kore changed his mind about him; he decided he would learn from him.

"What does the institution think of me?" He asked in a hesitant tone.

"They have no any formal opinion about you," he said easily. "However, make no mistake, they will find one soon." he added. "At the moment," he reminded Kore, "you are neither mad nor sane; you are in a state of limbo - so to speak. The state in which you are in is comparable to a soul in a purgatory, waiting for it to be released, ready to enter either hell or paradise. You are yet to be institutionalised; that means your presence here must be formalised through a decision that need to be made by people considered experts on mental health issues. Their recommendation regarding the state of your health would determine your fate."

As soon as he finished saying those words, he stood up and left. What the man had just said made Kore see the light at the end of the tunnel.

If a panel was going to discuss the state of his mind, he saw no reason for not getting vindicated, he thought.

Hence, such possibility sent his spirit soaring high up in the air. This happy state of mind, unfortunately, didn't last long; a few days later, following the interview the panel of experts had made with him, they released the following report on him:

For his own safety, as well as the safety of the society in general, Kore should be kept in an institution, where he is going to benefit from a treatment offered by a team of expert doctors. We have found Kore to be suffering from a state of paranoid schizophrenia, which requires that he is kept under a constant surveillance. His relationship with the following persons and institutions is an example of the poor state of his mind: Ingrid of the Social Welfare office; the police; Hadio, his ex-wife; Peter Wells; University authorities; Jakobsson of the labour office; Hadio's lawyer; the judge in the family court etc.

Furthermore, there is a pent-up anger in Kore, which poses a great deal of danger to people who might get into contact with him. We have managed to trace this anger to a time he had spent in jail in his country, where he had undergone a severe torture. As a victim of torture, it is quite possible for Kore to cause harm to other people, as a way of getting even with society. People that are in danger of becoming victims of his deranged state of mind are particularly people that he knows them well, including Hadio and Peter Wells, who he had been pestering.

In conclusion, we recommend Kore's case should come up for a review in a year or two. Meanwhile, Kore is expected to undergo a treatment, involving both medication and therapy."

When this decision was conveyed to Kore, he felt as though the whole world had come crushing down on him.

# Chapter Thirty Nine

# *Emil*

The letter from the social welfare office to Peter's residence came on time, as expected. In it, the family members were requested to visit the social welfare office, beginning with Hadio and Peter first, to be followed by the children, at a later date. On his way to the social welfare office, on a late Friday afternoon, accompanied by Hadio, Peter was far from feeling enthusiastic about the visit. As a matter of fact he was angry; one could easily notice this from his reckless driving. He had once or twice deliberately ignored some important traffic regulations.

At the social welfare service offices, they were directed to an office, at the end of a long corridor. Standing in the doorway was a short man whose face looked as if the blood had been drained out of it; he had put on a pair of jeans and a checked blue flannel shirt that looked a little too tight on him. He shook hands with Hadio and Peter; afterwards, he let a wide smile to cross his face that Peter reciprocated with a smile of his own. Soon the two were hugging each other with such great warmth that, watching the spectacle with interest, Hadio found quite strange to see Peter express himself in such a passionate manner. She had never experienced such a moment with him.

"By gosh, Emil, you haven't changed a bit;" Peter said.

"You haven't changed much yourself," Emil said.

Making a point of introducing Emil to Hadio, Peter said, "Meet Hadio." He told Hadio afterwards, "This is Emil, my former classmate from the undergraduate days; centuries ago now, it seems."

Perhaps out of a sheer feeling of excitement for meeting his former classmate, Emil said as he addressed Peter further, "As I was addressing the letter to your family, it never occurred to me it was to you, my friend, Peter, I was writing the letter."

"Well, here I am now," Peter said pompously in reply.

They got inside an office with a spacious look. Emil requested his visitors to sit on the chairs, from where they faced him across from the table.

"Let us see now," Emil said, and added, "Where do we start from?"

He pulled a letter out from a drawer, and then kept it on the table. Afterwards, using quite a lucid expression, he said, "This letter, the copy of which has been forwarded to you, is from the school board. The school authority believes that all is not well in your home front, especially, because of the changes taking place in the children's lives, both in terms of poor school performance and a growing aggressive behaviour. This is a reason the school authorities have requested us to have a word with both of you, to determine if together we could come up with some sort of solution to benefit the children."

He paused briefly to give them a curious look, and then he said, "The case has been discussed here, and it is our view that a separate discussion with the children, after you, is necessary."

Both Peter and Hadio nodded their heads quite at the same time.

Peter wished the man would go on with his speech. As long as he spoke in general terms, the speech meant little to him. He knew, however, any moment now, he would focus on Hadio and him, and he never liked what that might entail. If Emil could read what was going on in Peter's mind, he would have gotten over what he was saying as quickly as possible.

Peter's dreadful fear of psychologists had influenced his attitudes towards them.

"They always speak with a kind of confidence that make them feel different from everyone", he told himself. "They ask one question after another, and seem to like what they find about you. They act as if their past is beyond any probing." He added.

As he sat there in the room, listening to Emil, he recollected a time when his mother had taken him to meet with one of them. He had hated the man, just as he hated Emil now.

He was jolted from pursuing his thoughts further by Emil who was saying, "Based on the information from the school authorities that we have here, I understand that the two of you are living together. How is your life together, if I may ask you?

With little effort, Peter said in reply, "It is good."

Emil was surprised to see how quickly Peter came up with the reply. To Emil, it looked as though Peter had been anticipating the question. Then Emil took a slow and deliberate look at Hadio and asked the same question.

Hadio's reply seemed evasive to him.

She said, "Not bad," to which Emil said, "Do you mean it is not good either. Is this what you mean?"

"It is good," she managed to say, looking at Peter out of the corner of her eye.

Emil subjected them to further questioning; he asked about their financial status, household choirs, as well as relationship with the children etc.

In the end, Emil nodded his head wisely and said, "I think a happy home is a virtue; however, due to constant conflicts, many of us fail to benefit from its blessings. If the parents do not respect and love each other, this is bound to have negative effects on the children.

Needless to mention to you is the fact that you are two fully responsible grown up people that can decide for yourselves what is best for you. We shall hold a separate meeting with the children, and would inform you of our decision soon."

From his speech, it was clear to Peter the meeting had come to an end.

Both Hadio and Peter stood up to shake hands with Emil. Addressing Peter, Emil cheerfully said to him, "Well Peter, it has been a pleasure meeting you. Please, in case you are in the neighbourhood, drop by just to say Hello?"

By now Peter was out of the doorway, heading toward the corridor, on his way to the elevator, as Hadio trailed behind. Peter never bothered to give a reply. In fact, far from reciprocating the friendly gesture, he was boiling with anger. As he walked into the parking lot, at the basement of the building, he said loudly for Hadio to hear him say. "What a fool; he wishes me to drop by in his office anytime in future; let him know I would rather drop dead than to drop by in his office."

They got inside the car and drove away. One or two kilometres down the road, on a deserted ground, Peter stopped the car suddenly; he opened the car door and pushed Hadio hard out of the car.

"Get out of my car. I don't want to see you," he said.

That a journey home, after having had a meeting with Emil, would be anything but a pleasant one had been quite clear to Hadio. However, what she hadn't been prepared for was that Peter would refuse her a ride home.

"What have I done to warrant such awful treatment from you?" She asked meekly.

"I hate you." He said. "You and your miserable children," he added impatiently, "have done all that you could do to destroy my reputation. I curse the day I sat my eyes on you, Get out of my car."

After that he drove away, leaving Hadio standing on the age of the road.

At no time in her life had Hadio felt so lonely, miserable and helpless. She realised that Peter's aggression towards her had been increasing in volume, as her ability to counter him diminished with time. She did this to avoid putting her position and that of her children to jeopardy.

It was enough that she had broken up with Kore; she didn't want the family to face further uprooting, in case she broke up with Peter, too. But was it worth it? She started doubting whether her perseverance was worth the price of losing her dignity, as a person. She felt gripped by anger towards Peter, such as she had never felt before now; she wished he was present there so that she could hurt him; she promised herself she would no longer take his harassment laying low; she would stand up to him, she promised herself.

She looked for a bus to take her home. By the time she got home, it was late in the evening. The moment she got there, she tried to get to talk to her children in their room; she wished to speak to them about their day in school; she had not spoken to them for quite some time now, because each time she tried to do so, the children gave her a cold shoulder.

This time the children refused to have anything to do with her, too. She went to her room, knowing quite well that, having already lost Kore, she was at a point of losing her children now. At that moment, Hadio felt there was nothing left for her to live for. She shut the door of her room, sat on her bed and wept, silently.

Several days later, the children went to visit the Social Welfare Office. Emil welcomed the children, and then took them to meet with a woman psychologist with a kindly face. The woman exchanged warm greetings with the children; she held them in her office, talking to them in great details about their home-life, relationships with parents and life at school.

Shortly after, a report on the outcome of the discussion that had been held with different members of the family was forwarded to the school authority; a copy of the same report was also forwarded home to Peter and Hadio. The report itself was quite brief, but it covered important items. It read as follows:

Having studied well the situation affecting the lives of the children, we are convinced that their school performances as well as their aggressive behaviour have been caused by an environment, which is not quite healthy enough for them to grow up in. Those constant quarrels taking place there, between and among various individuals, have precluded any kind of improvement from taking place in their lives.

The children feel vulnerable due to lack of a proper care, assistance and love. They have been quite scarred psychologically watching the humiliation of their mother by Peter. This has strengthened their hatred for Peter, but had also made them to despise their mother for failing to stand up to him.

Moreover, the children have developed a feeling of great hatred for both Peter and Hadio for the fate that has befallen their father, who now is in a mental hospital, and whom the children have shown to have a deep love.

In conclusion, more than anything, we feel the children would need love and care to enable them to feel confident in themselves. Since they could have secured this love from their father, who now is in the mental hospital, this office recommends an alternative home for them, to enable them to have the love they disparately need in life.

The family court upheld this decision and made it into law. When the children were informed of the decision, they became happy; they were happy that they were getting away from a home that they had increasingly come to despise and hate so much.

# Chapter Forty

## *Alvarez Speaks His Mind*

From the day the decision had been made to formally keep him in the institution for undergoing a treatment, Kore had remained locked inside his room. One day, as he enjoyed an early morning walk in the hall, he met the man he had spoken to quite a few days earlier.

"Hello there!" the man said.

He never waited for Kore to return the greetings, but said further, "Well?"

"Well, what?" Kore said.

Perhaps due to a feeling of embarrassment for being so direct in his speech, the man said politely, "I am sorry, but I just wished to know if you have received any word from the panel of medical experts?"

"Yes. I have," Kore said quickly.

"What is the decision?" He asked a little anxiously.

"I have been institutionalised. Isn't that what you would call it?" Kore replied, sounding frustrated.

"Welcome home," the man said, not quite so enthusiastically.

They walked side-by side, as the cold wind that filtered through the half-opened windows blew across their faces. Suddenly the man accompanying Kore stopped; without much fanfare, he introduced himself to Kore as Ricardo Alvarez.

In due course, Kore and Alvarez would become good friends. Their friendship, however, would become a subject of much speculation among the orderlies, who had no doubt in their minds that the two men were truly mad in every sense of the word; perhaps, it was for this reason they referred to them as, "The Two Crazy Musketeers."

Nevertheless, whatever opinion those minders might have been having about Kore and Alvarez, what they had no way of knowing was that both Kore and Alvarez had opinion of their own about their state of mind that was not quite flattering.

About the state of their mind, Alvarez liked to make a joke. He would tell Kore, "The only difference between them and us is this: while we permanently live our lives on this side of the wall, on some nights they go home to sleep."

Alvarez was quite short and had short thick limbs; he was in his late-thirties; he had a round face and thick strong jaws, giving his face a shape of granite that required polishing; he wore thick glasses on a dull looking face, which, otherwise, would sparkle easily in a moment of joy.

A long time ago, Alvarez had decided to store away in a Swedish ship that took him to the port-city of Gothenburg, Sweden, from where he had sought political asylum.

The decision made by Alvarez to store away on a Swedish ship hadn't come at a spar of a moment, according to him. For two long weeks, prior to the departure of the ship to its destination, Alvarez had made a thorough study of everything he had wished to know about the ship. He had made note of the departure date for the ship, the type of cargo it was going to carry, the number of crew in the ship and the final port of call. In doing all of these things, he obtained the support of groups to which he belonged that was opposed to the ruling government.

At this time, he had identified a place to hide, and there he had kept food provision to see him throughout the number of days he hoped to stay hidden.

Given his perceived knowledge of the Swedish human rights track record, the choice he had made of letting the Swedish ship take him to Sweden had made him secure in his belief about gaining political asylum there.

One morning day, after he presented himself to members of the crew, five days after the ship had left the port, he was taken to a captain of the ship – a giant of a man with side whiskers and a long ginger hair that reached his shoulder; the captain wished to know what he was doing in his ship; to the surprise of Alvarez, he also wished to know if he was hungry. He was hungry, he had told the captain, who immediately took him to a dining hall, and had ordered breakfast made of salami, bread, eggs and coffee that he consumed with a great relish, since he had been extremely hungry; the food he had stashed away had lasted him no more than three days.

As he ate his breakfast, the captain took coffee and sat there watching him with curious eyes. Encouraged by the positive reception he had received from the captain, Alvarez became eager to speak to the captain about himself, but the captain wouldn't let him do such a thing between mouthfuls of food. He would speak to him, he had said, once he finished eating, which he did, later, in his office, in a company of his assistance that had acted as a witness.

The conversation had been carried out in English, which, as a language, was familiar to everyone in the captain's office. The warm reception in place of a harrowing one he had been expecting to get from the captain, the saintly figure of the captain, the warm coffee, not to mention the brightly-lit room, as well as the enticing sweet smell of both the ocean mixed with the sweet smell from the mangoes piled up on the plate on the table in the captain's office, had a soothing effect on his nerves, which were on edge.

As soon as he finished speaking to the captain about himself, the captain informed him that it was not for him to decide his fate; that would be done by people who deal in immigration issues in Gothenburg, he said. While waiting for that day to come, the captain reminded Alvarez that he would be required to do some job on the ship, for which he would be paid a salary.

There were two more ports in North America left to visit before the ship heads off to Sweden, the captain reminded Alvarez. The next day, Alvarez took a job as a kitchen boy, helping to keep both the kitchen and the dining hall clean.

In Gothenburg, he was handed over to immigration authorities to whom he explained his situation. He told them where he came from and had further said, in his home country, he had fought for the rights of the indigenous people that he belonged. However, before escaping to Sweden, he had killed two policemen there in self-defence, he had told the authorities.

His home government, following his case closely, had accused him of murder and pillage, and had called for his extradition.

Notwithstanding requests for his extradition, made by his home government, the Swedish Government had decided to offer him political asylum. After gaining political asylum in Sweden, Alvarez had lived a simple life in his new home country until his world came to change suddenly and quite dramatically, one day.

It was a hot summer-day, with scarcely any breeze in the atmosphere, when his life took a new turn for the worse. He was reading a book, sitting on a bench, in one of Stockholm's many gardens when he saw someone from his home-country – someone that he thought he would never live to see him again.

At first, he was not sure that the man was who he thought he was. After watching him, for a while, he became quite certain that the heavily-built short man, dressed in light khaki trousers, a white shirt and leather sandals, eating a con ice-cream, while enjoying an afternoon-walk in the garden, was none other than Pablo Gutierrez – 'the butcher.'

He noticed that he had grown a beard, perhaps in an attempt to give himself a disguise. Gutierrez, in his homeland, had earned notoriety for torturing and killing people thought to be opposed to the government, for which he had been working as a senior security officer.

On setting his eyes on him, Alvarez knew quite well what he was going to do next. He had reached a decision, there and then, that he was going to try to kill Gutierrez, to avenge his brother's murder, Pedro, which took place in his hands.

Once he made up his mind, he set the task of studying his every movement, to its smallest detail. He discovered, in due course, Gutierrez's presence in Sweden had something to do with the embassy in Stockholm. Alvarez had also discovered that Gutierrez had a fixed schedule that he had been meticulously following.

From the embassy, he would take a walk to the nearest shopping-centre from where, around five, he would be doing some shopping. Usually he bought some food-stuffs and other odd items. From there, he would take a walk to his apartment, two blocks away, where he lived alone. Apart from visiting a neighbourhood gym club, he had no any extra curricula activities. He had no friends; no one visited his apartment, except for a middle-aged woman cleaner.

One day, when Gutierrez was on his way home, Alvarez approached him quietly from behind, and then spoke in Spanish to him. "Good day," he said.

To make sure that the man was indeed none other than Gutierrez, Alvarez remembered to add, "Mr Gutierrez."

Gutierrez turned abruptly to look at him, and could sense danger, somehow.

"Who are you?" he asked; he was trying, at the same time, to reach for something in his pocket. Alvarez drew a knife; with an agility that comes from first-rate-training in the art of physical combat he drove the knife deep into Gutierrez's throat; he died before he could hit the ground. Thereafter, he made no any attempt to run away. He kept the knife on the ground, sat down beside the dead-body, waiting for the police to arrive.

Alvarez was taken into police custody, charged with the murder of Gutierrez. Notwithstanding several appeals made by his lawyers, as well as human rights organisations, calling for the government not to carry on with his extradition, it seemed luck had not been in his side.

This time around, the conservative section of the Swedish press had advised the Swedish Government to deport Alvarez back to where he came from, or face the possibility of having Alvarez's home government renege on a timber trade agreement that had offered Sweden favourable terms of trade, they wrote.

And so, a plan had been underway to secretly send him back to his original homeland, one day, when Alvarez acted mad by biting his defence lawyer's left ear, took a sizeable chunk off the ear and swallowed it, living his defence lady-lawyer reeling in pain, while bleeding profusely. The rest is history.

Kore thought what Alvarez did to the lawyer was quite disgusting, and told him so in their discussion that took place in Alvarez's room.

"I think what you did to that lawyer is a horrible thing. You should not have done it," Kore said.

It was raining outside; the raindrops, furiously pelting against the glass window had made a disturbing dull-sounding noise in the small room.

"I do agree with you," Alvarez said. "However," he added, "I wish to tell you that that lawyer's ear has done a lot of good. Because of what I did, I am now considered to be a mad person. But am I mad? No, I don't think so. Yet, can you imagine what would have happened to me had Sweden sent me back? I had to feign madness to save my life.

Had Sweden sent me back home, in defiance of international law, Sweden would have faced a political embarrassment of a highest degree. As for the people in my despised home government, they are perhaps happy to know that I am living my life in a mental institution. And here in this institution, it is immaterial what they wish to think about me.

As for you, my friend, think what you want; just remember this: that lawyer's ear has served many purposes."

Although Alvarez was not always in a state of cheerful mood, yet he managed to somehow make his burden look lighter, especially if compared to other people caught in a similar situation as his. And as Kore came to know him well, Kore discovered that he was given to brilliant ideas, which he often expressed them with a conviction of a preacher. He seemed to have answers to many questions.

When Kore got admitted into the institution, he found Alvarez there. And yet, nothing much had changed in him, to make him feel disgusted with life.

Sitting in his single room, talking to Kore, from out of the blue, he said, "From a whole gamut of emotions, I still wonder why the three-man panel of doctors should insist that I display the feelings of regret and remorse."

"Why don't you do it?" Kore challenged him.

"You are not being serious, or are you?" He asked. "Do you know," he said further "what price I would have to pay for being remorseful, or full of guilt for what I did? I would have to disown my principles and everything else for which I have fought for. I never killed anyone just for the love of it. I am not a psycho-path they say I am, for not showing guilt or remorse for my actions."

Somehow the conversation between the two men had forced Kore to think of the reason for which people, like him, were there in the mental institution; he was curious, and so he wanted to hear Alvarez say something.

"Why are we here?" He asked Alvarez.

Replying to Kore's question, in a sombre tone, Alvarez said, "Our being here is a measure of our powerlessness in a society we are living in. Power, my dear Kore, is the name of the game. I mean real power; power to make important decisions in a society."

Alvarez must have detected in Kore's face what to him appeared like a shadow of doubt, regarding what he was trying to say to him; hence, to appeal to Kore's intellect, he said, "Yes, it could be done. Why not? As immigrants we need to come up with some sort of solution to change our own destiny, by ourselves. We don't need anyone to remind us about our situation as it is often done here, either through documentary programmes they run on us, or research work they carry on us.

It is true that we are leaving in run-down neighbourhoods; joblessness is rife among us. These are the facts of our lives; they have since become a way of life to us. However, the question is: why are the concerned authorities not doing much to change this dismal situation that affects our lives?"

He remained quiet briefly.

Meanwhile, Kore was eager to hear what more Alvarez had to say to him. His previous statements, however, had made Kore's mind reel back to a time, at a refugee camp, on his arrival there, when he had watched a programme in which the fate of the immigrants had been a subject of discussion.

Watching the panel of experts on immigration acknowledging failures in the integration policy had made Kore feel encouraged; he had been convinced then that acknowledging policy failures was the first step toward undertaking corrective measures. From the TV room that evening, in the refugee camp, he had gone to his room, and had slept a deep sleep, hopeful that efforts leading to integration of immigrants into the mainstream Swedish society was bound to take place, one day; today, a decade later, integration still is a subject of discussion in the country.

"If the past is anything to go by," Alvarez jolted him from following his thoughts further, "there is no reason for hoping that change is coming soon."

"Integration is about marginal groups in a society, having access to national resources; at present, despite all existing laws and regulations put in place to bring equity in the society nothing much has changed; crucial resources, such as job opportunities as well as bank credits are still denied to those who are less privileged." Kore said.

"It is essentially for the same reason," Alvarez said, "I am convinced there is a need for members of the immigrant community to have their own political party to represent their interest here. If the Green is a party that belongs to people who share a common interest in the way of gaining a better environment, I see no reason, as immigrants, why we should not have a political party?" Alvarez said.

"Unless, those holding crucial resources in their hands change their minds, at the individual level, the quest for integration will remain an elusive dream, even if you have a party that speaks for the less privileged in the society." Kore said.

For a moment he stayed quiet, and then said, "If you ask me, I have more fear of a faceless bureaucrat, who in public platforms seem to support efforts leading to integration, but would look at my job application and then caste it aside, merely because I have an identity different from his, than a skin-head waiting in a street corner to cut my throat with a sharp razor blade. The former will condemn me to leave a life of a perpetual circle of poverty, degradation and humiliation, while the latter will send me to my early grave. Between the two, if you ask, I would rather meet the latter of the two fates

Alvarez displaying a sign of disappointment at Kore's statement said, "So you don't believe a political party can offer solution for the less privileged."

"Yes; it is impossible, at the practical level," Kore said.

"Why do you think so," Alvarez asked.

"Seeing that immigrants are in a minority here, while democratic elections make fetish of numbers, how do you overcome the anomaly?" he asked.

"It is quite simple," Alvarez said. "Don't forget," he added, "we are a population of one million in a country of eight million people. We may not be able to win an outright majority vote; however, through our votes, we could decide on who wins the elections and who loses them. To succeed, however, we must reject multiculturalism, since it amplifies our differences in multicultural name."

"Are you not in favour of multiculturalism?" Kore asked anxiously.

"I know well that in this country different immigrant groups don't like each other. They hate and despise each other. While each group thinks it is better than the other, the fact is that they share a common culture of marginalisation, derived from a position of powerlessness. In a fight to improve their conditions, this is what immigrants need to keep in mind. However, unless they forge unity and forget divisions based on their cultural differences, immigrants will never be able to share a common platform," he said.

"But cultural differences are real. Don't you think so?" Kore said.

He had not been expecting Kore to interfere with the flow of his ideas, it seemed. He searched for an answer to give and then he said, "let us keep to our separate cultures – our traditional dances, our foods and our dress, all of which are a source of personal and communal pride. Let us not, however, allow cultural differences from stopping us working together."

Presently, Alvarez excused himself; he went to the bathroom. Like Kore's own single room, Alvarez's room had a single chair, a bed and a table. Nothing fanciful; one felt comfortable in it, just the same. Compared to his life outside of the institution, apart from losing his personal freedom, and the fact that he couldn't see his children or his wife, Kore had little else that he missed.

Back from the bathroom, a moment later, Alvarez said, "Well, where were we?" And then suddenly, he remembered.

He said, "Yes, we must ask ourselves the following crucial questions: what does this multiculturalism means? Does multiculturalism means keeping our traditional dances, our dresses or our foods? I believe there is more to multiculturalism than what a mere style of clothes or food could suggest."

Kore admired Alvarez for the way he expressed himself; it seemed obvious to Kore that Alvarez seemed not to want to force his view-point on him, but to make his point clear.

For a moment, he stayed quiet, which had made Kore eager to want to hear Alvarez say more.

"In all the discussions made on multiculturalism," said Alvarez, "the role that ethnic Swedes play in this multicultural society is all but ignored, which leaves the discussion half complete. Multiculturalism is not only about whether migrants should feel free to practise their culture, and to what extent, but it is also about how much the mainstream ethnic Swedish society is exposed to the immigrants' ways of thinking and behaviour. If society could succeed in this objective, it would help lessen the speed with which people, like us, are made to end up in here," he said cogently.

"You are not saying, by any chance, these institutions are places reserved exclusively for immigrants? Surely, there must be a scientific reason to justify our presence here," Kore said, feeling uneasy.

"That is right." Alvarez said promptly."

He took a keen look at Kore and then said, "I doubt what role science has played in your case, if any at all."

"What do you mean?" Kore asked, looking as if the statement had disturbed his feelings.

"Psychologists whose decisions have brought you here may not be charlatans, but then their science is not an exact science in a way that mathematics is," he said. He posed briefly to see if Kore would say something. Kore stayed quiet, but gave Alvarez an intense look that made hard for Alvarez to read any meaning into it.

"Their theories," he went on with his exposition, a moment later, "come and go."

"In this case, could you tell me how our presence here gets justification from the concerned authorities," Kore said, knowing well that he had managed to put Alvarez in a corner; thus, he became more than curious to see what Alvarez would do to wriggle out of this one.

"It is simple," Alvarez said laughing lightly. "I believe," he added, "those who have judged the state of your sanity did it not from any scientific perspectives – even though they assumed this to be the case – but from a subjective evaluation of your behavioural tendencies, drawn from what their cultural norms, beliefs and practices are."

He stayed quiet afterwards, as if to give chance for Kore to digest his point of view.

"Your madness, according to them," he added, after a while, "is a result of your displaying the emotions of anger toward the police and any other source of authority you might have encountered; for them, your belligerent attitude denotes a behavioural tendency akin to madness." He let his eyes rest on Kore for a long while before saying, "It might be too late for you; in Sweden the ability to contain your emotion, in any form, is a sign of a well-balanced mind."

Having seen some sense in what Alvarez had just said to him, Kore engaged Alvarez in further conversation.

"Where do you think the solution lies, in this case?" Kore asked.

"Since science is incapable of generating a kind of knowledge which calls for tolerance, understanding and human brotherhood, I think it is wrong to put much reliance on science to understand human actions in a social setting. True knowledge is an antidote to all forms of false knowledge which might lead to misconception, distrust and misunderstanding in a society; only from out of philosophy a true knowledge is possible.

After this conversation, a few days later, Alvarez's case came up for a review; a reprieve was denied.

# Chapter Forty One

# *Burning Sensation*

While in her office, working on one of her pet projects, Hadio received a letter. Unlike other letters that had often been kept for her to collect in the pidgin-hole, this letter was delivered in person, by the office secretary. She had a hunch that the letter holds a message that would cause her to feel disappointed. But, on the second thought, she admonished herself, and urged herself to think positively. She took a deep breath and opened the envelope in a hurry. After reading the letter, Hadio was deeply shocked; her knees grew weak, while the rest of her body shook like someone suffering from a debilitating bout of fever; she also had a feeling of suffocation.

From the office, she ran blindly to the bathroom, locked herself inside the bathroom, cried and vomited. In the letter, she was given a notice of three months in which to vacate the office. The letter carried the signature of Peter Welles. She read the letter, once more; however, each time that she read the letter, the message in it remained quite the same.

In fact, three weeks earlier, the board running the project had sat down to discuss the future prospect of the project. As a

Senior Consultant to the project, and an important member of the board, Peter had a major say on the issue. He had called for the termination of the project on the ground that the project had succeeded in its mission of letting people have knowledge on the subject of female circumcision.

He had said the project couldn't do more than what it had so far done; the eradication of the practice of genital mutilation, he had said, didn't fall under the purview of the project activities, which must be left to the law enforcing agencies to do, by apprehending individuals breaking the law, prohibiting the practice of female genital mutilation.

From the bathroom, she returned to the office to phone Peter.

"Someone is going to visit the office. I want you to make inventory of each and every item in the office. Keep a table and some chairs for a temporary use; you may need them," Peter said when he received Hadio's call.

In response, mortified by the prospect of losing her job, Hadio said, "But, Peter, why?"

The disbandment of the project Stop Genital Mutilation Now had also affected two other people - a thirty-year-old man and a girl of twenty-five years old, both had acted as assistants to Hadio.

Hadio wanted some sort of clarification from Peter; she wanted Peter to put things in a perspective for her; she discovered, to her dismay, Peter was one person least concerned about her fate. By phoning Peter, Hadio was also looking for some sort of consolation from him; instead, she received a heartless remark - one that made her spirit to sink to its lowest possible point of desperation.

"Did you not think the project would end up, one day? He sarcastically said in response to her desperate attempt to talk to him. "You must accept," he maliciously added, "the decision with all your heart." He chuckled afterwards.

At that moment, Hadio recollected a conversation that once she had had with Kore. In replying to a statement she had directed at him that had caused him to feel offended, Kore had said to her, "You are cheated into believing what you are not; you are merely a puppet; whoever is pulling the rope he or she will bring the show to the end…"

"Why didn't I listen to him when I could do so?" She asked herself.

She wished she had asked the same question before it got too late. She could hardly bring herself to do such a thing, because by then Kore had already become irrelevant to her scheme of things

When faced with a choice between a man that had promised security of job, but had nothing else to offer her, and another one that had respected her, but couldn't provide for her, she had opted for the former; in choosing Peter, she had opted for security, not love and respect.

To make up for her past actions, she wanted to shout for the world to hear her asking Kore for forgiveness.

Hadio imagined herself without a job; such a thought had made her feel terribly worried. She felt like having a rest, and so she decided to take a day off. From the office, she took a bus home. Inside the bus, on the way home, she thought she heard Kore's voice sounding in her head, taunting and mocking her. She held her head between her hands, and gave out a loud hysterical shout. The rest of the passengers in the bus, staring at her with a look of bewilderment in their eyes, were visibly shaken.

Once she reached home, she went to lie down on her bed and thought of Kore. Each time she found herself in a bind, she couldn't help thinking of Kore. Such thoughts made her feel sad and also made her want to cry; she found refuge in listening to a sound of music when faced with such a moment. Hadio was not someone who could be considered to be a lover of music, but she found the music of BB King to have had a calming effect on her mind and body. She left the bed to fetch a bottle of whisky from the kitchen cabinet and poured a generous portion of whisky into a glass.

She took the glass, and the bottle, and entered the sitting room; she sat down in one of the sofa sets and took a long sip from her drink. As the burning sensation of the drops of whisky went past her throat, and into her stomach, she felt an instant relief from a pain in her mind that had been exacerbated by thoughts, each one more severe than the other one.

She approached the music cabinet, picked an album that she wanted to listen to and let it play the song, GHETTO WOMAN, by BB King. As she listened to the music, she got up from her chair, and did what she had always done when she got drunk; she danced to the tune of the music, while tears fell down her face. She listened to the same music again and again, as she continued dancing, until she reached a point she couldn't dance any more. She went to her bedroom, carrying with her the drink. While in her bed, she continued taking her drink until she finished the bottle, and then she blacked out.

In the evening, when Peter came home he found her in bed, unconscious of everything in her surroundings.

On the following morning, she woke up feeling awfully sick and tired. She had just entered the kitchen in order to try to get a cold drink of water when she came across Peter taking breakfast. He threw a wicked glance at her, and told her not so inspiringly, "You will kill yourself, if by taking alcohol you think you could solve your problems. Drinks are there for you to enjoy, not drawing your sorrows in."

Hadio neither had the strength nor the inclination to argue with him. Instead, she stared at him with a tired look in her face. As soon as he finished taking his breakfast, Peter went away, leaving Hadio in the kitchen, feeling she had no desire for anything. She thought of a long day ahead of her, and how tired she was. At last she pulled herself together; she decided to report to duty, even though she was tired and feeling miserable.

Hadio continued to feel indifferent to everything in her surroundings, including her job, to the extent each time she went out to work she felt she had no desire to do anything, because of a condition of tiredness hanging on to her quite irrevocably.

Two months from the day when she received the letter that had conveyed the bad news to her, Hadio left the office to go out to have to breathe a fresh air. Outside, she came across people enjoying sunshine after a long winter season. It was a perfect bright spring day, the sky was clear; birds were cheeping incessantly as they kept jumping restlessly from one tree branch to another. This favourable change of season had meant nothing to her. Hadio felt an unrestrained urge to do something – to shout, to cry or to fall down and die.

"Why is everybody's face but mine is shining bright with happiness?" She seemed to think.

She was crossing the road when her attention was drawn to a bar, its lights beckoning at her. On the way there, her mind became suddenly filled with a sudden determination to get drunk. The thought of getting drunk made Hadio develop an instant feeling of wellbeing. It was 12 Noon. Inside the bar, which also served food to customers, she ordered for a large mug of beer, and took a long sip from her drink of beer.

At that moment, she remembered her friend, Gudrun Helmut Waldorf. The thought of her friend triggered a memory in her mind about the time when she and Gudrun had occupied this very same table, and had talked and drank together. They had talked about their work to each other. With the memory of her friend deepening in her mind, Hadio developed an urge to speak to Gudrun, and so she went to ask the bar tender in the counter to let her use the phone. She dialled Gudrun's number.

A moment later, a voice on the other end of the line said, "This is Gudrun."

"This is Hadio," Hadio said carefully. "How are you?" She added.

"I am fine; good to hear from you; and how are you?" Gudrun answered enthusiastically.

Hadio hesitated for a moment and then she said, "I am fine."

Hadio's dull sounding voice might have convinced Gudrun that something was not quite right with Hadio. Addressing Hadio further, she said, "Are you not feeling well?" to which Hadio replied in a soft voice, "I am fine."

Seconds later, sounding quite agitated, Hadio said, "No; I am not fine. In fact, I feel quite miserable."

"What is wrong? Tell me, please," Gudrun said in a pleading tone.

"Yes; I am not feeling well. I have been fired from the job," Hadio said.

"Where are you? I am coming to see you, right away," she said, giving her statement an urgency of finality.

Fifteen minutes later, she was inside the bar. On seeing her friend, Hadio gave a cry of pleasure, and then the two ladies hug and took their seats. Gudrun ordered for beer, took long sips from her drink before the two ladies sampled the food they had just ordered.

"I am so sorry Hadio," Gudrun said. "When did you receive the news?" She added.

"It has been two months now," Hadio said, trying to wipe tears off her face.

"I am sorry. You have lost a job, but society has lost a voice of change; how can that happen to you?" Gudrun said.

"I don't know; I feel I have no reason to blame society; there has been a wonderful collaboration between society and myself, you could say" Hadio said, trying to sound convincing.

"What does Peter think?" Gudrun asked.

"I don't think he cares," Hadio said.

"Why?" Gudrun said, looking somewhat astonished.

"For quite some time Peter and I have never been on good terms," Hadio said. As she spoke about Peter, she felt she had no reason to not candidly speak about him to her friend. She had never spoken to anyone about him before.

"Although Peter and I live together under the same roof," she said, "yet our lives have come to increasingly resemble that of strangers. We make every effort to avoid meeting each other; we don't take our meals together; in the sitting room, we don't sit down to watch TV together. I don't know whom to blame for my family's current life of misfortunes. Sometimes I wished I could blame Kore. If Kore had not been such an obstinate person, in his views, perhaps the family would still have been together, and not scattered to the wind as now.

"It is easier to blame others for our misfortunes than putting the blame on ourselves," Gudrun said. She added, "I have every reason to trust you, but have you ever posed to give thought to your role in this your family drama?"

"I took a critical look at my role, occasionally, and could not help holding myself responsible for the misfortune that has befallen my family," she said looking down on the floor, in despair. "After all," she added, eyes still caste on the floor, "was it not I who had walked out of a married life, and went after a man I barely knew anything about? I failed to understand the reason that got me attracted to Peter. I must have been influenced by the power in him. Indeed, it was through him that I had secured a place in the project 'Stop Female Genital Mutilation Now.'

She stopped to give a sigh of grief and went on with her speech. "However, I had often wondered as to how long I would be allowed to keep my position, and whenever this happened, I had felt fear gripping me."

"He is the one who got you the job, in the first place; I think he should feel concerned," Gudrun said, a slight sign of anger crossing her face.

"His signature was in the letter in which my employment got terminated. I don't think he cares much about me or my children," Hadio said.

The more she spoke about Peter, the more she developed a feeling of relief from a pain in her mind and heart, and the more she felt free to talk about Peter to Gudrun. She could even afford to smile.

"I have no reason to doubt you, but what made you stick to him for so long? Didn't ever occur to you there was something erroneous in the type of relationship that you two were in?" Gudrun said.

They had just finished taking their meals. Gudrun had ordered spaghetti Bolognese and a beef steak; Hadio had her favourite Swedish dish of boiled potatoes, brown source and beef. When it comes to food, the two ladies had one thing in common: they never let the much-publicised information, available in all fashion magazines, idolising thin female bodies, to influence the desire they have for food.

They had gone through their first round of drinks, and now they were embarking on their second round. Half way through the second round, Hadio found herself in a happy state of mind, and felt quite relaxed.

"Though I felt humiliated, nevertheless, I thought I must persevere for the sake of my children. I thought Peter was a source of security for me," Hadio said, as she offered Gudrun a sheepish smile.

"Is there no anytime in your relationship with Peter that you could look back with tender feelings? Getting that moment right might tell you when things started getting wrong; not that it matters now, anyway." Gudrun said.

"Peter had been nice and considerate to me only during the first few months of our relationship. With time, I never liked the way he conducted the physical relationship with me; he considered my body as an object to be used for his gratification, without giving any due consideration for my feelings," Hadio said resignedly.

Giving Hadio a sorrowful look, Gudrun said in an anxious tone, "Oh; poor Hadio."

Still in a mood to let the steam off her chest, Hadio would not let Gudrun to finish what she had in mind to say to her.

"Peter," she said vigorously "wouldn't allow me to dress up the way I wished to. He would insist on dressing me up, according to his own whims and caprice, and felt happy whenever some of his friends said nice things to him about the shape of my body. Each time that took place, he often became extremely delighted and proud. That, however, was long before I became fat."

"That sounds to me as though Peter is someone that hungers for admiration. I am afraid to say, happiness drawn from such circumstances may not have a lasting effect on him," Gudrun said boldly. "What happened," she added carefully, "after you became fat?"

"That is a long story," Hadio said. The more they sat there talking and drinking, the more Hadio talked from the depth of her heart and the more she felt the need to open herself even more to Gudrun.

"Soon after I became fat," she said, "every time he came across me taking food, Peter never held his tongue."

The waiter came and took their order of beer for a third round.

"When he came across me taking my meal, two months before getting the letter that ended my assignment, he wanted to know why I was eating food. When I said I was eating to stay alive, he disagreed with me. He told me I was one of those people who live only to eat, but don't eat to live. I never got used to Peter's hateful remarks. Occasionally, I tried to match his stinging remarks with one of my own.

When he said he hated to see me eat food which had made me to become fat and ugly-looking person, I told him I was fat, not him. Looking quite depressed, he told me that I was making him look bad in the eyes of his friends who, he said, laugh at him. And when he said to me he would think what to do with me, I told him he was free to do whatever he wished to do. Whereupon, in a heartless manner, he told me to watch my tongue; he called me, nigger. Immediately after he uttered the words, he said he didn't mean it.

I had become so annoyed with him by now that I told him he was behaving childishly. Unlike in the past when I would remain quiet every time we argued I was determined to counter him. He was shocked; he looked quite perplexed, and had resembled a little poodle whose favours he had been accustomed to having had been suddenly withdrawn. I told him in a categorical manner that if my identity is what he was commenting on, he should know that I was not a figment of his imagination that he calls *nigger*. I told him that my name is Hadio, and that I am an African woman.

Hadio posed to take a sip from her drink, remained quiet and looked at Gudrun with inquiring eyes, to see what she would say.

As Hadio talked to her, Gudrun had many thoughts crossing her mind. About Peter, she was convinced he had been driven by a desire to assert his own personality over Hadio, and consequently this has had a negative effect upon Hadio's psychological wellbeing.

However, mindful of the fact that Hadio might accuse her of trying to psychoanalyse her, if she said something meaningful, in relation to her plight, she stayed quiet. She wanted, for example, to tell Hadio that Peter's mistreatment of her was a reason she had developed a compulsive behaviour, which made her to have a limitless desire for food and drinks, and therefore the reason for her becoming fat.

"This is not the direction I have been expecting your life-journey to take. I am sorry," Gudrun said, instead.

"Never mind that; it is enough to know that you are here for me," Hadio said, giving Gudrun a timid smile.

Gudrun approached Hadio, and let her arm rest on Hadio's shoulder and said, "I am sorry I can do little to help you. I am deeply saddened by what happened to you. Tomorrow I will leave for Nairobi where I have been offered a position to work for UNICEF. I shall keep in touch from there. I kept postponing telling you about my new assignment in Nairobi. I am sorry, Hadio."

Hadio was lost about what to say. The news had come as a shock to her. She nodded and said, "Good."

They ordered another round of drinks, talked to each other further until five in the evening. Gudrun hugged Hadio, for the last time, before she went away, leaving Hadio to sit alone.

Hadio was not in a hurry to get back home; to her, home had lately become a place only fit for sleeping, a place for taking shower or changing into new clothes; it had ceased to be a place of refuge; it had ceased to be a place to get away from the daily chores of the office work; above all, it had ceased to be a place for relaxing, and for feeling free to dream the dreams of happiness, now seemingly quite beyond her reach.

# Chapter Forty Two

# *Why Are You Killing Me?*

Hadio took her drinks, sitting alone well until past nine in the evening, when she hired a cab to take her home. She paid the cab driver and limped into the bright-lights of the apartment. There, to her shock, she came upon Peter and Karin locked in a loving embrace. The moment she saw Hadio, Karin freed herself from Peter's embrace, stood up abruptly, and said something to Peter that Hadio couldn't hear it well; thereafter, she left the room in a hurry, avoiding looking at Hadio.

Hadio had always suspected there was something going on between the two. What had never occurred to her, however, was that Peter would have the temerity to invite Karin - his personal secretary - inside their apartment, to indulge in loving affairs.

The sight of Peter with another woman had caused pain in Hadio's heart. However, the pain she felt had been caused not by a feeling of jealousy; she was aware of Peter's lack of any feelings for her, and neither did she have any feeling for him; however, she was saddened by the fact that Peter didn't have any residue of respect left in him for her.

"Have I sunk so low that I have reached a point of no return? What has become of me?" She told herself.

She looked out the window and realised, except for a sound made by the wind, brushing against the leaves of the trees, it was extraordinarily quiet outside. She wanted to leave, but she had nowhere to go.

She was contemplating what to do next when Peter told her, "If you remember, two weeks ago, I had given you no more than a week to get yourself a place to live in, after which I had said I wouldn't want to see you here again. This house is out of bounds for drunkards. Get out,"

"How do you expect me to do that when you know well I have no place to go to?" She offered a feeble response.

"Yes, you have; but none of that is my business," he told her furiously.

"Before I met you, I never took a drink. You made me to drink; don't forget that" she said, her voice trembling with anger.

His face flushed; he felt a knot in his throat and stammered as he made attempts to address her; after a long struggle to contain a mounting anger in him, he was finally able to once again make a clear speech.

"I wanted you to be part of a civilised society that enjoys a drink, occasionally, he said. "However," looking at her with a sneer of disgust, he added, "you went a step further; you have become an alcoholic; it is a choice you have made; you can get off the drinks, if you try; however, because you are lacking in a resolve to do something, you will not do it. I don't care what way you choose to take; all I want is that you should get out of my life. You are disgusting to look at," he jeered her.

She approached him slowly; her face clouded in a burning rage, and then slapped him hard in the face, twice. The slap in the face drove Peter mad. He stood up, got hold of her head, and then smashed her head against the table; well before she could recover from the pain, he grabbed her hair and pulled it quite so hard that she felt the hair was getting ripped off her skull. After that, once again, he punched her.

Each time that he punched her, Hadio gave a horrifying cry of pain, and pleaded with him not to further hurt her.

"Please, don't hurt me," she begged him.

He didn't give any heed to her cries of pain; her pleading for mercy went unnoticed. Instead, he beat her to a point he became fully exhausted. Breathing heavily, a moment later, he went to sit in the couch, from where he looked at Hadio, lying down on the floor, sobbing, blood gushing out from the nose and the mouth, and in a most cruel manner said to her, "That should be enough a lesson for you not to repeat a similar mistake again."

Hadio could not put up a fight to retain her place in the house, let alone fighting Peter physically. She felt mad at Peter for being so cruel to her. She couldn't stand looking at Peter, sitting in a coach, looking at her, a contemptuous smile crossing his face. The look in Peter's face had made something in her to snap. She stood up and went inside the kitchen; from there, she walked back to where Peter was sitting, his back against her.

Holding a bread knife in her right hand, Hadio took one last look at Peter before she sank the knife deep into his chest. Peter gave a loud crying-sound of pain; he looked at Hadio with pleading eyes, and in a feeble voice said, "Why are you killing me?

Hadio bent forward to a point where she let her face almost touch his; and then quite loudly said, "Die."

Suddenly, it was quiet in the room.

Hadio felt an overwhelming sense of euphoria. Looking at the dead body, bathed in blood, its lifeless glassy-looking eyes staring at nothing in particular, made Hadio have a sudden urge to do something – to cleanse the evil spirits that she had picked up while living with Peter.

She took off her clothes and remained nude; like someone enacting a long forgotten ancient ritual, she danced a kind of dance that resembles the one performed by the whirling dervishes. As she danced, she mumbled something to herself. She danced until she reached a point she couldn't dance any more.

Exhausted, her body covered in sweat, froth coming from out of her mouth, she fell hopelessly on the ground, next to the dead body; there she remained for a long time.

Upon regaining strength, she managed to stand up, and went to fetch a bottle whisky from the cabinet in the kitchen, and then poured a couple a long shot for herself; from the kitchen she went back to the sitting room, put the TV on in order to watch her favourite program, "The Simpson's," while she went on sipping her drink of whisky.

An hour later, she dialled the police. A female voice on the other end said, "Yes? What can I do for you?"

"I wish to report murder," she said.

She gave the information about the location of the murder scene. Thereafter, she went back to the sitting room to watch the program. Still naked, she sipped her drink of whisky, unmindful of the dead body on the floor that laid next to her feet. She couldn't believe she was capable of taking life of any kind; even an animal life had been a sacred thing to her. She felt nothing for Peter; nor did she hate herself for killing him.

When the police arrived at the scene of murder, they found Hadio in her clothes. After they finished asking Hadio some routine questions, they took her to the police station. In order to make sure that the scene of murder is not tempered with, the police sealed off the area.

To show respect for Sarah, the Bissell family allowed Peter's body to be buried at the Bissell family graveyard, followed by a private ceremony attended not by so many members of the family.

A few days later, the country's major media-outlets released quite a great deal of information concerning the brutal murder of Peter. In keeping with the laws of privacy, other than the information given on the murder of Peter, nothing in the media disclosure of the murder case had mentioned Hadio by name.

Hadio was put under police custody for interrogation purpose that had lasted several days, at which point she revealed to the police that she murdered Peter. The police forwarded their report to the prosecutor's office that charged Hadio with a murder of Peter, and called for the case to go for trial at the District Court in Uppsala.

This was a straight forward case. Not only was the suspect identified but the suspect had also pleaded guilty of committing the murder. Forensic test revealed a stub by a knife, which was in the possession of the police, with Hadio's fingerprints on it, to have caused Peter's death.

After the case went through several preliminary hearings, finally today was the day the court was going to deliver the verdict on Hadio's case. While still in remand, Hadio had given thoughts to her life, and could look at it from every angle. But at whichever side of her life's angle that she chose to look at, she was left with one unanswered question, which was this: who was she? If once she was a wife and a mother of two children, now she was neither; instead, she was a prisoner waiting for judgement to be delivered, in a court of law, for a murder that she had committed of another human being.

The past, it occurred to her, was out of her control, and the future was not in her control. She felt helpless. Like other people in a similar situation as hers, she wanted to enlist God's help, but couldn't bring herself to do such a thing.

She had either forgotten how to do it, or she hated what she thought was hypocrisy involved in the act of praying to God, only when in need of God. When the goings was good, God was out of her mind, after all. Why would God listen to her now when she is in such dire strait? She reasoned.

From the corridor outside, she heard footsteps coming in her direction; it was her keepers coming for her in order to convey her to the court, where she would face her judgement; she felt ready for any eventuality.

Present in the courtroom was the main judge, three lay judges, the prosecutor, the defence lawyer, the court-clerk and finally, Hadio, the defendant. However, the court had made a special provision allowing anyone wishing to attend the court proceedings to do so; among the attendees was Sarah, Peter's mother. A group of journalists talking to each other and smiling was also present in the courtroom.

Once everyone involved in the case was present, including the defendant, the judge declared the court open. Oaths were administered and the proceedings in the courtroom went on smoothly.

The presence of the public in the courtroom made Hadio develop a feeling of both anxiety and shame. She looked at the people with her eyes partly cast down. Except Sarah, Peter's mother, she saw no one among the attendees that she knew; she wished there were more people in the court that she knew. Hadio regretted having lost contact with people from her community; Peter didn't want to have anything to do with them; however, by obliging Peter in his wish, she felt she had been complicit in his decision.

At this point, she was convinced that she had never in all her life felt as lonely as she felt now. Some of the people present in the courtroom were drawn to the case for curiosity sake. Some, she believed, had sympathy for her, while others were baying for her blood.

Her defence lawyer, dressed in a straight skirt, a blouse and a brown jacket, took a seat beside Hadio. She looked at Hadio, smiled at her, and told her not to lose courage; she assured Hadio that all would end up well. In response, Hadio gave a shy smile and directed her gaze at the judge, who, she thought, gave her a dull look. The other three judges that assisted the main judge presiding over the case sat there quietly

In the courtroom, a short and ferocious looking woman, in her forties, acting as a prosecutor, depicted Hadio as an opportunist as she rested the case.

Pointing to Hadio she said as she addressed the court, "That woman, Your Honour, is not someone to be trusted. She is not to be trusted, because she has double-crossed her husband who, in getting her to come to this country, had helped her get away from the abject poverty of her homeland.

Not mindful of her husband's love for her, she left him for another man. Your Honour, it was not the love she had of Peter which had made her to leave her husband, but for the love of money she had been dreaming of having, once she moved in with Peter, which had made her to leave her husband.

When she realised that her dream couldn't be attained, out of both frustration and malice, she was left with one option, and the option was to kill Peter, which she did mercilessly. Moreover, at no time has she ever given thought to what might happen to her two children, now living in a foster-home. This woman has sacrificed the love of her children and husband at the altar of financial greed. Justice can be served only by giving her a maximum life sentence. Thank you."

As the prosecutor continued to present her case to the court, Hadio kept looking at her with tearful eyes.

Soon it was time for the defence to take to the floor in order to rest her case.

"Your Honour," in a thoughtful sounding voice she said, "what my colleague has presented in this court, I am sorry to say, amounts to nothing short of conjectures, innuendos and rumours, all of which, unfortunately, could have the effect of tarnishing Hadio's good name. Your Honour, allow me to tell the court who the real Hadio is."

She took a brief pose to give a sweeping glance at the people present in the courtroom.

"Your Honour, Hadio is a woman of impeccable character," she said, giving Hadio a reassuring look. "When faced with all kinds of adversities," she added, "Hadio had remained patient; she gave love, even when that love hadn't been well received. With the public, she generously shared knowledge about a subject very few people here in our country have known little about, and for this reason many people are thankful to her."

Once again, she took a pause, and giving the prosecutor an incriminating look, she said, "Your Honour. I wish the court to also know that Hadio is not a gold digger, as it has been suggested here in this court. She came out of Africa because she was meant to join her husband here. And once she got here, she sought employment and was able to get one.

She did all of this, and much more, so that she could take care of her family, whose head of the family had refused to take any job, on a spurious pretext that all job offered to him were beneath his dignity. She left her husband because she had reached the limit of her patience. To continue living under the same roof with him would have resulted in a situation far worse than anything imaginable.

Furthermore, she moved in with Peter because she wanted to have a peace of mind, so that she could dedicate her efforts and time to the welfare of her children, as well as her work. As to her children, she wanted them to grow up in an environment where she could provide for their needs well. In all of this, she had envisioned a role for Peter to play; she thought Peter had a love for her, which proved to be not the case.

Peter, instead, turned out to be someone worse than anyone she had ever met before. Not only did he refuse to keep his promise of a marriage to her, but he had also made life difficult for her in every possible way. Hadio, in the end, found refuge in the drinks, which, unfortunately, proved to be her undoing. One day, while drunk, she took a knife and stabbed her tormentor.

There is no doubt, Your Honour, that Hadio killed Peter. But was this a premeditated act of murder? No; it was not. Your Honour, Peter died in the hands of a woman that due to an unenviable situation, to which Peter had subjected her, had lost all her reasoning capacity. In Peter's death, however, she found redemption; she was able to regain her lost freedom, as well as her dignity. I kindly ask this court, Your Honour, to consider the case based on the above-given facts, and be lenient to her.

The court adjourned briefly to enable the judges to retire to a private place for deliberations. When the court met once again, Hadio was declared not guilty of the offence for which she had been accused, and so the case was dismissed to the jubilation of many people.

As soon as the court declared the verdict that had set Hadio free, Sarah approached Hadio. She shook hands with her and then told her, "I am sorry for what happened to you. You are welcome to get in touch with me whenever you wish." She let Hadio have her full address and then left.

Although Hadio was now free, yet the struggle to regain a place in the society had just begun. First, she had to get a place to live in, and look for a job, afterwards. She went to Social Welfare

Office responsible for Sunnersta area; there she met Emil who gave her a begrudging welcome.

Hadio made her intentions clear to him, whereupon, he said, "I am quite sorry to inform you that your current poor income situation can't allow you to rent an apartment anywhere here in this high-cost residential area. Neither is this office able to pay any subsidies to enable you to have a place here."

He gave her a contemptuous look and added sarcastically, "I recommend that you look for support elsewhere. I suggest you approach the office of the social services, in your former low cost residential areas. I am quite sure a place could be found for you there, where you could be happy among your own people. "Good day," he said; he never bothered to stand up and to see her off. The meeting was short. Emil acted as if he didn't know her.

Hadio left the office in a depressed mood. As a Project Manager for the now defunct project, "Stop Female Genital Mutilation Now," she had been well paid, of course. However, there had been an oversight on her part regarding payment to her trade union office. Because she had not been paying her dues quite regularly, for a period close to a little more than six months, she had forfeited her unemployment benefits.

Hadio went to Gottsunda's branch-office of the social services. There she met with Ingrid, who offered her a room that ironically had once belonged to Kore.

As a jobless person, she was entitled to a monthly sum of money to cover her basic needs. Hardly a week into every month, she would be broke, having spent all her money on drinks and food.

Because of this state of reckless expenditure, Hadio never had much money left for anything else. And yet whenever it came to drinks, she had a generous supply from friends whose hospitality knew no bounds.

Many of her new friends were people like herself; they held no jobs of any kind. With time, drinking for her became a way of life. Drinks made her feel hilarious; it gave her a confidence of sort. In the evenings, she would always be in her best, cruising into the city bars, hoping to receive offers from friends.

On such occasions, she would talk about her past to anyone ready to listen to her stories about female genital mutilation. In her circle of friends, she was known as Mama Circumcision. On more than one occasion, she was hospitalized because of having too much alcohol in her blood stream. However, when she was hospitalized, for a long-term treatment, she promised to finally reform.

# BOOK THREE

# Chapter Forty Three

# *Medical Report*
## 1995

Ingrid received Hadio's medical report that explained how drinks had negatively affected her health, and felt quite sad. The report recommended that Hadio should undergo a long-term treatment for alcoholism, in a specialised clinic. Ingrid had never forgotten, on more than one occasion, how Hadio had helped the Social Welfare Office deal with issues concerning female genital mutilation.

After she finished reading the report, Ingrid was overwhelmed with a feeling of grief. Ingrid was convinced that given her contributions to society's knowledge, concerning the subject of genital mutilation, Hadio deserved a better fate than the one at present.

Keeping this in mind, she sent a copy of the letter that she had received from the hospital to the senior most head of her department; attached to that letter was a memo she wrote, in which she requested the most senior officials of her department to do everything possible to get Hadio gain access to a medical-treatment.

In less than a week, Ingrid received a favourable response to her request, in a meeting in which she also took part. As soon as she received the green light, Ingrid got in touch with a treatment centre that she knew something about, in order to see if a place could be found for Hadio there. There was a single vacant position, she was informed, the treatment-centre would be quite happy to reserve for the patient sponsored by Social Welfare Office.

After she secured a place for Hadio, at the treatment centre, Ingrid thought about how to break the news to her. From her experience with people who had been in a similar situation as Hadio's, Ingrid was aware of how such people would rather suffer consequences of alcoholism than acknowledging the problem to themselves. Happily, when Ingrid relayed the news to her, Hadio welcomed the offer with all her heart. Encouraged by the response, Ingrid requested Hadio to see her on the following day, at ten.

On that note, Ingrid gave a sigh of relief. The prospect of getting Hadio back on rail had made Ingrid feel good. This should not be taken to mean that Ingrid had not been regularly helping people with problems similar to Hadio's. Indeed, as a social worker, it was her duty to assist people get over their problems. Nevertheless, whatever assistance she had rendered in the past to people with social problems, she did it to discharge her duties, which had been part and parcel of her bureaucratic assignments. With Hadio, it was altogether a different case; she brought passion to bear on the task.

In the following day, at ten sharp, Hadio stood at Ingrid's office, knocking on the door.

"Come in please," Ingrid said.

Ingrid had met Hadio a month earlier, when the latter had been to the office to collect the monthly cheque, for her upkeep. It was an unusually cold spring-day; Hadio, dressed in a shapeless tight-fitting black overcoat, took it off and then placed it on a hanger beside the doorway. She removed what looked like layers of scarf from her neck, and placed them on top of the overcoat. Still not saying anything, she removed a handkerchief from the handbag and used it on her face and mouth. She was breathing heavily and unevenly.

Hadio had grown double her previous size. Puffy eyes, on a face thick with layers of fat, had diminished the size of her large eyes to look like two puncture holes on her face. Her total appearance gave an impression of someone that had lost hope in life.

"Come. Sit down." Ingrid said.

Hadio sat on a chair facing Ingrid, across from the table. She looked at Ingrid with shy and sleepy eyes.

"What would you like to have?" She asked Hadio

"I will have tea," Hadio said.

Ingrid went to the kitchen to fetch tea that she poured into a large porcelain mug; she had biscuits placed on disposable paper plates; she placed the wooden-tray with its contents on her working table and told Hadio to help herself. Seeing how swiftly Hadio had disposed of the biscuits and the tea, a moment later, Ingrid told her, "Would you like to have some more?"

"No, thank you," Hadio said politely.

"Here are some documents that I would like you to sign," Ingrid said as she addressed Hadio further."

Hadio didn't say anything in reply. However, she kept staring at Ingrid, her eyes half closed. Hadio looked like someone that was neither fully asleep nor quite awake.

"Hadio," Ingrid shouted, almost in despair. "Do you hear me?"

"Yes," Hadio gave a feeble reply.

Ingrid gave Hadio some documents to sign. When it was over and done, Ingrid said, "Be ready tomorrow, at ten. Wait for me by the roadside, outside your home."

Hadio was about to leave when Ingrid remembered to tell her, "Pack up a few things."

On that note, promising to meet on the following day, the two women took leave of each other.

At ten sharp, in the following day, Ingrid went to fetch Hadio. She found Hadio waiting for her, at the point agreed upon by the two of them. Hadio had put on the same tight fitting black overcoat of the previous day. Ingrid wound down the car window; from her position inside the car, she drew Hadio's attention. While crossing the road, Hadio approached the car slowly. An exchange of greetings followed between them, and then they drove away.

The health centre was situated less than a half an hour's drive away from the city centre; it was situated in an almost isolated area, far removed from any sign of civilisation. It was surrounded with an open field, dotted with pine trees. Branching off from the main road was a small gravel road, cutting across an open field, from where one could observe the treatment centre, from a long distance, as one approaches it.

The treatment centre was made up of two buildings, placed adjacent to each other, and separated by an open space of about thirty meters, covered with a snow that showed signs of receding. The offices were housed in the smaller of the two buildings, while the larger of the two buildings provided sleeping rooms and other social amenities; both faced the driveway.

A smiling young-looking man in a brown pair of trousers and a pullover of the same colour, standing on the steps of the office building, waived at them, as they approached a parking lot. Ingrid parked and got out of the car. Hadio remained seated. Later, Ingrid opened the door for Hadio.

As he shook hands with both Ingrid and Hadio, the man said smiling, "I am Doctor Lars Svedberg; head of the administrative section and a Doctor."

"I am Ingrid Kaufman of Social Welfare Office," said Ingrid.

Pointing to Hadio, Ingrid said, "This is Hadio Hebe."

Hadio nodded but remained quiet.

"Welcome to Bohman Rehabilitation Centre," Lars said cheerfully.

Addressing Ingrid further he said, "The name Bohman, in case you wonder, it is homage to the first director of the clinic."

Ingrid nodded her head and said, "Oh, really."

Lars pushed the main door to let Ingrid and Hadio get inside the administration building. Together they walked in a long hallway till they reached a place at the end of the corridor, where Lars had his office.

At Lars's office room, there was a table by the window; its yellow curtains had sketches of colourful flowers drawn on them. On top of the table was a computer set. On the table, there were papers that had been kept to one side. At the middle of the room, there was a black leather sofa-set, arranged in a circular pattern, with a round shaped-glass table placed in the middle.

"Please sit down. Would you like to have tea or coffee?" He said.

"Tea for both of us," Ingrid said.

Lars went to fetch tea in the kitchen; he returned, bearing in his hands a wooden tray. He placed the tray with cups of tea on the table, and then told his guests sitting on the sofa set "Help your selves."

"Thank you," both said quite at the same time.

Between sipping her tea and talking to Lars, Ingrid had found time to rummage through her brief case, from which she retrieved some documents that were kept inside a folder.

She took out the documents, gave them to Lars, and said, "These documents here deal with Hadio's case. They hold my reports, Hadio's medical reports and finally a letter of authorisation from the Social Welfare Office; appended there is also Hadio's signature."

Lars accepted the papers, went through them briefly, and then put his signature on each one of the documents. Once the formalities were over between them, Lars could now think of Hadio. Turning his gaze at Hadio, he said, "Can you speak Swedish Hadio."

"Yes, I can speak some Swedish," Hadio replied in a low tone.

"Nonsense," Ingrid said in a light-hearted manner. She added resolutely, "Hadio speaks excellent Swedish."

His eyes alight with excitement, Lars said, "Splendid."

Addressing Hadio further, he said, "At Bohman Rehabilitation Centre, we are like a family. I hope you will enjoy your stay here."

Hadio remained silent. Directing her gaze at Hadio, while talking to Lars, Ingrid said, "I have no doubt that Hadio will enjoy her stay here."

"Getting Hadio to come here," Lars said, "was an excellent idea. You have played well your part. Ours is about to begin now."

"Good; seeing that we have nothing more to talk about, I ought to take leave of you," Ingrid told Lars. "Duty calls," she added after a brief silence.

She stood up in a hurry; facing Hadio, she said, "I am sorry, but I must leave you now Hadio."

Ingrid hugged Hadio and reminded her that all would turn out well for her. However, before taking her leave, Ingrid said, "You have my telephone number. Call me. I will try to phone, from time to time, to see how you are doing. Good luck."

On that note, Ingrid left, accompanied by Lars, who went to see her off.

Back in the office, a moment later, addressing Hadio, he said "Come with me. Let me take you to your accommodation."

The two of them walked in a long corridor, heading on to a door through which they went out. They took a small path, cutting across an open field, separating one building from the other. At the building, next to the one from which they came out, they made their entrance through a large revolving door. Posing at the hallway, inside the building, Lars addressed Hadio.

"Here, on the ground floor of this building," he told Hadio, "you will find a gymnastic hall, dining hall, conference hall, TV room, guest room and a library." He took a pause and said further, "You will get to see them well tomorrow. As for now, let us take the stairs to your accommodation."

A broad staircase took them to a first floor, causing Hadio to breathe heavily. On the second floor, they walked through a wide corridor, on either side of which were sleeping rooms. Half-way the corridor, Lars stopped; with a feigned fanfare, he opened the door of a room on his right side and said, "Welcome home, Hadio."

"Thank you," Hadio said lazily.

"As you can see, it is not a Ritz. However, I like to think we have everything necessary for adequate living," Lars said.

"I like it," Hadio said.

"You may want to take a rest now. Lunch is anytime soon. Feel free to use any of the facilities in the house. See you tomorrow," he said and left.

Hadio was left to contemplate her place at the treatment centre. She felt tired, every part of her body paining her; she was thirsty. She approached the bed, but changed her mind. Though the warmth of the bed was enticing, she knew the lure of the sleep to be an unattainable dream. Hadio hadn't been getting a good sleep, lately. She hated going to sleep every night, only to wake up a couple of hours later, stomach paining her.

She would do anything in life to have a good sleep. Apart from not sleeping well, due to worries, she also had been suffering from constant headaches that made her want to cry. Those headaches were caused by thoughts of her children.

Every time such thoughts took control of her mind – as it was the case now – she panicked, her whole body drenched in sweat. To calm her nerves down, Hadio had to leave the room to have something to drink. She knew exactly what she was looking for, but tried to cheat herself into believing that she was looking for nothing more than a bottle of cold water to drink.

At the entrance to the dining room, she saw a machine with all sorts of bottles of drinks in it. Hadio looked hard at the contents in the machine, but failed to find in the machine what she was looking for. Facing the machine, she wanted to shout, to cry, to break the machine, and to scatter its contents, far and wide. She dared not do any thing wrong out fear of getting accused for being a candidate not fit for the treatment of alcoholism but madness.

Back in her room, she sat on her bed and cried. She approached the bathroom slowly and carefully, having made up her mind to take a bath; she took off her clothes, filled the bathtub with warm-water, and lay down in the bathtub.

She stared at the ceiling above, trying to banish away all sorts of unwanted thoughts from entering her mind, but without any success. She realised that the only good thoughts were those from her childhood days; with time, she was afraid, even those would fade away. After a long rest in the bathtub, she left the bath-room in a bathrobe.

In the past, a scenery such as the one unfolding before her eyes, standing by the widow, watching birds in large flocks flying high in a mid-morning clear sky, would have had a soothing feeling on her troubled mind. Not now. Now she was not feeling anything. She was good as dead. She lay down on her bed and wept, and wept, until she fell asleep. A sharp knock on the door woke her up.

"The door is open. Come in," Hadio shouted from the bed.

Slowly the door opened to let a blond middle-aged woman get inside the room; she gave a broad smile that offered Hadio a feeling of comfort.

"Sorry for waking you up," the woman said politely.

"I am not asleep. Come in," she said.

The woman entered the room carefully and said, "Good morning. May I sit down?"

"Good morning. Sit please" Hadio said. She said, afterwards, "What can I do for you?"

"I am Helena Akestrom. I am the Head Cook," she said. She waited to see what Hadio would do.

"I am Hadio Hebe," Hadio said.

Helena picked up the only available chair in the room and placed it by Hadio's bed-side, and then sat down. The room was thinly furnished. It was devoid of anything that might suggest to someone that it was a place intended for a permanent habitation. A small wardrobe, a table, a chair and a bed are all there were in the way of furniture.

"I am trying to keep a register of all foods available in the kitchen for our guests to choose from. You will be surprised to know what a broad range of food is available for our guests to select from. While some of our guests consider eating certain types of food a taboo, others refrain from eating them, for reasons of allergy and religious beliefs," she said.

"I eat almost anything, though I prefer certain types of food over others. No; I place no taboo on the food I eat, and I don't suffer from any form of food allergy either," Hadio said.

Helena nodded while taking notes on a notebook she had in her lap. When she finished, she stood up and told Hadio, "It is good to put things in their proper perspectives, before it is too late."

She took a deep look at Hadio and said to her, "what do you say?"

"True," Hadio said in a feeble voice.

On her way to the door, Helena turned around to have a last look at Hadio and said, "Welcome to Bohman Rehabilitation Centre." Before going out, she said, "Lunch is ready. Dinner is between six and seven; breakfast between seven and half past eight."

Hadio looked the time on her watch; it read 11.30. She took the stairs down to the dining hall. There were already a few people in the dining hall having their lunch, sitting in a group of two and three people; a few stood in a line waiting to receive their food.

Hadio went to stand in line. When her turn came up, she asked to be served spaghetti. Water, juice, milk, and fresh salad were separately kept on a long table, somewhere in the middle of the dining hall. Hadio carried the plate of spaghetti on a tray, went to fetch milk and salad and then looked for a place to sit alone. She ate her food slowly, drank two glasses of milk and then left for her room.

At six, she went to the dining hall to have dinner. Later, in her room, she switched on the TV to watch one boring programme after another, she went to sleep afterward, and had horrible dreams from which she woke up, sweating profusely.

# Chapter Forty Four

# *Bohman Rehabilitation Centre*

In the following day, at seven in the morning, Hadio took shower and then changed into fresh clothes. She looked at herself in the mirror, but never liked what she saw. Hadio had changed; she had become excessively fat. One day, a few days before coming to Bohman Centre, she had seen a close friend of hers in the street who couldn't recognise her, even though the two had been known to each other well, once before. Hadio was convinced that her friend hadn't seen her, and so she called her name. Her friend had stopped; took a look at her, but having failed to recognise her from three meters away, went away.

Becoming fat, initially, had never bothered Hadio much, for it had been obvious to her that wherever one turns to look, one comes across people who are either fat or skinny. She had despised Peter for insisting that she should change her physical appearance to look skinny; she had despised him for failing to understand that irrespective of her physical shape, she would always be the same.

If there was a time her fat physical profile had mattered less to Hadio, that time was now long gone. Now, because of the way she looked, she hated herself. How did Hadio come to feel this way? She remembered the conspiratorial look and the laughter that people had directed at her every time she went out shopping. She remembered people avoiding coming into close proximity to her, as if that would change their physical status to look fat. She recollected people breaking silly jokes in her presence about fat people by saying how careless fat people are. At first, it mattered little to her what people had been saying about fat people, like her. With a passage of time, those comments, those furtive looks, slowly but surely, came to penetrate every single pore of her body, finding a place in her mind, finally. With a passage of time, except when she went out in the evenings, looking to have drinks with her friends, she had developed the fear of going out, knowing well what awaited her, out there.

Hadio left the room to go to the dining hall. In the dining hall, she took her favourite breakfast of porridge, boiled eggs, a glass of juice and tea. There were new faces in the dining hall she hadn't seen on the previous day. It was quiet in the dining hall.

Presently, Lars got inside the dining hall, and in his usual cheerful manner said, "Good morning everybody."

He never waited for the diners to reciprocate, but said further, "I wish to inform you that we shall meet in the conference room for a group introduction, at nine. Meanwhile, please enjoy your breakfast."

He left after that.

The time was 8.30 a.m. Hadio had half an hour free to spend. From the dining hall, she went to her room; there she waited. As she had nothing special to do, she went to stand by the window; she left the window, a few minutes later, and went to the bathroom to look herself in the mirror; she left the bathroom, only to rummage through her beg, to see if she could find a dress other than the one she had put on, which would fit the occasion, but changed her mind. Finally, exhausted, she fell on her bed, breathing heavily, while sweating profusely.

At nine sharp, she left for the conference room.

The moment she entered the room, Lars said, "Finally, Hadio is here."

She felt embarrassed. Everyone looked in her direction but remained silent. There were altogether ten people, six men and four women, forming a circle. Placed on a makeshift table, in front of each person, was a battle of water. Standing outside the circle, holding a bottle of water in his right hand, was Lars.

Hadio looked for an empty chair, while giving a sweeping glance at the people forming the circle; from their looks, it was clear to her that they were society's damaged goods, which needed some mending done on them.

"Welcome to Bohman Rehabilitation Centre," Lars said.

With thick curly brown hair, large pair of eyes, full mouth, and a baby-looking face, Lars could easily stand out from the crowd.

Lars let his eyes scan the people he was about to address, then he said, "Ladies and Gentlemen, we are here today to undertake a journey together. Our metaphorical journey is fraught with dangers of all kinds; it is also a long journey; there are no short-cuts to our destination.

There will be some of you who will fall by the wayside; they shall not be left to perish. A reward such as none of you had ever experienced awaits you, at the end of what is a long and tedious journey. There is no better reward than the one that comes from your ability to look right into the face of the demon tormenting you, and with confidence say, "At last, I am free." When I talk of the demon, I am not talking of the Biblical demon. There is no demon in the drinks that you take. The demon is in your desire to have a drink; look there and you would find one."

Following what Lars had said, the room became electrified with a sound of conversations.

"I want each of you to stand up and say, I have a desire to drink that I shall not let it to take control of my actions. Are you ready?" He said.

The room resonated with the crying sound of, "Yes. Yes. Yes"

Lars smiled and said, "Now then, let us do it."

Lars had deliberately avoided letting his clients utter the conventional statement, "I am an alcoholic."

He was convinced a more appropriate therapeutic tool to begin the treatment of alcoholism is not for someone to say I am an alcoholic, but to instead say I have a desire to drink that I shall not allow it to take control of my action.

According to him, while the former of the two propositions constitutes a statement of fact, the latter is a statement of intent. The former is neutral, while the latter is proactive in outlook.

Pointing to one of the men in the circle, he told him, "You shall begin the exercise."

In his 40s, but looking older than what his real age was, the man stood up and said what he had been instructed to say. As soon as he finished speaking, before he sat down, he looked suspiciously at the people around him as if he was expecting applaud or a criticism.

The confessions went on without a hitch until a woman in her early thirties, tall, with tussled brown thick-looking hair, mild brown freckles on her face, stood up to speak. As she spoke, she mentioned neither her name nor did she express any determination to fight the demon in her. She spoke in a hoarse voice of someone suffering from cold.

"I beg to differ with Lars," she said firmly. She added, "Let me be clear about one thing here; the culprit is not to be found in my desire to drink; instead, the culprit is a society allowing the sale of the drink to take place."

She was about to proceed on with her speech when Lars said in an unusually sharp tone, "Do I get you right? Are you calling for a total prohibition of the alcohol sale?"

"Yes; that exactly is the point," she said promptly. There was a sign of defiance in her voice.

"Alcohol industry," she said further, "is a backbone of many economies. Governments earn huge sums of money through taxation. Thousands of people earn their living through its production. But let us face it; if alcohol is available in the market place, the desire to drink will be present. So, stop alcohol sale and there would be no people like us here. Putting the cart before the horse will not do," she said vehemently.

Before seating down, she said, "By the way, my name is Anna. Anna Blomquist."

Bravo," Lars applauded. He smiled and said, "You have a point. Without the sale of alcohol, Bohman Rehabilitation Centre would be empty of people, and out of business. However, you must bear in mind, not every alcohol-drinking person is at Bohman Rehabilitation Centre. Compared with others who can control the urge in them to drink, individuals such as you are few."

He took a short breath, looked at Anna, and went on with his speech.

He said, "Are we to let a few people to determine what majority of people should and shouldn't do? Let us not forget that we are living in democratic society, where the right of the individual is clearly enshrined in the constitution of this country. However, I can understand your concern well. There was a time when alcohol consumption had posed a serious problem in our country. Instead of eating, we made alcoholic beverage out of potatoes. Hence, in due course of time, large-scale consumption of alcohol, by many people in our country, had led to poverty, disease and lethargy.

Alcohol consumption had become a national problem. A way had to be found to deal with it. In mid-nineteenth century, some form of restriction on how much volume of alcohol individual was allowed to consume was put in place.

By mid-twentieth century, it was possible, once again, for people to begin drinking freely. However, in order to discourage excessive alcohol-use, the price of alcohol was kept high, compared to that of the other European countries.

From this point on, alcohol consumption had ceased to be a national problem; instead, it had become something that individuals are expected to deal with. And here is where people like you and us come into the picture; in your case, it is making a choice to get rid of the urge to drink. Bohman Rehabilitation Centre is here to help you do it effectively. I kindly ask you to give us your trust to enable us together to do the job well."

Here, the audience applauded him. Anna Blomquist stood up and said in a friendly tone, "You have my trust. I too have the urge to drink that I must fight against."

"Thank you, Anna," Lars said.

He leaned against the table in front of which he stood, picked up the papers on the table, and started distributing the papers to his audience, one by one. As he did so, he said, "The papers contain a weekly programme, tailored to fit in with your individual need. Clearly stated, therein, is where, when and by whom to get both therapy and medication.

We lay emphasis on physical health, and so we have a gymnastic hall that you may want to make use of its facilities. We have a library well stocked with all kinds of books that may serve your needs well.

Books that are not available can be ordered. Above all, we don't underestimate the bond of social ties, and what this could mean for your health.

You shall each have a separate paper to write down the name, telephone number, and the physical address of someone you might like to pay you a visit. Leave it at the office when you are ready."

He took a short pose and said, "That is all I have to say. From here onwards, the time-table will direct you what to do, when to do it, and with whom to do what. Follow your programme closely, and all will be fine. Thank you.

If any of you have any question, please feel free to ask."

No one asked any question, and so the session came to a closing end. Immediately, thereafter, the audience introduced themselves to one another. Hadio and Anna were together whenever they had a free time. Since their rooms were placed next to each other, a visit to either's room became easy to undertake. After some time, they opened to each other and felt free to tell each other what neither could tell anyone but the psychologist. However, the struggle to overcome the urge would be a constant reminder to them of how close they were to the abyss.

# Chapter Forty Five

# *Sarah to See Hadio*

It was 10 p.m., several days later. Hadio was about to go to bed. She had quite a hectic day; she was tired, yet she felt quite alive. She had just finished watching a motivational movie about how a human spirit has the capacity to emerge victorious, if faced with problems. It was a story of a girl, abandoned by her parents, misused and abused by society, nevertheless, went on to become a useful member of the society; she built a worldwide organisation for helping needy children.

While still searching for sleep, it came to Hadio's mind that she had yet to submit a name of someone she would like to pay her a visit. She couldn't think of any person. Hadio had lost contact with people from her country that she knew. She couldn't keep a close touch with any of them for fear of annoying Peter, who had never wished to see them. At the same time, Hadio had also been busy in her work, and could barely have spared enough time to be with someone. Her friend Gudrun had left for Nairobi.

Hadio had almost given up hope when she remembered Sarah. Hadio never had the opportunity of getting to know

Sarah well; she liked her, just the same. She never wished to speculate much about Sarah. To her it was enough that in the courtroom Sarah gave her telephone number, and had even encouraged her to get in touch.

In the following day, she woke up early. She rummaged through her hand-beg, and was able to retrieve the form she had received from Lars, in which she was expected to fill in the name of someone she would like to keep in touch with.

On a blank space, showing name, she wrote down the name Sarah, with capital letters. Immediately, in a space below her name, she wrote down the telephone and the physical address.

At 8 a.m. she went to have breakfast; at nine sharp she submitted the form to the office secretary, who was to initiate the contact between Sarah and herself. She had a gymnastic session to attend at 9.15, followed by a therapy session, which would last until 11.45 a.m.

A week later, Hadio received a call. Hadio had just finished taking lunch at 12 noon; she was hoping to take a short nap in her room when the telephone rang.

"Hadio, could you please come over to the office," the secretary told her.

Hadio shut the book, put her shoes on, and then left for the office. As she entered the office, the secretary said, "Someone wants to speak to you," and then she handed Hadio the telephone.

"Hello," Hadio said carefully.

"Hello. Is that Hadio?" the voice said.

"Yes, Hadio speaking," she replied.

At that single moment, before saying a word, Hadio searched frantically in the files of her mind for anything that would let her know something about the voice reaching her from the other end of the line.

"I am Sarah. How are you, Hadio?"

Hadio was happy to hear Sarah's voice. When she took up Sarah's name, she feared her effort would amount to a long shot in the dark. She never expected Sarah would respond to her wish favourably; and now she was on the phone.

"I am fine, really," Hadio said nervously.

"I received a letter from Bowman Rehabilitation Centre, almost a week ago. I wanted to get in touch with you, but couldn't. I have been busy. Sorry. Anyway, how are you?" Sarah asked carefully.

"I am getting better; thank you and how are you?" Hadio said.

"I am fine. I wish to tell you the note I recently received from Bowman Rehabilitation Centre says that you want me to come and see you. I want you to know that I will be very happy to do so. I will write Bowman Rehabilitation Centre to give my official assent, and shall also inform them of when to come. Thank you for giving me the chance. I am looking forward to seeing you soon. Bye," Sarah said in an enthusiastic tone.

Hadio didn't know what to make of the new surprise in her life. She was going to meet a woman whose son she had killed. She was quite certain that Sarah held no grudge against her. She remembered the day in the court-room that Sarah let her have her address and even encouraged her to get in touch.

From the moment she finished speaking to Sarah, she thought of how the meeting would turn out. Hadio had met Sarah only twice; the first time that she met Sarah it was in Sarah's own house; she met her in the court-house, the second time. Both times, she thought Sarah was nice to her.

When she and Peter paid Sarah a visit, Sarah had taken time to listen to her, talking about her work. Hadio had never wished to know the kind of relationship mother and son had been having. Peter, of course, had spoken much about his mother, but had never said anything good about her. As it was their problem, and theirs alone, Hadio had never wanted to be judgemental.

One day, a week later, walking in a hallway, on a Friday afternoon, the office secretary saw her.

"Hadio," she shouted.

Hadio got inside the office, and went to stand behind a large wooden counter.

"I have received a message from Sarah Bissell," she raised her eyes up to look at Hadio, and said, "Do you know her?"

"Yes," Hadio said nonchalantly.

"Well; Sarah had phoned to let me tell you that she would like to come for a visit tomorrow at 11 a.m. She would like me to confirm it with you," she had said.

"Tell her I will be happy to meet her," Hadio said and left.

That evening, after dinner, Hadio spent time at Anna's room; the two talked mostly about men in their lives. For the first time, Anna told Hadio about the feelings of love she was having for one Jonas Olsson. Despite many attempts she had made to win his love, he rejected her, Anna said.

"What I couldn't get over," she said further, "was the fact that he had got together with my best friend, Magdalena.

"Was that not enough a reason for you to hate him," Hadio told her.

"My heart is filled with a feeling of love that I still have for him. In it, there is no room left to fill in with hate," Anna said.

"Oh, poor Anna," Hadio said.

Hadio left her place in the chair, approached Anna, and then held her up in her arms, trying to plead with her not to feel sad. That evening, Hadio had stayed in Anna's room longer than usual, trying to bolster Anna's spirit with stories and jokes.

Finally, she left to go to her room to catch a sleep before facing the challenge that the following day was going to usher into her life.

In the following morning, Hadio woke up early, took a shower and changed into fresh clothes; she put on a windbreaker, and wore a colourful turban. She took breakfast and then off she went for a walk, out in the woods. Spring had come; everywhere, nature was undergoing a process of rejuvenation.

From beneath layers of snow that once had covered the ground-surface, there emerged patches of wet green grasses; trees no longer had a gaunt and naked look of the winter season; the sound of water streaming down on pebbles and rocks on the river, along with the sound of birds cheeping loudly, made Hadio feel extremely happy.

"If nature can celebrate the coming of spring, should not I be doing the same thing?" Hadio reasoned.

After a long walk in the woods, she went back, feeling quite refreshed. It was now 10.30 a.m. She had a half an hour left to meet Sarah; she felt nervous. She went to see her friend Anna in her room. Anna had already taken breakfast; now she was in her room, ironing clothes. It was a Saturday, a free day.

As Hadio entered the room, Anna put aside the iron she was using to press the dress and said, "Aren't you early this morning, seeing that you are in your best dress? I didn't see you at breakfast."

"I had my breakfast quite early, this morning. After that, I went for a walk out in the woods. I am meeting with Sarah," Hadio said.

"Yes, of course. You are nervous, I guess," Anna asked.

"That is the understatement of the century, "Hadio said.

Anna laughed.

"Don't laugh. I am so nervous my stomach keeps turning. I am afraid I might throw up," Hadio said.

"Take it easy. Don't work yourself up like that. It is not good for your health," Anna said.

"Easier said than done," Hadio said.

After spending several minutes in Anna's room, Hadio left to go to her room, promising Anna to meet her soon.

"Good luck," Anna said.

As soon as she got inside her room, she went to the bathroom to refresh. Minutes later, she looked at the time on her watch, and realised she had only five minutes left to meet Sarah. She locked the room and took the staircase down.

She wanted to be on the spot, to welcome Sarah.

Presently, she saw a car approaching. She held her breathe. In another second, that car was negotiating a turn, on its way to a parking lot.

The driver packed the car, put the engine off, and got out of the car. As the driver emerged out of the car, Hadio could recognise the figure of Sarah. Sarah approached Hadio smiling. Soon the two women were holding each other in a tight embrace. Afterwards, Sarah took one steps back. With arms akimbo, she took a good look at Hadio.

"You look good, Hadio," Sarah said.

Sarah was far from looking good. She seemed to have aged tremendously. The colour of her once glowing skin had acquired a dull hue. Her hair had become thin and had lost its lustrous quality. Her cheeks had lost their rounded shape.

There was something about her overall countenance that had made Sarah to look not healthy. Since there was nothing to gain by telling Sarah about what her observation were on her appearance, Hadio said, "Well, thank you. You look good yourself."

Soon after that, Hadio led the way to the guest room.

"Do you like it here?" Sarah asked Hadio, scrutinising the room with her eyes.

"Oh, well, it is OK," Hadio said. She added, "In fact, I am happy here."

"Good. It is your attitude more than anything else which is important," Sarah said.

"And the people here, they are all nice to me," Hadio said smiling.

"How long are you staying?" Sarah asked.

"Two months. I have spent close to a month already," Hadio replied.

Sarah had put on a yellow skirt, and had a sweater which fitted her loosely. She had boots for shoes.

"When I received a call from someone at the rehabilitation centre to ask me if I was willing to visit you, I never hesitated to say yes. I have always wanted to see you. Unfortunately, for one reason or another, I have been lacking the courage to make it happen. Had I known the path your life was going to take, I would have taken steps to get in touch with you, much sooner," she said.

"I presume it had been ordained that it should happen this way; that we should meet here under these present circumstances, rather than those under which I had been living," Hadio said.

"You are not a fatalist by any chance; or are you?" Sarah said lightly.

"No; I am not. A realist, maybe, is what I am," Hadio said.

They both laughed.

"Do you have any plans? Sarah said.

"I live one day at a time. I can't afford speculation. I don't know what turn my life might take tomorrow," Hadio said.

"I guess you know where you have come from, you should know where you want to go," Sarah said.

Sarah looked at the time on her watch. She let her arms rest in her lap and gave Hadio a curious look.

"I am curious Hadio. Do you mind if I talk to you about Peter?" Sarah said, giving Hadio a restrained look.

"Oh, I don't mind, 'Hadio said cheerfully. "What do you want to know?" She added.

Of course, she minded a lot, but she never gave a sign of any of that; instead, she hid her feelings behind a cheerful smile. Any discussion about Peter had made her conjure up some of the awful moments she had undergone in Peter's hands, which she wanted to put behind her. Yet, there was no way she could let Sarah down.

"Did you have any feelings for Peter?" Sarah said without mincing words.

Hadio had no straightforward answer to give, and didn't know what exactly would satisfy Sarah's sense of curiosity.

"That is a hard question," Hadio said. "I would do my best to answer, nevertheless," she added.

"Your best should be more than enough," Sarah said, feeling relieved.

Hadio sat straight on her chair, gave Sarah a cautious look and said, "I was tired of my life with Kore. When Peter came along, he swept me off my feet with his kisses, dinners and nice titillating talks, all of which I had never experienced before. I learned to appreciate him; eventually I came to like him. Very soon all that changed suddenly and swiftly."

Sarah gasped for air as if she choked on something. "I am sorry." She said, using a voice that sounded heavier than usual.

It was quiet in the room; sounds of birds cheeping, and a humming of machines coming from behind the walls were the only sounds that reached them, from outside.

Hadio frowned; she gave a picture of someone thinking hard about something she didn't want to be reminded about.

In the end, she said, "I think what Peter did was human, even though I found hard to come to terms with what he did. You see, as human beings, we tend to appreciate things we don't have; they bore us once we have them; we search for greener pastures that we assume are on the other side of the fence; we look for new things; newer challenges fascinate us; these things happened to Peter. He fell in love with Susan, his secretary."

"Oh, poor little girl," Sarah gave a cry of lamentation, and took Hadio in her arms; she held her up in her arms for quite a while before she took her seat.

"That is cruel of him?" She said, looking seriously concerned

"What Peter did to me, when seen in retrospect, is a blessing in disguise. I think his action which were cruel, to say the least, had opened up my eyes, and now I see things differently. I have come to appreciate Kore, for example. Both Kore and Peter were two men in my life; yet no two people on earth were so different from each other," Hadio said.

"Different; how different?" Sarah said impatiently.

Hadio took a short breath; looking Sarah in the face, she said, "While Peter was determined in his desire to induce a change in me, such as a change in the food I eat, the clothes I put on, my hairdo, the friends I keep, Kore never did any such things. On the contrary, it was me who fought to induce a change in him.

When I spoke in a campaign against the practice of Female Genital Mutilation, I wanted him to agree with me in everything I said. I refused to acknowledge his point of view. I had been hard on Kore, while Peter had been hard on me."

At this point, her eyes had tears that she wiped them off with the back of her arm.

Once more, Sarah left her position to console Hadio. "It is over now; please, don't weep."

Still in an agitated mood, but trying to take control of her emotion, Hadio said, "I didn't find getting away from Kore hard to do, but it was a different case with Peter. From my association with Peter, I drew a sense of security; he offered me the job that I valued greatly; it is for this reason, I left my job in the hospital. I wish I had walked out of his life much sooner; it would have saved me from the sin of'...." At this point, she became tongue-tied.

"That would have saved you from killing him. Say it. Don't shy away from saying it. You must come to grips with it, if you want to heal." Sarah said, looking Hadio in the eyes

Hadio nodded; moved by Sarah's encouraging words, she offered Sarah a genuine smile, and said from the bottom of her heart, "Thank you, Sarah."

Sarah smiled.

"We all have secrets that we carry in our heart. May be, one day, when we come to know each other well, I will tell you what mine are," she said, which made both women to smile.

Sarah spent full hour talking to Hadio.

Before leaving, Sarah told Hadio, "You have my telephone number; please feel free to call."

From meeting with Sarah, Hadio went to look for Anna. She found Anna in the dining hall where Hadio joined her for lunch. Anna might have noticed changes in the way Hadio looked. Hence, she told Hadio, "Well, say something."

"The meeting went on well. Sarah was nice to me. Sarah was like a mother-in-law that I have never had," Hadio said. "I never met Kore's mother, you know," Hadio added.

"Do you think she was making effort to be nice?" Anna said.

"Why should she want to do that? Has she not come to see me on her own free accord?" Hadio said.

"Have you bothered to know the reason that had made her to want to see you?" Anna said.

"Is it necessary, really?" Hadio said.

"I was just wondering." Anna said. "Here is a woman," she added, "whose son you have killed, yet she takes pain to pay you a visit; to me that looks odd. I am not begrudging you for having Sarah coming to visit you. I am sorry if that is how I sound, but I try to understand things rationally," Anna said.

"Not each and everything in life has a rational meaning," Hadio said cogently. "For example," she added, "our belief system can't be explained rationally."

After a moment of silence, Hadio said, "There is nothing that is odd in her action. You shouldn't forget that we were two women in Peter's life, Sarah as a mother, and I as a friend, a wife, or a concubine - take your pick. While Peter is dead, both Sarah and I are here. Try to understand Sarah's visit in this given context," Hadio said.

"Oh, you are being philosophical now," Anna said, trying to laugh.

"I am not a philosopher, but I am free to speculate. If that makes me into a philosopher, then count me as one," Hadio said, joining Anna in laughing.

"Will she be coming to see you in future?" Anna said.

"I hope so," replied Hadio.

They changed the subject and talked of permission to visit the city on the coming Saturday. They parted afterwards; both had chores to attend to. Hadio had clothes to wash, while Anna had a book to read, which she had promised herself to finish at the end of the week.

Apparently, the two women became so much preoccupied in their respective duties, during the following week, they barely meet each other.

Sitting and talking to each other, on a Friday evening, a week later, their conversation focused on a town trip, which was going to take place on the following morning.

"To tell you the truth, I don't know how things would turn out tomorrow for me," Anna said.

"Anything can happen, of course," Hadio said.

"I thought about it many times. Here at Bohman Rehabilitation Centre, where there are no drinks to lure us, it is easier to abstain from drinking," Anna said.

"Is it out of self-control we don't drink, or it is because we are not presented with an alternative choice that we don't drink? I dread the moment," Hadio said.

"What is your fear? Is it freedom to make choice that you fear?" Anna said.

"I fear a bad choice I am likely to make, using the freedom I have," Hadio said.

"Would you, in this case, not rather have freedom to make a bad choice than to have no freedom to make any choice, at all?" Anna said.

"What choice do I have?" Hadio said.

"Here at Bohman Rehabilitation Centre you lack an alternative choice to test your resolve. Tomorrow you will have one," Anna said.

"What will you do with your freedom, Anna?" Hadio asked.

"To be honest with you, I don't know," Anna said.

# Chapter Forty Six

# *Harold*

Hadio had been at the Bohman rehabilitation centre for the past six weeks now, and could already notice signs of improvement in her life. She was getting less and less tired. She had lost couple of kilos, which had enkindled a spark of hope in her. She looked forward to evenings when she hold talks with Anna, joked and laughed. With personnel she was in good staid.

Nevertheless, Hadio still had the urge to drink, but never had those panic attacks she used to have, if she couldn't get a drink. Through telephone calls, she kept in touch with Ingrid of the Social Welfare Office.

Tomorrow, on Saturday, permission will be granted for anyone wishing to visit the city-centre to do so. Hadio had made up her mind to pay Ingrid a visit. She would visit her room after that, just to have a look at it. From her room, she would take a leisurely walk through the streets; visit one or two restaurants; walk through the vast malls to determine what items were new in the market-place, and then finally go back home.

She would love to undertake the trip, accompanied by Anna. Anna, however, had her mind already set up; she was going to pay her parents a visit.

Tacked under the bed cover, feeling warm, Hadio looked on Saturday morning with a mixture of fear and anticipation. She was restless all throughout the night; in the early hours of the morning she fell asleep, and then the long-awaited Saturday morning was here, at last. She woke up quite early in the morning, took shower, put on her best dress, looked at herself in the mirror and then went out to have breakfast. In the dining hall she met her friend, Anna.

The atmosphere in the dining hall was electric. People talked and laughed loudly, they patted each other's back; they were ready to leave. Lars, in a jovial mood, was there to see them off.

Most of the patients had their own friends or relatives there to pick them up. A few, including Hadio, had a van waiting – a property of Bohman Rehabilitation Centre - ready to convey them to the city centre. By six, they were supposed to embark of their return trip.

Anna's parents were there to pick her up in their vintage Mercedes Benz car. Anna remembered to introduce her parents to Hadio. They neither seemed friendly nor overtly distance; they were preoccupied with their daughter.

Once, in their conversation, Anna had told Hadio about her parents; she told Hadio that her parents had acted as international diplomats, both serving as economists for various international organisations, but had retired from active duty since.

Anna, who was a doctor of medicine, had earned half her education living with her parents abroad. Hadio and Anna wished each other well before parting.

At 10 a.m. Hadio and other three passengers were on their way to city centre. The air in the atmosphere was just perfect for outing; a slight breeze of wind was blowing up in the air, but the skies were clear. Passengers in the bus were quiet. Hadio looked from one passenger to the other, and wondered what might be going on in their minds. One of them had caught sight of Hadio looking at her and quickly looked away.

Hadio looked forward to having a meeting with Ingrid. She had phoned Ingrid two days earlier to tell her about the trip to the city-centre, and the fact that she was hoping to meet with her. The trip to the city-centre took twenty minutes. The driver packed the van at the old university packing lot where the passengers disembarked and left, thereafter.

Ten minutes later, Hadio was knocking on Ingrid's office door. Ingrid gave Hadio a warm welcome. She offered Hadio a chair, and then went to fetch tea in the kitchen. With Hadio, Ingrid knew, it was tea or nothing. Afterwards, the two ladies sat down, taking their time, making conversations, sipping their tea casually.

"You look well, Hadio," Ingrid said.

"Thank you. I am happy to hear you say it. I often look myself in the mirror, but don't see much change," Hadio said.

"Well, you better believe it. You have changed. What do they do up there to make you look the way you do?" Ingrid said.

Hadio faltered and said afterwards, "I don't know really,"

"You don't have to say anything you don't want to say; in fact, you shouldn't say anything at all," said Ingrid and smiled.

"I wished you could stay the night; we could go out and have dinner together," Ingrid said.

"There is always another time, but thank you," Hadio said.

For a short while, the two women remained silent, and then abruptly Hadio said, "Have you remembered to pay the rent for my room?"

"Don't worry. My office has taken care of it. Moreover, I have sent someone to help clean it up for you. I have written a cheque in your name too; it is for this month," Ingrid said.

"Once again, thank you; you have been very kind to me," Hadio said.

"You deserve it, it is how everyone else here in this office feels about you," Ingrid said.

"I am glad to hear that," Hadio said.

"I will keep the room for you until further notice," Ingrid said.

"That will be sometime next month, if all goes well for me," Hadio said.

"Splendid," Ingrid said.

"By the way," as if what she had in mind next to talk to Ingrid about had come to her at a spur of a moment, Hadio said, "How is Kore? And how are my children? I am curious, you know."

Ingrid looked at Hadio and felt sad. She would have liked to be of some help; however, feeling discouraged by existing rules and regulations that do not allow her to say anything to Hadio, or anyone else in a similar situation, Ingrid said, "I can't help you; I am sorry."

"Why?" Hadio said feeling quite demoralised.

Hadio had kept this topic of discussion last, because the subject had been of utmost importance to her. She had been thinking about members of her family, and couldn't keep them out of her thought system. She had been hoping for information that would assuage the feeling of high anxiety in her.

Ingrid developed a feeling of dejection from knowing that she had nothing to say which could make Hadio feel good. Delivering bad news to people had always left a bad test in her mouth, even to a person of her position, who wasn't strange to giving bad news.

She pulled herself together, nevertheless, and said, "Kore made it strictly clear to us that he doesn't wish anyone to pay him a visit. I think he is trying to avoid having people feeling pity for him. As for your children, they are somewhere out there;

the law does not allow us to reveal their whereabouts to anyone, including you," she said.

Hadio held her head with both her hands – a habit often favoured by people from her country, when they are in a state of physical or moral pain; she leaned her elbows on the table and remained in the same posture for quite a long time.

Seeing Hadio in such a desperate situation had made Ingrid develop a feeling of tormenting anxiety. For a short while, Ingrid was lost on what action to take. She pulled herself together finally; she went around the table and, encouraging Hadio to stand up, gave her a warm hug. At last, when she was convinced Hadio's body was trembling no more, Ingrid went and took her seat.

"I am sorry; this is my problem; I shouldn't have got you involved," Hadio said, using a handkerchief to wipe tears off her face.

"Don't be silly," Ingrid said. She added, "What are friends here for?

"I feel so helpless that I don't know what to do," Hadio said in a beseeching tone.

"I don't pretend to have right answers to your problems, but one thing I know to be true," Ingrid said. "Right now," she added, "I know you have an uphill struggle to make, which is to get off the drinks, and I think it is one issue that should matter most to you. Everything else, I am sorry to say, is beside the point. I am convinced your future depends on making the right decision, right now, right here."

Looking at Ingrid through wet-eyes, her mouth trembling, Hadio said, "Thank you for everything; I promise to do my best."

"I know you will," Ingrid said confidently.

On her way out, Hadio posed next to the door and said, "Goodbye."

"Goodbye and Good luck. Don't forget to phone me," Ingrid said looking jovial.

Hadio went to visit her old room, situated a few blocks away from Ingrid's office. In the corridor, she met some people with whom she exchanged greetings. She opened the door to her room, put the lights on, and by the bed-side found a chair that she sat on. She let her eyes to scan the room for something new. The room looked clean; clothes strewn all over the floor, before she left for the rehabilitation centre, she found they had been kept inside a wardrobe.

Retrieving a key from her handbag, she opened a small wooden chamber built inside a wardrobe, and took out a photo album that she perused through. The photo album held pictures of Kore, herself, the children and friends the family had acquired over the years.

There was a picture showing one of the children sitting in Kore's lap while the other one stood beside him; Hadio was in a seat next to Kore's; both parents looked at the children with loving eyes. The pictures looked like they had been taken a century ago, their colour showing signs of fading; however, their smile in the picture was as breathe-taking as it was contagious. Looking at the pictures, Hadio laughed and wept quite at the same time.

Further images of Kore and the children made her wonder if she will ever see them again. The thought of the children and Kore brought more tears in her eyes.

As she sat there sobbing, she had a feeling of suffocation. She returned the album to its place of origin, in the wooden chamber, built inside the wardrobe, and then left the room in a great haste; she was in a state of panic; she locked the door from outside, took brisk steps towards the main gate, heading out. Twenty meters away, there was a bus stop.

She took the bus to Stora Torget; from there she went straight to a bank, to cash in the check. It was one in the afternoon now. Hadio had five hours left for her to return to the rehabilitation centre.

She was hungry. She visited several restaurants, but liked none of them. None had reflected in them what they claimed to be, she seemed to think. She searched for a restaurant to have lunch made of one of the traditional Swedish dishes (common in most of the European countries) Meatloaf eaten with boiled potatoes and brown source was her favourite dish.

Her love of the Swedish traditional food was such that she couldn't get enough of it. When she couldn't find any such place, she felt sad. She realised that such eating places in Sweden have dwindled to a point now they have completely ceased to exist. She was not a fun of fast foods, or those ethnic inspired type of foods, both of which seemed to have mushroomed everywhere in the city.

She remembered a restaurant located in the industrial area of Uppsala, where, accompanied by Kore, she had often visited. The restaurant had been managed by a middle-aged lady from Hungary, who had been providing wholesome meals to her customers. She took a bus there, and hoped against hope that the restaurant would still be there, and that it had not gone the way of all the other ones. Happily, she found the restaurant, and discovered that, like in the past, it was still managed by the lady from Hungary.

The restaurant with a low-lying ceiling, a wide dining hall, with polished wooden tables and chairs, was located inside a white painted two storey building. To get there, one had to take the stairways, meandering its way up to the first floor, where the restaurant was located. She exchanged warm greetings with the restaurant's proprietor – the middle-aged lady from Hungary with amiable personality. Hadio placed her order, afterwards.

She was eating her meal quite slowly, relishing every bite of the meatballs, eaten with mush potatoes, when her eyes fell on someone she knew. The man had been one of her drinking buddies. She decided to keep him company. As Hadio approached him, the man raised his face up to look at her and shouted, Mama Circumcision,

People in the dining hall turned to look at him. Their response, Hadio thought, calls to mind the look in the face of a hunter, whose prey gets away, following a sound in the bush; it was a look of dismay, mixed with shock and anger.

"Come, come. Sit down Mama Circumcision," he shouted again. Hadio sat down, facing him across from the table and said, "Hello Boldie." His real name was Felix. Boldie was in reference to his bold head.

"How are you Boldie?" Hadio said.

"I am fine, and how are you," Boldie said in reply.

"I am fine Boldie," Hadio said.

"Where have you been? We missed you," Boldie said.

Hadio remained quiet. Later she said, "How is everybody, Boldie?"

"Everybody is fine, except I am sorry to inform you, Harold, our American friend, has passed away; a car accident. I am off to the funeral. Would you like to come with me?" He asked.

Harold, Hadio recollected, was a fine man; he had been quite fond of telling dirty jokes. He was one of the Americans that had refused to fight in Vietnam, during the Vietnam War, in the 70s, and consequently had to seek political asylum in Sweden.

He had strong nostalgic feelings for his country that came out in the open every time he got drunk, which he liked to do a lot. He had racist tendencies he fought against, but had betrayed him whenever he got drunk. Like his friends, when he was not drunk, he called Hadio Mama Circumcision. However, the moment he got drunk he called her black wench.

Hadio had never let herself get bothered by any of her friends calling her Mama Circumcision; nevertheless, she always took exception when, like Harold, someone referred to her as a wench. She liked to believe that she was nobody's wench, and, therefore, no one had a right to give her the name. To get even with him, she could have labelled him as a trash or a trailer American. She had refrained from calling him any such names out of a respect she had been having for him.

Hadio was not bothered by his or anyone else's racist tendencies. It was clear to her that people tend to be racists when more than one race shares a common space. When she lived in her native land, and the only race there was her own, people were not racists; they acted in a tribal or a clannish manner, instead.

If Sweden didn't have immigrants, feelings of prejudice would have probably been directed towards something else, she believed. It would have been the northerners against the southerners, and the easterners against the westerners, and so on and so forth, for people will always find a reason to hate someone, and when they can't get someone to hate, they will find one, by any means necessary; this is how, the devil has come to be; was not the devil persona invented living inside the peaceful atmosphere of what was the Garden of Eden? Hadio imagined.

She was aware of her own held prejudices that she constantly fought against. Her own people were not free from racial prejudices too. They vehemently disapproved of her action to themselves when she went to stay with Peter, though they never said anything to dissuade her from taking the action. To her, it seemed, what they hated most about her action wasn't that she had left Kore for any man, but for a Swede - a white man.

Boldie ate up his food and took his drink in a great haste. He didn't want to be late for the funeral.

"I am coming with you," Hadio said. She wanted to pay Harold her last respects. Soon the two were on their way to the funeral, after disembarking from a bus at Stora Torget. At the cemetery, dotted with tall trees, Hadio had the chance to meet once again with many of her friends. Among the mourners, she realised, not only was she the one person not dressed up in black, but that she was also the only black person there. Others that were not in black dress had a mourning black arm-band.

As the burial ritual got underway, people became quiet; they stood at attention, making effort to look sad, which had made Hadio to wonder. She had been at funerals before, where she had noticed a display of similar sentiments. She wondered, each time, what such state of mind really denotes. Do people in the funerals wear solemn look out of feeling sad for the dead, or it is because coming face to face with death reminds them of what is in store for them, therefore, making them want to look sad?

There were very few people who came to bury Harold; mostly, these were his friends, including his two children, and their mother - his divorced wife - as well as a priest. No high sounding words of eulogies were made to honour his memory. Harold was as lonely in death as he was when he lived.

This sad state of affairs made Hadio to think of what was in store for her when she dies. Would there be as many people to bury her on the day she dies? She realised that she had more in common with Harold than she would like to admit. Harold, like her, was an immigrant; they shared common drinking friends; each had patted ways with a spouse, and had the children taken away from; both were alcoholics; she was undergoing treatment; Harold had relapsed and is now dead. The similarity between them was so close that it shocked her.

As soon as the casket was delivered to the ground, the people beat a hasty retreat.

She was jolted from pursuing her thoughts further when someone put her arms around her shoulder.

"Hello, Stella," Hadio said.

"Hello Hadio," Stella said.

By now her friends had reconstituted their group; they were proposing to go to a pub, to drink there, to remember, and to honour, Harold, their dead friend; they asked Hadio to give them company.

Once inside the bar, at the city centre, no longer were they quiet and solemn-looking as they had been at the cemetery. As they searched for a nice place to seat, they joked with one another and laughed loudly. They were a group of seven people, including Hadio; three women and four men.

A waitress, with a tired but a friendly smile took their order of beer; she was back in no time, bearing in her arms a wooden tray, full of bottles of beer and glasses. They took each their drink; for a moment, except for the gurgling sound of the beer going past their throats, it was quiet. Hadio, feeling anxious, sat quietly in her chair; her drink of beer remained untouched.

Shortly after quenching their thirst, they focused their attention on Hadio.

"Why don't you drink? Come, let us drink," Fillip, one of her friends, told her.

"Yes, why don't you drink? Drink Hadio," they said in a single voice.

"What are you waiting for?" They shouted.

"Why are you not drinking? Come, let us drink," Fillip told her.

"Yes, why don't you drink? Drink Hadio," they said together.

"What are you waiting for?" they shouted again.

Hadio was so much overwhelmed with the cry "DRINK", "DRINK", "DRINK" that automatically she reached for the glass of beer on the table, and directed it to her mouth. As she was about to take the drink, against the background sound of the cry DRINK, DRINK, DRINK, Hadio felt the situation quite disquieting; her body trembled uncontrollably; the glass in her hand slipped through her fingers, spilling its contents on the ground, forcing her to stand up and leave the place in a hurry; her friends remained glued to their seats.

"What is the matter with Mama Circumcision?" Fillip asked.

"Perhaps, she has seen the devil. The devil is after her," Stella said.

"Mama Circumcision has always acted strangely," Lennar said.

They decided to make a song out of what Stella had said. They sang in a chorus, repeating the same lines, over and over again. "She has seen the devil. The devil is after her."

By now Hadio was walking alongside the city's old police station, on her way to the old university parking lot. Inside the van, she met the driver and a single passenger. She exchanged greetings with both and then went to sit next to a window.

It was 6 p.m. now; for another 15 minutes, the driver waited for the missing passengers to arrive. At 6.15 p.m. when neither of the two missing passengers showed up, the driver announced the departure of the vehicle to its destination.

In the morning, there were altogether four passengers in the van; now they were two; two people were missing. Hadio never wished to know why they were missing. It could mean anything. Somehow, she was happy she wasn't one of them. Hadio looked through the window as the van picked up its speed on its way out of the town, and caught sight of people on bicycles and cars, their light shining dimly against the fading light of a late spring day; pedestrians took walk on their way to somewhere. She felt quite happy that she was heading back to the clinic.

Inside the bus, she thought of how close she had come to drinking. She was amazed by people who would look for any excuse to just have a drink. Most people will drink when they are in a happy mood, but drink when they are in a sad mood too. She was glad she didn't let her emotional needs stand in the way of her better judgment. She had been tempted but had overcome the temptation to drink. However, she wouldn't let this little success of hers to get into her head. Hadio was woefully aware of the difference between winning a battle and winning a war.

Hadio liked the way she looked and felt; everybody she met told her how nice she looked. Therefore, was she willing to trade everything for a drink? She would like to keep free from drinks, but she wasn't sure she would succeed. She had a few more weeks to go. Those would be three crucial weeks of her life-time.

A half-an-hour later, they were at Bohman Rehabilitation Centre, where Hadio hoped to meet Anna. Anna, however, was nowhere to be found. She wasn't in the dining hall, and she wasn't in her room either. Hadio took her dinner; later, she went to her room to take a shower, slipped into her pyjamas and waited for Anna. At 10 p.m. she thought she heard the door to Anna's room getting opened. She got out of the bed in a great hurry, put on the pair of slippers and went out. She was more than eager to meet Anna; she wanted to talk to her about the trip. The door to Anna's room was locked. Hadio knocked on the door; it was silent inside; she went back to her room, and back to the comfort of her bed; that night she slept her deepest sleep in years.

# Chapter Forty Seven

# *Go Away*

In the following morning Hadio went to the dining hall, to have breakfast and to meet Anna. However, Anna was still nowhere to be found. Hadio took breakfast and then went in search of Anna. Last night, Anna's door remained locked, even as she knocked on the door, more than once. Was Anna in her room? It was unlike her not to respond when there is a knock on the door. If Anna was in her room, there must have been a reason for her not wanting to open the door. Perhaps she was not feeling well.

Anna was on her mind as Hadio approached the door to Anna's room. She wanted to go past the door and head to her own room but decided otherwise. It was coming to 8.30 now. Once more, Hadio was greeted with silence after she knocked the door, more than twice. Hadio was about to go away when the door finally opened. Behind the door stood Anna in a night gown; her hair was unkempt, her eyes looking puffy and red. Anna looked tired; she looked as though she hadn't had enough sleep.

"Good morning Anna," Hadio said cheerfully.

"You have made it. I can see from the way you look. I have failed," said Anna hysterically.

"Are you going to let me in or not?" Hadio said.

"Do as you wish," Anna said.

Hadio entered the room and sat on a chair by the bedside; Anna sat on the bed, her legs touching the floor.

"What makes you think you have failed?" Hadio said.

"Oh. Come on. Don't patronise me, please. I relapsed, you haven't. What does that mean to you?" Anna said in a gloomy spirit.

"That may be true, but it could happen to anyone?" Hadio said, trying to look convincing to Anna.

"No amount of logical reasoning would ever change the fact that I have relapsed. I have failed," Anna said and gave Hadio a tired look.

"You talk as though it is the end of the world. Your life isn't going to end, merely because you have relapsed. Take control of your life," Hadio said seriously.

"What are you? Are you my mother; Are you my father? Are you my teacher? You are someone I met here; I don't even know you well; you have no right to talk to me the way you do; go away, please," Anna said angrily.

"I thought we were friends," Hadio said and left quietly, feeling sad.

From Anna's room, Hadio went to attend the therapy session; later, she visited the gym.

At half past eleven, Hadio left the gym to go to her room; she took a shower and sat down on her bed, thinking of Anna. To her relief and comfort, she realised that she held no any grudge against Anna. Anna, she thought, was a typical child of her culture, in a sense that success and failure are not seen to be two sides of the same coin. Whenever any endeavour made by a person is expected to result only in success, whoever fails, he or she is not well thought about.

Hadio read for a few more minutes and then went to have lunch. She was hoping to meet Anna, but Anna was not in the dining hall. Knowing Anna well, Hadio was convinced she would soon wither away the storm.

On the same day, in the evening, sitting on the bed inside her room, while reading a book, Hadio heard a knocking sound on the door, and went to open it; there, standing on doorway, was Anna; her face gave impression of someone not sure about what to do. More than once she turned to look behind, as if she was contemplating leaving.

"Come in," Hadio said. "It is a happy surprise," she added.

Anna made no effort to get inside the room, but gave Hadio an anxious look.

"Come in Anna," Hadio insisted.

Finally, as she entered the room, Anna said, "I am sorry. I know you meant well. Will you, please, forgive me?"

Anna's present disposition was a far cry from the one in the morning. Now she seemed quite relaxed and appeared to be well groomed. She had put on a pair of clean jeans, a blue sweater and sandals. Hadio left the bed to hug Anna; Anna wept uncontrollably.

"Shh, don't weep," Hadio said.

After a while, Anna stopped weeping. She held a blue handkerchief in her right hand that she used to wipe tears falling down her face. She went to sit on the chair by the bedside, where Hadio was sitting. For a short while, the two women remained silent. Hadio had no wish to start a discussion of any sort.

While still in a state of agitation, a moment later, from out of the blue, Anna shouted, "He doesn't want me, He doesn't want me. Jonas doesn't want me."

Hadio, this time, said nothing. She let Anna do all the talking.

"Yesterday, I met Jonas," she said in a halting manner. "I was inside an ICA shop, looking at some items to buy when I saw him. I ran to him. He responded favourably with a warm hug; the response encouraged me to talk to him further. I asked him, if it was OK for us to find a restaurant to sit down, have coffee and talk. He accepted my proposition."

At this point, she stopped talking. She took the handkerchief she had kept in her lap and wiped her face with it.

After a moment of silence, she said, "I was very happy to see him. I thought that he had come round, and that we were going to be together, like before. I became delirious with happiness."

She kept silent for a long stretch of time, and then she resumed her conversation abruptly.

"I became frustrated when he tried to convince me to come to terms with the fact that he had acquired the friendship of Magdalena - my friend - and that he liked me only as a friend - a platonic friendship is what he meant. I asked myself, is not that statement a sort of a cliché? A line everyone seems to remember to tell each other, whenever a relationship fails to work out?" She said.

"For me to understand and appreciate his position in a rational manner," she went on, "I need to use my brain; it is not, however, with my brain that I love him; my love comes from my heart. I wept, I begged, I implored him to resume our love. The more I tried, the more he refused, and the more I became frustrated. In a fit of anger, I went away, leaving him to sit alone; from there, I walked straight into a bar, where I ordered one drink after another. The rest is history."

Hadio remained quiet. She wasn't in any hurry to speak. Does she have something to say to Anna that could befit the occasion? Would it not look better if she remained quiet, instead of saying something that would make her look like she was a fool? Yet she had to say something; at least it is what social etiquette demands of her; it is what Anna would expect her to do. Would comforting Anna with nice words do? Would telling her to forget Jonas be the apt thing to say? To ask Anna to forget Jonas would amount to saying the same thing to her that Jonas had told her, once before, which was to accept her fate as a foregone conclusion. Was Anna able to forget Jonas?

She was not, of course; that is why she had to drink; to try to get over what is an impossible situation. She realised, sometimes, silence is a more effective means of communication than thousand words.

Hadio approached Anna, held her up in her arms and stayed that way for a long time. Anna was a strong girl. Hadio hoped Anna would overcome her problem. Later, Anna left for her room.

In the week that followed, Hadio and Anna kept contact with each other, in the same way as before. Anna never spoke about Jonas again. Life at Bohman Rehabilitation Centre went on, as usual. Hadio attended her therapy sessions quite regularly; she found physical training to be satisfying, emotionally, physically and spiritually. If the fear of relapsing once had hanged like the sword of Damocles on her neck, she felt she had less to fear for, as time went by. She had phoned Sarah twice; each time, it seemed, Sarah had been happy to hear from her. Then, finally, the day for her to leave Bohman Rehabilitation Centre came.

This was one of those days the weather gets so cold, damp, windy and grey that most people end up becoming depressed. Hadio wasn't feeling depressed; in fact, she felt quite cheerful; happily, her buoyant demeanour had a contagious effect upon the mood of everyone else surrounding her, this Monday morning day. Ingrid was in place to convey her to the city. Lars was also present; the three of them met in Lars's office.

---

Addressing Hadio in his cheerful manner, Lars said, "Dear Hadio, there is a time for everything. Two months ago, you came to us; today, you are leaving us. During your stay here with us, we got the opportunity of getting to know you well. I am happy to say your presence here has been a great honour for us here at Bohman Rehabilitation Centre. We shall miss you, now that you are leaving us. On behalf of the Bohman Rehabilitation Centre, I wish to say goodbye, and good luck."

Tears welled in Hadio's eyes, as Lars spoke to her; she had much to thank Bohman Rehabilitation Centre for; and so, in her short speech, she said, "No words are enough to help me convey my sincere gratitude to Bohman Rehabilitation Centre. When I came here, I was a wreck. I can't say I am a hundred per cent cured person, but I can say with full certainty that today I am different from the person you had received here, two months ago." Throwing a bright look at Lars, she said, "I want to thank you for everything you have done for me."

Now directing her gaze at Ingrid, she said, "I also wish to thank my friend Ingrid for making it possible for me to be here, and to benefit from the treatment offered at Bohman Rehabilitation Centre. Thank you all."

Both Lars and Ingrid left their positions to hug Hadio.

On that note, Hadio and Ingrid left; Hadio carrying with her good memories from Bohman Rehabilitation Centre. A night before her departure took place, Hadio had said goodbye to Anna. They had promised to get in touch with each other, if possible. Anna was going to leave on the following day, in the morning.

# Chapter Forty Eight

# *Unique Qualities*

Hadio had to look for work. She went through all kinds of job advertisements, hoping to find one. She never had in mind the exact kind of job she was hoping to have; she would take any job so long as it would enable her to pay the bills for her food. Also, she would love to have to earn a little extra money to make it possible for her to afford an accommodation other than the one now paid for by the social welfare office.

She took an inventory of her qualifications to determine if she had something special she could offer. She realised that, other than having an experience working as an Assistant Nurse, she had nothing else to offer. She had, however, always taken pride on her duties, working in her capacity as an Assistant Nurse; she was good in taking good care of people; her greatest asset was to have empathy for people she had been assigned to take care of; she would look for such a job, it came to her mind.

On a visit to the Labour Office, one day, Hilda, the Labour Officer, told her about an available job opening that fitted her profile.

"A well to do lady is looking for an assistant to help in her day-today-work. I think you will be the right person for the job, but there will be an interview," she said.

She handed Hadio a note that she told her to read.

"Thank you," Hadio said.

"Good Luck," Hilda said.

A month before, Hadio had gone through a psychological evaluation test to determine her mental status and was found to be healthy.

Hadio knew how important having a job would mean to her. Not only would the job enable her to regain her lost self-confidence, but it would also take her a step closer to having contact with her children. Without a job, she realised, any chance of having her children with her was quite remote. She went to a restaurant to have tea and read the note she received from Hilda.

From the note she read, Hadio learnt that the job requires a female candidate of the age, ranging between 25 to 40 years; one who has a high school education; has a training dealing with taking care of older people; has computer proficiency, has a driving license, has had no any criminal record and is trustworthy.

Hadio believed she would be able to do the job, if given the chance. To be able to do the job, however, was one thing; to get a chance to do it was quite another thing altogether; not all people, she realised, who can do a job have a chance to do it.

In her case, she had a hurdle to overcome. She doubted she would go through the interview successfully once the secret of her past record, dealing with the murder she had committed, was brought to the knowledge of the prospective employer.

In this case, she reasoned if indeed it was wise for her to appear for the interview. If she took the interview she might stand a chance of winning the job, even though that chance would be less than 00.1 per cent. If, on the other hand, she failed to appear for the interview, she would have no chance at all. Would it not be better for her, she asked herself, to take the interview, rather than not to take the interview, at all?

At the end, she decided to appear for the interview; subsequently she phoned Hilda, who made arrangement for her to take part in the interview.

A week later, on a Wednesday morning, at 8.30 a.m., Hadio was inside a bus, marked with letters Arlanda, as its destination point; she was on her way to the interview. It was raining lightly; the absence of wind, coupled with skies that were almost clear, had made the day look promising.

Hadio forced a nervous smile and started counting backwards from one hundred. That was her personal way of keeping worries at bay. Kore had taught her how to do it. At Bohman Rehabilitation Centre, she had practised doing it constantly; it had worked miracles for her.

At a bus stop several kilometres away from Knivsta, six women passengers got off the bus.

By now Hadio had come to realise that, like her, the women that got off the bus were on their way to the interview. A mixture of fear, loathing and jealousy crossed her mind. Some of the women looked more presentable than others, in terms of the way they looked and in the way they dressed. All of them looked younger than her; all were ethnic Swedes.

On the opposite side of the road, there was a van parked on a shoulder of the road. Leaning against the car bonnet, facing the road, was a tall young-looking man.

"Are you on your way to the interview?" He asked the moment they got off the bus.

"Yes," they all answered, at once.

"Well, come over, I will take you there," he said.

They crossed the road, got inside the van, took their seats, and remained quiet. The van went off the main road and drove on a countryside gravel road that Hadio still remembered from the trip she had made, accompanied by members of her family. Close to the building, Hadio met the same atmosphere of solitude that paradoxically had been amplified by birds cheeping restlessly. The tall old oak trees were there in place too; nothing seemed to have changed; it was as though, at Sarah's home, the law of change never applied.

A moment ago, Hadio had almost given up hope; now chances of winning the job looked much brighter. If the women had the age going at for them, and the fact that they were native Swedes, none knew Sarah as well as she did; that was her bright card. She felt the situation quite encouraging.

As soon as they got off the van, the driver led the way towards a building, which was some sort of an annex. He pushed the door wide open for them to get in. A single table and chairs stood in the middle of the room. Placed on top of the table were trays of biscuits; thermos flasks of hot water for tea and coffee, jugs of drinking water and empty glasses were on the table. The women sat in the chairs placed on either side of the table.

"Help yourselves. I will be back in a jiffy," he said and left.

The women never helped themselves to anything; they were too anxious to eat. When he returned, he had white sheath of papers that he gave one each to the girls, on which he requested them to write their name, physical address as well as email address. After they wrote down the information, they handed the young man the paper. He left the room, carrying the papers with him.

To Hadio, the atmosphere inside the room was quite unnerving; it looked to her as though the candidates were deliberately avoiding talking to each other. Perhaps they had nothing to say to one another; they didn't know each other well enough for them to talk, Hadio imagined.

Do people, it occurred to Hadio, must know each other well enough to say the general things that people say to each other whenever they meet in public - say at a train station, or at the airport.

"Kristina, would you come with me?" the man jolted Hadio from following her thoughts.

Before leaving the room, he said, "The interview has just started. I will be calling your individual names as they appear in the list. When the interview is over, I will drive you to the bus stop. Good luck to you."

He left afterwards, accompanied by Kristina.

The interview went on quickly. Hadio had every reason to believe that whoever was doing the interview, he or she must be quite thorough. Each time one of the candidates returned from the interview her face looked listless.

Soon it was Hadio's turn to finally face the interviewer. As usual, she was led to the interview by the same young man with a mechanical approach to his work. He led her all the way up to the sitting room, and to the place of interview. Hadio noticed that the room looked much the same as when she saw it last. The walls had the same colourful framed pictures of birds taken from every part of the world.

Sarah had a desk and a chair in a corner of the room, from where she interviewed the candidates. Once they got inside the room, Hadio's escort left her to face Sarah alone.

Hadio approached Sarah while conscious of the situation she was in. It was clear to her that her visit was not a social one; she was there not to exchange niceties with Sarah; she was there in search of a job; job seekers are expected to approach the would-be employers with care and tact, knowing full well that everything they say or do would have to be analysed, interpreted and filed. Keeping this knowledge in mind, while avoiding the display of any kind of emotion, Hadio faced Sarah.

"Come in Hadio," Sarah said cheerfully.

She never bothered to stand up to shake hands with Hadio.
Hadio sat on a chair, facing Sarah across from the desk.

Sarah had eye glasses on the bridge of her nose; Hadio had
never seen Sarah with glasses on before; Sarah looked different.

"Welcome Hadio," Sarah said casually.

"Thank you," Hadio said.

Hadio remained quiet.

"Why do you want this job for?" Sarah asked suddenly.

"I want it for the same reason which makes everyone else
wants to have a job; to make a living and be of service," Hadio said.

"Do you have any of the qualifications required for you to
do this job?" Sarah asked.

"I think I have most of what is required to do the job. I am
literate in computer. I worked as an Assistant Nurse; hence, I
know how to attend fairly well to the needs of those who need
care. As a person, I think I am trustworthy. However, as you
know it well, I have a criminal record," Hadio said.

Sarah gave a chuckle. Later she said, "What you refer to as
a criminal record, to me it is hardly a secret; was not the person
you killed my son? However, I am also aware of the fact that
the court of law did set you free. I must trust the laws of this
country; in my mind, you are not guilty; so, let us forget about
it," Sarah said firmly.

"I am sorry," Hadio said.

Sarah ignored the remarks. She said instead, "Every single
one of the qualifications that you have, others have them too.
Therefore, my question to you is this: what more do you have
that is unique?"

"I don't know what may constitute qualities you would
consider unique," Hadio said. "However," she added, "I would
like you to know, for whatever it is worth to you, I happen to
have a special regard for people I am entrusted to take care of;

and although such a job demands a lot of energy and time, I enjoy doing it, nevertheless."

"Let us assume, for a moment, you get selected to the post for which you are getting interviewed; as Hadio, how are you going to relate to the new job, given your last job had made you into a celebrity of sort," Sarah said.

"It is not unusual for the so-called celebrities to believe that they are a special breed of people because society is bestowing high status in what they do. In any case, I never considered myself to be a celebrity of any kind," she said.

To Hadio's relief, a moment later, Sarah offered a warm smile, and said, "I am happy you have come for the interview. You will hear from me soon?"

Shortly after, the candidates were driven to the bus stop. Throughout the short journey to the bus stop, they remained silent. From the bus stop, they took a bus to the city centre.

A week later, Hadio received a letter from Sarah. The letter said,


Dear Hadio,

I am happy to inform you that you have been selected for the job for which you have been interviewed. The appointment will be officially conveyed to you as soon as all necessary procedures between my office and the relevant authorities have been finalised.

Sincerely yours,

Sarah Bissell


On receiving the letter, Hadio was overwhelmed with a feeling of happiness

# Chapter Forty Nine

# Zeal, Zest and Vigour

Once the formalities Sarah had spoken about were over, it was time for Hadio to report on duty. She was expected to report on duty on Monday, at 9.30 a.m., two weeks from when the interview took place. The excitement of having to begin a new job had robbed her of any sleep, during the previous night. Nevertheless, in the morning, Hadio was full of energy, zeal, zest and vigour as she took the bus. At a junction, where she got off the bus, she noticed a car; beside the car, there stood the young man, who had conveyed both she and the girls to Sarah's mansion for the interview. The young man waved at her. She crossed the road to meet with him.

"My name is Roger. I am visiting Sarah. I am her nephew's son," he said casually, as he shook hands with Hadio.

"Oh, I am Hadio Hebe. I am going to work for Sarah," Hadio said smiling.

"I am happy for you. Sarah speaks highly of you," he said in a low voice.

"I hope I can measure up to her expectations," Hadio said.

After exchanging those brief remarks, both remained silent. Meanwhile in her silence, Hadio had many thoughts crossing her mind. She was thinking, if Sarah had spoken highly about her to Roger, what more did she say to him. Did she let him know how Peter died? If she did, there was nothing in Roger's expression to indicate that he knew something.

She was afraid that society might regard the murder she had committed as a bloat on her character. She was aware of how unyielding, uncompromising and unforgiving society can be in its attitude towards people accused of murder. She is not an evil person; she even considers herself to be kind and considerate to others.

Must she, therefore, let herself get bothered by the irrational, undignified and unguided societal attitude towards her? Yet if society is not willing to take her for who she is, that is not her problem; it is the problem society must find a way to deal with, she reached a conclusion.

Sarah watched Hadio from the veranda of her house, as Hadio alighted from the car. For a moment, Hadio's memory was transferred to a day, together with her two children, accompanied by Peter, she visited Sarah. A mix shudder of fear and excitement gripped Hadio. As she climbed up the long staircase, she offered a smile that Sarah reciprocated.

"Welcome Hadio," Sarah said.

"Thank you," replied Hadio.

"You are quite on time. No doubt you have met my nephew's son, Roger? Roger is visiting. He has been of great help these past few days. Unfortunately, he is leaving - come this evening," Sarah said.

By now they were at the sitting room.

Pointing to the same sofa set in which Hadio had set in once, Sarah told her, "Sit anywhere." She added, "What would you like to drink?"

"I have just had tea. Thank you," Hadio said.

Hadio refused the offer without thinking; in her culture having to accept the offer of food, or drinks, quite readily, is taken to be not a sign of good behaviour; one is expected to refuse the offer, once or twice, but accept on a third or fourth time, if insisted upon by the offering party.

Though Hadio knew how much truth there is in the saying, "Old habits die hard," she promised herself not to allow old ways to hold her back, especially, those that people follow merely because they had to show respect for the tradition.

Sitting beside Hadio in a long couch, Sarah said cordially as she addressed Hadio, "I have a few things in mind to say to you. As we age, we change. We can't do things in much the same way as we used to do when we were younger; what we once enjoyed doing, suddenly we avoid doing them, either because we find no fascination in doing such things, or they become difficult for us to perform. You are neither going to get me interested into doing new things, nor are you going to instil any form of energy in me to enable me to do things. But you will help me to do things I must do, even though this will require energy, which I happen to have it in short supply, currently. I can't point out everything to you now; nevertheless, we will improvise as we face the future together. However, there are a few things that come to my mind quite readily." She posed to take a breath and then said, "Can you drive?

Before Hadio could say a word, Sarah told her, "Do you have a driving license?"

The logic behind the two questions was not lost to Hadio. You could drive, but without a license you would drive at the risk of getting caught by the police for breaking the law; this much truth was clear to her.

"Yes, I can drive, and I have a driving license," Hadio said.

"Good. In this case, I would need your driving service, from time to time. You will get me books from various libraries as well as procure medicines and other miscellaneous provisions from the city centre; you will drive me to my bank, to my lawyer's office or to the hospital, if need be. If I should attend a meeting somewhere, which I seldom do these days, you will take me there. You will also help me with household chores. I will need you to stay here, though. For you to stay in the city, and having to come up here, every day, it is going to be a difficult thing to do. In my case, I will miss your service at night-time; that is the time I might need your services most.

So, I will make an offer you can't refuse. I will provide you with accommodation, for which I am not going to charge you anything. What do you say?" Sarah asked.

Hadio couldn't hide the feelings of utmost happiness the statement had caused in her.

Hence, she said, "I accept the offer with all my heart. Thank you very much."

Hadio offered her thanks quite so profusely that Sarah was forced to say, "Oh, don't be so melodramatic," She added, "It is a simple accommodation; you must sleep somewhere, after all."

Hadio remained quiet. Although Sarah's offer might have looked quite effortless, it meant quite a lot to Hadio.

"Come with me. Let me give you a tour of the place, to familiarise you with your new home," Sarah said. She added, "It is my hope that this place will be your home, at least, for the time being. What is your hope Hadio?"

"I am hoping for the same thing," Hadio said and offered a shy smile.

As she led the way, undertaking the house tour she had promised Hadio, she let Hadio see the kitchen, four self-contained rooms, an attic and a basement. From there, followed behind by Hadio, Sarah led the way out of the house and into the next building. Hadio noticed that the building had all the qualities of the other building, except the rooms in this building were not as large as in the other one.

"This house," Sarah told Hadio once they were inside the building "has always been reserved for my guests, who are members of my family as well as old colleagues, from my working days. Nowadays, they don't come as often as they used to do. The old generation have all passed away. Except for Roger, and one or two other young ones, the rest choose to live in their own world, which is far removed from the dreary world that I live in myself. You will have a room of your choice in this house. Keep the keys with you every time you are here. Leave them with me, when you leave," Sarah told Hadio.

From the guest house they went back to Sarah's house.

"Tomorrow you will officially begin the job. Go, get all your personal belongings, and be ready at the junction, at 9 a.m. I shall be waiting there for you," Sarah said. Roger will drive you to the bus stop now," she added.

"I will see you tomorrow," Hadio said.

As Hadio was about to leave, Sarah told her, "Wait; don't leave, yet.

She disappeared inside a room that stood next to the sitting room; a moment later, holding a check in her right hand, while addressing Hadio, she said, "I imagine you may have some needs you would like to be taken care of. You will pay me another time"

Hadio thanked Sarah for the offer. Afterwards, leaving Sarah smiling, standing in the middle of the room, she left. Outside, Hadio met Roger. From the time that he took Hadio to meet with Sarah for the interview, she never saw him again. He must have been lurking in the shadows. He looked quiet and distant. Is he the same way with Sarah? Roger drove her to the bus stop.

From there, she took the bus to the city centre. Hadio was in a jovial mood. She was so happy that she wanted to sing; she wanted to let everybody know how happy she was. Her happiness, she felt, called for some sort of indulgence. She went to cash in the check in the bank; Later, Hadio went shopping for clothes to suit the late spring season; she also bought body lotion, perfume and other accessories used by women, mostly to enhance their physical health and give them a fashionable look.

At 3 p.m. she went to a film show; later she went back to her little room; there, she packed clothes into a suitcase she had just bought, took a shower and then sat on her bed, feeling delirious with happiness. At seven, she went to a restaurant and treated herself to a sumptuous dinner of large sized margarita pizza.

The need to have a drink crossed her mind, and even though the idea was tantalising to her, the consequences of what this might mean to her life discouraged her from pursuing the idea further. From the restaurant, she took the bus home, looking forward to a good night rest.

# Chapter Fifty

# *Grounded*

At Fair Breeze Rest Home, a decision had been taken to have Kore's case come up for a review. Kore was in his room, having an afternoon-nap when one of the orderlies with a perpetual look of an angry bull knocked on the door.

"You are wanted in the office," the orderly told Kore. Except once before when he met a group of doctors, who elicited answers from him on wide range of issues, this was the second time he got summoned to the office; Kore didn't know what summoning to the office would mean for him.

Kore approached the office carefully, accompanied by the orderly. Inside the office, he found Doctor Olson along with three older-looking men waiting for him: all were dressed in large fitting black overcoats.

"Mr Kore, for the benefit of the gentlemen here with me," Dr Olson said, not offering Kore greetings of any kind nor a chair to sit on, "I shall address you in English. I know you speak English. I hope you don't mind. These gentlemen here," he said pointing to them, "are from U.S; they are on a tour of our institutions."

Kore remained silent.

"What would you say, Mr Kore if I tell you that you have a good chance of getting away from this institution?" He asked suddenly.

"Why, of course, I would welcome the decision," Kore said, feeling astonished.

"How are you going to deal with world outside? He asked.

"I have changed now;" Kore said.

"What do you mean?" Doctor Olson asked, not believing his ears.

"I am going to accept what I can't change. I am also ready to re-evaluate my values, and arrange my priorities accordingly," Kore said.

At this reply, Doctor Olson took a sudden look at his colleagues who, looking back at him, nodded their heads quite at the same time, as if the statement Kore made had given them an overwhelming feeling of pleasure.

"You have just earned your discharge, Mr Kore. Let me tell you the reason," Doctor Olson added in a jovial tone.

Before Doctor Olson could speak up, one of the visitors addressing Kore said, "Mr Kore, my name is Christopher Huntington. I wish to let you know that it is my pleasure meeting you. You are from Africa; aren't you?"

"Yes," Kore said nonchalantly.

"What part of Africa are you from?" He said.

"East Africa," Kore gave a short reply.

"I like East Africa with its beautiful scenery, plenty of wild-life, as well as friendly natives," he said, giving his colleagues a gratified look. "Gentlemen," he said, as he addressed his colleagues further, "have you ever seen the African elephant, in all its majestic splendour, in its own habitat: the African bush? It is a sight to behold, I guarantee you that."

Kore could not help getting annoyed with a man who gave to the elephant and the bush an African identity but refused to do the same thing for the people; he called them natives, instead. Yet it was not lost on Kore that he had been generous with his definition; it could have been worse. In America, but also in Sweden, nigger and *neger* respectively (the latter is a Swedish version of the word nigger in English) are terms used by some people – though not all - to identify any black person - be they from America or Africa.

"Who give such people the right to label other people in the way they do? Calling a person from Africa by any other name, it means denying that person a sense of belonging and identity. Everyone in this planet belongs to a place, which he or she identifies with. A person from Europe is European, the one from Asia is Asian; another from America is American and a person from Arabia is Arab. Why can't a person from Africa be African?" Kore said to himself. It seems to Kore quite obvious that such people have so much admiration for the continent of Africa because of its beauty and immense resources, but have so little respect for people, that they find hard to dignify the people with the name of a continent they admire so much.

"What a waste of breath and time," Kore, feeling annoyed, seemed to think in relation to the person talking to him.

"Thank you, Mr Kore. Just curious," he told Kore. "Please go on," he added, addressing Doctor Olson.

"Mr Kore," Doctor Olson said, "I wish you to know that before me here is a report dealing with the state of your health. I am quite happy to inform you, based on the observation regarding the status of your mental-health condition that had been made by expert doctors a decision has been reached to get you a discharge. The following are the observations made on your health condition:

You have been responding well to both therapy and medication. You have been interacting well with medical orderlies.

You have proved to be in total control of your angry emotions.

With other patients, as well as other personnel, you have been helpful and cooperative.

Hence, based on the above-mentioned factors, as well as the information you have just given here, this panel has decided that you are healthy enough to resume your life outside the compounds of this august institution."

Kore almost laughed at the use of the word august. He was quite familiar with the word which is often used to describe outstanding international institutions; he had never expected the man could use such a word to describe the lacklustre social environment of a mental institution.

"We will send a separate letter to the district hospital authorities to enable you to continue getting treatment for the speech impairment, as well as the hip and the back problems. Do you have any question, Mr Kore?" He said.

"No," said Kore

"Good luck to you," he said.

"Thank you," Kore said.

"I called the Social Welfare Office to talk to someone there – one Ingrid; she is responsible for you. If you go there now, you will find her in her office, waiting. Outside, there is a car waiting to take you there. Good luck," Dr Olson said.

Kore went to look for Alvarez and found him in his room. He was quite lost on how to break the news to his friend. What state of mind should he display? Should he display a state of happiness for receiving a discharge while his friend is still locked up in the institution?

He met Alvarez in his room. The door to the room was open. He found Alvarez sitting on his bed; in his hands he held a paper, with a sketch of a woman drawn on it; the woman's right arm outstretched towards a tree, as if making attempt to pluck a fruit.

"I didn't know you were an artist," Kore said, trying to locate a chair to sit on.

"Ah," Alvarez said with a grin, "it is a hobby that I abandoned, a long time ago, which I am trying to resume so as to better deal with the stifling boredom of the institution."

He added after a shot pause, "I have been trying to locate you, but you were not in your room," he added,"

"I was in the office. The Board has given me a discharge," Kore said casually.

"Wait! You haven't told me any of that," Alvarez said, looking startled.

"The whole thing has come as a surprise to me," Kore said.

"What did you say?" Alvarez asked.

"I have changed, I told them so." He added, "I have also told them that I am ready to accept what I can't change."

"Do you actually mean it?" Alvarez asked.

"Oh Yes, I do; why are you asking? Kore said.

"How is it possible?" Alvarez said.

"I had an opportunity to make changes once, but I didn't. I dared to dream. I shouldn't have done it." Kore said.

"Is it wrong to dream?" Alvarez said.

"Yes, unfortunately," Kore said.

"How?" Alvarez asked, looking confused.

Take a look at me; I am not any longer the person that I once used to be. The cost of dreaming about a better future has resulted in the loss of my limb," Kore said.

"I can see that; but what has become of your spirit? Has that changed too? Alvarez said.

"Since I am not a student of metaphysics, I am averse to discussing with you anything to do with spirits or the spirit. I walk with a limb and stammer when I talk; in case you haven't noticed. It can never be worse than that." Kore said.

"In that case, am I right to assume that they have succeeded in making you toe the line?" Alvarez said.

"Maybe," Kore said. "Good-bye Alvarez," he added in a sad tone.

"I wish you good luck, Kore" Alvarez said sincerely. "I will be happy to hear from you. Write or phone me, if you can; let me know something about life, out there, in the concrete jungle," Alvarez added cheerfully, but obviously feeling quite sad to be losing his friend.

And so, the two men who differed from each other, in all sorts of ways, but became very good friends in the Fairview Rest Home, parted ways.

Kore went to his room; there he packed his meagre clothes in a rag-sack and then left.

On his way to meet with Ingrid, Kore acknowledged to himself that he had known only troubles ever since the day that he left his home. He knew well that problems were not something new to people. He knew also that when dealing with problems confronting them, some people would spend time talking to psychologists; others would talk to God, through payers.

And despite different mechanisms they choose for coping with their problems, what most people share, it occurred to Kore, is a role they assign to external agents for helping to bring positive changes in their lives. Neither of the two methods could apply to him, he believed. While psychologists scare him, speaking to God through prayers, on the other hand, requires faith in God that he had very little of it left in him.

From the day he left his home, Kore believed he had ceased to be in control of much of anything, in his life. His life, subsequently, like a floating piece of wood on a river, had become uncharted, unhindered and uncontrolled. Thus, as someone in a position not to do much to change his fate, Kore had lately come to accept the outcome of life with almost a fatalistic sense of resignation; he had come to accept what he can't change.

Once again, Kore came face to face with the Social Welfare Office. He found Ingrid waiting for him inside her office. The moment he got inside the office, she stood up to shake hands with him. Waiting for him there was Jakobsson of the Labour Office.

In the past, dealing with them separately had posed a great challenge for him; together, they would be a formidable fighting machine. The good thing was that he was not there to fight them; he was there to listen to what they wished to say to him, and hence do their biddings, whatever the case may be.

"Welcome Mr Kore," Ingrid said as she gave him a warm smile.

"You look quite good," she added, to Kore's utter surprise.

Kore couldn't recollect Ingrid having any interest in his physical appearance. In the past, their relationship was far from being a friendly one; it was not even a cordial one. Perhaps, a change had lately come over her, or was it a change in him that had prompted her to act that way; what could it be?

Kore was jolted from following his thoughts any further by Ingrid who was saying in her usual commanding voice, "Mr Kore, both Social Welfare Office as well as Labour Office have worked out a plan to get you reintegrated into the society, from which you have stayed away for quite a long time."

Jakobsson nodded his head in agreement and offered Kore a cautious smile that Kore reciprocated mechanically since his mind was wondering far afield, thinking what more surprises Ingrid and Jakobsson had up their sleeves.

"You see Mr Kore," Ingrid said, as she addressed Kore further, "since as a physically disabled person you need a special care for which both my office as well as Jakobsson's office have acknowledged to be the case, therefore, my office has got a new place for you to live in - a place considered to be most convenient for someone with a physical disability, like yours." She stayed quiet after that, but gave Kore what had amounted to a pitiful look.

"We have moved you to a place closer to the city shopping centre," she said, a moment later, "to enable you to do your errands easily."

To show that he was in total agreement with Ingrid, Jakobsson nodded his head, even more vigorously than he had done previously.

Meanwhile still addressing Kore, Ingrid said, "Someone will pay you a visit every other day to help with household chores."

At this point, Ingrid had fully finished conveying her message.

Now, it was the turn for Jakobsson to address Kore.

In a slow but conscious manner, Jakobsson said, "Welcome Mr Kore. I have with much regret noticed that since we met last, you have undergone quite drastic changes; these changes have posed some challenges to us about how to carry our new relationship with you; one of the most challenging aspects of this relationship is how to get you integrated into the society, and, in doing so, make you feel confident in yourself. Ingrid, in this regard, has done her part; my role is to see that you get some work to do - an employment of sort. It may not be an employment of your dream, but an employment nevertheless."

Kore sat upright in his chair and offered to keenly listen to Jakobsson. Ingrid nodded her head, looked at Kore and smiled. As she smiled, it occurred to Kore that the number of times that Ingrid had smiled, in just one sitting today, had by far exceeded the number of all the times that in the past years Kore had seen her smiling.

"Mr Kore." Jakobsson jolted Kore from his reverie.

"You will report to the local office of Charity for All, which is a non-governmental organisation, offering support to newly arrived refugees; there, someone will assign you a duty," Jakobsson said. When he was left with nothing else to say, Jakobsson looked at Ingrid and stayed quiet. To Kore it was obvious the meeting had come to an end.

"Do you have something you wish to say Mr Kore?" Ingrid asked.

He wished to say what has he done to deserve such consideration from them? Is their consideration like the one extended to the vanquished by the victor? Or are they showing him pity for being someone that had spent time at Fair Breeze Rest Home, and now is pretending to fit in?

He realised he had nothing to gain by saying such words that might be construed by both Ingrid and Jakobsson to mean that he wasn't grateful; after all, the offer proposed by them was something they had thought well about.

"I have nothing to say," he said. Later, he remembered to add, "Thank you.

The room allocated to him by Ingrid he found to be a far better place for him to live in than his earlier room. It was a self-contained apartment, having a sitting room, one sleeping room, a toilet and a shower room. Installed in the kitchen were gadgets necessary for cooking and restoring food; in the cupboard he found well-arranged set of utensils required for all kinds of use. The bed was large enough to accommodate two people; beside the bed was a night table; next to the night table was a dressing table.

One thing Kore liked most about his new dwellings was the privacy it had afforded him; he was made happy by the fact that he was not going to share facilities made available to him with someone, unlike in the past when he was forced to share such private facilities as toilet, bathroom and kitchen, with people who had no regards for other people's feelings.

His presence at the offices of The Charity for All will turn out to be another milestone feature marking a life-long-journey Kore had been making in his effort to give his life a clear meaning. The building from which the local branch of The Charity for All had been running its activities was a modest looking building, located at the historical part of the city. A middle-aged woman, with a friendly smile, welcomed him into the office.

"Come in, please," she said in a cheerful tone. "My name is Lena," she added.

As one enters the office building, through the main entrance, Lena's office stood on the right-side. Standing at the middle of a large hall was a long table, with chairs placed on both of its sides; the hall had an appearance of a classroom; there was a copying machine set against the wall; there was also a small kitchen in a tiny room connected to the main hall.

Lena's office looked simple; a single table occupied by Lena and several chairs were the most visible items in the room; to one side of the wall was a map of the world. The walls were surrounded with framed pictures, showing older female immigrants undertaking various activities.

"I am happy to have you here with us," she said the moment he got inside the room. "Ingrid of the Social Welfare Office and Jakobsson of the Labour Office," she added, "have both spoken highly of you to us. We are not a profit-making organisation; our job is mostly done on a basis of volunteering, and as such we don't pay salary to people here.

Your salary, which is in a form of a stipend, will be paid to you through the Labour Office, in an association with Insurance Office. Your duties with us here would involve helping us with simple administrative and other miscellaneous duties.

This is to say, you would print out copies of documents for our guests; these are older female-immigrants who are new comers; you would give them company when they go out shopping; you would help them feel in forms; you would make coffee and see that the kitchen stays clean, all the time," Lena said and stayed quiet for a while.

"Do you have something that you wish to say? She said, afterwards.

"I am happy to have the opportunity to work as a volunteer here" Kore said.

Those words he didn't say just for the formality sake. Indeed, he was quite happy to be of service to someone.

The women that he served seemed happy that they had found a new home, something that every new comer to the country had once felt about it. He himself had similar feelings once.

At this point, happiness comes with the knowledge that all things that matter in life is taken care of; housing agency supplies a home to live in; Social Welfare Office takes care of the education of the children; money for the family's upkeep is paid through the same institution.

In the beginning, everyone is thankful for what they get. With a passage of time, however, the sense of gratitude diminishes to a point what is offered as a favour it is demanded by force. Thus, it is not uncommon for the Social Welfare Official to be threatened for not making enough payment to their clients.

Kore looked at these women and wished the best for them. Most of them were middle-aged. They joked with each other, and never hesitated to order him to make tea for them, whenever any of them felt like having a cup of tea. Kore knew they joked about him.

From those among them who came from South Asia, they called him Langra, a derogatory Urdu/Hindi term, used for a person with a limp, like him. Sometimes they joked openly about him, by imitating the way he walked and the way he talked, and laughed in his face, thereafter.

Despite his hatred for them for making him a butt of their joke, Kore did everything else to serve them well. He didn't want to spoil what was a honeymoon period for them; it is one period in their lives they will like to remember.

At the hospital, the doctor was quite nice to him. This was Dr Andrea. Dr Andrea was a man of medium height; he had a well-trimmed body that might suggest that he was someone who took good care of his body. Nevertheless, the signs of wrinkles evident in his forehead and around his full mouth had made him to look older than what his real age at forty-nine would suggest. He was a type of a man who said little but liked to listen.

After he came to know Kore well, he took liking to him, and felt free to tell him about an account of his life in Africa. In Kinshasa, Congo, he told Kore, he had been a doctor, appointed by the World Health Organisation (WHO) to work in the Democratic Republic of Congo, as an advisor to the country's Ministry of Health.

He told Kore of his travel adventures in Africa that he had undertaken when he was in his mid-twenties; he told him of a long boat journey that he had taken to Kisangani, sailing on the mighty River Congo, and how he had been awe-struck by the enormous sight of Mount Kilimanjaro, as well as the rich wildlife he had seen in Ngorongoro Crater, and in the Serengeti plains of Tanzania.

Dr Andrea had been taking good care of Kore from the day he got admitted into the hospital for the treatment of his injuries. The treatment that he offered Kore had included a spinal cord operation that he had performed on him, twice. Kore had come a long way since then; now the two men had become friends - almost.

Currently, Kore was under a regular care of a physiotherapist. As such, he never saw Dr Andrea as often as he used to do. On this day, however, Dr Andrea had made a special arrangement for Kore to see him. Kore met Dr Andrea in his large office, sitting, waiting for him.

"Come in," Dr Andrea said. "How are you doing today? He said, as he stood up to shake hands with Kore.

"I am fine and how are you," Kore said cheerfully.

"I am fine," Dr Andrea said.

Dr Andrea sat facing Kore across from the table. A pen and a leather bounded note book of a brown colour lay on the table; the note book had long hand-written notes on it. Dr Andrea looked at those notes; in a business-like manner, he said afterwards, "I will come to the point, right away; I am not going to beat around the bush."

Kore wondered what Dr Andrea wished to say to him; he waited impatiently to hear him speak.

"Are you still doing a volunteering work in the offices of The Charity for All.'"? Dr Andrea said.

Now that Dr Andrea has spoken the words, Kore felt relieved from a mounting feeling of anxiety.

"Yes," Kore said.

"Do you enjoy working there?" Dr Andrea asked.

"I have no other alternative, 'Kore said.

"Let's say that you do have a say on the matter, what would you have done?"

"I don't know really," he said.

He wanted to be frank with Dr Andrea, who must have valid reason for asking him the question, but felt confused what to think about his new assignment.

"In this case, what do you say if we ground you?" Dr Andrea said, shifting his gaze away from the note book he was writing something on, to focus on Kore.

"You don't mean in the same manner as when a plane is grounded?" Kore said.

"Yes," Dr Andrea said, laughing.

Having observed in Kore's facial expression what looked like a sign of disappointment, following what he had just said to him, Dr Andrea tried to reassure Kore by telling him, "Why, it happens every day to people of your health condition. I could recommend the issue to relevant authorities, if you say so."

"Why do this for me?" Kore asked.

Although Kore never doubted Dr Andrea's good intention, he wanted to know the reason; he was entitled to it, he believed.

"You are doing a volunteering work, which is quite a noble thing to do; the question is, what do you hope to achieve?" Dr Andrea asked.

Kore didn't have an answer to that question, and so he remained silent.

"You are not a student that enriches a CV. You are a qualified man, who can do what you have been trained to do; if you can't get a normal work to do, it is just fare you should be given disability pension. What I don't like here is the state of a legal limbo you are made to find yourself in; it is unfair. If you are neither a working person nor a student, what are you?" Dr Andrea said, giving Kore a kindly look.

He stood up abruptly, turned to have a look at Kore, and said in a hurry, "I am thirsty. I am going to have some water. Will you have some?"

Kore nodded his head. Doctor Andrea went out of the room; from the water machine in the corridor, he filled two plastic cups with water; he gave Kore one, and took his drink of water in one gulp.

"What do you say?" He asked Kore.

At that moment, Kore decided to put his pride aside; he gave a critical look at his chances of getting a proper job.

"If I couldn't get a proper job when my health condition allowed it, what chance do I have now when I am almost a broken man? Furthermore, as someone who had spent time at Fair Breeze Rest Home, wouldn't my record undermine any chance of getting employment?" Kore reasoned.

"Well, what do you think?" Dr Andrea said.

"Let's do it," Kore said, as he gave Dr Andrea a wide smile.

On his way to the bus stop, several meters away from the hospital's main gate, Kore considered critically the option presented to him by Dr Andrea; once having seen a clear meaning in it, he thought, "I don't need to sit home and brood about chances I had never had, or one that I would never have. Yes, my limbs are broken, and so too is my hip; I have also sustained severe injuries to some of my internal organs, but so what? I better stand up and create my own chances."

He realised he had many things in life he had wanted to do but had been unable to do. Learning how to play chess was one thing that he had wanted to do; how to master computer was another thing. Was he too old at 47 years of age to indulge in such activities? Both activities demand time and the use of brain; a challenge that Kore was willing to face.

Three weeks later, he received a letter from the Labour Office, requesting for his presence there.

As he opened the door to Jakobsson's office, Kore caught sight of Jakobsson reading a book. The moment Jakobsson saw Kore, he put the book aside, raised his face up to look at Kore, and smiling lightly, he said, "Good morning."

"Good morning," Kore said.

"How have you been keeping?" Jakobsson said.

"I am fine?" Kore said.

Kore sat down on a chair facing Jakobsson across from a table.

Immediately after he sat down, Jakobsson addressing Kore told him, "I have with me here a report I have received from the district hospital as well as a letter from the insurance office." He opened the drawer of his desk and took out a folder, inside of which were papers. "What I have here," he said, pointing to the items he held in his hands; "is a report from the hospital, which is a quite straight forward one." He posed to give Kore a look.

"The report," he went on, "is about the strain you feel due to injuries on your limbs and on other parts of your body. The report has also made reference to speech impairment. All in all, it is the opinion of Doctor Andrea, at the District Hospital, that to avoid putting further strain on your mind and body, you should be absolved from doing all kinds of duties.

Given Doctor Andrea's report, the Insurance Office wishes me to tell them what chance you have of getting employment - if any. They want to know if you are worth anything in the market." Jakobsson said.

Throwing his arms up in the air in a manner of someone in total despair of something, he told Kore. "I don't know what to say. Can you help me out?" He said.

"I can't help you there. It is your job," Kore said.

Jakobsson laughed nervously. "What should I say?" Jakobsson said.

"Say anything. I know you mean well. But there is no way I could commit myself,"

"This thing is putting me in a very awkward situation," he said in voice belonging to someone consigned to a position of hopelessness.

"If it is of any help, I am open for any suggestion," Kore said.

"Are you serious, really?" Jakobsson said.

"Yes," Kore said.

"Then, in this case, leave it to me," he said.

A month had gone by when Kore received a letter from the Insurance Office, requesting his presence there. By circumstances beyond his control he was less known to officials there. He must have felt awkward that he was heading there now.

At the office, he met a middle aged woman who looked at him as though he was a creature from out of this world that by accident had just fallen off the roof of the office-building and now it is confronting her, sitting across from her desk. The lady never bothered with social formality of exchanging greetings with Kore. She went in for attack, right away.

"Who are you? She said and never looked Kore openly in the face.

The look was not of a person who was shy; there was something in the furtive look she gave Kore, coupled with a grimace on her face, that betrayed a high level of aggression.

"Oh, I am Kore," Kore said.

"May I have your civic number, please?" She demanded.

Putting his hand in the breast pocket of his jacket, he fished out a battered identity card bearing a civic number. Handing the identity card to her, he said, "Yes, but of course, here is my identity card,"

She took a quick look at the identity card and said in a plain language, "You have had no business with us here. You are one of those souls who always remain invisible to us."

Kore wished to tell her she shouldn't be surprised; didn't she know that all souls are invisible to the naked eye? He wanted to tell her that she should be complimenting herself for having finally come across one, like him. He decided not to say anything.

"I will come to the point. I don't like this, and I don't understand what this world has come to. I find quite disturbing that people like you retire themselves before their time is up," she said as she continued giving Kore the same furtive look.

"I haven't retired myself; I have had nothing from which to retire. I had no work. For some reasons known only to you, I know you don't like me; however, that is not my problem. So kindly please concentrate in what you are doing, and let us go through the charade," he dared say to her.

This conversation was not heading in the right direction, he imagined to himself. He felt that while he was there to have a problem solved, he had turned out to be a problem. What a better way to finish this conversation except by storming out of the room, it occurred to him.

He was contemplating doing just that when he heard the woman say, "I don't have much to say except to tell you that upon a recommendation made by the authorities at the district Hospital, as well the Labour Office, this office has accepted to an early retirement for you. From now on, all future disability pension schemes offered to you will be directed from this office. For the technicalities involved, read this information," she handed him a brochure. She added, "I have nothing to say."

On that note she left Kore sitting alone in the room, thinking how his life ambition had met its inauspicious and inglorious end at the hand of a humourless official, inside a dour looking place, and felt sad that fate had not favoured him with a smile.

# Chapter One

## *Point of Reference*

Hadio took to her new job like fish to water. Sarah wanted Hadio to have comfortable feelings, even as she worked for her. A walk in the woods, every morning, before breakfast, was something that both ladies looked forward to. The walks in the woods were full of eventful episodes. It offered them the opportunity to pick mushrooms as well as watching birds by making use of the binoculars that Sarah had constantly carried with her, in her walks.

One time, during an early spring season, while taking their early morning walks, Sarah pointed to a little yellow bird. Sarah told Hadio that the bird had just arrived from East Africa. Hadio immediately felt a special kinship with the bird; taking a keen look at the bird perched on a branch of a short tree, not far from where the two women stood, Hadio shouted the following words: "Karibu."

"Did you say something?" Sarah said, giving Hadio an odd look.

Hadio smiled and told Sarah that those were Swahili words meant to welcome the bird.

"Birds and fishes are truly transnational creatures. They are creatures of the air and the sea. They are here today; tomorrow they are not. They don't belong to anyone but to the world - a world we must do everything to save from getting destroyed," Sarah said.

Hadio couldn't agree more with her, she told Sarah.

From taking a walk in the woods, a breakfast made by Hadio of porridge, bread, butter, omelette, cheese, orange juice, coffee and tea followed. Sarah ate sparingly but encouraged Hadio to eat well. After breakfast, Sarah would often retire to her room to write on her computer, leaving Hadio to do household chores.

Hadio had noticed quite early in time that if there was one thing Sarah hated most, it was a sloppy work. Hadio had also taken note of the fact that Sarah wanted things to be kept in their place of origin. A vase that stood on the side table, for example, must remain where it is, and nowhere else; chairs in the sitting room must be kept in their place.

Sarah never liked someone to tamper with her things.

What is more, Sarah liked everything to be attended to as scheduled. Flower-pots must be watered at six every evening; afternoon tea ready by four; laundry needed attended to every Wednesday.

Once a week, on Friday, Hadio went to Karolina library, either to return books or borrow new ones. Once a month she travelled to Uppsala in order to procure food and other necessary provisions, such as Sarah's medicines.

At day time, the two women were always busy, and could seldom spare enough time to talk to each other much. However, after supper, they enjoyed watching TV together, and talked.

Hadio, one evening, was in the sitting room, knitting a sweater that she had promised to give to Sarah as a present. Beside her sat Sarah. The two women were watching the TV together when they were treated to a news bulletin that announced someone's death. The news affected Sarah in a way that was quite hard to describe. Considering that Sarah was not someone to flaunt her emotions easily, it came as a surprise for Hadio to see Sarah in such an agitated state of emotion.

Presented on the television screen was a recorded video of a tall-looking man; the man was taking a stroll on a meadow; trotting in front of him was a dog on a leash. The man had a wind jacket that fluttered against the wind; his face was in a pensive mood; thick hair, driven behind by the wind, revealed an exceptionally large forehead.

As she kept watching the video, it dawned on Hadio that she had seen the man before. When she was convinced of who he was, she emitted a crying sound of agony.

"What is it?" Sarah asked.

"I know the man in the video," Hadio said.

"What do you mean?" Sarah asked.

"Mr Mikael Holmberg was the man who had made it possible for me and my children to come to Sweden," she said. "He was a kind man," she added.

The news bulletin dealing with Holmberg's death was immediately followed with an interview, in which one of the Swedish most prominent social and political commentators gave answers to questions asked by a journalist.

"Who is Mikael Holmberg?" asked a clean-shaven journalist, in his late twenties, who belonged to a crop of young journalists that have just come of age, and were now ready to take over the place of the retiring old journalists.

"Holmberg was a man of his generation," said the commentator. "He belonged to that generation of people in our country's political history," he added, "whose political ideals had brought far reaching socio-economic changes to our country."

He stayed quiet, for a while, as if reflecting on what more he wished to say. "When he was a young aspiring politician," he said finally, "Tage Erlander, the most prominent post war Swedish Prime Minister, took him under his wing, both for his talents and for his strong commitments to the values of the Social Democratic Party. Olof Palme was yet another young man that Tage Erlander took under his wing, for the same reasons. By the way, the two young men had gone on to become life-long friends."

"Holmberg is also remembered today for his recent work in Africa, helping Africans to achieve their development dreams. What would you say to that? He asked.

"Had he been with us here, Holmberg would have chastised you for thinking that he was working for Africans, which he saw as a way of demeaning their efforts, by denying them the role they play in the development of their continent. Instead, he would have liked you to think, together with Africans, he worked to achieve development there.

He believed no one section of humanity can have a clear conscience if another one is living in poverty. He was an idealist. Above all, he was a good man. The likes of him, we will never see again," he said.

"In a world," he added, "where political idealism in our society is being substituted for cheap political cynicism, Holmberg had become an endangered species; perhaps, death has come to him at the right time." Tears lingered in the commentator's eyes.

Two days later, in a car driven by Hadio, Sarah attended a burial ceremony held in Adolf Fredrik Church, one of the prominent Stockholm churches; there, Sarah had the opportunity to once again come into contact with her former colleagues with whom she had lost contact.

If Peter was someone known to both women, Holmberg was yet another person who would provide the two ladies with a common point of reference. Hence, the death of Holmberg, it seemed, would bring the two women much closer together.

In the following week, their discussion would centre more and more round Holmberg; it wasn't that they had intended this to be the case, except that one topic had led to another one, so that in the end they ended up discussing Holmberg.

"If Holmberg is responsible for your coming here, I am also partly responsible," Sarah said. "At the time," she added, "I had been a Director General in the Ministry of Foreign Affairs. I had followed every twist and turn the struggle to bring you here had taken."

Sarah held her left hand against her mouth; her eyes wide open, she said, "What a coincidence!" Whenever Sarah assumed that posture, she acquired a look of a young innocent girl.

"Yes, what a coincidence," Hadio said, repeating Sarah's words.

"Given the nature of problems you and your family have encountered here in this country, do you still think he did a right thing to get you to come here? Sarah said.

"I don't know what to say. All I know is, with good intentions in mind, Holmberg did his best to get us to come here. If my life now is what it is, I dread to think what turn it would have taken had we not come here," Hadio said.

"I have never wished to know anything about your past for fear of disturbing your feelings. Anyway, are you not in touch with any of your family members?" Sarah said cautiously.

"The last recollection I have of my husband," she said, "is that he was in a mental asylum, and my children are currently living with another family elsewhere. I don't know exactly where" Hadio said, tears lingering in her eyes.

"Oh, I am sorry," Sarah said. She added, "I never meant to cause you to feel sad."

"It is OK," Hadio said.

"What are your plans now?" Sarah asked.

"I have started thinking a lot about my children," Hadio said. "Thanks to you," she added, "I have a job now that gives me a credibility of some sort. Ingrid, my former social welfare officer, knows the whereabouts of my husband; he doesn't wish to have any visitors, according to Ingrid," Hadio said sounding sorrowful.

"Given what has taken place between you and your husband, would you be willing to meet him?" Sarah asked.

"Yes; that would make me happy. I am not sure, however, if he would be willing to forgive me. I caused Kore a lot of pain," Hadio said.

"Would you be equally willing to forgive Peter?"

The mentioning of the word Peter threw Hadio off balance. This was the second time Sarah was speaking to her about Peter; she didn't know what Sarah herself thought about Peter, but now she must give Sarah the answer she was looking for. Maybe, one day, she might ask Sarah what she thought about Peter.

Hadio recollected her composure and said, "That is a hypothetical question." "Peter," she added, "had caused a lot of harm to me. He is dead now. Had he still been alive, I wonder if he would have forgiven himself for making me suffer so much. My life was consumed with guilt, after his death, which had made me want to even drink more, to forget.

Besides, I felt ashamed because of what he did to me. I have since changed my mind. I have come to a realisation that those that cause harm to people they must grapple with feelings of shame and guilt, not their victims," Hadio said.

She stayed quiet after that, giving thought to whether she should say more. There was no need keeping her feelings about

Peter to herself; the person she was talking to is his mother, after all. Sarah deserves to know.

"Sometimes, I feel that I must forgive Peter," she said. "Peter," she added, "was a tormented person. I saw him cry in secret; he often cried in his sleep. I don't know what he saw in his dreams. Even as I lived with him and getting tormented by him, I could not help feeling sorry for him, and now you have mentioned him to me, I still feel sorry for him" Hadio said.

"You have mentioned some very important point to which I personally can relate," Sarah said not so-enthusiastically.

"I have been contending with a feeling of shame mixed with guilt, throughout my life, which I have never wished to share them with anyone, but I will be happy to share them with you now. Those feelings," she added quite solemnly, "I am sorry to say have had a negative bearing on my emotions, to a point of causing a distortion over my personality."

Later, she told Hadio everything regarding the kind of relationship she had had with Bacchus, Peter, her son, as well as her own family members and the society in general.

"I believe what has happened can't be wished away; one must accept what can't be changed. It is through coming to terms with the past that we are able to let the past rest, by not allowing it to come and haunt us," Hadio said philosophically.

Getting the jist of the meaning, Sarah said, "Those are inspiring words that only philosophers and such other similar gifted people can put them to action. I can't."

After this discussion, Hadio became Sarah's most trusted confidante.

By the time they finished talking it was 11.30 a.m. Hadio saw Sarah off to her room, and then left to go to sleep in the little house. There was a little house and a big house. That was how Sarah had referred to the two houses, placed adjacent to each other.

Several months later, Hadio received two phone-calls, both of which had made her feel very happy. The first call came from Anna. Hadio was about to serve breakfast when the telephone rang. She went to answer the call. Sarah had let Hadio answer all calls made to the house.

Hadio picked up the phone, and said, "Sarah's residence. Good morning,"

"Good morning. This is Anna," Anna said.

"Good morning Anna. It has been a long time," Hadio said.

"Yes, indeed. If you wonder how I managed to trace you down, I got your address from Ingrid. I hope you don't mind," Anna said.

"Don't be silly Anna. Why, I am more than happy to hear from you," Hadio said.

"Ingrid informed me that you are gainfully employed now. I hope you are happy," Anna said.

"Oh, yes. You can't imagine how happy I am. Sarah is nice to me," Hadio said.

"What about you? What are you doing now?" Hadio said.

"I wish we could meet somewhere, instead of talking on the phone. I am calling to let you know I am leaving for Kathmandu, Nepal. I have volunteered to do work as a doctor for the organisation known as Doctors without Borders. I am leaving tomorrow. The whole thing has been rushed through. I will be away for a while. I hope to see you when I get back. Take care," Anna said.

"Good-bye and take care," Hadio said.

On the same day, in the evening, Hadio received a second call; this one came from Ingrid. Sarah and Hadio had been sitting watching television together, as usual, when the telephone rang. Hadio went to get the call; after a brief exchange of warm regards, Ingrid said, "I have a surprise for you."

She never gave Hadio time to contemplate what the surprise was about.

"Kore came to see me. He wants me to give him your address. What do you say?" She said.

"Wait. I don't understand. Where is Kore?" Hadio said anxiously.

"I am sorry. I have been taking things for granted. Kore has long been discharged from the institution; he has a disability pension; he lives here, in Uppsala." Ingrid said.

That piece of information took Hadio by surprise. She was flabbergasted. It was too much of an emotion. She wept and smiled, all at once.

"Are you there?" Ingrid asked, not sure if Hadio was still on line. It was quiet for another few more seconds, and then Hadio said with a trembling voice, "I am sorry. How is Kore?"

"Kore is fine," Ingrid said.

"I will be in town on Friday. Tell him to meet me at Landings Restaurant, at St Pers. Tell him at 11 o'clock," Hadio said.

"I hope you don't mind if I come along," Ingrid said. "You know," she added, "anything can happen."

"Nothing will happen. Kore has never been aggressive to me," Hadio said.

"I hope you know what you are doing. I will pass the message to him, just the same. Take care," Ingrid said.

For several months, well before he set up his mind up to see Hadio, Kore had been thinking about whether getting in touch with Hadio was a right thing to do; he remembered those circumstances under which they had parted ways and felt quite discouraged.

He liked Hadio; he admired her, especially, because of her determination to make success out of her life, but felt with much sadness in his heart that her job had not allowed her to think of anything else. The decision she took to leave him for another man had caused so much pain in him that he couldn't get over it.

He often took time to think about his own actions, and how that might have impacted his marriage-life. He realised that his greatest undoing, in his relationship with Hadio, was that he had failed to express his true feelings to her. He realised that he and Hadio were more alike than they were different; they had each cared more about themselves than they had cared for each other's welfare.

One day, he decided to forget all of that; he went to see Ingrid and inquired if she could make arrangement for him to meet with Hadio.

Every time someone phoned the house, Hadio made sure to let Sarah know where the call was coming from.

"The call is from Ingrid, my former social welfare officer," Hadio said.

"What does she want?" Sarah asked.

"She said Kore wants to meet me," Hadio said.

"Where is he?" Sarah asked

"He is in Uppsala; he has a disability pension." Hadio said in reply.

"What are you going to do?" Sarah asked

"I will see him," Hadio said.

"Good. Follow your heart?" Sarah said and smiled.

Hadio reciprocated the smile.

Hadio saw Sarah off to her room. Later, she went to the little house. She thought of Kore. She had two days left to meet with him. She was happy about the prospect of meeting him. But would he equally be happy to meet her? She recollected circumstances under which they had parted ways; nothing much there to encourage her, she realised. Would he be willing to have her back? In her case, she would do anything to be together with Kore.

She had spent half the night contemplating a meeting with Kore before falling asleep, and dreamt of life with him and the children.

She dreamt of the joyful moments they had once shared together. She dreamt of the day the family went to Stockholm, on a summer day, and how at the famous Swedish summer park, at Gröna Lund, the children became happy listening to singers as they sang their beautiful songs.

Outside Gröna Lund, in another venue, they watched children most favourite show - the circus. In the circus, the children enjoyed watching the elephant riding a bicycle and enjoyed watching the clown in action.

When she woke up, she had tears in her eyes. It was 3 a.m. She couldn't go back to sleep after that. Hadio couldn't let the feelings go.

# Chapter Fifty Two

# *You Are Fat*

Soon Friday was here; this was the day Hadio was hoping to meet Kore. Hadio accompanied Sarah on her short morning walks; the two ladies had breakfast, afterwards. Hadio remembered to make some sandwiches for Sarah to use, during her absence.

Hadio had two hours left to meet Kore. Before leaving for the city, she decided to take shower. While in the shower, Hadio took a deeper look at her body. She noticed with regret that she was no longer covetous, since her curves had been lost to layers of fat that had engulfed the rest of her body; she wished she wasn't fat and that she had a voluptuous body. Hadio was well aware of how men from her community admire a woman if she is voluptuous.

Ever since she gained extra weight, Kore didn't see her; the last time he saw her, she looked like her old self, except with age she had put on weight on her rear and thighs. When this happened to her, it caused Kore no alarm; in fact, he seemed amused, and had told her that he thought she looked good. But that was then. What would he think of her now? She was going to get the answer soon.

She finished taking shower and now she was selecting clothes she was going to put on. Hadio was not someone willing to sacrifice comfort for looks; a brown coloured woollen gown, a white turtle neck sweater, a leather jacket and an old pair of shoes is all she had put on. She sprinkled on her neck a perfume present Sarah gave her. At ten, after bidding Sarah goodbye, she left. She drove away, using one of Sarah's cars.

The chill in the air, combined with the grey sky, made Hadio develop a feeling of hopelessness that she fought against. Today, it was too important a day for her to let such a sentiment influence her feelings. She must look good and feel good for Kore.

A half an hour later, she was parking the car in a basement of a large building, in one of those pay-to-park packing lots, which lately seemed to have mushroomed throughout the town.

From there, she went to keep appointment at Landings Cafe, situated inside one of the largest city malls, known as St Per's. She liked Landings Cafe for its broad glass windows, bright lights, easy accessibility, excellent services and spacious atmosphere, not to speak about its products that are of high quality. She selected a table for its strategic value, facing ICA shop; she wanted to have access to a view that would enable her to see Kore clearly, as he enters the cafe.

She bought a cup of tea and waited for him, meanwhile, juggling several ideas in her mind, all at once. No sooner had she thought clear of one subject then she let her mind to wander far away, thinking of another subject altogether.

At this moment, for example, thinking of how to react to Kore's presence, she changed her mind suddenly and started thinking whether Kore would wish to have anything to do with her.

Her mind had kept jumping from one thought to another so that in the end she almost forgot keeping a look out for Kore, now approaching the entrance to the restaurant, and then her eyes fell on him when he was only three meters away. Responding to her reflexes, she stood up and ran to him. She fell into his arms, and the two hugged each other.

Perhaps for lack of saying something meaningful, Kore told Hadio, "You are fat."

"You are limping," she said.

He smiled.

"What happened?" She said.

"Oh, that is a long story; it is a chapter in the history of my life I want to forget about," Kore said.

The absence of a free gaiety in his steps, Hadio had noticed, was not the only sign of a physical change in Kore; he also stuttered as he spoke to her. Kore seemed to have grown shorter, which could have something to do with the limb, and the fact that he had grown fat. His hair had become thin and grey. Kore had changed; he looked too old, she thought. When he smiled, it was only then that something of the old Kore appeared. She started weeping.

"Oh, come on; stop it," he said.

She nodded her head in silence, retrieved a handkerchief from her hand beg, and then used it on her face.

"You have changed," she said, despite herself. "Oh, forget it," she added in a hurry

"Forget what? It is registered in my mind, already. I have no way of wiping it off my mind," Kore said.

"I have never wanted to comment on the change in you. I am sorry," Hadio said.

"It is obvious that I have changed; so, has the rest of the world, including you," Kore said.

"Please, let us talk of something else," Hadio said.

"I am happy to see you Hadio. I have never given up hope of ever seeing you again," he said.

"It has been a long time; we both have gone through a lot," she said.

"Yes, a lot," he said.

Hadio started weeping again, but then abruptly took control of the situation by saying "I promise I shall not weep."

"I know how hard it is for you to have to come to terms with the way I look," Kore said. "After all," he added, "you have not been prepared for a new me; you will adapt bye and bye, nevertheless,"

"I have changed too, as you can see it," Hadio said.

"Yes, you have changed; to me, however, you are still the same Hadio that I knew once and loved. I still love you Hadio, despite everything," Kore said.

"I was unkind to you. Will you forgive me Kore?" She said, tears streaming down on her face.

"I haven't been without any blemish, myself. Yes, I will forgive you, if it so much matters to you, but on condition that you too forgive me," Kore said.

She left her place in the chair to hug Kore, while all the while tears kept streaming down on her face.

"Shh; don't weep now. It is OK," Kore told her.

A few minutes later, Kore went to fetch tea for both.

Back in his seat, Kore said, "I am now a pensioner Hadio."

"I know; Ingrid told me," Hadio said.

"It is funny, the image that I have in my mind of a pensioner has always been made up of a slow-walking old man, in an oversize overcoat, holding in his hands several plastic bags, which have nothing of importance in them, looking for a bench on which to rest, before resuming the never-ending journey," he said.

"The image is that of a homeless person, more or less, not that of a pensioner. Anyway, have you ever come across such a person in real life, or have you yourself become one such a person"? Hadio said jokingly.

"Oh no," Kore said, laughing. "That image has stuck into my mind, somehow," he said.

"Why are you limping? Couldn't they fit you with some sort of shoes that could give you a balance?" Hadio said.

"Keeping the limp is my own choice. This is a society that is obsessed with immaculate looking things. Society thinks the sight of a limping person is a blight on the fair face of their city's beautiful social and physical landscape. They don't like it, but I don't care, because this is who I am now.

"You remain obstinate as before," Hadio said.

"And you have not lost any of the biting wits," Kore said.

They laughed at the jokes.

"What do you do now?" Hadio said.

"I am doing things I have wanted to always do but couldn't do. I have taken piano lessons, and I am learning how to play chess; I am hoping to do many other things besides,"

"Do you have time or energy for all that?" Hadio said and laughed.

"If I must avoid fitting into the profile of the imaginary pensioner figure that I have in my mind, I must do all that and more. But let us talk about you now," Kore said.

"I work for Sarah Bissell," Hadio said.

"Who is Sarah?"

"Sarah, you know her well. She is Peter's mother," Hadio said.

"You don't mean, Peter's mother, Sarah?" Kore said.

"Yes,"

He leaned backward in his chair, kept the tea cup on the saucer and said, "Surprise, surprise."

"I know what you think. She has forgiven me," Hadio said.

"I presume it wasn't that difficult for her to have to do that; there was no love lost between them, after all," Kore said.

"How do you know?" Hadio said.

"Peter had told me everything," Kore said.

"Sarah and I hardly talk about Peter," Hadio said.

"We will not talk about him either," Kore said.

For a moment they remained silent. Finally, Kore said, "Do you have any information regarding the whereabouts of our children?"

"There has never been a single day that went by I haven't thought of them. They are here somewhere; their exact whereabouts, however, is a guided secret of the Social Welfare Office; we are not supposed to know," Hadio said.

"They are our children," Kore said.

"They are our children, biologically, not legally and not socially either. They belong to someone else now. We have forfeited our right when we let them go," Hadio said.

"Who did it? Was it not you who did it? You left me for someone who cared neither for you nor the children," Kore said loudly, attracting the attention of people in the restaurant.

"Keep your voice low, and don't shout at me, please," Hadio said.

"I am sorry. I shouldn't have shouted. No use crying over spilt milk. What can we do now?" Kore said.

"When we have sorted out things, and have put our house in order, then we will see," Hadio said.

"Where do we begin?" Kore said.

"I don't know really. I am not a lawyer," Hadio said.

"Common sense tells me that we shouldn't expect much until we have put our relationship in an even keel. If we were a husband and a wife once before, what are we now?" Kore said.

"Since Peter and I had never married formally, and we two never divorced, I think we are still married to each other," Hadio said.

"Until the law says otherwise, let us keep it that way," Kore said.

They ordered another round of tea; they talked of their past life together; much of what they talked about had focused on issues concerning their two children. They had spent about an hour at the restaurant. It was now 12 noon. Both were hungry, and so they went to take launch at the restaurant for the pensioners that Hadio had paid for.

After launch, they took a leisurely walk through the streets. Kore invited Hadio to his single room apartment, reserved for pensioners; the room was conveniently placed right in the middle of the city, not far from where they took their launch. Hadio liked the place, but thought the room could do with new curtains, which she promised to bring along next time when she would visit him. At 4 p.m. Hadio left.

On her way back home, she thought of Kore and wondered what Kore would think of her. She admonished herself for being selfish to think of herself alone, when she should think of Kore - his health, and his current social position in life. Such selfish behaviour is what had killed their relationship, in the first place. Does she want a repeat of the same situation in her life? She promised to be generous in her feelings to Kore.

# Chapter Fifty Three

# *Patient Enough*

Sarah looked frail and depended on Hadio for a physical support, more than ever before. The two women had ceased taking those long-distance walks in the woods that they used to take together, every morning. Nevertheless, they still took a walk together that were confined to areas closer to home. Sarah seemed to have lost all appetite for food; not even the exotic dishes Hadio had been making for her had managed to entice her to eat well.

If Hadio used to take Sarah once a month to the hospital for check-ups and for the treatments of blood pressure, the visits had become quite a regular thing now. In the evenings, after filling the bathtub with warm water, Hadio would be there to make sure that she helped Sarah get in and out of bathtub.

As time went by, more and more visitors came to see Sarah. Sarah introduced those visitors to Hadio; some were members of her family; others were her old colleagues.

Sarah spent long hours writing on the computer, despite poor health.

"You need to conserve your energy. You spend a lot of time writing," Hadio told Sarah while serving warm milk, mixed with a spoonful of honey, for Sarah to drink before going to bed.

"At my age, you realise how short life can be. I might not have enough time; I am writing my memoirs, and I am trying to set the record straight; I intend to be as objective as I could be," Sarah said.

"Can you not cut short your working hours?" Hadio insisted.

"I am almost there. A slight change here and there is all that I need to do. It would take several months before I could give the manuscript to the publishers," Sarah said.

"With all due respect, I still think you should take it slow," Hadio said.

"Yes, of course. I respect your concern for my health. I need to put the record straight, nevertheless," Sarah insisted.

"One of the most difficult things I know is writing," Hadio said.

"Honest and sincere writing is even more difficult to do," Sarah said. She added, "I have been wrestling with this fact ever since the day that I started writing my memoirs. However, one thing that you mentioned, during our conversation, about guilt and shame, had helped settle the issue in my mind,' Sarah said.

Whatever she might have said to impress Sarah, Hadio felt proud to know that Sarah had treasured her words; she felt honoured.

"What did I say? Hadio asked.

"You said those who cause other people harm they should be ashamed of themselves, not the other way round. Well, in my case, I have lived all my life in total shame, because of what Bacchus did to me, as well as having guilt feelings for being unkind to my son, Peter," Sarah said.

"Can anything be achieved now? Wouldn't it be better to forget about everything? Hadio said.

"My conscience is a holy thing to me. I don't want to die having feelings of guilt and shame. I want to be free when I die," Sarah said and gave a weak smile.

Hadio tended to the needs of Sarah well, and still found time to communicate through phone calls with both Ingrid and Anna. Anna had phoned her twice from Kathmandu; she had spoken to Hadio about her work, the people there and Nepal, as a country. She told Hadio how happy she was, and how much she was looking forward to meeting her on her return home.

Hadio had been to the city centre twice to visit Kore; for the sake of a better relationship, they had each worked hard to put a lid to suppress their simmering emotions, which had threatened to come up to the surface every time they talked to each other.

Once or twice, Hadio invited Kore whom she introduced to Sarah. On his second visit, while Hadio was preparing lunch, Sarah and Kore spoke to each other. To the astonishment of Hadio, when Kore left in the evening, Sarah talked to her about him. She told Hadio that she admired Kore for being sincere about his feelings. She also told Hadio that Kore was free to stay with her, if it is what she wished to do.

The proposition made by Sarah had encouraged Hadio to give further thought to the idea which had not been far removed from her mind. She liked the idea of having Kore staying with her, even if it was going to be a temporary stay. However, she was not sure how she would take it should Kore make any physical advances towards her.

Would she be willing to accommodate his feelings? She wouldn't mind recapitulating to his amorous advances, if she knew how to do it. It had been quite a while since she had been with someone; her last physical experience with Peter had emptied all the desire in her to want to have physical relationship with someone.

She was afraid Kore would misunderstand her reasons for not responding favourably to his advances and might end the relationship.

One summer day, Kore had stayed late, helping with the garden work, planting and watering the flowers; later, he racked up the fallen leaves and helped to trim the bush.

In the evening, as they enjoyed taking their desert, after a light dinner of chicken soup, bread and salad, Hadio asked Kore to stay the night.

"There is no use leaving now; it is late," She said. She wanted to look polite; she didn't want Kore to feel he is not wanted, or he is a burden. The moment after she offered the invitation, she realised that she had let herself open to a challenge that she didn't know how she would relate to it.

"Who are you trying to cheat?" She admonished herself. "In your subconscious mind, you have wanted this, all along," she told herself.

"Yes, why not," Sarah said and gave Kore a friendly look, to reassure him of the concern she had for him. Hadio's face brightened up, knowing that she had Sarah's support for letting Kore stay the night.

"You will like it here," Sarah said. "The nights," she added, "are most enjoyable time in this rural homestead of ours: you will come to discover that listening to owls hooting has a way of inducing a quick sleep in most people."

"That is right," Hadio said. "Sometimes," she added, "I think I have come to rely on that sound to gain sleep,"

"By the way," Sarah said addressing Kore, "Do you have owls in your home country?"

"Oh yes," he said. "However," he added, "Owls are considered by some people to be a bad omen."

"Ah, is that so?" Sarah said, looking astonished. "Hadio," she added, "didn't tell me anything about it."

"It is hard for Hadio - a city child - to have knowledge of such a thing," Kore said, giving Hadio a smile, which Hadio reciprocated with a smile of her own.

"They are," Kore said, "taken to be harbingers of death. Most people believe if someone is ill in a house, and an owl hoots, death will follow."

"Let us hope that no one gets sick here," Sarah said jokingly, which elicited laughter from both Kore and Hadio.

"I am retiring for the night," Sarah said, standing up. Hadio accompanied her to the room and saw her in bed.

Later, when she was assured that everything was it should be, Hadio bade Sarah goodnight.

"Good night," Sarah said in reply.

"Come," said Hadio, addressing Kore, once she got back into the sitting room. "Let me take you to your room, in the next building, at my accommodations," she added in a jovial spirit.

Once there, she directed him to a room reserved for guests. The room had a bed, several chairs and a wardrobe.

From inside the wardrobe, Hadio drew out a clean, well pressed pair of pyjamas and a pair of sandals.

"We keep these for our guests, in case of emergencies," she said as she handed the items to Kore. "For pyjamas," she added, "we have all three sizes for you to choose from. These are medium, large and extra-large. I guess the medium size will fit you. In the bathroom, you will find everything else that you need."

"Feel comfortable and have a good night sleep," she said. Before she left, she said, "I am in a room, next to yours. "If you wish, just come in."

Kore was left to contemplate his place in his new surroundings. He was happy that Hadio had the opportunity to work for Sarah. Sarah was nice to him. However, it was Hadio who he thought most about, and tonight as she sat there in the dining hall, across from the table, she looked more desirable than any other time.

As he sat on the bed, thinking about her, the desire to hold her face in his hands became irresistible. At that point, he was faced with either one of the two propositions; to throw care to the wind, go and face Hadio in her room - even at the risk of being sent away by her - or forget and go to sleep, in which case he would be forced, on the following day, to brood over a lost chance.

He left for Hadio's room; he knocked on the closed door. Hadio opened the door; in her hand, she had a comb; her hair had a dishevelled look; he might have caught her at a point where she had just started combing her hair.

The moment she opened the door, Kore held her in his arms and gave her a light kiss in the mouth. Hadio responded to the kiss, but there was reluctance in her to go all the way that didn't escape the attention of Kore, who pulled back and said, "I am sorry."

Hadio didn't exactly know what to say; she became tongue-tied; she felt embarrassed. She didn't intend to act in the way that she did, and wished she had acted differently. "I am sorry," she said. In her desire to say something more meaningful she added, "I will do better next time."

"I don't mind waiting for ever," he said smiling. "Like all women," he added, "you are different from men, whose visual image of a woman can be a cause of major sexual attraction. You need to get used to me, again. Until then, I promise to be patient."

On hearing Kore making that kind of statement, Hadio felt a special respect for him, and felt that there was a redeeming feature in Kore's words of wisdom that augured well for their future relationship.

A few days later, they became physically intimate, and from that point on, Kore paid Hadio visits, more often.

# Chapter Fifty Four

# *Memoir*

During the whole of the winter season, Sarah had worked very hard on the book; in early spring, she handed the manuscripts to the publishers. Apparently, the book had taken its toll on Sarah's health. During winter season, Sarah had spent time in and out of the hospital for check-ups and for the treatment of blood pressure.

The book came out in mid-spring season and received favourable reviews. Hadio was happily surprised to see her name in the acknowledgment section of the book, where Sarah had expressed her thanks for the contribution that she said Hadio had made to the success of the book.

In the memoir, Sarah had never let any part of her life story remain secret, to the public. She let bare all her secrets for the world to see. She wrote in great details the encounter with Bacchus in Paris and what followed thereafter. She mentioned the bumpy relationship she had had with Peter, her son, and wrote about the years she had kept away from her family. On the day that she held the first copy of the book in her hands, she shaded torrents of tears; those were tears not of sorrows, but they were tears of relief, for having gotten all secrets off her chest, and felt lighter for it.

She received messages of congratulations from various sources; the one message she treasured most in her heart came from her family, which stated, "Sarah, we love you."

As summer approached, on her doctor's recommendation, Sarah undertook preparation for travelling abroad. She had a cottage in the island of Crete, Greece, which, in the past, had afforded the opportunity for her to get away from the extreme cold winters of her Nordic homeland.

During the past few years, however, because of a poor health condition, she hadn't been spending her winter holiday there. Three weeks before her trip to Crete took place, she got in touch with the man taking care of the house, to let him know of her impending visit there.

In his fifties now, the man whose name was Nikos was someone she had employed to take care of the house, which he had been doing regularly now for the last twenty-five years.

On her way to the island, Sarah planned to have a stop-over of three days in Paris.

Two weeks before her departure to Greece took place, she told Hadio, "Have you ever been to Greece?"

"No," Hadio said.

"How would you like to have to visit Paris?" Sarah said.

"I would like it very much," Hadio said.

"Get ready then; you are going to give me company. We are leaving for Greece on a holiday. On our way there, we shall make a stop-over of three days in Paris. Meanwhile, get your passport ready," Sarah said.

Finally, a day for Sarah and Hadio to leave for Paris came. From Orly Airport, they hired a taxi that took them to Grand Hotel du Palais Royal.

The trip to the hotel brought memories of Paris in Sarah's mind about the time when she was young, and feelings of happiness came to a girl of twenty-two years of age, like herself, quite naturally.

Because it was quite late in the evening, by the time they got to the hotel, they ordered from room service a light supper of broccoli soup and bread, followed by hot chocolate drink; not much later, they went to sleep, as they wanted to conserve their energy for the following day.

At 8 a.m. in the morning of the following day, they took breakfast in the dining hall. By nine, they were in the hotel lobby arranging for a taxi that would convey them to places Sarah wished them to visit.

Outside, the sun cast its shadows on the streets that had long seemed to have come to life. From the hotel, the taxi took them to a building Sarah had once occupied, which had been managed by Lesia, at arrondissement 4th. She also visited the building at arrondissement 6th on rue Bonaparte, where she had spent time with Bacchus.

With permission from the tenants, Sarah got inside those buildings, accompanied by Hadio, and saw changes in both places. The hostel at arrondisement 4th was no longer there; there were apartments in the place of the hostel, instead. The single room, at arrondissement 6th, was still there. In both places, none of the tenants there knew the history of the place they lived in. When Sarah told them something about it, they were amused.

While inside those buildings, Hadio looked at Sarah's face for any sign of anguish and had found none. Away from there, Hadio brought up the issue by asking Sarah politely, "How do you feel?"

For a moment, Sarah remained silent; however, this was not a kind of silence denoting a lack of something to say. A few days earlier, had Hadio asked Sarah the same question, she would have elicited from her an ambivalent reply.

"Contrary to what you may be thinking, I have nothing to be distressed about. In fact, I am in an ecstatic mood," Sarah said in a happy tone.

As much as she was eager to avoid having further discussion that she was afraid would bring back memories of humiliation that she knew Sarah had undergone in Bacchus's hands, she was nevertheless forced to say, "What do you mean?"

"I am happy to be in Paris, and to have this opportunity in which to relieve my past experiences; indeed, without any exaggeration, I can say the cathartic effect of this visit on me is quite clear," she said cheerfully.

Seeing Sarah in such a joyful mood must have tempted Hadio to have further discussion with her.

"Is not the presence of Bacchus," she said quite carefully, "a necessary thing, if the healing process is to have any meaning to you?"

"If you want to know," Sarah said, "the truth is Bacchus has always been present in my life. His phantom figure had never allowed me to enjoy a moment of peace"

"I am so sorry," Hadio said, feeling genuinely sad.

"Don't; that belongs to the past now," Sarah said, her eyes twinkling merrily.

"My presence here," she added, "has enabled me to put Bacchus in a context from which he ceases completely to be a phantom figure that I have been imagining him to be. As a matter of fact, I feel that I have nothing to fear from. Even if Bacchus himself were to materialise before my eyes, I would fear him not."

Later, when the two ladies went to visit Café du Dome, at Montparnasse, to her surprise, Sarah discovered the café was still operating just like it did once before. Nothing seemed to have changed; everything resembled those she had once seen. Even the arm wicker chairs that they sat on, as well as the slight-looking round wicker table, on top of which sat pots of coffee and plates of pastries, were similar in appearance to those of the past.

As for people in the café, they took coffee, talked to one another, and laughed. Having settled the issue of Bacchus in her mind, Sarah was in a Café du Dome, this time, for a reason that had nothing to do with him.

Sarah knew Café du Dome as a venue where artists and writers visiting Paris had met, during the roaring twenties of the 20th Century.

Today, the names of those artists and writers sound like a roll call from a list of people that had made astonishing successes in their fields of endeavours. Among them are Ernest Hemingway, James Joyce, Pablo Picasso, Henry Miller, Samuel Beckett, Salvador Dali Jean-Paul Sartre and many more others.

Sarah was happy to be in Café du Dome which afforded the opportunity for her to relive a piece of history. Even though time is what has put a wall of separation between her and the above-named artists and writers, nevertheless, Sarah was happy to be occupying the very same space that those people knew well. Here, they had sat down to enjoy taking a cup of coffee, to gossip, to fight, to love, to dream and to inspire each other to greater heights of achievements.

Toying with Le Mond that she had bought on a news stand on their way to the café, Sarah took a deeper look at Hadio's eyes that she assumed must have seen more than their fair share of troubles and then said, "Tell me something about Paris. What do you say?"

Hadio felt she was destitute for words that would enable her to express the wonders of Paris, and so she remained quiet. Meanwhile, Sarah gave Hadio an inquiring look, as if saying to her, "What are you waiting for? Speak up."

Hadio, finally, plucked up courage and said, "I wish I were a poet to sing the many virtues of Paris, among which are, the broad boulevards, the beautiful cafes, the architectural wonders of the buildings, the fashionable Parisians, the multicultural setting quite unique to Paris, and the numerous wonderful historical monuments; alas, since it is beyond my ability to do so, I would leave all that for others to do. As for me, I feel privileged to be in Paris, and to have a chance to share this magnificent moment with you, which I promise to keep and treasure in my heart, for the rest of my life."

"Oh, I feel I am the one who is privileged to be with you," Sarah said. "You have been a good companion and a helpful friend," she added.

"Thank you for giving me a new chance in life," Hadio said honestly.

"Away with sentimentalism," Sarah said playfully.

Changing the subject of their discussion, a moment later, Sarah said, "As the wheel of time changes, it alters the perception that we have of our environment and ourselves in such a way that it becomes quite hard for us to come to terms with."

Not knowing what to actually say in reply, Hadio simply said, "What do you mean?"

"What I mean," Sarah said, "is this: when I was in Paris, and still young, to me people looked old and tired. But now since I am the one looking at people, through the prism of my old tired pair of eyes, I am the one feeling old and tired, and everybody else look young, fresh and full of vigour."

"Old age is not a disease; unless one dies young, which is a tragic thing, as human beings, it is our fate to grow old," Hadio said.

"Well said; but you know what; growing old does not make one feel happy," Sarah said.

"How is that so?" Hadio asked.

"Notwithstanding such a phrase as 'growing old with grace,' there is nothing graceful in getting old," she said.

"At an old age," she added, "you cease to walk in a graceful manner; besides, many old people cease to be polite and pleasant."

As soon as she uttered those words, Sarah had doubts if she sincerely meant what she had just said. Does she, for example, believe what she had just said to constitute the truth? And if so, as an old person herself, do all the qualities that she had claimed belong to old people apply to her as well? She asked herself.

She was jolted from pursuing her thoughts further by Hadio who said, "I agree with the first of your two propositions. It is true that most old people do not walk in a graceful manner; it makes you feel pity for them, watching them as they bumbled along the street.

However, when it comes to your second point, I beg to differ with you. Old people seem to be impolite and unpleasant, only when society chooses to neglect them, by making them feel that society has no longer any need for them. In the society from which I come, however, old people are revered for their wisdom, and so they feel wanted.

"I wished I lived in your society," Sarah said joyfully.

"But on the second thought," she added quite seriously, "why should I want to do that when part of that society is here; you are here with me; other immigrants, like you, are in my country; I feel we have much to learn from you, just as you have much to learn from us."

After a brief moment of silence, she went on with her speech. "Many years ago as I sat in this very same cafe," Sarah said, "I prayed, one day, Sweden could have a multicultural society, similar to the one in Paris, so that it could add colour to what I then considered to be grey and drab Swedish surroundings

"What do you make of multiculturalism in Sweden today?" Hadio said, infused with excitement.

Sarah stayed quiet; contemplating what would constitute an honest reply to Hadio's question.

"Today, thankfully, Sweden is a multicultural society," she said enthusiastically. "Sweden, today," she added, "has ceased to have a grey and drab surrounding. Multiculturalism has infused colour into our society; this, however, is an observation anyone can make."

Before she could go on with her speech, she posed briefly to take a sip from her coffee; she said after a while, a slight smile crossing her face, "However, to my shame, what multiculturalism means at political, social and economic levels is something to which I have never given much thought about. I have taken multiculturalism for granted, even as I worked for the state. I need to grow out of that when I get back home."

"Until then, meanwhile, I am hungry; what about you?"

"It is twelve noon. Let's go have lunch," said Sarah.

# Chapter Fifty Five

# *Crete*

At the end of three hectic days in Paris, the two women left for Greece. There, they found the weather was warm. For a moment, the heat in the atmosphere had reminded Hadio of her homeland; there, all throughout the year, the weather is warm. Every time feelings of her homeland came flowing into her mind, Hadio had fought those feelings; she would never allow the feelings to take control of her mind; such feelings triggered memories of sufferings she had undergone at the hands of Bobe Haigan.

The plane landed at the Heraklion Airport at three in the afternoon. From there, they took a chartered plane to Paleochora, located at the extreme southwest part of Crete. From there, they drove to Sarah's sea-side villa.

On hand, waiting to receive Sarah, was Nikos - the house keeper - a pot-bellied man with a thick moustache. When not involved in the business of taking care of the house, Nikos keeps a stall, where he sold fresh fishes in the market place.

Nikos hugged the two ladies, and then addressing Sarah he said, "Welcome home Sarah,"

Nikos looked at Hadio and said to her, "And you too,"

"Thank you," Hadio said.

"It has been a long while since you were here. How are you Sarah?" He said.

"I am fine," Sarah said.

Pointing at Hadio, Sarah told Nikos, "Hadio is my assistant." He nodded his head and smiled.

"I am quite happy to see that you have made some renovation that has given to the house a new face lift," Sarah said.

"I thought the house could do with some renovation. How was your trip?" Nikos said.

"It was fine. I don't like, however, when the plane hits pockets of air. I can't get used to it," Sarah said, taking off her pullover that she let it rest in one of the sofas.

"How is your family keeping?" Sarah said, looking genuinely concerned.

"Oh, they are fine. I wrote to let you know, Calix, my second son, had got married to a girl from our town. Alisa is expecting a baby this month," he said.

"I remember that. And now soon you will be a proud grandfather. But again, you are not new to the feeling. How is your eldest son, Alexander? Still working for the same shipping company?" Sarah said.

"The same company, yes. He is now acting as a captain of the ship," Nikos said, feeling proud of his son's accomplishment, remembering his days as a sailor when becoming a captain was a dream, quite impossible to imagine.

Suddenly Nikos looked at the time on a clock in the wall and said, "You need a rest; you must be tired; see you tomorrow morning."

As he was about to leave, he turned around to look at Sarah, sitting in the sofa, and told her, "There is fresh food in the fridge.

I could get something for you to eat, from somewhere outside, if you wish."

Before Sarah could give a reply, Hadio said, "No, but thank you. I will manage something."

"Well, that is all then; see you tomorrow," Nikos said and left.

"He is a fine man. I have known Nikos, his wife and their three children, now grown up, for as long as I can remember," Sarah told Hadio.

Presently, Hadio approached the fridge to see the things it contained. She was happily surprised to discover the fridge was packed up with all kinds of foods imaginable.

"I am making a tuna salad. Would you like to have some? Hadio said loudly from the kitchen for Sarah to hear her.

"Yes. Tuna salad and Greek bread will be fine. It would be nice to have wine to wash it down with. Please, check if Nikos has remembered to buy some," Sarah said.

"I can see all sorts of wine Nikos has kept them on the kitchen table," Hadio said.

"That is Nikos for me; he is prompt, efficient, considerate and care about details," Sarah said.

Soon the two women were taking their dinner that Hadio had prepared. After dinner, Hadio served fruit dessert that they took with coffee.

The villa, Hadio noticed, had three rooms, with bathroom, a store and a kitchen. The house had all the gadgets necessary for modern living. Beautiful turquoise-coloured tiles covered the rest of the space in the house, including the sitting room, the sleeping rooms, the bathroom and the kitchen. On the front porch of the house, overlooking the sea, there was a small garden of flowers that looked tidy and well cared for. Other houses in the neighbourhood exhibited similar features.

From the dining room, Hadio visited Sarah's sleeping room to start making preparation for her to take bath; she laid down new bed sheets on Sarah's bed.

When she was done, she let Sarah decide what she wanted to do. Sarah, feeling tired and exhausted, told Hadio she was ready for a long hot-bath, and would be ready to retire for the night, afterwards.

Hadio assisted Sarah to take bath; later, she saw Sarah to her bed. From Sarah's room, Hadio went to her room, took bath and, like Sarah, retired for the night.

On the following day, Hadio woke up at 6 a.m., peeked through the door to Sarah's room to see if everything was fine, and then left for the kitchen to make breakfast of buttered bread, cheese, milk and coffee.

From her position, inside the kitchen, the delightful mild sea-breeze, the distant sound of the sea-waves breaking into the sea-shore, the enticing smell of the sea-weeds, reaching her through the open kitchen window, all had made Hadio feel quite delirious with joy.

At 8 a.m. Sarah was at the breakfast table. The two ladies ate their breakfast quietly, while each was contemplating what their first day in Greece would be like.

At around 8.30 p.m. Nikos, boisterous as his usual self, came in.

Addressing no one in particular, he said, "How is everybody? Have you slept well?"

"Oh, yes; thank you," Sarah said.

"Yesterday, on my way home, I remembered that I had yet to install the hammock out in the veranda, from where you have always liked to watch the sea. I am now going to fix it, for you," Nikos told Sarah with an exaggerated flair of his arms.

"Thank you for remembering," Sarah said. "Make it a bigger one; this time, Hadio might want to have a feel of it also," she added.

Leaving Nikos to install the hammock, they left, driving Nikos's car that he had let Sarah use during the duration of her stay there. Hadio drove the car. Sarah had quite a few places in mind she wished to visit. They went to the market-place, directed by the map they found in the car; from there, they went to the beach; it was a hot day; the clear skies gave the sea its intense blue colour. There were swimmers basking on the sand; plenty of them. Neither Hadio nor Sarah took a swim; instead, they chose to loiter around on the sandy beach, like so many other people did, who like them never swam.

Hadio had remembered to pack some sandwiches that they nibbled on, after every while. At 4 p.m. they went back home, Sarah feeling quite tired and exhausted.

"Thank God; beaches here still maintain their pristine form, which is not the case, elsewhere in the world. I hate the new crop of tourists, flocking en masse into all sorts of tourist resorts, taking advantage of cheap travel arrangement, with their cameras, their money and a new silly pattern of consumption," Sarah said, feeling quite angry.

She took a short breath and said further, "Somehow they have managed to change the bucolic atmosphere of every single place they have visited to a degree that today it is no longer feasible for anyone to have a moment of rest for contemplation. Beauty is meant for one to admire, or to write poems about, not to devour and destroy it."

Hadio didn't know what to tell Sarah. Did Sarah expect her to react to her statement? What could she tell Sarah? Should she tell her that she had enjoyed the outing, which she did, in fact? She decided to stay quiet and assume that Sarah was merely talking loudly to herself.

From that day on, the visit to the town-centre became less frequent. Instead, they spent more time in the house, sitting in the hammock, out in the veranda, from where they watched the waves fall and rise in the calm blue waters of the Aegean Sea.

Occasionally, accompanied by Nikos, they went out to a secluded beach for a walk, far from the cottage, just to breathe a fresh air; Hadio liked the feeling of warm sensation she felt whenever the warm sea water touched her naked legs; the heat from the sun was for the most part quite unbearable, and so they kept their walk short.

At other times, accompanied by Nikos, they went to the countryside, where they came across relics of the Second World War.

Most of the evenings, they spent time talking to Whitefield, their neighbour. Whitefield was from England; he was in his eighties. Whitefield had a long administrative experience, working for the British Colonial Office, and later as a British Ambassador at various world capitals. He retired to his English country-side home, where he played host to his grandchildren, whenever they paid him a visit;

During summer, and much thereafter, he spent time in Paleochora, at his sea-side home, writing the history of First World War; his special area of interest being the war that took place in Eastern Africa, between the German and the British forces.

The visit to the island had done much to improve Sarah's health, it seemed. She exhibited unusual signs of swiftness in her bodily action; her appetite showed signs of improvement, and she laughed more often. Hadio, on her part, was happy that Sarah had made it possible for her to visit places, such as she might never have visited before. Up till this point, Paris and Greece had existed only in films and books.

Three weeks had gone by, and their journey back home was approaching swiftly.

Two or three days before their departure, Nikos invited them to have dinner in his house, which turned out to be rather a feast than a usual dinner. There was so much variety of food to choose from that they never knew where to begin.

Sarah who normally ate sparingly had given full rein to her appetite. While Sarah found dakos, which is a salad unique to Crete irresistible as an appetizer (dakos is constituted of barley rusks soaked in water, topped with grated fresh tomatoes, goat milk cheese, olive oil, salt and oregano spice for seasoning) and enjoyed the fish, Hadio liked the taste of gamopilafo, which is a rice dish prepared in a rich meat broth from a goat.

It has been quite a long time since Sarah saw Anastasia, Nikko's wife. Anastasia, Sarah noticed, had retained her youthful looks, and was as shy looking as before. She spoke little English, and so every time she addressed Sarah, she would do it in Greek. Niko, her husband, would do the translation.

Their third son, Corban, talked briefly to Sarah about his laundry business before resuming his conversation with Chloe, his wife, whom he seemed to be in deep love.

After dinner, Sarah gave presents to members of the family.

Later, Hadio would learn from Sarah that the dinner, and the exchange of presents that followed, were a form of ritual that took place each time Sarah made a visit to the island.

A day before their journey back to Sweden took place Whitefield invited Sarah and Hadio to his residence, to a simple dinner of roast chicken, mush potatoes and gravy, which he took pain to prepare.

After dinner, they spent time talking in the sitting room, where Sarah took coffee and Hadio and Whitefield took tea. Framed pictures surrounded the walls of the sitting room. Bookshelves, holding books and papers of various types, covered parts of the wall. Scores of other books and papers neatly piled up on the floor were scattered across the room. At either side of the main door, leading to the sitting room, there were two large old wine jugs of the Bronze Age.

In the sitting room, they discussed all manners of subjects. The discussion, which took place mainly between Whitefield and Sarah, was done on a friendly basis, even though on more than one occasion when their discussion veered into a subject with ideological undertone, it resulted in a heated debate taking place between them.

One such subject was Margaret Thatcher's conservative economic policies and their impacts on the English working class. Sarah said those policies were ruinous to the country's social fabric. The two were bound to disagree on their views, since they had differed in their ideological beliefs. Sarah was a socialist and Whitefield a conservative.

Colonialism was yet another subject that was hotly contested. When Sarah showed disapproval of colonialism by saying, "Colonialism dehumanises people, and shouldn't have been undertaken under any pretext," it made Whitefield laugh and almost choked on the tea he was drinking.

"Excuse me," he said.

He produced a handkerchief from the pocket of his dinner jacket and then used it to wipe his mouth. He coughed slightly and said, "Colonialism is a product of a set of mind shaped by forces unique to the 19th Century European history. In Europe, this was a period of industrial growth; countries looked for resources to develop their industries. During this period, mind you, only those seemingly powerful European countries, such as England, France and Germany, could contest for colonial territories. Your country, Sweden, didn't take part in this colonial race, not because it was concerned with issues of morality, but simply because it was weak."

Sarah felt uneasy with the type of reasoning made by Whitefield. She was not the kind of person to give easily to arguments, but in this case, she had seen some meaningful points in what Whitefield had said, which she found she had no reason to argue about.

In the end, she said, "Sweden might not have taken part in colonial expansion; however, I am proud to say it contributed to its down fall."

Whitefield smiled and said, "I give you that." He added, "Colonialism is gone and buried. I don't pretend to defend it, but I take issues with people who, when offering their criticism of colonialism, lose sight of trees for the woods."

"I beg your pardon," Sarah said.

Whitefield contemplated his situation and was convinced that whatever he might say in relation to the subject of colonialism, as someone who once had been part of a colonial administration, he would appear as though he was determined to stand in defence of colonialism, at any coast.

He gave a worried smile, raised his cup of tea to his mouth and took a sip from it. Afterwards, while considering whether to go on with the discussion, or not, he remained quiet. It would look ridiculous, he imagined, a moment later, if he stayed quiet when Sarah was expecting him to say something. He looked at Sarah and thought she looked quite attentive.

"Colonialism," he said suddenly, "had a good side and a bad side to it."

"But that is just natural," Sarah interrupted in her heavy sounding voice. While genuinely seeking more information, she added, "I know it isn't quite easy to give the list of everything good in colonialism in a single sitting, but I would appreciate to hear you naming just one good thing you may want to share it with us here about colonialism."

The challenge from Sarah which he had all along been imagining in his mind was finally confirmed through the statement that Sarah had just given. This had spurred in him the need to pick up the gauntlet, and do something about the challenge.

"It is a hard task you have given me," said Whitefield, keeping his eyes on her. "I could speak to you," he added quite half-heartedly, "about what our civilising mission has meant for Africa."

The moment after he uttered those words, he realised, though quite belatedly, that he had left himself open to a challenge.

"What civilisation are you talking about? Sitting upright in her chair, Sarah shouted. "Whose civilisation are you talking about?" She added looking quite agitated.

"To answer your question, I must go into a philosophical discourse, to which I have neither an inclination to do it, nor have I any love for doing it," he said slowly and in a measured tone. "Let us leave it for another time," he concluded.

"Another time," Sarah agreed with him.

What other way for them to conclude their hot discussion than to promise each other "next time," knowing well there may never be another time.

On her way back to the cottage, accompanied by Hadio, after bidding Whitefield farewell, Sarah's attention was drawn by Hadio, who said, "Isn't a person entitled to his nostalgia?"

Hadio never gave Sarah a chance to react to her statement. "Don't you think so?" she said smiling somewhat.

They were taking a walk on a small pavement where at every few meters street lights shined from the lamp post, guiding the ladies on their journey home.

From a short distant away, they could hear the lapping sounds of the waves breaking into the sea-shore; far out in the sea, tiny specks of lights coming either from ocean liners or fishermen boats were visible to them.

"But, of course, from time to time, as individuals we are subjected to feelings of nostalgia," Sarah said.

"What makes you feel nostalgic, Sarah? Hadio asked in an inquisitive tone.

"Let's see now,'" Sarah said, as she slowed down steps to a halt, almost.

"I yearn for a time now long gone, when my society had achieved an almost impossible task of building an equal society; an equal society you could say is a utopia. We may not have succeeded completely, but we came closer," Sarah said.

"I know of no other society that is more equal than the Swedish one," Hadio said.

"There was a time when the country had such a dream, and the mandate to create such a society was entrusted into the hands of the Social Democratic Party; this explains the reason, after the Second World War, why the party could stay in power for such a long period of time. Sadly enough, this is not true today, where parties that are promoting fascism and such other like ideologies have increasingly become part and parcel of the Swedish political landscape," Sarah said looking sad.

After this discussion, the ladies remained silent, as they continued with their short journey that took them home.

Suddenly, Sarah stopped, which made Hadio to do a similar thing. "Tell me Hadio," Sarah said looking straight at Hadio, "What is your nostalgia?"

"My feeling of nostalgia," Hadio replied readily, "have nothing to do with a high value that has failed, or one which is in the process of failing, like Whitefield's and yours respectively. In my case, I yearn for a return of my childhood days, surrounded by my relatives and parents. I see no relatives here, my parents have passed away, and I have no shoulder to cry on. If it had not been for you, I would have felt both lost and lonely."

Sarah approached Hadio and gave her a warm hug.

"We have each other, Hadio," Sarah said, holding tears back.

On the following morning, they woke up early. After breakfast, Hadio got busy packing their belongings in their suitcases. Soon it was time for the two women to leave. However, up to the last minutes, while Hadio was busy packing, Sarah enjoyed watching the sea from her position, sitting in the hammock.

Hadio was eager to know what had made Sarah fall in love with the hammock. Hence, on their flight home, she told Sarah, "Seeing that you have such a great fascination for the hammock, why not have one installed in your house?"

"It is not the hammock par se that holds my fascination," Sarah said, sounding quite animated. "Were it the case," she added, "I would have one built in my house in Sweden; as you know it well, I don't have one there."

Following a moment of silence, she added, "Mind you, while sitting in the hammock, in the veranda of my Paleochora home, not only do I enjoy watching fishermen making their daily catch of fish, but I also try to imagine what different generations of people, sitting on the same position as myself, a thousand years ago, would have imagined, as they watched soldiers from Greece sailing on a mission to bring a wayward territory back into the folds of the Athenian rule, Phoenicians ships plying the sea in search of people and territories to trade with, Roman ships looking to expand frontiers of the Roman empire and Crusaders on their way to the Holy land to fight, kill and get killed – all in the name of God."

"You have quite a fertile imagination, I must say," Hadio said.

"Maybe," Sarah said smiling lightly.

After this brief conversation, the two ladies never said anything to each other for the rest of the journey home

# Chapter Fifty Six

# *The Grey Uppsala Skyline*

From the day Sarah returned from Greece, accompanied by Hadio, her health seemed to have suddenly changed for the better. Instead of taking the usual short walks, in the woods, at morning hours, accompanied by Hadio, the two resumed their long walks.

The visit to the hospital became less frequent. Sarah started showing interest in social life. Twice, accompanied by Hadio, she visited Uppsala's famous theatre to watch the play by August Strindberg, Miss Julie. When she went for the second time to watch the same play, Hadio couldn't stay quiet out of curiosity.

"What is quite irresistible in the play to make you want to see it twice," Hadio asked Sarah.

They were on a way to the theatre, inside a car that Hadio was driving. As it was in a midst of a winter season, the light in the atmosphere was already showing all signs of fading away, at three in the afternoon.

Sarah gave a hearty laughter and said, "Between my life and Miss Julie's, there is an astonishing parallel, which is hard to believe. We both come from upper layers of society; each of us had relationship with men that ended in alienation from our respective families."

When Hadio wished to know if the play might not evoke memories that she may wish to avoid having, Sarah took a passing look at Hadio holding the steering wheel with steady arms, and felt she was in safer hands.

They reached a point on their journey to Uppsala, where if she were to look on her right, Sarah would see Denmark Church, from which position generation of past travellers to Uppsala might have drawn their direction; and if she were to look straight ahead, she would have a clear sight of Uppsala's grey skyline. That grey skyline, with its iconic structures of the church and the castle, must look the same today as it might have looked to someone, centuries ago, approaching Uppsala from a southern direction, sitting on a horse driven carriage.

For the benefit of posterity, some things need be kept the way they have always been. Sarah was convinced.

"The world is a hard place to live in," Sarah said. "How else could you successfully overcome life's myriad challenges," she added, "if you allow the past to weigh heavily on your conscious"

Hadio took a quick look at Sarah and smiled.

"Of course, those are not my words; they are yours; in our discussion, you had mentioned them to me, in relation to something, if you remember; I don't exactly know what it was," Sarah said.

"They are not my words, either, I read them," Hadio confessed.

"Never mind who said what," Sarah said. "What is important," she added somewhat enthusiastically, "is that now I live the words."

Hadio gave a light smile and said. "Splendid,"

As days went by, Sarah's interest in the social life grew. From a wardrobe inside her bed room, Sarah retrieved some of her long-forgotten clothes that she had once admired and loved putting them on; she decided there was nothing wrong if she indulged her vanity; now after putting them on, she asked Hadio to comment on how she looked in them. Hadio was overjoyed to see Sarah gaining interest in life; hence she looked forward to having better days with her.

Happily, Sarah's enthusiasm for life had a contiguous effect on Hadio's own mood; it energised her feelings. Yet, what had made such a positive change to take place in Sarah's life, both in physical and psychological terms, had been a subject to which Hadio gave much thought about. Does the answer to this intriguing question to be found in Paris or in Crete?

Whatever the reason, Hadio felt happy to see Sarah enjoying life. It seems as if Sarah had suddenly come upon the elixir of life.

One Saturday morning, while Sarah was in the study room and Hadio was in Sarah's bedroom, sorting out clothes that needed laundering, the telephone rang. Hadio went to answer the call. "Sarah's residence; Good morning," she said.

"Good morning, Hadio; this is Gudrun," Gudrun said.

"Good morning to you. What a surprise," Hadio said.

"I am here on a vacation of one week. I wish to let you know I have come home to celebrate my 40th birthday, which is due on this Saturday. I am planning to hold a small celebration at my apartment; Alex, my girlfriend, will be present for the celebration; I hope you could come," she said in an anxious tone. "Afterwards," she added, "we will dance the night away at Katalin."

"Of course, I will come;" Hadio said laughing at the phrase, "dancing the night away," which reminded her of the disco culture of the seventies.

"I have two friends of mine I would like them to join us for the occasion; that is, if it is fine by you," she added.

"Don't be silly Hadio," Gudrun said. "You friends," she added, "are my friends; let them come."

"Good; I will talk to them and let you know what they say," Hadio said.

Before meeting Alex, Gudrun had spoken to Hadio about her: she had referred to Alex as her girlfriend. Then, one day, Hadio met Alex in a meeting the three of them had had in down-town restaurant.

It was a summer day; they sat under the shade of a willow tree, its leaves swaying gently afforded them a shelter from the heat of an exceedingly hot summer afternoon day. Gudrun and Alex had set on one side of the table facing Hadio sitting on the other side of the table.

"Meet my girlfriend Alex," Gudrun had said over a cup of coffee, as she introduced Alex to Hadio, and then Gudrun gave Alex a full kiss in the mouth.

With a slight measure of amusement Hadio had watched the two women kissing.

"Say something," Gudrun had said, addressing Hadio, after they finished kissing.

"What do you mean?"

"The kiss,"

"What about the kiss?"

"Aren't you embarrassed?"

"Should I get embarrassed by the kiss?" "To me," she had added, "a kiss is a kiss as long as you are not kissing me."

"What if I kissed you?"

"I wouldn't enjoy it; that is all; my sexual preference being of a different nature, of course," Hadio had said, looking Sarah in the eye.

"I had been confined to a closet for such a long period of time that when I officially came out of the claustrophobic confinement of the closet, I couldn't believe it. It is for this reason I test myself in a way you have seen me doing, just to make sure that I am not dreaming, though no one needs to do such a thing today" Gudrun had said.

Hadio laughed; both Gudrun and Alex joined her.

Afterwards, Gudrun had told Hadio how she met Alex.

"Alex," she had said, "had been an exchange programme student from Australia. We met in a bar; it was love at first sight."

Alex gave Gudrun a shy smile and had said, "Gudrun had convinced me to stay and take a job, which I accepted. The rest is history."

"I am happy we met," Gudrun had said, looking at Alex with loving eyes, and the two had kissed again.

In physical terms, Alex looked different from Gudrun. Whereas Gudrun was of medium height, had a rounded shape, blond hair and a voice that was heavy, Alex was tall, had long limbs, had hair the colour of chest-nut, and had a soft voice. She spoke Swedish with an Australian accent, to the admiration of everyone she came across; knowing this to be the case, Alex never lost a chance to play the part to the maximum.

Two days before receiving Gudrun's call, Anna had called Hadio to let her know that she was home, back from Kathmandu; she said she had come home to spend Easter Holidays with her parents. Anna and Hadio had planned to meet on Saturday – on the same day that Gudrun was going to have her birthday celebration.

Gudrun had never met Anna before; Hadio hoped the two would like each other.

She phoned Anna, the minute after she finished talking to Gudrun, to tell her about Gudrun's birthday and, on behalf of Gudrun, gave her the invitation; Anna accepted the invitation readily. Anna and Hadio agreed to meet outside Uppsala's main train station, and together leave for their destination, on a car driven by Hadio.

From finishing talking with Anna, Hadio went to see Sarah in the study room, to extend the invitation to her.

"I haven't attended any birthday celebration for ages," Sarah told Hadio. "Nevertheless," she added, "I am eager to see how this one will turn out. I am excited."

Sarah's favourable response made Hadio feel quite happy; she was happy about the prospect of having Sarah meeting her friends. She had no doubt in her mind that her friends would take a liking to Sarah.

From the moment that Hadio finished speaking to Sarah about Gudrun's birthday, a measure of curiosity about the birthday and her place in it took control of Sarah's mind. Sarah gave thought to clothes she would like to wear for the occasion; which present to give to Gudrun, and whether she would enjoy the company of people half her age.

In the evening, while Hadio and Sarah sat watching TV programme together, Sarah brought up the subject of Gudrun's birthday and said, "I am thinking of how to dress up for the occasion."

Lamenting a lack of suitable clothes to wear for the occasion, Sarah said, "I combed the whole wardrobe and noticed that everything belongs to another age."

Hadio sighed, raised her head up and said, "I anticipate a meeting of a likeminded people for whom the dress code may mean something, but it is not everything."

"Since I am old fashioned, etiquette demands I should dress up for the occasion," Sarah insisted.

"What do you have in mind?" Hadio asked.

"I need to redeem myself. Tomorrow, on Friday, we shall have to do some shopping," Sarah said.

## Chapter Fifty Seven

# *Svertsbackgatan*

On a Friday afternoon, of the following day, they did the anticipated shopping in Uppsala. Afterward, they took a leisurely walk through Svartsbeckgatan – popularly known as Gågatan, which in English stands for walking alley. As its name implies, Gågatan is reserved strictly for pedestrians; the street is flanked by shops and fancy looking cafes, from which point customers on a summer day enjoy taking coffee, watching the world go by.

The overwhelming evident pace of changes seen in this street, however, had confounded Sarah's mind. Because of the nature of her job, which had confined her movement to Stockholm alone, Sarah didn't have the opportunity to visit Uppsala, as much as she would like.

"I recollect a time when only ethnic Swedes took to this street; it seems days have changed; there are more people with foreign background in the street now than any other time that I can remember," she said in relation to her observation.

"Is it good or bad?" Hadio said, giving Sarah a shy look.

"What?" Sarah asked.

"The changes you have noticed; are they good or bad?"

"I don't know really," Sarah said. "What I know," she added, "in the past, I must have lacked the ability to foresee changes ever taking place here."

Hadio gave Sarah a careful look and said, "Here I am taking this walk with you, and I am glad."

"I know. But, what a lovely afternoon this has turned out to be," Sarah said, eyes twinkling with pleasure.

"The weather," she added, "warm and bright in this early april month, the happy looks in the faces of shoppers anticipating the joys of celebrating Easter Holidays with their loved ones, and you beside me, all of which making my spirit to swell with immeasurable happiness, is a moment I would like to treasure in my heart," Sarah said in an ecstatic manner.

"I feel the same way too about everything; I wish I could live in this moment, forever," Hadio sounded happy.

"Sadly enough, all good things must come to an end," Sarah said.

Giving Sarah sheepish smile, Hadio said, "Sometimes, I let my sentimental emotion take control of my mind."

"Emotion, sentimental or otherwise, it is what makes us who we are: human beings," she said.

Hadio remained quiet.

It was getting late, and so the two ladies felt the need to get back home before dusk fell was a necessary thing to do.

At home, Hadio helped Sarah get the shopping items placed in a wardrobe, inside Sarah's bedroom; later, she went to her own quarters to refresh. Later, they took their evening meal together.

On the following morning, the two ladies got up quite early, anticipating Gudrun's birthday celebration with pleasure. After breakfast, Sarah went to the study room to write on her computer. Minutes later, Hadio heard Sarah calling her. Hadio was busy doing the dishes.

Hadio took the apron off, washed her hands, dried them up with a towel, and then off she went to see Sarah in the study room.

It was not often that Sarah asked Hadio to see her in the study room, except when she called Hadio to get her a cup of coffee, a habit that she had ceased carrying on with, ever since she got back home, following a visit to Greece.

As soon as Hadio got inside the study room, Sarah said, "Sit down, please."

Hadio sat down on a chair facing Sarah across from the desk. Meanwhile, she anxiously waited to hear what Sarah wished to say to her.

"I have the newsletter, BIRDS here," she said. "You know what it is," she added, sounding nervous.

Hadio nodded her head. BIRDS, Hadio knew to be a newsletter belonging to Swedish Association of Bird Watchers, to which Sarah was an important member. It formed part of mail consignment that came with the postman, a day before.

"There is a piece of information in the newsletter stating that yet there is another area in East Africa, favoured by birds of passage from Europe, which has been lost to them," Sarah said in a sorrowful tone.

"What a pity," Hadio said, feeling genuinely sad. "What happened," she added.

"We have information that once the lake which had acted as a source of attraction for those birds dried up, the migration of the birds also ceased from taking place," Sarah said.

"Poor little things," Hadio said, "they must have become disoriented."

"What will you do now?" Hadio added nervously.

"My organisation has commissioned a study on the subject; we want to save the situation from getting out of hand; we are going to cooperate with WWF," Sarah said.

"That sounds great," Hadio said.

"Of course, such undertaking would require painstaking efforts that need to be made, with a view to generating knowledge, not only about factors giving cause to the destruction of such rich natural environment, but also how to find a way to stop further destruction from taking place,"

Sarah said this with confidence, as if to reassure Hadio that, hard as it may look, the job will be done in the end.

"I believe the study would envisage also how people living in the study area will benefit from recommendations to be made," Hadio said, giving Sarah a shy smile.

"I get your point," Sarah said. "We would make clear to whoever is going to be commissioned to do the study," she added, gazing at Hadio, not taking her eyes away, "to consider people first and last."

Following a moment of silence, Sarah said, "On Monday, our association will have a meeting. You will take me there. There is so much to be done,"

In the afternoon, Hadio went to the kitchen from where she prepared a fish fried plantain dish, cooked in coconut milk. At Bowman Rehabilitation Centre, she had once cooked the same dish that Anna liked it.

She hoped that Gudrun and others would like it, too. She kept the matter secret; she would not let even Sarah know about it. After she finished cooking, she kept the food in a portable container that she later kept it somewhere inside a fridge.

On the way to their appointment, in the evening, they stopped by a florist shop to buy each a bouquet of flower to give as a present to Gudrun.

Not only did Sarah got dressed up modestly, but she had also avoided choosing clothes that are identified with older people, while trying, at the same time, to not look as if she was dying to look young. The only luxurious item she had allowed herself to put on was a necklace, embellished with tiny precious stones.

Hadio, on her part, opted for a look mostly associated with African women. She had wrap around made of African prints, a half-sleeved blouse of the same colour made from the same material as the wrap around, and a colourful head gear and a shawl.

At the entrance to the main Uppsala's train station, while searching for a place convenient enough to park the car, hoping to wait for Anna there, Hadio saw Anna waving. Hadio stopped to let Anna get inside the car; Anna took the back seat. Meanwhile, Hadio introduced the two ladies to each other. At the word Sarah Bissell, Anna's face brightened up; she directed her eyes at Sarah, concentrating on the road ahead, sitting beside Hadio, and said, "It is a great honour meeting you,"

Sarah turned to have a good look at Anna; while looking genuinely pleased, she said, "I feel the same way about you, Anna."

"Hadio had told me that she was working for someone called Sarah, but that is all I know," Anna said. "I didn't know," she added, "Hadio is working for you - Sarah Bissell. Hadio is lucky"

Sarah gave a subtle smile and said, "Don't be so sure; I may not be who you think I am."

"I would not have anyone else for an employer," Hadio said, smiling somewhat, while looking sideways at Sarah.

"Reciprocating the smile, Sarah said, "Thanks for the warm and kind thoughts."

# Chapter Fifty Eight

# *To Katalin*

Gudrun had an apartment of three rooms, situated a few blocks away from Uppsala's main train station. It was six in the evening by the time Sarah, Anna and Hadio got there, where the three met their host eagerly waiting for them. Standing beside Gudrun, in a brightly lit sitting room, was a young-looking woman that Hadio remembered her as Alex, from the organisation Gudrun had been involved with before leaving for Nairobi.

Gudrun introduced Alex to Anna. Hadio took her turn to introduce Sarah and Anna to both Gudrun and Alex.

Once the formal introduction was over, addressing the ladies, Gudrun said in a happy tone, "Feel comfortable, please." She added, "You can sit anywhere, while I go and fetch drinks."

The ladies took their seat in a sofa-set made of black leather, arranged in a secular pattern, a shiny black mahogany table placed in the middle.

"I am coming along," Hadio said.

Soon the two ladies were on their way to the kitchen. Inside the kitchen, Hadio let Gudrun into her secret, concerning the food she had prepared.

"I have made the food without letting you know it," Hadio gave Gudrun a worried look.

"I wanted to surprise you with the food; it is my special birthday present to you; what do you say?" She added.

"I am sure it is going to give an exotic touch to what essentially is drawn from a traditional menu," Gudrun said.

"Thanks for your thoughtful consideration," Gudrun added, feeling proud of Hadio.

On that note, Hadio went out to fetch the food that she had kept it in a secret place, inside the car, and came back in time to help Gudrun convey the assortments of drinks to the drawing room.

From there, once again, the two ladies excused themselves; they went back to the kitchen, to get the food to the dining room. The food was quite rich, in all its variety. It consisted of slices of French bread, varieties of cheese, salmon, tined stuffs; meat balls, boiled potatoes, Hadio's fish fried plantain etc.

From the kitchen, the two went to join the rest of the group in the sitting room, to light the candles for the birthday-cake, and for the guest to offer Gudrun congratulations for her 40th birthday.

Later, except Hadio who had a driving to do, the rest sat down to take their drinks. One or two rounds of drinks later, the ladies felt comfortable in the company of each other, and so they started discussing what life look like outside Sweden.

"How do you like Nairobi? Sarah asked Gudrun. "Hadio told me," Sarah added, "you are U.N. personnel."

"Nairobi is different from what you and I read in papers or see on TV" Gudrun said.

"Do you mean to say there is hardly any truth in what we see on TV or read in papers?" Sarah said. "What about those heart rendering images of poverty and sufferings we see on TV? Are you saying there is hardly any truth in them?" She added.

"Of course, there is truth in what we read in papers or watch on TV," Gudrun said. "However," she added, "what we see and read about Africa is only one part of the truth,"

"What is the other part of the truth?" asked Alex.

"The other part of the truth is the state of joy people know well in Africa," Gudrun said.

"I never thought in Africa people know the meaning of joy," Alex said, looking quite astonished.

"Joy and sadness cannot exist without the other. They belong to different sides of the same coin," Gudrun said.

"They go through a lot of suffering, nevertheless; you cannot deny this," Sarah said forcefully.

"So are we here in Europe. Are we immune to human suffering merely because we are rich? Poor or rich, we are subject to the same laws of nature," Gudrun said.

"Wait a minute," Sarah said. "In Europe, we are blessed with robust institutions that help ease our sufferings; you can't say the same thing for people living in Africa," she added.

"Yes, they have their traditional institutions that take care of them; although they may not look anything like the European institutions, nevertheless, they are there," said Hadio who had decided to make her contribution felt on the on-going discussion

"I doubt it very much if those institutions are effective enough to take care of all their needs" Alex said.

Anna had been quiet for all the time that the conversation was taking place in the room. She liked the different points of view that the protagonists in the discussion had presented to counter each other's point of view, and so she thought rather than partaking in the discussion she had more to learn by lending her ear. However, Alex's statement had a darker side to it, which had made Anna want to get involved in the discussion.

"No one entity, big or small, has the capacity to provide to its society all of its human needs," Anna said. "Traditional societies," she added, "have the capacity to engender a spirit of collective responsibilities to its members."

"The communal spirit to which you have referred could work out well for its members in their own homeland," Alex said. "I doubt if communal spirit as we know it here," she added sharply, "could be of help to anyone."

"Why do you have doubts?" asked Anna looking a bit disturbed.

"Communal spirit that engenders collective responsibility and action, as you have put it, goes against our culture. It makes it quite hard for us to integrate immigrants into our society," Alex said.

"What aspect of culture are you talking about," Gudrun said.

"What do you mean?" Sarah asked. "Culture to me is culture," she added.

All eyes in the room were directed towards Gudrun. For a moment Gudrun stayed quiet, perhaps thinking about how to express her point, avoiding getting mistaken for being pedantic.

"I speak of culture as we practise it, and culture as consisting set of values that we believe in," Gudrun said.

"I will appreciate if you can further elaborate on the point," Sarah said.

"We, in our country, take issue with how immigrants practise some of their culture; we don't like it when some men, from among them, kill their women in the name of keeping the honour of their family members, or when they practise female genital mutilation; these practices we abhor, and we have every right to do so, because they go against one of our most important cultural values; namely, the right to life. However, because of these cultural anomalies, some of us draw a conclusion that there is something immutably wrong with their culture," Gudrun said and looked at her colleagues to see if they had something to say.

"Call a spade a spade; if it is bad it is bad" Alex said in a blunt tone.

"A bad cultural practice is one that goes against our values; not all cultural practices of the immigrants fall into this category. What purpose would it serve, let us say, should immigrants choose to abandon their culture and follow ours," said Anna, offering a challenge.

"Why, it will help getting them integrated into our society," Sarah said.

"I don't see how consuming seal-fish, or running around a tree at a mid-summer-day, will speed up the integration of the immigrants into our society." Anna said, trying to look convincing.

"In this case," Sarah said earnestly, "if they don't practise our culture, tell me, what else should make the immigrants get integrated into our society."

"I suppose," Anna said easily, "practising our cultural values will do the trick."

"Whatever they are, they are our values; not theirs," Alex said, looking agitated.

"They are universal values; they include the following: belief in human equality, the right to life; and a life free of discrimination," Anna said.

Anna was taking a short breath, intending to have a drink of water, when using a tone full of excitement her attention was drawn by Alex saying to her, "But that exactly is the point. Every one of those values you have mentioned is our value,"

"The right to life is a right every human being aspires to. However, how the West differs from other communities, in relations to these values, is that we have codified them, made them into canons, cherished them, preached them and fought for them," Gudrun who was drawn into her own thought, and was quiet for quite some time, said abruptly.

"That may well be the case." Anna said. "However," she added, "it is important to bear in mind that no one is born believing in the values of the society to which they are born in."

There was a slight murmuring in the room; soon, it was quiet again, as everyone in the room directed their attention at Anna who, after taking a quick sip from her glass of wine, said in connection to what she had said earlier, "None of us here is born believing in the values of our society. To have to believe in them requires a certain level of moral courage, as well as an acceptable level of intellectual depth. This is the reason why those in the right of the political spectrum make a mockery of themselves each time they speak of culture in abstract form, and then use this abstraction to censor immigrants for not practising it.

"I thought there was something missing whenever those in the right of political spectrum here in our country speak about culture without specifying what they mean," Sarah said feeling impressed with views presented by Gudrun and Anna. "I fear," she added, "these are people who believe in neither Judeo-Christian nor Enlightenment values, both of which are pillars of our Western civilisation. If they are neither of these, what are they?"

"Nothing," Anna said. "Simply put," she said, "they are purveyors of hate."

"Next time," she added, "when they speak to me of culture, my question to them would be this; do you believe in the important cultural values of your society? I know they don't, because if they did they wouldn't act in a way they are acting, promoting acts of discrimination, which goes against one of the most important cultural values of our society."

Following Sarah's statement, Gudrun exchanged meaningful glances with Anna. The confession made by Sarah must have reassured both women that if Sarah could acknowledge and uphold their views, those views must make quite a sense in themselves.

Sarah took a sip from her drink and, addressing both Gudrun and Anna said afterwards, "I find the views you have expressed here to be quite meaningful. For how long, I wonder, have you been holding those views?"

"I must confess to you," Gudrun said, "I learnt a lot while working for UNESCO that had broadened my mind. Before leaving for my assignment abroad, I had held ideas quite different from those that I hold now. For example," she added, "in relation to the immigrants, I had always thought in terms of us and them."

She turned to give Hadio a quick look and said, "I am sorry Hadio."

She stayed quiet for a moment and said afterwards, "However, my short sojourn to the continent of Africa, and what I had learnt from there, had made me realise that, as human beings, we are more alike than we are different." She reached for Hadio's hands, clasped them tightly in both her hands, and then said, "For any of you wishing to confirm my statement look no further than Hadio, who to me is everything a human being could wish to be."

The women looked at Hadio and offered a smile. Hadio returned the smile and looked down on the floor, feeling ill at ease.

"Are we not all of us here in this room, apart from the difference in our colour, alike in our humanity? Gudrun said.

The ladies, including Sarah, all at once, left their position to go and hug Hadio.

The overwhelming expression of love directed at her brought tears in Hadio's eyes; Hadio felt she had no words to express her gratitudes for the love shown to her by her women friends; in a trembling voice, she said, "Thank you very much."

Presently, Gudrun got up from her seat; in a cheerfully sounding voice she said, "Time for dinner; ladies, please, let us proceed to the dining table," whereupon the ladies proceeded to the dining room, as requested by Gudrun.

In the dining room, the ladies took their seats around a table, covered in oil-cloth. As the women became busy serving a portion of food each into their blue chinaware plates, which Gudrun said she had inherited from her mother, who in turn inherited from her mother, there was a silence in the dining room. The women ate their food with great gusto; in the end, they praised Gudrun for the good food. They reserved their special praise, however, for the fish fried plantain dish that they ate to the last bit.

"Taking a look at the ladies, at the same time pointing at her Hadio, Gudrun said, "Fish fried plantain is the brainchild of Hadio,"

Without any reservation, the diners showered Hadio with praise; Gudrun requested Hadio to furnish her with the receipt from the dish. As soon as they finished taking their dinner, the ladies went to have coffee in the sitting room; while there, they continued their discussions until nine thirty in the evening.

The ladies, evidently, felt quite so comfortable in the presence of each other's company that they almost forgot they were expected to be at Katalin soon. Gudrun had already booked a table for the occasion, and so perhaps the fear of not getting a comfortable place to sit in couldn't arise in their mind. They felt they still had time left to refresh before leaving for Katalin.

At ten, they were inside Katalin night club. A well-known jazz-club in the city, Katalin had the distinction of inviting well-known musicians, from around the world of blues and jazz music, to come and play there.

At Katalin, tonight, there was a band from the U.S, playing Chicago Blues, which for the beauty of the music had kept some of the audience tapping their feet, while others let their heads move with the beat of the music. Most of the audience, it seemed from their age, which was not so young, were connoisseurs of the blues music; rather than taking to the floor to dance, they enjoyed sitting and listening to the music.

Occasionally, however, from the audience, a couple would take to the floor to dance. Once in a while, one of the ladies from Sarah's company would offer to dance with someone,

When the band played Buddy Guy's famous number, "Damn Right I Have Got the Blues," Hadio took to the floor; as she danced alone, letting her waist to wriggle to the beat of the music, while her right arm raised high above her head moved like a cowboy in a rodeo about to lasso a cow ensnare the bull, she was joined on floor by one of the band members; together they danced as the audience clapped and cheered.

As for Sarah, she savoured every minute that she spent in Katalin. The music brought to her mind sweat-sour memories of Paris when she had been to a night club, accompanied by Lesia, where she had enjoyed watching black musicians from the U.S playing wonderful jazz music, to the joy of the audience. The band at Katalin tonight was also made up of black musicians. Throughout the evening, the ladies enjoyed listening to the music, talking to one another.

When the band stopped for a short rest, Hadio went to talk briefly to the man leading the band. As they were preoccupied in their talk, none of the women had noticed Hadio sneaking away and now talking to leader of the band. Before the band resumed playing, the band leader, tall and hefty looking man, in a black suit, a white shirt and a black bow tie, posed to give a short speech.

"Ladies and Gentlemen," he started in his baritone voice. "Are you in a mood for celebration tonight?" He asked.

It seemed the audience never exactly knew how to react to the question, and so while a few gave a reply of "Yes," others stayed quiet.

"Ladies and Gentlemen, we know what a true friendship means to us," he said.

"We all have friends." he went on in his baritone voice that listening to him talking made you believe the voice was coming from inside your bowels.

"We love and honour our friends for their friendship to us, for their dedication to our wellbeing, and for the selfless efforts of their deeds, all of which things make our societies a better place to live in," he said.

For a moment he stayed quiet. It was now quiet in the hall; not even a sound of whisper could be heard.

"Ladies and Gentlemen," he said, "Hadio, the lady in an African outfit," he pointed to a place in the hall where Hadio was seating with the rest of her friends, "wishes to express the feelings of love that she has for Sarah Bissell, her friend and benefactor, and also want to wish her a long, healthy and prosperous future."

The name Sarah Bissell must have aroused attention of the audience to the extent that it was no longer quiet in the hall; people looked here and there to try to locate Sarah.

The brief disruption of the quiet atmosphere was brought to a quick end by the speaker who was saying, "We have received a request from Hadio to play the famous tune "Amazing Grace," to wish Sarah happiness and a healthy life,"

The moment after he finished giving the speech, someone from the management approached the ladies; in his hands, he had a Champaign bottle. Everything happened quite so fast the ladies didn't know what to say; the whole thing came as a surprise for Sarah, who looked at Hadio with a wonder in her eyes.

Hadio had kept her intention to herself; she wanted to surprise her friends with her action. As the band started playing the tune, a man from the management opened the bottle and handed it over to the ladies; they poured the Champaign in special glasses, and then toasted to the happiness of Sarah, who held back tears; the rest of the audience in the hall toasted with them.

At one o'clock, the women left Katalin. From there, they took a walk together to a parking lot, where Hadio had the car parked, in a parking lot.

Hadio drove Anna to the train station for her to take a bus home. The night was clear, and the traffic on the road was light, all which things had made Hadio feel quite relaxed, as she drove Sarah home.

Considering the long evening hours that Sarah had spent with the women at Katalin, talking and drinking, far from feeling tired, Sarah didn't exhibit any sign of exhaustion; to the contrary, looking quite animated, she spoke merrily to Hadio about her friends, whom she showered with much praise; she hoped to have more of similar nights with them, in future, she told Hadio.

At home, Hadio made sure that in Sarah's room everything was conveniently set up for her to have a good night rest; she put new bed sheets on Sarah's bed; she remembered to fetch and then place the glass of milk laced with honey on the night table, which she had let Sarah take every night before she went to sleep. Ever since Hadio succeeded in convincing Sarah to have the glass of milk, which she had told Sarah would induce a good night sleep, Sarah never kept away from the ritual.

At the door steps to her room, Sarah turned abruptly; using brisk steps, she went to face Hadio. Her arms stretched, she held Hadio in a tight embrace.

In a voice full of kind emotions, she said, "I wish to think you for the nice evening, which has awakened a lust for life that I thought to be dead in me. I give my special gratitude to you, if not for anything else but for being here for me, and with me. I also want you to know that you will always have my love and trust."

Knowing how easy it is to love than to trust someone, Hadio was overwhelmed with a feeling of love and respect for Sarah, who gave unconditional trust to her. Hence in reply Hadio said, "I feel honoured to have this opportunity to work for you. I thank you for giving me your love and trust; I hope to prove to you that I am worth the trust you have bestowed on me. Thank you, once more."

"You will always have my trust and love." Sarah said smiling. "Have a good night sleep," she added.

"You too," Hadio said in reply.

Inside the room, Sarah changed into sleeping pyjamas, and then her eyes fell on the glass of milk on the night table. Tonight, she felt she had no desire for the milk. Nevertheless, for the sake of keeping the ritual, she took a few sips and then went to the bathroom.

Suddenly, the urge to take a bath took control of her mind, but she must brush her teeth first, she thought. She took a long look at herself in the mirror and was pleased with signs of improvement showing in her face. She took a comb and then used it to brush her greying and thinning hair; a moment later, she returned the comb to a place inside a small wooden cardboard built above the mirror; looking herself in the mirror, she sighed, made faces and smiled.

She took off her pyjamas, opened the tab to let the water run until the bathtub was half-filled with warm water; she closed the tab and eased herself down into the bathtub quite slowly and carefully.

As she rested in the bathtub, feeling comfortable, Sarah shut her eyes to let herself enjoy feelings of warm sensations creeping into every pour of her body; Sarah felt happy to be alive and healthy.

She leaned sideways to pick up the soap when she felt an excruciating amount of pain gripping at her chest; she felt as if her body was getting subjected to thousands of electrical currents; she gasped for air to breath; moments before a total darkness descended over her, she saw the image of herself when she was a child, her father bending to kiss her good night, on her forehead.

Early in the morning, of the following day, Hadio did what she had always done; she pushed the door to Sarah's room wide open, to see if everything was fine. Sarah, she found out, was not in her room, and in bed. This hadn't come as a surprise for Hadio; she took for granted, being healthy enough to take care of herself, since she came back from Greece, Sarah might be taking a shower, and so she shouted her name.

When she received no reply, Hadio approached the bathroom carefully; she pushed the door wide open; there, sprawled inside the bathtub, half-filled with water, she saw Sarah's body. Hadio emitted a loud frantic crying-sound of despair.

After recollecting her composure, however, moments later, she took Sarah's-limb body into her arms, checked for any sign of heart-beat, and discovered there was none; mouth to mouth self-aid resuscitation techniques proved useless.

She went to get the telephone in the living room and then dialled the ambulance; she dialled the police at the same time. The paramedics – three altogether – came after awhile, took a long look at Sarah's body and declared her dead.

In keeping with rules and regulations, the police made sure that the scene is not in any way tempered with, pending police investigation. Hours later, Sarah's body was officially taken to the hospital, where she was officially declared dead.

The statement released by the hospital authorities, based on the post-mortem made on Sarah's body, stated that Sarah's death had been caused by a heart attack.

Several days later, following the police investigations on those circumstances leading to Sarah's death, Hadio was freed from any suspicion that could have connected Sarah's sudden death to her, since Hadio was the only person present at Sarah's house, at the time when Sarah died.

Hadio was invited by the Bissell family to attend the burial ceremony. She drove one of Sarah´s car to Stockholm; once there, she parked the car at a most convenient parking lot, not far from the wharf owned by the Bissell family. Later, she got into a boat marked with the letters Bissell, which took her on brief sea journey to Bissell family's estate. At the other end of the journey, she found a car waiting. After she identified herself to a young driver in a uniform, they drove on a well kept gravel road. On either side of the road, the landscape was dotted with a mixture of trees, consisting of pines. On either side of the gravel road, beautiful looking horses were visible, feeding on sparse vegetation made of grass.

Hadio caught sight of an imposing building, on a hill-top, looming large. On the stairs of the building, Hadio saw Sarah nephew's son, Roger, standing there, waiting for her. He held an umbrella that offered him a protection from the rain that had just started falling. After warm greetings, Roger led the way to a small chapel with red bricks. Hadio found herself a pew to comfortably sit in; with her in the pew were two people. Hadio, meanwhile, listened with a keen mind to sermons given by a young looking priest.

Away from the chapel, at the family's well kept graveyard, standing quite isolated from the rest of the crowd, watching the casket holding Sarah's body getting lowered into the grave,

Hadio became quite happy for Sarah, whose spirit, Hadio assumed, had finally found a dwelling place, alongside those of her ancestors. Sarah was buried next to her son and opposite her father's grave. Hadio felt, in death, both Sarah and Peter had become true members of the Bissell family - a family from which they had been alienated for the most part of their lives.

When the burial ceremony got over, a lady with austere angular plain face, dressed in black, approached Hadio and politely told her, "My name is Ulla. I am spokesperson for the Bissell family. The family members want you to know how much they appreciate your services to Sarah, and wish to thank you very much."

"Sarah was quite nice to me; I will miss her a lot," Hadio said,

"We shall request you to take care of the house until further notice. The family will continue to pay your monthly salary," she said.

On that note, Hadio left. She was in a hurry to leave; she wished to keep her grief to herself. Sarah's death had been a great blow to her. In Sarah's death not only had Hadio lost an employer, but a good friend and a trustworthy confidant. Kore, Anna, Alex and Gudrun came to give her company, as she mourned Sarah's death; Kore's presence, particularly, helped lighten the burden of grief that Hadio had been carrying in her heart.

# Chapter Fifty Nine

# *The Will*

Less than a month later, Hadio received a letter from an advocate that she knew. She had driven Sarah to meet with him several times, the latest occasion being two weeks before leaving for Greece. That lawyer now requested her presence at his office.

On the way to his office, driving one of Sarah's cars, on the appointed date, Hadio speculated the reason that could have made the advocate wish to meet her. Of all the thoughts that had crossed her mind, the most ominous of them all was the one pointing to a possibility of her job-tenure ending.

The uncertainty of what that trip to the advocate's office would entail for her future had made Hadio develop a feeling of anxiety. To ward off the gloom that had engulfed her spirit, she hummed her favourite song, which didn't help much.

At the office, she was received by a big beaming advocate in a blue suit, a white shirt and a tie with white dots to match colour of the shirt. Sitting across from his desk was Ulla. On setting eyes on Ulla, dressed in skirt suit, Hadio's worst nightmare seemed to come true in her mind. Even though the room was properly heated, yet Hadio shivered with cold, her stomach turning up. She felt like throwing up, but refused to succumb to the temptation.

"Welcome Hadio," Erik, said.

"Thank you," said Hadio

Pointing to Ulla, he told Hadio, "I believe you have met Ulla before."

"Yes" Hadio said nervously.

Ulla looked at Hadio and smiled.

Ulla and Hadio set facing the lawyer across from the table. The two women sat so close to each other that Hadio caught an enticing perfume scent on Ulla, which had been so captivating that in wanting to have more of the scent Hadio had almost lost track of the lawyer's speech.

"Good," he said, "As you may know," he went on, "Ulla is spokesperson for the Bissell family, to which Sarah was an important senior member. Ulla is here today to act as a witness concerning a statement in a form of a will that Sarah had left before her death." He remained quiet briefly and then looking at Hadio, he told her, "Is that clear"?

"Yes," Hadio said.

"I can't go through all the provisions covered in the document in their entirety. I shall, however, mention the gist of the matter to you, but leave a copy of the documents to each of you to keep, and, if you wish, go through it at your leisure.

Suffice to mention here is that before her death, while in a healthy state of body and mind, Sarah left a will in which she stated that in case of death occurring to her, all property belonging to her personally, both movable and immovable, together with bond and shares, including any amount of cash in the bank, as well as any amount of loyalty emanating from the sale of her memoirs, will all pass to Hadio. In case of

Hadio's death, preceding hers, and after her death, all the above-mentioned assets will be owned by Society for the Bird Watchers of Sweden, to which Sarah had been an active member.

The will, however, is quite clear about one thing: Sarah's share of the property, owned by Bissell family, belongs to Bissell family only; no one associated with Sarah, including Hadio, can have any claim upon it whatsoever," he said.

Addressing Ulla, he said, "Do you have anything to say?"

"On behalf of Bissell family, I wish to let you know that the family intends to honour and respect to the letter Sarah's last will," Ulla said.

"And you Hadio; do you have anything to say?" He asked.

Hadio said nothing, but started sobbing. After a while, she stopped sobbing. She became suddenly aware that, looking at her weeping, someone would readily say that those were crocodile tears. She nodded her head, but stayed quiet.

"Good." The lawyer said. "I have nothing more to say except to remind you that for the will to become effective, a period of no more than three months is required, so that anyone wishing to contest the will could do so," he added.

In the national media, Sarah was honoured in a way reserved only for people who once had made large-scale contribution to national welfare. Her achievements were recounted in great details, and the government decided to name the old Department of Zoology at Stockholm University in her memory, in recognition of her financial contribution to the Department.

When her death was made public, however, the media came up with a story that shocked the nation. The reports made by the media didn't want to acknowledge a mild heart attack to be the cause of Sarah's death. The media instead pointed fingers at Hadio. The headlines in the newspapers said it all.

"SHE HAS DONE IT AGAIN," one such print media wrote. Referring to Hadio's history, the story beneath the